Outside, A Gun Barked Three Times...

Alessandra and Sarah both jumped up and ran for the door.

Fifty other restaurant patrons reached for jackets, pushed back chairs and prepared to follow.

The big maître d' barred the exit, but Al got the heel of her hand up under his nose and shoved him back out of the way like someone peeling open the lid of a tin of sardines.

Outside, about ten feet from Costello's front door, a man lay dying on the sidewalk. At the far end of the block a set of red taillights vanished around the corner to the howl of tires pushed beyond their ability to hold traction.

Sarah's husband, Frank, was nowhere in sight.

Neither was the shiny black Suburban.

Sarah Waters stared at the dying man.

Al grabbed her by the arm.

"Time to go," she said.

In the distance, a siren wailed.

NORMAN GREEN

is the author of six novels, including *The Last Gig* and *Sick Like That*, which both feature private investigator Alessandra Martillo. According to *Booklist*, "It's Al's no-holds-barred combination of toughness, savvy, and hidden vulnerability that drives the series...."

SICK
LIKE THAT
NORMAN GREEN

W✹RLDWIDE®

TORONTO • NEW YORK • LONDON
AMSTERDAM • PARIS • SYDNEY • HAMBURG
STOCKHOLM • ATHENS • TOKYO • MILAN
MADRID • WARSAW • BUDAPEST • AUCKLAND

Recycling programs
for this product may
not exist in your area.

ISBN-13: 978-0-373-06278-2

SICK LIKE THAT

Copyright © 2010 by Norman Green

A Worldwide Library Suspense/June 2013

First published by St. Martin's Press, LLC

www.Harlequin.com

Printed in U.S.A.

SICK
LIKE THAT

the sun went down last friday and now all it does
   is rain
haven't felt a smile since i last saw tommy paine
so raise a glass you sinners, down on your knees
   you saints
the world is one man thinner and it wears a
   darker taint
not enduring but embracing and in embracing,
   burned
a small man's feckless caution thomas casually
   spurned
bow you kings and princes and kneel shouldered
   with the mob
pray into the silence to rouse the sleeping god
let's hear it for the common extraordinary man
who never lost his courage or ability to stand
sing now you thieves and pirates to salute the
   turning page
stand crying all you stalwarts for your brother
   passed this way

on the death of thomas paine,
who should have gone home on 9/11/01,
but did not

d.e.kellogg

Acknowledgments

My thanks to Bill and the doctor, without whom I would not be here. Thanks also to the Liberty Street Irregulars, who do their best to keep me sane. And, finally, thanks to Christine, for everything.

ONE

ALESSANDRA MARTILLO DID not like Marty Stiles, she thought
he was a pig, but if so he was a pig with many useful skills
and she had learned a lot from him. In short, she owed him,
and she hated that, which was why she sat on the hard plastic seat of a southbound A train that was headed for Coney
Island where Stiles slumped motionless in a wheelchair and
waited for death.

Death, it seemed, was taking her own sweet time.

Please, his sister had begged, tears in her eyes. Please…I
flew all the way up here from Valdosta, he won't even look
at me, he won't even press the call button for the nurse when
he makes a mess in his…

Oh, Jesus, Al told her, uncomfortable under the weight
of obligation. I ain't trying to hear about that.

Please, oh God please, I'll pay you whatever you charge,
please just go talk to him, I can afford it…

All right all right all right, Al told her, not too graciously,
but she knew it was something she needed to do. I'll go. I've
got business this afternoon, but I'll get down there after I'm
finished. About nine-ish.

Thank you, thank you, the sister told her, sick with gratitude. I'll call ahead, I'll make sure they let you see him,
they won't care if it's late, I'll make sure… How much do
I owe you?

Don't worry about it, Al told her.

Christ.

And they got hospitals all over town, Al thought, but no,

they have to send Marty's fat sorry ass to some rehab all the way down in Coney Island, God ever decides to give Brooklyn an enema, here's where the bone goes in...

Guy in a stocking hat sitting across the aisle stared at her, she stared back until he finally looked away. Your own fault, she thought, the dress was the shortest one she owned, but she had her reasons for that. This dress don't wake Marty up, maybe he's better off dead after all. Still, it was late, it was dark, and she and Mr. Personality were the only two passengers in the car. One other guy riding between cars, he peered through the dirty door glass, made eye contact with Mr. P, then looked away.

Al felt a flutter somewhere between her stomach and her throat.

So it's like that.

Well, baby, you ain't gonna outrun anybody in those high heels...

She picked up the camera bag she used in lieu of a purse. Not heavy enough for a weapon, she thought, nothing in there to stab someone with or shoot them or otherwise inflict bodily harm. Shove a lipstick into his eyeball, maybe...

Al got up, walked over and stood in front of the center set of exit doors. Mr. Personality got up, too, stood smirking at his reflection in the glass of the rear exit doors.

You could lose the shoes and run, she thought.

Buck eighty for those babies, yo. How long's it take you to clear a buck eighty to piss away on a pair of shoes?

The train slid into the empty station and stopped with an echoing jerk, and then all the exit doors rattled open simultaneously. Al stepped out, watched as Mr. Personality did the same. She stood, waiting, and he stayed by his doors, too, just in case she decided to try and jump back in when they began to close. Al guessed that Mr. Personality's associate, the guy who'd been riding between the cars, had gotten off, too, but he had to be a bit farther away and so she focused on the first guy.

The doors closed behind her, the train lurched into motion.

The guy turned to her and smiled. "Hey, chica," he said. "Where you goin', baby? All dress up nice like that? You like to party?"

She turned her head to look at him. "Yeah, I do," she said. "I'm going to a party at my cousin's house."

He took a step in her direction, patted his rear pocket unconsciously before spreading his hands out wide. Probably got a knife there, she thought. "You don't got to go no place, chica. We gonna party right here."

She heard unhurried footsteps coming from the other direction, but they weren't close yet. "Don't you wanna know who my cousin is?"

His smile faded. "So? Who is he?"

"Rocco Parisi," she said. Parisi, a mobster with a well-earned reputation for violence, was known from one side of Brooklyn to the other.

He considered that, but after a few seconds his smile returned. "Well, you know what, baby, that jus' mean we got to cut you, after." He reached into his pocket and pulled it out, it was a butterfly knife, it flashed as he flipped it open.

SHE WAS TEN.

An old-fashioned pork shoulder roast with the skin still on and a thick bone sticking out of one end sat on the corner of the kitchen counter. Victor Martillo, her father and the toughest Puerto Rican in the shore patrol, stood in front of her with a six-inch knife in his hand. He was dressed in civilian clothes, but to Al it seemed that everything became a uniform when he wore it.

"Are you watching?" he said.

"Yes, Papi."

One quick step, he spun, swung the knife in a glittering arc, and the pork shoulder fell over so the round end stared at her.

Victor laid the knife aside carefully. "Come here," he said. It was not a request.

"Yes, Papi."

She stepped up.

He knelt down, the pork shoulder in his hands. The knife had gone deep, Al could see white bone behind the severed muscle tissues. In her imagination a pig screamed, made whatever noises a pig makes when you cut it just about in half.

"This is what a knife can do to you," he said. She could see her mother silent in the kitchen doorway, her face white, but her father's brown eyes never left hers. "You don't need to be afraid of a knife," he said, "but you can never forget what it does."

"Yes, Papi." Her voice was barely audible.

Victor put the meat back on the counter, picked up the knife. "Are you paying attention?" he said, even though he had to know that she was.

"Yes, Papi."

"Good. Now you're going to take this knife and try to cut me with it."

THE GUY BEHIND her was closing in, but she had no time for him. "Attack the weapon." Her father had drilled it so deeply into her that she didn't need to think about it now, and when Mr. Personality slashed at her he had merely performed the opening steps of a dance she had done a thousand times.

"Circles," her father's voice said. *"You see how the knife moves? It's going in a circle because my shoulder is still, my arm is the radius... Are you listening to me? Do you*

know what a radius is? Don't they teach you anything in that school you go to every day? Pay attention, we'll do it slower this time."

The knife missed her midsection, went by like a ball on a string, clockwise if seen from above. She spun counterclockwise, faster than her assailant, doing the next step of the dance, and then she had his wrist and she twisted, hard. He tried to turn away from her, instinctively trying to relieve the sudden pressure, but that left his arm extended, elbow locked, exposed.

Only two more steps.

Her momentum carried her.

The heel of her left hand slammed into the back of Mr. Personality's elbow and it broke with an audible snap.

She released him, he tripped and went down, silent, eyes wide. His knife skittered away, slid over the lip of the platform and down onto the tracks.

The pain hadn't hit him yet.

The second guy, the one coming up behind her, he must have had a nanosecond of indecision, she could hear it in the cadence of his footsteps, but his momentum brought him right to her, off balance…

"Do you see this circle," her father's voice said. *"This circle is you. This dot in the center, this is your center of gravity. Do you understand what that means? Now listen to me. When you do something stupid, okay, like you attack another person, this dot moves. It's not in the middle anymore, it's near the edge of the circle. That means you are out of balance. And the dumber it is, whatever this thing is that you're doing, the farther out the dot moves, and the easier it becomes to beat you. Are you getting this? Your opponent doesn't need to attack you now, you've already done the work for him. All he needs to do is push, just a little bit, right where that dot is, and you will fall over.*

"You see what I'm saying?
"Doesn't matter how big and strong you are.
"It's just physics."

HE WAS SO close she could smell the detergent his mother used to wash his clothes.

Or his girlfriend.

The woman who cared for him, whoever she was.

Let him sleep in her apartment, on her couch.

Or in her bed.

The one who went bail for him.

Who washed his fudgy shorts.

The one who would scream when they found him, after his idiot life was over.

"Oh, God, why? Why?"

SHE GOT HIS belt and a piece of his shirt, and she pushed on the dot.

She swung with him, they were two dancers waltzing, but then she pitched him away from her, he stumbled, cracked his head on a steel support column and bounced off, went down hard on the concrete platform.

BEHIND HER, the first one screamed.

SHE RIPPED THE stocking hat off his head and shoved it into his mouth, pushed hard, got a surprising amount of it into him.

Didn't hardly sound like screaming anymore.

His good hand flailed at her, but he had nothing left.

She rolled him over onto his belly and knelt on his back. The sounds in his throat went high and squeaky, then stopped.

"Bet that hurts, huh," she said.

He didn't try to answer.

She fished his wallet out.

"Diego Ponce," she said. "Is that you?"

He made a sound then, it might have been an affirmative.

"Diego," she said. "You wanna know what really pisses me off about this? Hmm?"

He held his breath, waited for it.

"You know what they're gonna say on the news tomorrow? 'Two Hispanic males.' In the paper, on the radio, and maybe even the television. Might not make the TV unless you both buy it right here in the station."

All she heard was his labored breath.

"'Two Hispanic males.' And in the morning when my father goes to work, all the white ladies on the bus are gonna look at him and wonder about all the bad things they think he would do to them if he got the chance. Do you hear me, you fucking piece of shit?"

The air whistled in and out of his nose.

You're wasting your time, she thought.

Diego Ponce kept no money in his wallet, but he had six hundred and change in his front pocket.

His buddy had about ten bucks less.

They must have had a good night, up until now…

She took it all.

I should do it, she thought. Relieve them of the burden of life.

Charitable act, really… If they were at all equipped to deal with reality, they wouldn't have gotten into this mess…

She could hear his mother screaming to God for answers why.

She stared at the back of Diego's head. You should have roasted his ass, she told the woman silently, the first time you caught him skipping school, the first time you caught him stealing money out of your purse, you should have beat him stupid.

You goddam cow, how can you still love him when he's like this?

Fucking women, she thought. Can't do what they need to do, always making up excuses.

We're sick like that...

"IT ISN'T CATATONIA."

"What the hell is it, then?"

The Filipino nurse stared at Alessandra reproachfully. "Some days Mr. Stiles is more responsive than others, but the doctors here think that he's basically in a minimally conscious state." She had soft brown eyes with an Oriental cast, a round Madonna's face, large breasts. Many men, maybe most men, would probably find her irresistible. She was beautiful, exotic, had a job, and she looked like she would yield to you, have your children, keep your house, care for your aging parents.

Well, if that was what you were looking for, Al was not your girl, and she knew it. She looked good enough if your tastes ran her way, she was tall, athletic, with dark brown hair, eyes, and skin, but there was little that was soft about her. You would probably guess that a relationship with Al might be a strenuous affair, perhaps of a somewhat predatory nature, and your enthusiasm might be muted just a tad by the knowledge that you could not be quite sure who hunted whom.

Hard to imagine her as someone's mom.

"I could never work here," she said.

The nurse just looked at her.

"I mean, I think it takes a special kind of person to do what you do," Al said.

The nurse, obviously unfamiliar and uncomfortable with

compliments, looked down at her hands. Typical female, Al thought. She pours out her guts in this place, nobody notices, nobody gives a shit.

"So anyhow, you're saying Marty won't recognize me."

"No," the nurse said, "I'm not saying that at all. He might respond to you and he might not. I do think he remembers me, but he didn't seem to know who his sister was. What I'm saying, Ms. Martillo, is that it's hard enough to adjust to paraplegia if one is mentally strong, but if a person is vulnerable…"

"Yeah," Al said. "I get it. You already fed him his dinner, am I right?"

"Yes." She glanced at her watch. "I usually take him a snack right about now."

"Marty does like his food," Al said.

"Yes, he seems to enjoy…"

"Let me take it to him," Al said. "And do me a favor, stay away for a while. Leave him to me."

The nurse stared at the hem of Al's skirt, so high in her lap that it barely kept her situation covered. "If you're thinking you can arouse him, let me assure you, it would purely be a physiological response. It won't do any good. A man in his state…"

"What I'm thinking is that I know Marty Stiles better than you do," Al said. "I know what he wants."

"And what would that be?"

Two things she knew he wanted: first, he wanted someone to feed him and clothe him and keep him warm and wipe his butt for him, and second, he wanted Al.

Always had.

"Just gimme his dessert," she said.

IT WAS AN odd-looking wheelchair, and it took her a minute to figure out why: it had small wheels at all four cor-

ners. There was no way a person who only had the use of
his arms would be able to motivate himself anywhere in it.
"Hiya, Marty," she said.

He didn't look at her.

At least, he didn't seem to. His eyes moved in what might
have been a random way, but she had known him for a long
time. It could have been her imagination, but she swore his
eyes had paused twice, once at the amount of leg she was
showing, and once again at the bowl of rice pudding she
carried. "You look like shit," she told him. She plopped
down on a windowsill about six feet away from his chair.
The spoon clanked on the bowl when she stuck it into the
rice pudding.

That could have been an involuntary jerk, she thought.
Like Pavlov's dog salivating. Maybe she was being unfair,
and mean.

Yeah, right.

She ate a spoonful of the pudding. Stiles swallowed.

"So anyhow, this broad comes into the office. I'm baby-
sitting, right, answering the phone and whatnot, because
Sarah, you remember her? Sarah Waters? You hired her
when you were gonna kick me to the curb, remember that?
Check this out, Marty." She paused long enough to eat an-
other spoonful of pudding. "Turns out she's really sharp.
You remember all those corporate clients you used to have?
You know, CFOs all worried about corruption and like that?
Managers with their fingers in the till? The CFOs love her,
Marty. Once I showed her how to do it, right, Sarah goes
tearing through that kind of work like a sailor with a free
pass to the whore house. Who knew?"

Marty Stiles swallowed again.

Al ate another spoonful of his dessert.

"Where was I? Oh, yeah, this broad comes into the office. I'm answering the phone because Sarah took the day

off. Kid had a soccer game or something, so I covered. People gotta have time for that stuff, am I right?" She ate some more pudding, then leaned forward and gestured at him with the empty spoon. "I had to give her a raise, Marty. I knew you were cheap, but Jesus. Matter of fact, she and I are sorta like partners now. I couldn't help it, Marty, she's really something, gets along with clients way better than you ever did, and we both know I'm no good at that shit. But Sarah, Marty, she's unbelievable. I'm telling you, Marty, she's bringing in more business than we can handle, I hadda hire a kid just to do the paperwork, can you believe that?" She was more than halfway through the rice pudding. "Marty, you know what, this stuff is not half bad. I mean, it's not really that horrible. You remember Daniel Caughlan, Marty? Your old buddy? He calls me the other day, he's in this arrested-living facility upstate somewhere, but he wants to pay up for that job I did. Wanted to know who to make the check out to. A hundred and fifty large, you believe that? I told him Houston Investigations, that's what we're calling it now. Me and Sarah."

He was staring at her now.

"Hey, come on, Marty, what the hell. It was me did all the work on it anyway. I mean, I know you got shot and whatever, but I let the money come to you, Medicaid's just gonna take it. What's the point in that?"

Both of Stiles's hands were clenched into fists, and he shook his head, just a little bit, almost as if he couldn't believe what he was hearing.

"So anyhow, this broad comes in. Stop me if you've heard this one. From Valdosta, wherever the fuck that is. She says her brother is in this rehab, but he's dogging it, won't do nothing, won't talk to nobody, poops in his pants. She wants me to check it out. I mean, it ain't really what I do, so I tell her it'll cost her two grand. Ain't got it, she tells me. So take it out of your brother's checking account, I tell her. I mean, why not? So basically, Marty, this is the most expensive bowl of rice pudding you never ate." She laughed at her joke, rattled the spoon around the bottom of the bowl and finished it off. She leaned forward and stared into Marty's face. She knew she was giving him a gap shot, but he was so mad he didn't look once. "Tell me something, Marty. Can you still get a hard-on?"

He swallowed again. "Bitch," he whispered.

"Didn't catch that, Marty. Because anyhow, that nurse out there, the one with the cannons, she told me she gets wet whenever she has to change your diaper."

Stiles lost control. "You fucking bitch!" He was much louder now. His hands, unused to sudden input from his brain, groped awkwardly for the nonexistent drive wheels on his chair. "You stole my business?" His voice got steadily louder. "You stole my business? You stole my money? What did you come down here for? You lousy fucking Rican cockteaser! You took everything from me!"

Al stood up, arranged the hem of her dress. She was not in love with the dress, but she found she was digging the freedom of panty hose over the constriction of blue jeans. "Why the hell not?" she asked him. "It's not like you're going anywhere." She tossed the empty bowl at him.

He swatted it aside as she walked out.

"Al! Goddam you, Al, get back here, you fucking bitch! Al, I swear to God I'll kill you if it's the last thing I ever do! Al! AL!"

She paused outside the door. The Filipino nurse, drawn by the noise, stood ashen-faced, looked at Al while Stiles continued his tirade. "Baby's first words," Al said, and grinned. She cocked an ear to listen, although it was not necessary, probably everyone on the floor could hear Stiles now. Maybe the whole building.

"MARTILLO! MAR-TEE-YO! DID YOU COME ALL THE WAY DOWN HERE JUST TO BREAK MY FUCKING BALLS? GODDAM YOU, MARTILLO!

Al looked at the nurse. "Minimally conscious, my ass," she said.

SHE STOOD OUT front, called Marty's sister while she waited for the car service. "I think he's gonna be all right," she said.

TWO

SARAH WATERS CLIMBED the subway steps out onto the street and headed for home. She lived in the basement of her mother's house in Bensonhurst, a largely Italian neighborhood down on the southern end of Brooklyn. She always found herself dragging when she got this close, the four blocks from the train station to the house always seemed the hardest part of the trip. You're always so happy to get out of there in the morning, she told herself, and so bummed when you have to come back. Is the basement really that bad? But it wasn't her mother's basement she minded, not really, it was her mother, right upstairs, and all too often, downstairs and in her face. "Frank is a good man." Her mother never got tired of saying it. "I don't know why you two couldn't work things out. Your father and I had our differences…"

Last night Sarah had finally had enough. "Frankie is only good for one thing, Ma." She slapped her left hand into the crook of her right arm and pumped her right fist.

"AAAAGH!" Her mother squeezed her eyes shut and crossed herself. "Don't talk like that in my house!"

"It's the truth, Ma." She glanced over her shoulder, but her son, Frankie Junior, was in his room with the door closed. She could just hear the sounds of his television. "Frankie could be fun sometimes, but you can only be doing that for about an hour a day, am I right? What am I supposed to do with him the rest of the time? When you have a family, you're supposed to grow up, bring home a paycheck, you're supposed to quit hanging out in the bar, drinking beers and chasing the waitresses. Besides, he's outa work two years now. I get back together with him, you're gonna have him in your basement, too. You want that? He's like a stray cat, you give him food, a soft bed, and a nice place to shit, you'll never get rid of him."

"Would that be so bad? Your father and I..."

"I don't wanna hear it." You can eat shit for forty years if that's what you want, but not me... But she couldn't tell her mother that, since his death her father had completely reformed his character and was now a saint.

Across the street, a guy pushing a small wheeled cart stopped at each ground-floor window he came to and rapped on the glass. "Eva?" he called. "Eva?" Sarah stopped to watch as the guy continued along to the next building. "Eva?" Looked normal enough, looked like a guy on his way home from the Laundromat, but apparently he'd lost his mind on the way. The world had become a different place since she'd started her new job. Or maybe, she told herself, maybe it had been like this all along and you never noticed. Even the sheltering arms of Bensonhurst seemed grittier than they once had, and she no longer fit there with the same degree of comfort.

It was all Martillo's fault.

Alessandra Martillo and Sarah Waters had grown up only a few miles apart, but they came from separate worlds. The small brick houses, tiny green lawns, and wrought-iron fences of Bay 19th Street were Eden compared to Browns-ville, where you had to walk with your attitude showing, where on garbage days you had to watch out for big black plastic bags that sailed down from the upper floors to land in the gutter. Kids from Brownsville, it seemed to Sarah, had no faith, they were natural skeptics.

They had seen it all.

Theirs had been an uneasy partnership at first, and in

some ways it still was. Sarah had begun to wonder what could have happened to Al when she was a kid, what had shaped her, put her on the road to becoming what she was. It wasn't so much that she was so hard, physically and emotionally, it was that she was almost reptilian in her approach to other human beings. You could never surprise her, if you pulled out your ice pick and tried to stick her with it you would only confirm what she'd already thought about you. Martillo did not trust you. She might, in time, suspend her judgments of you and your motives, but such suspensions were conditional and temporary. It made Sarah uncomfortable, but things had gotten easier between the two of them after Sarah had decided to quit trying to make friends and let Martillo think what she wanted.

Still, it had been something of a shock to her system, becoming the only student in the Alessandra Martillo School of Human Nature.

Sarah had been hired by Marty Stiles, hired to take Martillo's place, but it had only been a matter of days after that when Stiles had gotten shot. Sarah had not seen him since. And in the meantime, Marty's corporate clients had continued to call and make their demands. She remembered the morning she and Alessandra had faced up to one another, and to the situation they were in…

THE ROOM SMELLED of the man, it was a little bit rancid, a little bit damp, and had been too long between washings. It was not dust that lay in the corners, but crud. "This place stinks," Al said, wrinkling up her face. "Smell like crack up in here."

Sarah Waters sat in her chair behind the receptionist's desk, elbows tight, hands in her lap, felt the worry eating at her gut. The chair had, until very recently, been Al's. She looked at Alessandra, who was probably five or six years younger than her, maybe in her late twenties, taller, more meat and less fat, nicer butt, better looking if you went for the dark, moody, and maybe slightly psychotic type. "Yes," Sarah said. "It does."

"When Marty hired me," Al told her, "he sort of automatically assumed I was going to clean it."

Sarah could not picture Al doing something like that. "I think he was figuring the same when he hired me."

"He figure incorrectly?"

Sarah sighed. "They outlast you," she said. "They beat you down. Guys like Marty, you think you can wait them out, but you can't. He would have gotten his way in the end. He kept asking me to clean up and I kept on saying 'yeah, yeah' but not doing it." She looked around the room in distaste. "Eventually I would have given in," she said.

"Too nasty, huh?"

"Well, yeah," Sarah told her. "That would be part of it. But the other part is that if he found someone to do what I do and they promised him they would clean, he would have let me go." She struggled to keep the emotion out of her voice. "I need this job."

"You figured Marty out pretty quick."

Sarah nodded. "He's a small man. And sour."

Al walked across the room, stood in the doorway to the inner office, and stared inside. "So what do we do now?"

"Have you thought about it?"

"Yeah. You?"

"Yes. Ever since he called me. It was back when he was still in the hospital, before they shipped him down to the rehab. He told me you were unstable. Ah, what else? Temperamental, irresponsible, and rash. Said no one had ever taught you how to act."

Alessandra turned, leaned against the doorway, and nodded. "I guess that's mostly true," she said. "But you *gotta admire the guy, he saw this moment coming, this con-versation. He got here before you and me."*

"I suppose," Sarah said. "He must have figured that we would get together to try and screw him, and he was doing what he could to keep us from trusting each other."

"Like I said."

"Yeah, okay," Sarah said, feeling her face grow red. "So what did he tell you about me?"

"Very good," Al said with a small smile. "Didn't take you long at all."

"So?"

Al inhaled, stretched, let it go. "Doesn't really matter," she said.

"Go on," Sarah told her. "I can take a punch."

Al shrugged. "Marty was never happy," she said, "unless he knew you thought he was the smartest guy in the room. And the baddest. And had the biggest dick. And all that."

"Don't sugarcoat it," Sarah said. "Go on, spit it out."

She watched Al's eyes, waited while Al decided how much of Marty's vitriol she really needed to pass on. "Well," Al finally said, "all right, he said you were nothing but a house-wife. Said you'd never amount to much."

"Asshole," Sarah said, with heat.

"Well, yeah," Al said.

"I have never*," Sarah said emphatically, "been mar-ried to a house."*

"Okay," Al said. "So what do we do?"

"Whatever Marty really told you about me," Sarah said, "do you believe it?"

Al walked back around to the front of the desk, sat down in the client chair, stuck her feet up on the desk. "Marty twists things around so that he can get what he needs," Al said. "You gotta remember that. So you and me, we kinda got thrown into this. You didn't pick me out, or anything.

Maybe you don't like me too much. Question is, can you work with me? Some of that stuff Marty told you, maybe it isn't exactly like he said, but I know I got a short fuse. I know I don't always think before I do something. We don't have to be girlfriends here, anyway. We just have to be able to work together. You know what I'm saying? If you wanna try this, I'm ready to give it a shot. I promise I won't lie to you or try to screw you over."

The light went on in the back of Sarah's head. This person on the other side of the desk, no matter how bad or how fine she looks on the outside, she might be a cast-iron bitch just like Marty said she was, but she's just as insecure as you are…maybe more. "Yeah," she said. "Same here."

"Okay," Al said. "How do we work it?"

"I figure it like this," Sarah said. "I can do all the paperwork he hired me to do in about three hours a day."

"Reports? Bookkeeping? Phone calls? All that shit?"

"Three hours," Sarah told her. "Four, tops. So say I come in at noon. I clear the phones, I do the billing and the reports, I'm done by four in the afternoon. That leaves me the next four hours to handle all the corporate stuff, you know, you know, the repeat stuff at the hotels and restaurants."

"Think you can handle that?"

"You could show me," she said. "Come on, how hard can it be? I been typing up the reports all along and it's the same bullshit over and over. 'The bartender wrote up a tab.' Or he didn't. 'The waitress was courteous and prompt.' Or she wasn't. 'The food was tasty and well-prepared.' Or not. You could teach me how to do all that."

Alessandra was nodding. "Yeah."

"And that would free you up to handle the rest of it."

"Sweet. What do we do about Marty?"

Sarah looked down at the neat stacks of paperwork on her desk. "He's never getting out of that wheelchair."

"Probably not."

"But we can't just take it over. It ain't right. Even if he is a dick."

"I suppose not," Al said.

"Besides..."

"Go ahead."

"This is a dirty business," Sarah said. "I mean, some of it is downright creepy. Marty is perfect for it."

Al nodded. "The guy is good at what he does. You figure we need him?"

"I figure, a guy like Marty, we're better off having him on our side than to have him out there trying to get even. Besides, you're not like him," Sarah said, looking into Al's face. "I mean, I hope you don't mind me saying. You might think you are, but you're not, if you were I wouldn't be sitting here. You still have a conscience. Listen, I'm a mom so I know about these things, okay? So yeah, we need him. But he needs us, too. Shit, Al, he can't even get in here, this place isn't wheelchair accessible, how's he gonna get down the frickin' steps? So I figure, the easiest and most fair way to do this is thirds. One for me, one for you, one for him. If he ever gets his shit together."

"He might not go for that," Al said.

"Maybe not," Sarah said. "But at least we can say we tried."

"Guess you been thinking some about this."

"I need the job, Al. I live with my son down in my mom's basement and if I don't get us out of there I'm gonna cut her gizzard out with a kitchen knife, I swear to God."

Al ran her tongue across her teeth. "Okay, well, there is one other thing."

"What's that?"

"*It's a dirty business, you said so yourself. It can also be, ah, hazardous. You understand what I'm saying?*"

Sarah nodded. "*I thought about that, too. Look, Al, I know I'm not like you, I don't know kung fu or any of that, and okay, I didn't grow up in the projects, but it hasn't been all that easy for me, neither. I been slapped, punched, kicked, cut, knocked down, spit at, and pissed on. I can do this.*" *She saw the doubt in Al's eyes.* "*Look, some people's lives can't be summed up in a two-page résumé. Not yours, and not mine, either. I can take care of myself.*"

Al nodded. "*All right. One condition.*"

"*What's that?*"

"*We keep you out of harm's way.*"

"*I can take care of...*"

"*Listen, I can't have some little kid running around hating on me for getting his mother killed or fucked up. That's my condition.*"

"*Okay,*" *Sarah said.* "*Deal.*"

A DAY LATER Martillo had taken Sarah out to her first job in the field. It was the Sheraton in Midtown.

"Watch the bartender."

Sarah had already known what to look for, she'd typed the reports over and over. "He didn't ring up that guy's tab," she said after a minute. "He just made change out of the cash he's got sitting on the register."

"You see how easy this is?" Martillo said. "You're a natural. Take us a week or so to get you up to speed on this shit, then I'll never have to set foot in one of these joints again."

"Doesn't seem so bad." Sarah was mentally adding up the bill she would send to the hotel's corporate parents. "But I'll never be able to drink Cutty Sark as fast as you."

"You'll be surprised," Martillo told her, "what you'll be able to do."

In an hour and a half they had it all, the bartender with his hand in the till, the salesmen ripping off their expense accounts, the prostitutes working over the drunks, the concierge retailing coke in the lobby. Once Sarah would have only seen a nice hotel where she and Frankie might have splurged for a room on a Saturday night, and now she saw a snake pit.

All on her first job.

"Do we tell Sheraton all of this?"

"Nah," Al told her. "The hotel leaves that pile of blank tabs next to the register on purpose, it keeps the businessmen coming back and nobody's paying us to catch those guys stealing. And we don't tell them the bartender's robbing them blind, we just report on what we saw, he only rings in about half of the cash transactions and he buys back every fourth drink so he'll get a bigger tip. And the concierge is the night manager's nephew, okay, so this time we have a phone conversation with the night manager, nothing in writing. When we come back next month, the guy's still at it, then we kick it upstairs. I know it sounds funny, they're paying us to find problems, but you don't want to find too many problems at once, you'll lose the account."

"Got it." She thought for a moment. "Is it always this simple?"

"Sarah. Honey. Most of these guys don't even see you. They just see your chest. You're a woman, they don't expect nothing from you."

And so it went.

In that first week, they photographed a wayward spouse, served two sets of divorce papers, repossessed one sports car, and bagged one crooked purchasing agent.

Sarah found it all exciting as hell.

And this was the boring stuff, this was the stuff Al didn't like doing. "Marty says this kind of business pays your overhead and keeps your door open," Al told her, "and he's right, but I hate it. It's like fixing flat tires, one after the other, all day long." But to Sarah, it was exhilarating just sitting in the client's restaurant, eating the client's food and drinking his booze, keeping her secrets. And it was the first job she'd ever had where she used her head. Marty had hired her to type, but Al was showing her a whole new world.

She turned the corner and headed up the hill on Bay 19th Street, had not gone more than a dozen steps when she saw him get out of a car and wait for her.

Before Al, she would have been afraid.

Frank Waters was six foot four and had the physique of a longshoreman, which he had once been. He might even be a match for Al, Sarah thought, and you are no Alessandra Martillo, you're a head shorter than her and you're round and you're soft. You should be afraid…

But she wasn't.

Like the old neighborhood, Frank Waters just didn't seem quite as impressive as he once had.

Anyway, she told herself, soft is not always a bad thing, soft can be nice if you know how to use it.

And Sarah Waters knew what she was good at.

So did Frankie…

"Sarah…" He spread his hands out wide.

"What do you want, Frankie? Court says three hundred feet."

"Do you see a judge anywhere?" He went from wounded and lonely to belligerent, just like that.

"What do you want, Frankie?"

A car turned the corner behind her, drove up the hill, and passed the two of them by. Frank deflated as he watched it pass. "I miss you, Sarah," he said softly, not looking at her. "God, I miss you. Don't you miss me?"

Before Al, maybe she'd have told him the truth, because

at night, alone in her bed as she lay listening to her mother snore, she did miss him. She ached for the feel of him in the bed next to her, the way his dick woke up before the rest of him when she went for him in the dark.

Yeah, she missed that.

The rest of him, not so much.

"What do you want, Frank? We're divorced. Dee. Vorced."

"Do you remember? You and me, riding the train up to Prospect Park? Doing it in the tall grass? What were we, sixteen? Those were the best times of my life. You can't tell me you don't think of me, now and then."

She stepped up to stand next to him. She could hear Al's voice in her head. "Open your eyes. Look at the details. It's all right there, you just have to see it."

Frank hadn't shaved in at least two days.

His clothes looked like he'd slept in them.

The backseat of his car was piled with junk, and something that looked suspiciously like a bag of dirty laundry was featured prominently right on top. And to think she'd been leaning, if he had played her right she'd be going for him right now...

"It's been a long day, Frank. I have to work tomorrow. Good night." She walked past him.

He spoke to her retreating back. "Glad you got a job, Sarah." And then, louder. "You're still my wife, Sarah, I don't care what anybody says. *My* wife."

"Get lost, Frank." She didn't like the way he'd leaned on the first word of that last sentence. It's too bad, she thought. He could be so good sometimes, but he was such an ass the rest of the time.

She went in the house and headed for her cold bed.

AT ITS WESTERN end Atlantic Avenue was a street where the tide had crested and was now receding. All the signs of re-

cent gentrification were there: brownstones with thermo-
pane windows behind ghetto bars, front doors painted in
colors that had been hot five or six years ago, chi-chi little
antique shops and restaurants all closed up, names hanging
over dusty windows with TO LET signs stuck to the inside of
the glass. One old neighborhood bar had survived, looked
like the kind of joint where time stood still, a dark and fragrant hole where the bartender knew what you wanted if
you asked him for a bat and a ball.

Things had gotten too hot for Al in her old building. Once
the night crawlers have climbed through your window, it's
hard to sleep there, no matter how many locks you install.
She'd crashed with a friend in Queens for a while, but that
had been a strictly temporary arrangement.

There are some creatures who must live alone.

Doesn't make you a bad person.

She looked through the doorway at the guys sitting on
the bar stools. Same guys, she thought, probably been in
the same places for twenty years. Maybe they hadn't even
noticed the neighborhood getting gentrified, probably
didn't see it falling apart now. They got what they needed
from the barkeep, and from the television high in the back
corner.

White guy behind the stick looked at her when she
walked in. The look didn't say "what can I get you," it said
"what the hell are you doing in here?"

"Looking for Mrs. Taylor," Al told him.

The guy wiped his hands on an off-white dish towel. "In
her office," he said. "Have a seat, I'll tell her you're here."

Al leaned on the bar and inhaled that bar smell, stale
beer and boiled cabbage. The television was tuned to CNN.
The sound was down, but the crawl on the bottom of the
screen told you what they were talking about: the Dow was
off over seven hundred points, and the same talking heads

who'd been promising a soft landing last year were now talking about points of no return. Wondering aloud where the bottom was.

Well, there's news, Al thought. Thanks for the heads-up…

Mrs. Taylor was a leathery white-haired old woman who moved with a surprising amount of energy. "You must be Miss Della Penta," she said, and she held out her hand.

"Alicia," Al said, and shook her hand. "Al for short."

"Nice to meet you, Al," Mrs. Taylor said. "Come on up-stairs and I'll show you the room."

The street-level entrance was blocked by a heavy metal door. Mrs. Taylor stuck her key in the lock and wrestled with the door for a moment, then the lock opened with a metallic snap and she hauled the door open. The hallway smelled like the bar, but it was clean, ancient marble floors, painted walls, no graffiti on the mailboxes.

Not horrible.

One flight up, Mrs. Taylor fought and won the same bat-tle with another metal door, held it open for Al to precede her inside. Didn't lie when you called it a room, Al thought. Plaster walls, creaky wooden floor, tiny bathroom, minus-cule kitchen, one radiator. "Lotta people don't wanna live over a bar," Mrs. Taylor said. "They think the noise will keep them up. I'm tellin' ya, it ain't that kinda place."

"Old guy's bar," Al said, thought better of it once the words were out.

It was hard to tell if Mrs. Taylor was offended by that. "Those folks downstairs," she said, "they already fought all the wars they gonna fight. Danced all the dances they gonna dance. It's quiet here."

Great, Al thought. I'm gonna be living upstairs from God's waiting room.

"You alone?" Mrs. Taylor asked her.

Al sighed.

There was a guy.

He was TJ Conrad, a musician of some repute. He was a gifted guitar player, and he knew it. Mediocre piano, according to himself. He was smart, opinionated, fun, arrogant, moody, frequently unavailable, had the face of an ancient Bedouin tribesman and the emotional maturity of a thirteen-year-old delinquent.

She couldn't quit thinking about him.

I am not gonna call him again, she told herself. I won't, if the sonuvabitch didn't get my messages, he knows how to find me.

She remembered his last voice mail, he'd left it on the house phone in her old apartment. Heard, again, his disembodied voice. "Hey, babe," he said, "listen, I'm sorry I been out of touch lately. I been busy, I been going through some shit. Too many hours. Gimme a couple of days, okay? Maybe we can hang on the weekend, okay? See ya." And then, just before he disconnected, there was a voice.

Not his voice.

She had played it back a few more times, just to be sure, but yeah, it was a voice, and no, it wasn't his.

Sounded like a chick.

A very young chick.

Listen, she told herself, it could have been anyone. I mean, the dude is a musician, he was probably calling from a bar, he spends half his life in them.

Could have been anyone.

Oh, really?

Then why didn't he call your cell? Hah? Because he

didn't want to talk to you, that's why, he just wanted to leave that bullshit message.

Men.

"Yeah," she said. "It's just me."

IT WAS JUST ANOTHER stinking project building, concrete and bricks, high-gloss enamel paint, one elevator, two stairwells that she was forbidden to enter. Cold day with a stiff breeze. She walked home from sixth grade by herself, an increasingly common occurrence these days. She hated it when she had to make the trip all by herself. It wasn't fear of what she might run into on the way, she was a Brooklyn kid and the streets did not scare her much. No, it was the change that frightened her, the newness of being on her own. Her mother had always been there, as far back as she could remember, but lately her mother had begun retreating, acting strange, sitting motionless and silent in the darkened apartment, staying in her bed with the covers pulled up high in the mornings and leaving Alessandra to fend for herself. She'll be all right when Papi gets home, Al told herself, but Papi was gone again, he was far, far away, wearing his uniform, doing his job.

Al couldn't get used to it, but she did her best to adapt. After a few hungry days at school she began making her own lunch. She tried to restore the apartment to proper order, she made her bed, cleaned the kitchen, tried to make things look, as well as she knew how, the way they always had. The fear pressed in on her, though, strengthened by her growing awareness that her mother was now as far away as her father had ever been.

The wind between the project buildings blew hard, leaching the warmth from her body. She shivered, somewhat from the cold but more from fear. Had she forgotten her coat at school? She couldn't remember, and if she'd left it there it was gone for sure. "You've got to take better care of your things!" her mother would howl, fighting not to cry. "Al, honey, we don't have money to keep on buying things for you just to have you lose them!"

It had been bitterly cold that morning, she couldn't have left her coat home.

Could she?

Maybe she wouldn't tell. Maybe she could wear two shirts and her hoodie, maybe it wouldn't get too cold this year, maybe she'd find another coat...

Maybe her mother wouldn't notice. She'd been acting so funny lately...

It wasn't much warmer inside her building. She rode the elevator up, silent and alone, pushed open the door to her floor.

Funny smell in the hallway.

Someone had opened a window somewhere and the cold wind was reaching in, feeling for her...

The door to the apartment was open.

Two firemen and a cop stood just outside, in the hallway. They didn't notice her until too late, she darted past them, saw her mother lying on the kitchen floor, the skin of her face an unearthly gray.

Oven door open.

One of the firemen grabbed her. She screamed.

ALESSANDRA CAME TO, gasping for breath on the floor next to the daybed in her apartment on Pineapple Street. The heat must have gone off again, she was covered with cold sweat, and she was freezing.

And alone, still.

She got up shivering, climbed back under the blankets, felt her twelve-year-old self sliding away.

My last night in this hole, she thought, shaking, and

the ghosts have to come out one more time. Maybe they wouldn't follow her to the new place over on Atlantic…

Yeah. And maybe Prince Charming would come along and make her feel warm all over. She waited for sleep, but it would not return.

God, she was cold.

THREE

ALESSANDRA STIFLED A yawn and tried to focus. The hard plastic chair in the office of Houston Investigations was the only thing keeping her awake, it had been a long night without much sleep. "Al," Sarah said, "this is Mrs. West. She's the woman I was telling you about." Al could not recall any mention of Mrs. West, this was probably just Sarah's way of making the woman feel comfortable. "We know you here, honey, and we've discussed your case." There was something of the Pied Piper in Sarah, people seemed to trust her. She must remind them of their sister, Al thought, or their favorite aunt, or maybe their first girlfriend from school.

The woman glanced at Sarah and nodded. She was a tall woman, and very thin, with long wispy blond hair that tended to float and blue eyes so wide you could see white all the way around the iris. She doesn't see herself, Al thought, when she looks in the mirror she probably sees what she looked like twenty years ago. Those eyes and that hair made her look somewhat demented. You could see how she might have been fine, once upon a time, but in another ten years she wouldn't look too out of place riding on a broom. Funny how youth and beauty can hide the dark spots in a person, but baby, when that tide goes out… Mrs. West sucked in a big breath of air as if it would help her tell her story. "I would like you to find my stepson," she said, looking down at her hands, which she held clenched in her lap.

She's fighting for control, Al thought, she's got her legs

crossed, got her fists ready, she's trying to keep herself very tight and hard in that chair.

Sarah made eye contact with Al and raised her eyebrows. She's asking me if we can do it, Al thought, and she nodded. No big deal.

"Your stepson?" Al asked, let the tone of her voice pose the question.

Mrs. West nodded without looking up. "Yes," she said. "My husband…Jake is my husband's youngest son. Jake and his brother were children when I married their father. Jake was twelve, his brother, Isaac, was thirteen. I thought they would warm up to me in time…" She finally raised her eyes and looked at Alessandra.

"They thought I was a trophy wife," Mrs. West said. "Maybe I was. I never thought so." She looked back down at her hands. "My husband was a wonderful man, simply wonderful, but I thought I brought at least as much to the marriage as he did. I had just completed my residency, I had joined a private practice on Madison Avenue. I was not as well off as Thomas, of course, but I certainly didn't need his money." Her voice had trailed off to the point where Alessandra and Sarah were both leaning forward to hear her.

A trophy wife, Al thought, God, do they give a trophy for second place…? "You're a doctor?" Al asked her.

"Psychiatrist." She glanced up quickly. "Not what you're probably thinking." Back on solid ground, her voice gained strength. "Until recently," she said, "most of my work has been with incarcerated women."

You'd have to be in jail, Al thought, to let a woman looks this crazy mess with your head. But you're being unfair, she thought. Maybe all she needs is a nice haircut. "Rehabilitation?" Al asked. "We still do that?"

Sarah held her thumb against the first two fingers of her left hand, shook her hand once, and looked at the ceiling.

It was typical Sarah: with one economical gesture and no words at all she told Al she was being an insensitive clod.

"We have never really bothered with rehabilitation, Ms. Martillo," Mrs. West said sharply. "We warehouse people for a longer or shorter period of time, we force them to live in conditions you wouldn't wish upon a stray cat, and when their time is up we turn them loose. And when they get into trouble again we pretend to be shocked."

"I'm sorry, Mrs. West, I didn't mean…"

"Oh, it's all right, I'm the one who should be sorry. I care deeply about my work, Alessandra, and to tell you the truth it has probably limited my usefulness. I wish I could have been more effective." She shook her head. "One of society's lesser problems. I guess we all have so many things to worry about. But if a disadvantaged or abused woman makes one small mistake, more often than not it can have a drastic effect on her entire life, and there's no need for it, no need at all. It just seems such a waste."

"Let me ask you one other question, Mrs. West. You obviously can afford any agency in town. Why us? Why Sarah and me?"

Something of a hawkish look came into Mrs. West's eyes. "Caughlan," she said, and she showed her teeth in what was meant to be a grin. Daniel "Mickey" Caughlan was a former client, currently serving time for tax evasion. "I know his wife very well, we share the same tennis coach. I know how much you did for them. I've already paid plenty, Ms. Martillo, looking for Jake. No one has managed to do the job. Daniel Caughlan couldn't have been an easy man to work for, yet you got the job done. Perhaps you might be able to help me."

Sarah cut in. "Mrs. West," she said, "why don't you tell us more about your stepson."

"All right." Mrs. West nodded, then went back to examining her manicure. "Such a mess. You won't understand Jake, or my relationship to him, unless I tell you the whole story. My husband, Thomas, had a partner, they were in the financial services business. Thomas was simply brilliant, he was the brains of the firm. His partner, Barrington Arthur Tipton IV, was the salesperson." She looked at Al and grimaced. It was almost a twitch, a facial tic, there for a second and gone. "To say that they did well for themselves and their customers would be an understatement." She glanced at her watch. "Ten years ago Thomas was in a horrible automobile accident. He was driving up the FDR late at night and, well, no one is completely sure what happened, but his car went off the road. He was killed instantly."

"I'm so sorry," Sarah said.

"Were there any witnesses to the accident?" Al said.

That strange look passed over Mrs. West's face again and was gone. "One person driving a taxi southbound said he saw my husband's Mercedes and another car going north-bound at a high rate of speed and then there was a loud noise. The police theorized that the two cars were racing, and… Well. Whether there was contact between the two vehicles or some sort of mechanical failure or if Thomas simply lost control, the only person who would be able to shed any light on that would be the other driver, and unfortunately he or she never came forward." She pulled out a handkerchief and dabbed at an eye. "He always found speed…intoxicating."

"It must have been a horrible shock," Sarah said.

"Well, yes," Mrs. West said. "But I'm afraid it gets worse. Two months later, Tipton disappeared. The firm's trust fund was looted to the tune of twenty-eight million dollars. Tipton left a note behind saying that he'd lost the money and that he could no longer live with himself, but his body was never found. So of course the insurance companies never paid. The business was left in a horrible state, with lawyers crawling over the wreckage like a pack of wild dogs. Tipton's family was ruined. Thomas had better lawyers when he wrote his will, but still, the bulk of his assets were frozen. Not that I care, truthfully. I'm well off by any rational standard. And I won't survive long enough to see the outcome of all the lawsuits, but Jacob might. More likely, I would think, his children will inherit someday."

"I'm sure there was a police investigation," Al said. "What conclusions did they come to?"

"The police were all too willing to close the case. Money gone, two men dead, end of story. Their experts claim that Tipton did write the suicide note. I hired an investigator, someone not unlike yourselves, and he traced Tipton to the Dominican Republic. Someone matching Tipton's description stayed at an oceanfront villa for three weeks before moving on."

"Wow, you're kidding. So you think Tipton…"

"It is impossible for me to be objective about this, Ms. Martillo, but if you're asking me what I think, in my heart of hearts I believe Tipton stole the money and ran off. I think he knew he'd never be able to liquidate that much cash or move it successfully with Thomas looking over his shoulder, so he had to deal with Thomas first. I have absolutely no proof other than what my heart tells me, but on my bad days I'm completely sure Tipton murdered Thomas and then disappeared."

"Any trace of Tipton since then? Ten years is a long time to stay missing. Most people slip up, they get careless or homesick or overconfident…"

"My investigator traced him to Monaco, and from there to Liechtenstein, but after that the trail went cold. I couldn't afford to continue paying the man if there was no reasonable chance for a resolution, Ms. Martillo, so I had to let it go. It almost destroyed me to do it, but I had no choice. And it wasn't about the money, either. I had dreams of clearing my husband's name, and I wanted to see Tipton punished for what he'd done."

"And now?"

"I don't think about it much anymore. I suppose I have accepted everything, finally. The insurance company involved pursued matters in their own way, but they did not choose to share their findings with me." She raised her head high. "Grief will not be denied, Ms. Martillo, it presses in, it wears one down. It dissolves absolutely everything if you let it, until all you have left is your sorrow. I stopped looking for Tipton years ago. I prefer to believe that he will pay for what he's done, but in a fashion and at a time of God's choosing. I have to live my own life, such as it is. Of course, I regret deeply that Thomas's name and reputation were sullied, but that is nothing, nothing at all, compared to the loss of the man himself."

Al let the silence hang in the room for a moment. "So I take it," she finally said, "that you are not interested in having us look for Tipton."

West seemed to think about that for a second. "No," she said. She dismissed Tipton with a gesture, a tiny wave of one hand. "He's gone."

"Twenty-eight million is a lot of money."

"I never made the sort of money Thomas did, Alessandra, but I have done well enough." She regarded her manicure again.

"So?"

"Six months ago I was diagnosed with ovarian cancer. If I submit to chemotherapy and radiation, I might have a year. If I refuse, I might have twelve months."

"Wow. That's tough."

"Yes, well." Mrs. West shrugged. "I've had some time

to get used to the idea. I feel fine right now, today, so I'm going with that. The thing is, after Thomas died, his sons blamed me."

"Why? That makes no sense."

Mrs. West sighed. "Oh, but it does, Alessandra. It's perfectly understandable. They needed to blame someone and I was the only available candidate. Isaac died in a boating accident some time after Thomas's passing, and Jake has chosen to cut me out of his life. I understand, really I do, and I have no desire to force the issue, but in view of the circumstances…" Her control finally slipped, and she pulled a monogrammed handkerchief out of her bag and held it to her face. Al glanced at Sarah, who held out one hand, palm out, telling Al to wait.

A moment later Mrs. West wiped her eyes and blew her nose before stowing the handkerchief. She cleared her throat. "In light of the diagnosis," she said. "Jake is all that is left of his father. Of my husband. There are certain things, things that belonged to Thomas, as well as certain facts about the aftermath… I'll feel better if I know I've left them in his hands. What he chooses to do with all of it, if anything, is his business. And there's my own personal estate as well. There's my apartment, my weekend house on the island, and some money. Not twenty-eight million, but a reasonable amount. One would certainly cross the street to pick it up. I've left a little something to my maid and to my chauffeur, but I would really… I don't care what Jake thinks of me, Al, I'm doing this for myself, not for him. I just think it will be easier for me to let go if I've given what I can to Thomas's only surviving family. I don't want to let the courts take it…"

"I understand," Al said.

"Do you?" Mrs. West swallowed. "If you succeed in locating Jake, please help him understand that I am not trying to inflict myself upon him. It's just, you know, he looked so much like Thomas…"

She lost it.

Sarah got up and went to her. *I got this,* she mouthed to Al, who decided to go for coffee.

AL STUCK HER nose into the steam coming out of the foam cup. Dunkin' Donuts, she thought. Can't beat it. "Okay, killer," she said. "What do you think?"

"Such a shame," Sarah said. "Ovarian cancer, God, it seems so unfair. She's so young."

"Really? Fifty, I thought," Al said.

Sarah shook her head. "Early forties," she said. "But with a lot of miles on her. Can you imagine? Your husband is killed, his kids think it's your fault, his money is gone, you're all alone, and then cancer? That's horrible. My God. I feel so sorry for her."

"Tough break," Al agreed. "What do you think really happened? You buying her story? You think Tipton took the money and ran?"

Sarah shrugged. "I would guess that it had to be a high-profile case. With that much money missing, I would bet that the police would want to be careful, particularly since there were insurance companies involved. How bad would the NYPD look if they took the suicide note at face value and then some wrinkled-suit gumshoe working for the insurance company finds Bats sunning his buns on the beach in Rio or something?"

"Bats?"

"Barfington Alistair Tipton whoever."

"Oh. Bats."

"Yeah. So, I mean, who knows, but if I had to lay money on this, I'd go with the NYPD, and according to her, they thought the suicide note was legit. Bats probably hired someone to off Thomas West, then killed himself. Case closed."

"What do you make of the Dominican Republic angle?"

"You mean the reports of some guy that looked like Bats down there? Sunning his buns?"

"Yeah. And then in Monaco or wherever."

"Al, this lady's got a chauffeur, bald guy, I talked to the him when I walked her downstairs."

"A chauffeur? You serious? He wear a uniform? And one of those little hats?"

"He wears a suit. And he didn't get it from no Sears and Roebuck, neither, let me tell you. You wanna know how her mind works, she's got a Bentley, she got tired of the thing being in the shop all the time so she went to the dealer where she bought it and she hired their chief mechanic. Haig, his name is, he's the guy driving her. He told me, she wouldn't take no for an answer, she just kept raising her offer until he took it."

"Wow. Okay, I guess she's got the bucks."

"And a maid, so she says. Owns her apartment, from the way she talked, got a house on Long Island, and she's got enough cash laying around to wonder who to leave it all to. She's a doctor, works in some Madison Avenue firm, might even be a partner. She's not exactly hand-to-mouth, you know what I'm saying? So she thinks that Bats killed her husband and ripped her off, she hires some stooge to go look for him, but after a while she has to call him off because she's not seeing any real results. What I think, this detective, whoever he was, he had to be soaking her good. I mean, he had to be hitting her pretty hard. What if the guy just decided to take a nice Caribbean holiday on her dime? Be pretty easy to find some tourist looks sort of like Bats, at least from a distance. Take a couple of grainy, out-of-focus shots, tell her you nearly got him but he dragged ass and split. I think it would be easy to string Mrs. West along, get some more money and a European tour out of her, too. I mean, you ever notice, people that spend all their lives in school getting to be doctors or lawyers or whatever, a lot of the time they got no goddam sense. Plus, I think she loved her husband. I think she definitely believes he got set up. But suppose she came to someone like Marty with this? He'd see dollar bills floating in the air. Unless I see something telling me otherwise, I think she got used."

Al dabbed at the corner of her eye. "Why, Sarah," she said. "I'm so proud of you..."

"Oh, shut up."

"Admit it. When you started here, you never would have sniffed that out."

"No. I'd be all worked up trying to think of a way to convince you to help me find Bats and smoke him out of his hole."

"And now?"

Sarah shrugged again. "She just wants us to find the kid."

"Think you can do it?"

"I'd like to try," Sarah said. "Should be mostly on-line anyhow. I'll keep track of how much time I spend on him, and if you think it takes too long we'll cut Mrs. West a discount. How about it?"

"Sounds fair. What's your angle?"

"Well, Mrs. West is gonna phone me with what she's got. She has an old address, and she's got his Social Security number, so I'll start with the credit bureaus. If they got nothing I can check with Seton Hall, that's where he graduated, and you know colleges like to bleed their alums for donations, he ought to be on one of their lists. Then there's court records and whatever. If this kid has gotten married, divorced, bought or sold real estate, went to jail, died or got a traffic ticket, I'll get him."

"Good girl. You okay with this?"

"Yeah. Why shouldn't I be?"

"I dunno. You looked kind of bummed this morning."

"Did I?" She chewed on that for a moment. "My ex dropped by last night."

"Yeah?"

"Yeah."

"He come by the house?"

"No. Not exactly. I mean, I got an order of protection, he's supposed to stay away, so he was waiting for me in the street. Up the block."

"Why did you have to get an order of protection? He get physical?"

"You mean last night? No, we just talked for a while. He used to, you know..." She trailed off.

"Nah, I don't know, Sarah. You're probably gonna have to tell me."

Sarah gave her a look, thought about it. "Well, he would get pushy. I mean, he never hit me or nothing like that, but you know, when he wanted his way..."

"He raped you, you mean."

"No!" She sounded outraged, just a little. "I mean, not really. It's not like I didn't wanna..." She looked at Al. "We were married."

"That make it okay?"

"No. I don't know. I never thought about it that way. I mean..." She looked around, checked the closed office door. "I didn't like being forced or anything, Al, but I miss..." She swallowed. "I haven't been with anyone since Frankie. I'm not an old maid yet. I miss, you know..."

"That's a separate issue, Sarah. You want a nice firm filet mignon, guys are a dime a dozen."

"Easy for you to say."

"Sarah, stop. You gotta be kidding me. You telling me

you don't see the guys that come sniffing after you? What about that piano player in the bar from when we worked the Hyatt last week?"

Sarah colored. "Yeah, I remember, but you can't just…"

"Why the hell not? Sarah, honey, if you're in the mood for a couple nice cheeseburgers, there's no law says you got to buy the whole fucking bull."

Sarah's face got redder. "No."

"You in the market for undying love, till death do you part, sickness and health, all that shit?"

She shook her head. "Not at this time."

"Okay. So this is still America the beautiful, babe, and that means you're in the driver's seat. No excuse for not getting what you need."

"Maybe not."

"Not an old maid yet."

"No."

"There you go. So you want me to scare Frankie away?"

"Alessandra, Frank is a great big sonuvabitch. He used to…"

"Sarah. Honey. You're on the team now. You understand what that means? Means you're with me. I'm with you. You want this gorilla to avoid your block like the plague, we can probably engage him in a little aversion therapy."

They stared at each other for a moment. "Thank you," Sarah finally said, and looked down. "But he's not really a gorilla."

"No? He just likes pushing you around."

"No, well, you know. All right, I'm probably making excuses for the guy, which I know is stupid, but it's just that…I was in love with him, Al. We were high school sweethearts. He's the only guy I ever had, almost. Even after everything, you know, I still got a soft spot for him, I can't help it."

"That soft spot, it ain't in the middle of your skull, is it?"

"Maybe it is. Frankie is a nice guy, Al, really, as long as he ain't with the guys. He's got these guys he hangs around with, and they talk him into things. It's the neighborhood, you know what I mean? Listen, in case you ain't figured it out, I'm Italian, okay, so I know what I'm talking about. Every kid from south Brooklyn got a vowel at the end of his name thinks he could be a wiseguy if he wanted. Frankie goes around with all these pretend gangsters, these loser jerks from the block, can't keep a job, always looking for an angle. They like Frankie because he is a tough guy for real, he's just not always real smart about it. If he would just stay away from those jokers…"

"If he'd grow up and be a man, you mean. I hope you ain't holding your breath waiting for that."

"No. Hey, listen, I did divorce the guy. But when he's not getting suckered into some stupid hairball scheme with Vinny the brick and Tony and Mick and Jones Beach Joey, he can be a nice guy."

Al snorted. "Jesus Christ."

"I know, I know."

"Women. God, I will never understand us. What makes us so willing to put up with this kind of bullshit? Can you tell me? Why do we hook up with these losers when there ought to be some grown-up individuals out there with normal lives who don't live with their mothers? Will you tell me that?"

"Oh. Oh, I get it. What about you? What about…"

"Never mind me. Listen, Sarah, this guy bothers you, I'm not kidding, we ain't having this."

"It won't come to that."

"I'm not kidding, Sarah."

"I know you're not. If I need help, I'll ask. I promise."

FOUR

TJ Conrad looked ten years older than he had the last time Alessandra had seen him. They sat on a park bench on The Promenade, a small city park that stretched for the space of four blocks over the top of the Brooklyn-Queens Expressway. You could see the whole Upper New York Bay from there, from the Verrazano-Narrows Bridge up to the Statue of Liberty, Jersey City away in the hazy distance, the southern tip of Manhattan in the foreground. "I heard you on the radio," she said.

He brightened a bit. "Did you? You heard the BandX single? I heard it was getting a couple of spins, here and there."

"No, no that, the other one." Conrad had contributed a guitar solo to a song recorded by the pop diva Shine, who was known within the music business as "God."

He deflated again. "Oh, yeah. My seven seconds of fame."

"Come on," Al said. "Don't sell yourself short, it was a nice lick. Besides, there was two more seconds right at the end."

"My nine seconds of fame."

"TJ, let me ask you something, are you always this down after you've made a hit record?"

"I don't know," he said. "It was God who had the hit, not me."

"What about the reviews you guys are getting for the BandX record?"

He nodded. "They're very nice. I suppose that ought to make up for the guys not talking to me anymore."

"Not even Doc?"

"He called back, I'll give him that much. He left me a message. Haven't heard from him since."

"Oh. You mean he called your house phone when he knew you wouldn't be home, is that what you're saying? Left you some bullshit message about how busy he was and like that? Wow, I bet that really sucks."

"Alessandra, I said I was sorry."

"Yeah, you did, but are you going to tell me what the fuck is going on?" Who is she? That's what Al really wanted to ask him. Who was the little chickadee I heard in that message you left? She ached to throw it in his face, to demand he man up and tell her if it was over, whatever it was they were doing. Problem was, she didn't have enough. Other than three-quarters of a second of a girl's voice rendered indistinctly on her voice mail. Nothing, in other words, just her suspicions.

"You don't want to hear about my problems," he said.

"TJ." You bone-headed, stubborn, arrogant sonuvabitch… "I wouldn't ask you if I didn't want to hear it."

"Ahh, Christ…"

"Goddammit, TJ…"

"All right, okay, you win." He looked away from her, stared out into nothing for a while.

She waited him out.

"I been playing music my whole life. I'm good at what I do. I don't take a backseat to anybody."

"I know that."

"The business is dead," he said. He turned and looked at her, his face bleak. "I mean, we used to joke about it, me and Doc and the guys, like making fun of your uncle, 'Yeah, he's had it, his liver probably looks like a piece of Swiss cheese,' meanwhile the old bastard will probably have a pint of T-bird in his pocket when he goes to your funeral."

"Yeah, but…" She heard the wonder in her own voice. "I heard you on the radio."

He nodded. "A small splash, a tiny ripple…and then nothing."

"Serious? Nothing?"

"A quiet darkness," he said, "a watery death at the bottom of the deep end of the pond. Maybe about a hundred years from now some future musicologist will dig up BandX and give us a listen, and he'll go, 'Wow, check this out!' and he'll write a paper or an article. Then we'll be hot for a month or so, and for a while after that, right, whatever the kids are playing, it will sound a little bit like the blues, just a little bit, and then it will pass. We'll go back to being dead."

"You know something," Al said, "when you told me all musicians are drama queens, you weren't kidding. Your phone was ringing off the hook. When I was by your place last month you had like a hundred messages on your machine. Are you telling me nothing came out of all that?"

He shrugged. "Nothing I can pay the rent with."

"But God gave you a co-writing credit, you told me so yourself."

He nodded. "Check's in the mail. That's what I keep hearing, anyhow."

"Yeah, but…"

"Al. Baby."

"Oh, don't you 'Al baby' me. Are you telling me you got on the radio playing for God, you got an album coming out with BandX, the record company has to want you guys to tour, don't they? Isn't this what you guys have been working for?"

"I'm afraid it is."

She looked up at the sky, silently asked for help. "You gotta, for crissake, TJ, you gotta explain that one for me."

"Alessandra, you know something, when you have a

dream, it's better if you stay ignorant, it's better for you if you just go ahead and build your rocket or whatever the fuck it is you wanna do, because when you get close enough to see how things really work, then you know. Okay? Then you gotta stop kidding yourself." He stared at her. "Haven't you ever had a dream? Didn't you ever want something so bad you stayed up all night practicing? Tell me, Al. Tell me there's something out there that you really, really want."

It was her turn to be quiet, his turn to wait. "My dream," she finally said, "is to win the fight I'm in today, and to show up for the one I'm gonna have to fight tomorrow."

"That's it?"

"That's it."

He shook his head. "Okay, it's all right if you don't wanna tell me. Because if you keep it safe, nobody can shit all over it. Keep it locked up safe."

"Play my guitar all alone up in my room?"

"Al, honey, you don't understand. The business is dead. Remember how I told you we used to joke about it? That was because we were too far away to see how true it was. But now, okay, now we been up close and we seen the body, and you know what, it's dead for real, and it's starting to stink. You want to know the future of the music industry? It's Guitar Hero. A video game. Guitar. Fucking. Hero."

Alessandra's paranoia kicked in and she wondered if all the angst might not just be a smoke screen to keep her away from the subject of TJ's new sixteen-year-old girlfriend.

His alleged girlfriend, she told herself. You got no evidence, you got nothing. "Well," she said, "at least you got something off that track you did for God. If the business is really dead, at least you made a couple bucks off the carcass."

"There's that," he told her. "You really know how to cheer a guy up, you know that?"

"You're telling me your record company doesn't want

BandX to go play some dates so you can hump this new record?"

"You remember Sandy Ellison, our A and R guy? He's in Tibet producing some kind of documentary for the Hitler channel. So, as of right now, there are no plans, no dates, and no word from any of the guys."

Maybe that's what is really wrong with him, she thought. He's not playing. "So you're not playing anywhere."

"I just told you…"

"Not BandX," she said. "You."

"Well, yeah, 'course I'm playing, you know, here and there. No big thing."

"Where? Can I come hear you?"

"Al, it ain't that kind of gig, I'm just…"

"Where are you playing? Why can't I come?"

He sighed. "Note to self: never date a cop, public or private. Of course you can come. Anytime you want."

"All women are cops, we have to be," she said. "So? Where's the gig? And what's it gonna cost me?"

One corner of his mouth curled up into the faint beginning of a smile. "Hey, baby, I can get you backstage, but you gotta be willing to put out, you know what I'm saying?"

"You ain't had enough time to heal up from the last time. For real, I can come and hear you play?"

He sighed again. "Wednesday night. Joint down in the Village, right on West Street." He told her the name of the club. "We probably go on around eleven or so. Name of the band is Indio."

"Indio?" She was surprised. "You going Hispanic?"

He laughed. "Indio is about as Hispanic as I am. The drummer's parents are from Mexico, but he doesn't even speak Spanish."

"Any good?"

"They're just kids."

"Yeah, but are they any good?"

He looked out over the water, took his time answering. "They got something," he finally said. "I don't know how deep it goes, and I don't even wanna guess if it's commercial or not, but they got something." He turned and looked back at her. "The guitar player and the singer asked me to sit in. These kids really want to learn. I mean, there's nothing in it for me, but when you run into desire that strong, it makes you wanna help out. You know what I mean? It makes you wanna jump in. So yeah, I'm playing, but I'd be better off painting houses with my uncle, you wanna know the truth."

SHE THOUGHT ABOUT asking him up, but then it occurred to her that if you had to think about it maybe you shouldn't do it, because if it was simply another decision based on logic and reason then the human race would probably be extinct by now, there being no sensible reason she could think of to let some guy get into your space, ever. What she wanted was that feeling at the pit of her stomach when her animal nature seized control, ignored her reason and did what it, or rather she, really wanted to do despite all of the reasons to do otherwise. The difficulty was that she wanted TJ to have it like she did, she wanted more than that half-conscious, semi-erect "who me, oh yeah, great!" state of readiness most guys seemed to walk around in, she wanted him to want her, goddammit, not just the next available slot, she wanted to see that light in his eyes, and she just didn't. Okay, she thought, I know, it's unreasonable to expect that rush of desire and insanity that makes your hands shake and your mouth go dry, not every time, but…

He put his hands around her and patted her shoulder. "I gotta go, babe," he said, soft in her ear. "I'm dead on my feet, and I got a big day tomorrow."

"Okay," she said, and when he patted her again it felt like

his way of saying, "I know, I know, it'll get better," but he didn't know, he couldn't, or else he would have shown her something.

Anything.

And what am I supposed to feel? she wondered as he walked away, what are you supposed to say when a guy seems to have one eye on the exit most of the time, other than, you know, don't do me any favors, pal? But she could tell that he was beat, and if the yin and the yang don't match up every time, couldn't she just let it go? Couldn't she wait for a better time?

Her nascent fever ebbed, replaced by an incoming, nagging uncertainty.

THE PHONE RANG once. Her mother snatched it up. Sarah Waters gritted her teeth. "Why, hello, Frank," her mother said, her face lighting up. "It's so good to hear your voice!" Sarah shook her head. If we were Eskimos, she thought, I could strand her on an ice floe. If we were Mayans, I could tear out her heart and offer it to the gods. If we were Inca, I could leave her up on top of some frickin' mountain... "Well, of course I've missed you, Frank." Sarah wondered if she would ever make enough money to have her own place. Whenever she looked at the numbers, it all seemed so impossible. "Yes, Frank. She's right here. I'm sure she'll talk to you." Her mother held out the phone, a look of childish triumph on her face.

Sarah took it silently, held it down at her waist, glared at her mother.

"Oh!" her mother finally said. "Oh! Excuse me. I'll, ah, I'll just go upstairs now."

"You do that," Sarah said, and she wondered if there might not be some traditional and ritualistic method Sicil-

ians used to deal with people who have outlived their usefulness. Ice pick in the ear, perhaps… "Hello, Frank."

"I'm sorry," Frank said, and he sounded it. "I'm sorry,
I didn't mean… I thought I'd get your answering machine,
I was just gonna leave you a message. I didn't mean, you
know…"

Sarah closed her eyes. "It's all right, Frank. What's up?"

"Well, I, uh, I didn't get to say what I wanted to say the
other night. I wasn't at my best. Whenever I see you something happens to me, I don't know what it is, but I get stupid."

There it is, she thought, he's giving you the line, go on
and tell him what a short trip it is from Frank to stupid.
She didn't, though. "That right, Frank? What was it that
you wanted to tell me?"

"Just that it was good to see you. I wanted to tell you
that. And that you looked good."

"Thank you." Come on, she thought. Enough bullshit,
get to what it is you really want.

"What I meant was, you know, you looked, uh, you
looked good, that's all."

Women, Sarah thought, we use about twelve thousand
words a day. Guys must average about eight hundred, and
Frank sounded like he was right up in the seven-nineties
somewhere and starting to run dry. She had to give the guy
credit, though, he was trying…

"Things have turned around for me, Sarah. That's the
other thing I wanted to tell you. My luck has changed."

"Your luck?"

"You know something, Sarah, you were right, it wasn't
luck. I was just saying. I mean, I can see it now. I got this
counselor at the VA and he told me I hadda get away from
the neighborhood, and I hadda get away from the guys. I
mean, I grew up with 'em and everything, but I just can't

hang with them no more. They weren't doing me no good. You know what I'm saying? Those guys are always gonna be what they always been, they ain't gonna change."

Sarah wanted to scream. Hadn't she been trying to tell him the same thing for twelve years? And did he listen to her? Noooo, but let some other sonuvabitch tell him the same thing, all of a sudden he has this giant revelation. "So you got your problems with the union straightened out? You back working again?"

"The union ain't all that, Sarah."

I knew it, she thought.

"They ain't the only place in the world to get ahead."

"No? You made good money with the Teamsters, Frank." An actual living wage…

"Sarah, honey, don't worry. I know I owe you a bunch of child support and stuff, and…"

"It's your son that you owe," she said, sharper than she wanted to. "He's the one you owe, Frank, not me."

"Yeah, whatever, I know, but what I'm saying is that I'm gonna catch up, I promise. I'm gonna get all caught up, you know what I mean? I'm sending you some money, not this week, okay, next week, most likely, week after at the latest. I'm gonna pay you back everything I owe you."

"What you owe me?" Don't start down that road, she told herself. Nothing good can come from it. You can lay up all night long thinking about what Frank owes you, and what you'll never get back.

"I'm gonna make it up to you, Sarah, honest to God."

"What happened, Frank? You hit the lottery? Where you getting all this dough you're gonna send me?"

"You know something?" He sounded almost thoughtful "I did. In a way, I did hit the lottery."

"Don't tell me," she said. "Frank, don't you dare tell me

that one of those idiotic friends of yours has talked you into some new scam…"

"No, no, it ain't nothing like that. Sarah, baby, listen to me. I know you want me to go back on the Teamsters, but I don't wanna work on the Jersey waterfront my whole life, I want something more. I want something better. For you. For us."

"Oh, yeah?" She could feel it building up inside. "So, what, Frank, tell me what, you went back to school and got your law degree, is that what it is? Hah? Now you're gonna…"

"Don't, Sarah, please stop. You know what your problem is, you got no faith in me. I got a job, Sarah, a good one. I show up every day, I work hard, my boss likes me, and for once in my life I'm making serious money. I mean, you were right, Sarah, I just had to quit looking for the next big deal, I had to get a real job and apply myself, and that's what I been doing, I promise. Everything is turning around for me, Sarah. I thought you'd be proud."

"Yeah, I'd like to be proud of you, Frankie, I'd like to believe you, but I been down this road before. You remember that time you were gonna buy used cars and export 'em to South America? You remember that? What a great idea that turned out to be. How about that time you were buying the franchise for that cell phone company? What was that, AmericanTellecell? How'd that work out? What am I supposed to do, Frank? Am I supposed to forget all that?"

"Sarah, it ain't like that this time."

"No? What's it like this time, Frank? Huh?"

"Guy I served with in Kuwait," he said, defensive. "Guy lives down South someplace now, he calls me up. He's got this uncle, Paolo Torrente, guy needs someone to show him around New York City. He's from Palermo, he's in the wine business. In Italy. I mean, the family's loaded, Sarah, they own vineyards, they own wineries, they run their own wine brokerage firm, all of that. So Torrente comes to New York, he's going to start selling over here, but he's never been to this country before. He knows all about wine, you know what I'm saying, you wouldn't believe how much he knows about wine, but he's really just a country guy, he knows his business, but he don't know anything else. He had this broker he was working with, but the guy put him up in this big hotel in Midtown, right, it's costing him two, three grand a day, the uncle is going ape shit. So my buddy remembers me, he knows I'm from here, he knows I'm a Brooklyn guy, he calls me, says can I help him out. So I go get Torrente out of the Plaza or whatever, okay, I put him into this nice little joint in Staten Island, I help him get incorporated..."

"Hold it, hold it, you did what?"

"Oh come on, Sarah, it ain't rocket science, I found him a lawyer, for crissake, the two of them sit in the guy's office jabbering Italian for half a day, now he's got a subsidiary corporation so he can do business in this country. No big thing. Next we go look at a bunch of warehouses, me and Uncle Paolo, and he buys one. I mean, he don't rent the fucking place, Sarah, he buys it. So he's legit. He's for real. Palermo Imports, that's the name of the company, we got contractors coming in a couple weeks to put in the cold-storage rooms and pallet racks and all that, got some fag decorator drawing up plans to re-do the office spaces. I found him the contractors, they're from the neighborhood, but they do good work and they speak Italian so Paolo can holler at them in his native tongue and all that shit. Anyhow, what I'm saying, Sarah, this is for real. You're talking to the new operations manager for Palermo Imports, 760 Richmond Terrace, Staten Island, New York."

Sarah's mind reeled. "Frank, are you sure... How do you know this isn't some kind of scam? How well do you know this army buddy of yours? How come he isn't the one up here helping Uncle Paulie? How come…"

"He hates the city, Sarah. You see, I knew you would say that. I know the guy, Sarah. You go to war with someone, you get to know them pretty good."

"Okay, fine, but how can you be sure these greaseballs are for real? Where my parents come from, okay, they don't trust nobody from Palermo, believe me. How do you know they're not trying to bring heroin into the country or something like that?"

"Sarah, listen, you met this guy, you wouldn't be worried, I promise. He just bought a house, big huge place up on the Jersey side of Staten Island. He's having all his furniture and shit sent over here from Italy. And you can't mess around with drugs in this place, Sarah, it's a bonded warehouse. Or will be, when I finally get Customs up off their ass to come and make the final inspection."

"Customs? United States Customs? How the hell do you…"

"I told you, it ain't rocket science, Sarah, it's just knowing some guys, that's all. And you gotta admit, I know a lotta guys. That's how business really works, Sarah, you gotta know people. It's about relationships. It's about knocking on the right doors."

She groped for a chair, sat down in it. "So you're getting paid? Like with a check, not in cash, under the table?"

"I'm on salary, Sarah. I work way more than forty hours for it, but I get a check every two weeks, taxes taken out and alla that. This is a regular job, for a real company. I mean, I ain't saying Uncle Paolo ain't kind of wack, okay, but he's legit."

Her head swam. "I don't know what to say, Frank."

He laughed. It was a sound she had not heard in a very long time. "No, listen, I understand. I know I ain't got the best track record. But this is different, babe, this is just about finding a place where I fit in, and it's about working hard. I just found the right place, finally. I wake up every morning before the alarm even goes off, and I feel excited about going to work. Can you believe that?"

"Wow. Well, I'm happy for you, Frank. Congratulations."

"Thank you. Listen, Sarah, I got some money for you. Call it a down payment on what I owe you. I'd like to come by and give it to you."

"Oh, yeah?" She felt a flutter in her stomach.

"I know, I know, you don't trust me. I understand. How about we meet? We'll have dinner at Costello's, you always liked that place." She could hear the longing in his voice. "You don't have nothing to worry about, Sarah, I'm a new man. I don't wanna do nothing to jeopardize my position."

They both managed to laugh over that.

"I work most evenings, Frank. Let me check my calendar tomorrow and I'll call back and let you know."

"That's all I can ask for," he said. "A chance. It's all I can ask for, right? And more than I deserve, probably."

FIVE

"ALESSANDRA," SARAH SAID, "what the hell did you do to Marty? We don't hear a word for ages and then all of a sudden he's calling up and screaming at me."

Al smiled.

"No, for real," Sarah said. "He called here like five times, I hadda quit taking his calls, he was so vile. There's a bunch of stuff from him on your voice mail. Didn't you talk to him about the deal you and I made?"

Al shrugged. "I didn't really get a chance. When he finally started to talk, he was so pissed I think you probably could have heard him from here if you'd had your window open."

"Al, he made some ugly threats. Are we really working on his license? I never thought about that."

Al nodded. "We are."

"He said he's getting a lawyer, he's gonna sue, he's gonna put us out of business and get back every cent we made since he got hurt, he's gonna see to it personally that you get put away for criminal impersonation and fraud... Can he really do that?"

"Who knows? You were right not to talk to him, though. Give him some time to cool off. I'll go back down there and see him again."

"You really think that's a good idea? He was really hot."

"I can handle Marty."

"Yeah, but what if he tries to go through with this? We

can't operate without a license. I need this job, Al. Besides, you know, it's been fun. I like doing what we do."

"Does have its moments, doesn't it? Don't worry, I'm not exactly rolling in it, either, I need the job as much as you do. Listen, if it comes to that, we'll go hire a license, Marty ain't the only dirtbag ex-cop in town."

"Can we afford to do that?"

"I don't know. Maybe we won't have to. Let's do this, let's let Marty cool his jets for a couple days and then we'll go talk to him. If he doesn't want to play ball, then we'll have to figure something out."

Sarah didn't look happy with that. "Okay," she said. "Do you honestly think, I mean…"

"Right now, Marty is a mess. Believe it or not, he needs us. Give him a little time to figure that out. Meantime, you get anywhere with your Mrs. West?"

"No. Well, not really. She faxed over what she had on Jake. I had some questions for her, but when I called her office I got some guy who was really nasty. He said he couldn't answer any questions or make any comments. I left a message on her cell, but she hasn't called me back yet. I'll get started on my searches tomorrow. Listen, tomorrow I think I have to leave early."

"Yeah? What's going on?"

Sarah told her about the phone call from Frank.

Al stared at Sarah, disbelieving. "Why can't he send you a check? Do you actually want to sit down and have dinner with this prick? After what he did to you? Why would any-one want to give someone like him another shot at them? What are you thinking?"

"I'm not sure." Sarah shook her head. "You must have heard the old line, 'he may be a son of a bitch, but he's my son of a bitch.' He's really not a bad guy, Al, and he sounds different, Al. He sounds like an adult."

"Yeah, okay, fine. You musta caught him on one of his good days. I still don't get why you have to meet with him. How much child support does he owe you, anyhow?"

"All of it," Sarah said.

"What? What? He never paid you at all? He never…"

Sarah shook her head. "Four years' worth," she said. "I never got a cent. He was pretty worked up when I moved out."

"Yeah, well, Jeez, I wonder why. Probably had something to do with him getting stuck washing out his own socks and shit. Probably missed having his own personal sex toy, too, even if it happened to be attached to you. You'd better not be going soft on me, Waters. You let this guy back in, I'm gonna hack off his balls, I swear to Christ."

Sarah started laughing, softly at first, but then harder, and it seemed to dissolve some of Al's foul humor. "Ah, Jesus," Sarah finally said, catching her breath. "I wonder if his voice would change back. He could be the world's last castrate tenor." She started singing an old Mario Lanza tune in a high thin Mickey Mouse voice.

"Very funny," Al said, trying to hang on to some of her anger. "You still haven't told me why you want to see him."

The laughter drained out of Sarah's face. "C'mon, you know how it is," she said. "I loved him once."

Al waited.

"Okay, maybe I hated him for the first two or three years after we split," Sarah said. "But you know something, I ached for him at the same time. Maybe not him, exactly, but for the guy I knew he started out to be. That's the guy I wanted. I guess I've sort of forgotten about him this past year. Right up until the other night."

"Good," Al said. "Call him back and tell him to send you a money order."

"Yeah, but…"

"Here we go," Al said. "Whatever comes after the 'but' has to be a real winner."

"When you really love someone," Sarah said, "I mean, when you sell out, when you really open all the doors, when you give everything you got, Al, it doesn't stop just because the guy turns out to be a bum. I will probably always feel something for Frankie. That doesn't mean I'm letting him move back in."

"No? What does it mean, then?"

"It means I want him to be okay. It means I want to believe that he got a real job, one with a future. I want him to be what he started out to be, I want him to find a nice fat girl and settle down with her and have a mortgage and kids and payments and all that. I want him to be happy. I want him to call me up saying he's taking my son to a ball game."

"Sounds like paradise to me. And that's why you gotta go meet him at this restaurant tomorrow night."

"I know I don't have to do it," Sarah said. "I'm not even sure I want to, but I think I need to. I need to let him see how it is."

"Yeah? What if he don't wanna hear about how it is? What if he flips out?"

"And acts like a two-year-old? It's a distinct possibility. But I got a plan."

"A plan. Oh, great. This better be good…"

TJ CONRAD STARED out the passenger-side window of the rented Malibu. "Tell me again," he said, "what are we doing down here?"

"Going undercover," Al told him. "Jesus Christ, TJ, I thought this would be fun. I don't wanna go to this place all by myself, it would look weird, so I need a guy, but if you don't wanna do it I'll drop you off, you can catch a cab home, I'm sure I can find someone willing to submit to a free dinner with me, it can't be that bad, for crissake."

"Relax, will you? I didn't say I didn't wanna do it."

"No? You had other plans tonight, you should have said."

"I don't have other plans, Al."

"What's the fucking problem then? You don't wanna do this for me? You don't wanna hang out with me, is that it? Because, believe me, if you find my company so—"

"Al, stop, I give up, you win."

"I win what?" she yelled. "What do I win? What's my fucking prize, huh?"

TJ put his hands in his hair and pulled. "God, please, make her stop."

"Stop what?" Al was getting louder. "What is it that you want me to stop doing? You want me to stop talking? Is that it? Why don't you go buy a goddam blow-up doll if that's what you want? You could sit her there in the passenger seat, she'll just stare out the window with her mouth open! How about that?"

"Al, you're making me nuts."

"I'm making you nuts? Listen, you jerk, I asked you if you wanted to come, you said okay, and now you're acting like you're gonna get your fingernails pulled out or some shit."

"Do they scream at you while they pull out your fingernails?" TJ mumbled.

"What? What did you say?"

"I said," TJ replied, in a nearly normal voice, "women are terrorists."

"That's not what you said." She was still steaming, but she wasn't yelling anymore. "What do you mean, women are terrorists? What the hell is that supposed to mean?"

TJ nodded calmly. "It's true, you're emotional terrorists, every one of you. Listen, the average guy getting into a fight with the average broad, it's like Gilligan picking a fight with Mike Tyson. He's gonna get his ass kicked, okay, he might get his ear bit off, too, and afterward he's still not gonna know what the hell he did wrong."

"Oh for crissake," Al said.

"No, it's true. Think about it. You guys, you think, that's what you do all day long, every day. I mean, we can't see into your brains, but we know it's very busy up in there, you got shit going on all the time. I mean, look at you! You ain't saying anything right this second, but them fucking wheels are turning up in that head, don't tell me they ain't, I can smell the smoke. But when you look at a guy, chances are you know exactly what he wants."

"Oh, really? Is that it? Is that all women are good for? You just wanna—"

"Listen to me, Al. Guys are basic creatures, that's all I'm saying. You see a guy sitting quiet in a chair all by himself, he's not into anything deep or dark. Chances are he's thinking about one of four things: sports, beer, sex, or cars. Maybe work. That's it, Al, we got that stuff covered, we're happy as shit."

"You're an idiot."

"That's a different topic. Come on, don't look at me like that, you know I'm right. You guys are not like us. We can never tell what you want. Hell, half the time you don't know what you want, either. We can't win. And you know what makes it even worse? I lose, that's okay, at least it's over. Right? Right? Wrong. It's not over, nothing is ever over. The thing might be dead, okay, but you're not gonna bury it, no, you're gonna take the body back home and stick it in a closet somewhere. And then when the fancy strikes you you're gonna haul out the stinking, mummified corpse and then we're gonna have to do this same dance all over again.

And I'm gonna lose then, too, and you know what? I still won't know what I did wrong."

Al watched him. What you did wrong, she thought, you didn't convince me that you aren't going out the back door and nailing some chick that has twice my bra size and half my IQ. That's what you did wrong. You never let me know if I'm good enough… She knew that she would never have the courage to tell him that. "Let's start over," she said.

"Good." He exhaled loudly. "My name is—"

"Cállate," she said. "Shut up, you asshole. Here's what's going on tonight. You and I are going to go eat dinner at this joint down in Gotti country. Supposed to be good. A friend of mine is gonna be there with a guy. Okay? She trusts the guy, sort of, and I don't. If he gets out of hand, okay, I'm gonna intervene. If that happens, your job is to run and have this car right outside the door to this place, engine running, passenger-side door open, your foot on the gas and your hot little hands on the wheel so that when I haul her out of the joint you and I can get her away from there before anything serious can go wrong. Got it?"

"Got it," he said. "Am I getting paid for this?"

"Yeah, right. Tell you what, you do everything right and you don't piss me off any more tonight, we'll see if there's something we can do for you."

"Oh," he said, sounding disappointed. "Freebie, then. In the meantime, can we talk about cars?"

"Anything you want."

"Or beer," he said. "Or sports. Or… What was the other thing?"

"I forget," she told him. "But you wanna talk sports, you better stick to baseball. I don't like football and I don't wanna hear about the fucking Knicks."

"Got it," he said.

COSTELLO'S OCCUPIED A long low building that sat on a narrow strip of land between Knapp Street and Shell Bank Creek in Brooklyn. FINE AGED BEEF, the sign said, as well as FRESH SEAFOOD and ITALIAN SPECIALTIES. In warmer weather the waterway behind the restaurant would be full of sport-fishing boats, but this time of year the water was cold, gray, and empty. Sarah Waters stood out in front of Costello's looking lost inside an oversized wool coat, her head turtled down inside the high collar. TJ Conrad and Alessandra Martillo sat inside the Malibu and watched her from a parking spot down the block. "How'd she get here?" TJ wanted to know.

"Dunno," Al said. "Took a cab, probably."

"Expensive cab ride," TJ said. "I guess she couldn't ride with us. Kind of spoil the surprise if someone saw her getting out of our backseat."

"Well, yeah," Al said. She was surprised that Conrad would think of something like that, she thought it unlike him to be concerned about the comfort of someone he didn't really know.

"Why's she standing out in front like that?" he said. "How come she don't wait inside?"

"I don't know. Maybe he told her to wait for him out front."

"So what? It's freezing. You wouldn't do it. You'd wait inside." He looked at her. "Especially wearing that jacket you got on. Ain't you got anything warmer?"

"I'd wait in the bar," Al said. "For about fifteen minutes, maybe."

"You figure she's more domesticated than you?"

Al shrugged. "Well, she used to be married to this guy. They got a kid together. You like that better? You think you'd be better off if I was more like her?"

"Lotta guys think that way," TJ said.

"What about you?"

He shrugged. "It is what it is."

"What the hell does that mean?"

"Don't start up yelling at me again. What it means, it ain't my business what you do. Just seems smarter to me to wait inside, unless you think you gotta follow this asshole's instructions." A big shiny black Chevy Suburban rolled up to the front door. It was lifted, had tinted windows and chrome spinners. The driver's-side door opened and a tall guy wearing black jeans and a leather jacket got out. "You figure this is him?" TJ said.

"Maybe," Al said. "How do you know he's an asshole?"

"Come on, she's our girl, so he's gotta be the bad guy. Besides, he made her stand out in the cold. Makes him an asshole."

"Are all you guys as primitive as that? I can't see him now, can you? What's he doing?"

"He's around behind the truck, he's greasing the parking valet."

A much shorter man came around the back of the truck, got in behind the wheel and drove it away, revealing Sarah Waters, her hands in her pockets, talking to the tall man. "Must be our man," Al said.

"Let's see if she goes in with him," TJ said.

"Why wouldn't she go in with him, after all this trouble?"

"She don't look happy. And you see the way he's standing? Kinda like, half bent forward? Either he's got a sore back or he was expecting her to hug him and she ain't coming across."

"Not bad," Al told him. "You looking for a job?"

"Always," he said, not looking at her. "Long as I don't have to paint, I hate painting. Look, they're going in, we better move it."

INSIDE, COSTELLO'S SMELLED like garlic, rare steak, fish, and tomato sauce. The maître d' was a broad-chested, big-bellied man with gray hair, a pockmarked face, and heavy-lidded eyes that looked like they'd seen a lot of history. TJ stepped away from Alessandra to shake the man's hand. Money passed smoothly as TJ murmured in the man's ear. The guy nodded once and led the two of them to a table by a window. Sarah and Frank Waters were seated about twelve feet away.

"Very good," Al told him. "What did you say to that guy?"

"Told him she was my cousin," he said. "Told him I was keeping an eye out."

"Didn't faze him," Al said.

"You kidding? Guy like that in a place like this? You ain't gonna show that guy nothing he ain't seen before."

"Maybe not."

"You figure he's carrying?" TJ said.

Al glanced back over her shoulder. "Depends," she said. "He might be a retired cop, he's got the look. If he is, a buck buys you ten he's got a piece on him, but if I had to guess I would bet that he ain't no cop, he don't take up space like cops do."

"What do you mean?"

"Cops always act like they got a piece of the joint," Al said. "This guy is too quiet. I'm guessing he's an old neighborhood pro, he made it through the drug wars alive, now he's just playing out his hand. He won't be carrying, but there's probably some iron back behind the bar there someplace. Besides, look around. The clientele in this place ain't exactly your average demographic. Bet you ten bucks there's four or five pistols in this room."

TJ glanced around, then looked over at Frank Waters's broad back. Sarah sat opposite, and her eyes never left Frank's face. "You might be right," he said. "You don't carry a gun."

"No."

"Why not?"

"Never thought I needed to," she said. "Besides, you carry a gun, only bad things can happen. You get into a fistfight, nobody really remembers what actually happened and nobody really cares, the winners run away and the cops take the losers. You shoot somebody, okay, you are married to the pistol, the round, the brass, the gunpowder residue, the stiff and all the rest of the forensics, and the cops got a long memory. You are not gonna walk away that easy."

"What if the bad guy has a gun?"

"Him? No way. Guy that size, he's too used to relying on intimidation."

"Well, all right, I meant the generic bad guy, not this one in particular. But what if you're wrong about this one?"

"Well," she said, "you stay fifteen, twenty feet away from the guy, odds are he ain't gonna hit you anyhow. Pistol in his hand in a public place, he's gonna be jacked, his hands are gonna be shaking too much for him to hit what he's trying to aim at. You get inside five feet, you know what you're doing you got a decent chance of—"

A car alarm went off.

Frank Waters stood up, motioned Sarah to wait where she was, then strode from the room. Most of the eyes in the dining room followed him out, then went quickly back to what they were doing. TJ Conrad patted his jacket pocket. "I need a cigarette," he said.

"Be careful," Al told him. "Watch your ass."

He nodded, shook out a smoke, stuck it behind his ear as he got up. Again, most of the patrons watched discreetly. Well, Al thought, Frank Waters might not know he's been shadowed, but everyone else does... She wondered if she'd been right to let TJ follow Waters out. She and Sarah made eye contact. Sarah shrugged, a tiny gesture that eloquently conveyed her lack of understanding.

And her disappointment. Outside, a gun barked three times.

Bang.

One, two, three seconds.

Bang-bang.

Alessandra and Sarah both jumped up and ran for the door.

Fifty other restaurant patrons reached for jackets, pushed back chairs, and prepared to follow.

The big maître d' barred the exit, but Al got the heel of her hand up under his nose, pushed his head up and back, shoved him back out of the way like someone peeling open the lid of a tin of sardines.

Outside, about ten feet from Costello's front door, a man lay dying on the sidewalk. At the far end of the block a set of red taillights vanished around the corner to the howl of tires pushed beyond their ability to hold traction.

Frank Waters was nowhere in sight.

Neither was the shiny black Suburban.

For about a third of a second, Alessandra Martillo was lost.

Sarah Waters stared at the dying man.

A Chevy Malibu slid to a stop at the curb, TJ Conrad behind the wheel.

Al grabbed Sarah by the arm.

"Time to go," she said.

In the distance, a siren wailed.

SIX

"Easy," Al told TJ. "Don't go too fast, don't run any lights, use your turn signals. We do not wanna get stopped."

"Got it," he said, and he slowed down. "What the hell just happened?"

Al glanced into the backseat at Sarah Waters. The color was gone from Sarah's face and she stared blankly at the back of the front passenger-side headrest. Better start with TJ, Al thought. "I don't know. What did you see?"

TJ shook his head. "It all happened so fast," he said.

"Step by step," Al told him. "You were sitting with me. You got up, stuck a cigarette behind your ear, and you walked away from the table. What came next?"

"Walked past the register," he said. "Old guy at the door said to go left, said there was a butt can down by the corner of the building. We were parked on the street up that way anyhow, so I went to the end of the building, like he said. I didn't see anybody. Wait, that's not true, the parking guy was walking back, he musta just parked a car. Had someone's keys in his hand. I took a couple steps toward the sidewalk, away from the building, then I heard the shots. One first, then two more, close together. Couple more steps, okay, I reached the sidewalk, the big black Chevy with the chrome rims went flying past me. And then I ran to get this car."

"Good job," Al told him. "You see how many guys were in the Chevy?"

TJ thought for a minute. "Two that I could see," he said. "The back windows were blacked out."

"Either of those two guys Frank Waters?"

"No." He glanced at Al, then in Sarah's direction.

"I know," Al said softly. "Okay, the two guys you did see, would you recognize either of them if you saw them again?"

"No. I only saw them for like a tenth of a second."

"White guys? Black guys?"

"White," he said. "Dark hair. That's all I got." He glanced in Sarah's direction again.

Al nodded, looked in the back. "Sarah, baby, are you okay?"

Sarah blinked twice, looked up at Al, tried to focus. "Well, I'm not shot," she said, and she hugged herself. "Do you think Frank's okay?"

Alessandra looked at her partner. She loved the business yesterday, Al thought. Said it was fun. "Probably," she said. "That guy on the sidewalk, he had at least one slug in him and he wasn't Frank, we know that much for sure. And we didn't see Frank anyplace else. Plus, there were only three rounds fired, so you'd figure one or two of them missed, so I'm guessing Frank didn't get hit."

Sarah hugged herself tighter.

"Sarah, listen, are you all right?"

"I always knew something like this would happen," she said.

"Something like what? We don't know anything yet, all we know is that one guy who ain't Frank got shot, so don't jump to conclusions."

"Okay."

"Did Frank have a gun?"

Sarah shook her head. "I never saw him with one."

"He know how to shoot? He's a vet, right?"

"Army," Sarah said, nodding. "But he was a motor pool

sergeant. Never fired a single round after boot, that's what he told me."

"He never carried when he was knocking around Brooklyn?"

"No. He was never that kind of guy. I mean, Frank's pretty good in a fight, and you saw him, he's a big man, but he always said if you thought you needed a gun you were probably in over your head. We knew a few neighborhood wiseguys, we went to school with them, but we were never tight with them."

"Smart."

"Do you think…" She was beginning to shake. "You really think he's all right?"

This is where we find out if she falls apart, Al thought. This is where we find out how much Brooklyn she's got in her. "We don't know, babe. Let's just decide to assume he's all right until we find out different. Can you do that? Until we find out otherwise, okay, he didn't do anything wrong tonight and there's a good explanation for all of this, we just don't know what it is yet. You all right with that?"

Sarah stared at Al's face for a moment. "If you were a cop," she said, "you'd think it was him that shot that guy."

"Yeah, but I'm not a cop," Al said. "I'm a person who wants to find out what really happened. Most cops just wanna get the paperwork filled out right and off their desk so that it's someone else's headache."

"Okay," Sarah said. "Are we in trouble?"

"We didn't shoot anyone, either," Al told her.

"No. But we're witnesses."

"To what? You see who popped that guy?"

"No, but—"

"But nothing," Al said. "We didn't see shit. I'm sure they're gonna wanna talk to TJ, but we can worry about that later."

Sarah blinked. "There was a security camera behind the cash register," she said.

"Fuck. Are you sure?"

Sarah nodded. "An old-fashioned one, white and sort of long and rectangular. It's pointed down at the cash register."

"Ah, Jesus," Al said. "Well, I doubt if they got a good enough picture to ID any of us."

TJ cleared his throat. "If they got my picture," he said, "they could compare it to the pictures of me that they've already got, if you know what I'm saying. Might go better for me if I went to them."

"And they're gonna ask you who you were with."

"Yeah. Probably make it go easier if we just tell them the truth."

"Or something like it," Al said.

Sarah was nodding. "They'll ID Frank, too," she said. "He marched with a group of vets against the war and a bunch of them got arrested a few times. I mean, they let him go the next day, but I'm sure it's in their records somewhere. Besides, they know him at Costello's. And they probably remember me, too."

"Oh, great," Al said. "Okay, this is our story. For tonight, we got scared and we ran out, just like all the other cockroaches in the joint. Tomorrow morning your conscience can bother you if you want. If you're ready to talk."

Sarah took a breath, sat up a little straighter. "Yeah, why not," she said. "Listen, can I ask a stupid question?"

"Go ahead." Al watched as Sarah pulled herself out of panic mode and began to function again. Maybe she'll be all right, Al thought.

"Um. Okay, your BF there, um, TJ, he said he saw the valet coming back from the lot with somebody's keys."

"Yeah, so?"

"TJ," Sarah said. "On your way out, did you see anybody on their way in?"

"No," he said. "The big dude by the door was standing there picking his teeth with the corner of a matchbook. He looked bored stiff."

"Okay," Sarah said. "So whose car did the valet park?"

Al and Sarah looked at each other. "Sonuvabitch," Al said.

"You think?" Sarah asked her.

"Maybe," Al said. "Assume the shooters show up, they give their car to the valet, then they hop up and down on the Suburban's bumper until the alarm goes off. Frank comes running out, they grab him and shove him into the truck. In the confusion one of them takes one for the team. By accident or not, we don't know. Not bad, Sarah."

"Why didn't they take the wounded guy with them?"

Al shook her head. "Easier to finish him off and leave him there."

"Ohmygod. Their own guy?"

"Dead men tell no tales," she said. "Especially if they're just hired help to begin with. Right now we gotta go back to Avis and trade this sucker in for something different."

"Why?"

"I gotta go back," Al said.

"Why?" TJ and Sarah asked it simultaneously.

"If Sarah's right," Al said, "after everybody goes home, the car the shooters used will still be sitting in that parking lot. I mean, they probably stole it for the occasion, but it's something. Sarah, you go home and—"

Sarah gritted her teeth. "If you're working," she said, "so am I."

But we ain't after a crooked barkeep here, Al thought. "Fine. You go sit down at your kitchen table and you write down everything you and Frank talked about tonight, and

the other night, too, when he fronted you outside your
mother's house. And then you write down everything that
you can remember about Frank's business deals and all of
his neighborhood buddies, Jimmy the Mick and Bobby the
Weasel and all of the other mutts he ever ran with, because
I'm betting the car in the lot angle goes nowhere. I mean,
I still gotta go check it out, but right now Frank is the best
lead we've got."

THE NEW RENTAL was a Mitsubishi and it was both smaller
and less comfortable than the Malibu. And since she didn't
want to leave the engine running for fear of drawing attention to herself, it was cold, brother, cold. To make it worse,
she had to leave both front windows open about half an
inch to keep the windshield from frosting up on the inside,
and the occasional crosswind whistled through and made
it seem even colder.

The cops did not seem to be in a hurry.

Cruisers were parked haphazardly up and down Knapp
Street, and the meat wagon sat, engine running, right in
front of Costello's front door, spoiling Alessandra's view
somewhat. It didn't matter, she was not going to be able to
learn anything from watching the crime scene techs, not
from this distance. About an hour after she'd found the
parking spot and settled in, they loaded a gurney into the
van and left.

Bagged and tagged, she thought. *Via con Dios,* sucka…
She searched her memory, trying to solidify her brief and
hurried impressions of what the man had looked like as he
lay there bleeding his life out onto the sidewalk. Mediter-
ranean, she thought. Not very tall. It was the best she could
come up with, and that not-very-helpful category included
Greeks, Corsicans, Arabs, Israelis, Italians, and who the
hell knew what else. Of course, Costello's restaurant, along

with the neighborhood that surrounded it, favored Italian-Americans. Means nothing, she told herself. Don't jump to conclusions. Seemed like the smart-money bet, though. If the guy did turn out to be of Italian persuasion, gunned down in front of Costello's, most people would figure it for a Mafia hit.

A car turned onto the block behind her. She slithered down low in the seat, dropping her head below window level. After the car passed she raised up enough to peer over the top of the dashboard. Two guys in a car, driving slow, taking their time, looking. Had to be cops.

The parking lot at Costello's was emptying slowly. Al wondered how constructive the conversations taking place inside were going to be. "No, officer, I didn't see nothing, I was eating my clams. Hey, what, you never ate here? My God, let me tell you, my friend, the clams in this place..." Still, the odds were pretty good that the cops already knew about the two couples that fled immediately after the shooting.

Normally Al's reaction would have been that she didn't know the dead guy, and if the police came knocking on her door she would talk to them, but she was not going to volunteer, no way, let them catch her if they could. This time things felt a little different, though, because her partner was involved.

Partner. There was a word for you. One thing to know how to use the word in a sentence, but it was another thing entirely to really get it, to understand in your gut what that really meant.

In reality, she didn't know Sarah Waters all that well. Knew she was of Italian heritage, knew that she had one kid, a boy whom Al had never met, knew that she lived in her mother's basement and was not thrilled with the arrangement, knew that she was not a dope, knew that she'd needed a job badly enough to agree to work for a guy like Stiles. Knew, now, that she did not fall apart in emergencies.

Knew, as well, that Sarah's ex, Frank Waters, was in deep shit.

Somewhere in the dark recesses of her mind a closet door opened, just a crack. The disembodied voice of a social worker she barely remembered snuck out just long enough to ask her how she felt about Sarah Waters. It was an old question, asked about everyone who entered her life, and it was never easy to answer honestly.

"I don't know" was, as usual, the best she could do.

Maybe things would have been different, maybe Alessandra would have been different if she'd come up the way normal kids do, but then you had to ask yourself what normal really was, what relevance it could possibly have had in a family like hers. In the witch's brew that was Brooklyn public housing, even the kids who'd had it relatively easy had to be fucked up, too.

The parking valet at Costello's hung in there, you had to give it to the guy, his take tonight was going to be a fraction of what it should have been, but he was working it for what he could get. Every little while a few more diners would emerge from the restaurant, presumably having done their civic duty and gained their release from New York City's finest, and the valet would accept the claim ticket and run for another car. Al resisted the impulse to count the number of cars left in the lot and try to figure how long this was going to take.

Anyway, how were you supposed to recognize normal if you'd never met the guy?

The military had shaped her father into a biological guided missile, you pointed Victor Martillo at whoever you wanted in custody and he would return with one former badass in tow, sporting the necessary minimum of physical damage and a new pair of shiny bracelets. Sign on the dotted line, please, he's all yours. But when it came to personal relationships, the man had no clue. He had been often gone, but even when he was home he was just as lost. He had done what he could, he had passed on to Alessandra everything he'd learned about controlling human beings through the careful and precise use of force. Some of his methods were traditional and widely accepted, others were unconventional and Draconian.

And rules? What rules? Here's your guy, he's coming to get you, you think he gives a shit about rules? You got maybe three seconds to decide what you're gonna do...

Alessandra's mother had eked out a lonely existence in the barren winter terrain of Victor Martillo's world, but eventually she'd had enough and she checked herself out. After that, Al got nailed with an indeterminate sentence in the custody of her maternal aunt. The memory of her introduction to Magdalena's labyrinth gave her a shiver that had nothing to do with the temperature.

Christ, she thought, TJ thinks I'm a terrorist, what the hell would he think of Mag?

ABOUT AN HOUR and a half later it looked to Al like all the restaurant patrons were gone. Most of the police cruisers were gone as well. Costello's parking lot was mostly empty. There was one group of cars parked down at the far end of the lot, Al figured they had to belong to the people who worked in the place. Some of them were leaving, too. The parking valet got into a Lincoln MKZ and started it up. The Lincoln wasn't down at the end of the lot with the other employees' cars, it was more toward the middle. You're the guy parking the cars, Al thought, you can put your ride wherever you want... The Lincoln pulled out of the lot and turned up her street. Al slid back down, waited until the

guy turned the corner at the end of the block, and then she
started the Mitsubishi, pulled a U-turn, and followed the
guy. She couldn't have said what made her decide to do it,
maybe she was just tired of sitting there freezing her nipples
off, but she figured, if the hit team really did leave a car at
Costello's, if it wasn't the Lincoln, the real one would still
be there in the morning. A quick ride back down Knapp
Street would confirm that.

It turned out that the Lincoln was pretty easy to follow.
The guy jumped onto the Belt Parkway and followed it
as it curled around Brooklyn's south and west shores. The
Mitsubishi started to warm up once they got onto the Belt
and Al turned the heat up as high as it would go. After they
passed the Verrazano-Narrows Bridge, the Belt turned into
the Gowanus Expressway. She was genuinely surprised,
though, when the guy got off at the Atlantic Avenue exit.

It was her street.

The bar, the one she lived over, was closed up tight,
lights out, ghetto grates padlocked securely across the door
and windows. She felt a momentary pang—for a second or
two she had an intense desire to ditch the Mitsubishi and
go upstairs to bed. Instead, though, she stayed behind the
Lincoln. The guy followed Atlantic Avenue up and over the
hill, past Brooklyn Corrections, eventually turned right on
Smith Street. He pulled into a small fenced-in lot next to a
Lebanese bakery and parked. Al stuck the Mitsubishi next
to a fire hydrant and watched the guy yak to the lot atten-
dant before heading off down Pacific. Al got out, stretched,
then crossed over and watched as the guy entered an ancient
brownstone halfway down Pacific. She walked down, took
a picture of the front of the building with her cell phone, got
another picture of the rear end of the Lincoln on her way
back to the Mitsubishi.

When she got back she found an orange-and-white

parking ticket flapping in the breeze under the Mitsubishi's windshield wiper. Five fucking minutes, she thought, are you kidding me? I couldn't have been gone longer than that. She left it where it was. Marty is gonna be seriously pissed off, she thought, when they trace this car back to his credit card… The ticket blew off as she passed Brooklyn Corrections.

SEVEN

IT WAS AFTER ten by the time Alessandra got out of the shower. Twenty minutes later she was dressed, but she still wasn't ready to face the day. She stomped down the stairs, yanked hard to open the heavy door to the street, was greeted by a blast of cold air. She'd looked for her winter coat the night before but had not found it, and how you could lose something like that while moving from one tiny apartment to another was beyond her, but it was gone. When she passed the entrance to the bar she looked through the window. Beads of water ran down the inside of the glass. It looked warm in there, and the dim bar lights seemed much more civilized than the harsh morning sun. She turned and went in.

Her landlady was behind the bar. There was one patron, he sat at a table and stabbed halfheartedly at his breakfast with a fork. "Good morning, Mrs. Taylor," Al said. "Is that coffee I smell?"

"It certainly is," Mrs. Taylor replied in her nicotine-stained baritone. "Have a seat."

It came in a thick white china mug with a blue stripe around the top. Al wrapped her hands around it, felt the heat seep into her, held it to her face, and drank in the smell before she finally took a sip. "God, that's good," she said. "Thank you."

"My pleasure," Mrs. Taylor said. "Rough night?"

Al nodded. "Yeah, sort of. I had to work late. Thought I was gonna freeze myself to death."

"What is it that you do?" Mrs. Taylor said. "I forgot to ask, before."

"I work for a security company," Al told her.

"You mean, like a guard at a bank?"

"No. Nothing as nice as that. When someone's getting divorced, they hire a lawyer. If the lawyer is smart, he hires us, or someone like us. We go find out who the husband is sleeping with and where he hides the money."

Mrs. Taylor laughed. "But sometimes it's the wife, right? It can't always be the guy."

"Can't always be the guy," Al agreed. "Gotta be some of us, too, else who would all the guys be sleeping with? Each other, maybe, but it seems like I always get to follow the guy."

"And are they always rats?"

"Ah, well, you know. I probably don't get to see a representative sample."

"Oh," Mrs. Taylor said. "So they are always rats."

Al shrugged. "I suppose you could look at it that way. I try not to judge, you know what I mean? Because who knows what their wives were putting them through. You live with some ice goddess for ten or twenty years, maybe when you finally decide to break out it's only right that you should go a little crazy. So I just try to do my job. If I had to try and figure out who was right and who was wrong I'd be screwed." She looked at the older woman. "Are you married?"

"Mm-hmm. Four times."

"Wow. No kidding."

"What could I tell you?" Mrs. Taylor said. "I like men. I enjoy their company, always did. And I never wanted to live alone, even though that's what I'm doing now."

"Yeah? You finally give up looking for a good one?"

"Nah. Not really. Number four has Alzheimer's."

"Oh. I'm sorry."

"Nothing to be sorry for. He was very good, and for a long time." She paused, and when she spoke again her voice rattled softly down in her throat. "He doesn't really recognize me anymore, so I try to hang on to what we used to have. He was a good man."

"You go to see him often?"

"I used to," she said. "It was awful at first. I mean, we went through four years of misery before I finally had to put him in the Veterans', you know, and when he got there he was very angry, he couldn't understand what he was doing there. He'd ask me a million times when we were going home, and no matter what I told him he'd forget and ask me again about two minutes later. It was tough. Then the disease took all that away from him. I don't know if that's better or worse. Better for him, worse for me, I suppose. He's lost now, but he's happy, and he's very sweet. I think that was what he really was all along, and the disease finally stripped everything else away."

"That must be some consolation," Al said.

"Not as much as you'd think," Mrs. Taylor said. "The last time I went to see him, one of the little old ladies in there was going down on him."

"Yikes! What did you do?"

Mrs. Taylor shrugged. "What could I do? He don't know who I am, I doubt he knows if he was ever married or anything. She probably don't remember who she is, neither. So I said, 'Excuse me,' and I closed the door and left them to it."

"Jesus. I don't know if I could manage that."

"No? Might surprise you, what you can do when you love somebody."

"Yeah, maybe it would."

"You must have someone," Mrs. Taylor said. "With a behind like you got? Don't tell me there's nobody after it."

Al nodded. "I been seeing this guy." She hesitated, wondered how much she really wanted to say, but Mrs. Taylor had told her about her husband's absentminded hummer, and that had to sting. "Maybe my job ruined things for me. Because I can't believe, you know…" She shook her head. "Maybe that's it. I can't believe. Maybe that's all it is."

"No way to live," Mrs. Taylor said, nodding. "Going around half pissed-off all the time, wondering if he's jumping the fence. But you know, honey, you can't tar 'em all with the same brush. What's he do?"

"He's a musician."

Mrs. Taylor laughed then. "Oh, shit. Forget everything I just said."

Al had to laugh with her. "You're not helping very much," she said. "One of yours a musician?"

Mrs. Taylor shook her head. "Actor," she said. "Number two. Same breed of cat, though."

"Yeah? Was he anybody I'd recognize?"

"Only if you liked daytime soaps." Mrs. Taylor eyed her. "Back when you were about five, maybe. Then you might remember him as Dr. Reilly, the heartthrob surgeon."

"No. Sorry."

"No matter. He was a nice enough guy, and great fun to be with. Very insecure, though. Spent half his time trying to convince himself that he was a talented thespian and not just one lucky son of a bricklayer who happened to have a good chin and a nice smile. And I think he tried his best to be a good husband in his own way, but when he quit acting and started to direct instead, he couldn't help himself. All these actresses, you know, all these perfect little tramps… And I wasn't perfect no more, not by then. So… But I didn't have to hire you guys to catch him, I did that myself."

"Men," Al said. "But you know what? I'm feeling you."

"Well, coffee's on the house. Good luck with yours." Mrs. Taylor started laughing, couldn't stop.

"What's funny?"

"At the Veterans'," Mrs. Taylor said, shaking her head, "that little old lady. She had Myron's balls in one hand and her teeth in the other."

Al finished her coffee, left two bucks on the bar.

AL CALLED SARAH WATERS while she sat in the Mitsubishi and waited for it to warm up. "Hey, killer," she said. "How you feeling this morning?"

"Better," Sarah said. "I'm worried sick about Frank, but I'm better. Starting to think a little clearer."

"Oh, really? How can you tell?"

"Well, I found Jake West, for one thing. And I'm having second thoughts about us going to the police just yet."

"Yeah? Cold feet?"

"No. Well, I don't think that's it. It just occurred to me that if we talk now, they're going to assume that it was Frank shot that guy, and they'll go stomping around trying to pin it on him."

"What if it really was him?"

"I can't believe he would do something like that. I mean, he can be ignorant, and crude, he can even be mean sometimes, but I can't see him ever killing anybody, not for any reason. How about this, how about we find Frank ourselves, and we get it from him? Then we can decide what to do. If he really did it, I'll testify against him myself."

"What if the cops come looking for us in the meantime?"

"Well, they might," Sarah said. "But the more I think about it, the less likely it seems. I mean, Costello's? In Brooklyn? You kidding me? Who's gonna say anything?"

"That was my initial reaction," Al said, "but I assumed that it was just my lack of moral fiber showing itself. I tell you what, I'll meet you at the office, you can give me what you came up with on Frank and I'll see if I can turn him up."

"You don't think that I…"

"No. Suppose he sees you coming? He doesn't know me. Besides, somebody's got to take care of the paying customers, else we'll both end up in your mother's basement. Speaking of paying customers, how'd you find this Jake character so quick?"

"Well," Sarah said, "you can get a MasterCard from any bank in the country, but there's only one American Express."

"You're kidding me. You hacked American Express's database?"

"No," Sarah said. "What happened, he changed his name a few years ago, from Jake West to John A. Smits, and he moved upstate, but he didn't pay off all of his bills first and American Express hired a collector to find him and get their money back. The way it works, the guy buys the receivable and then what he collects is his. So he doesn't find Jake, but three months later AmEx calls him up and says, 'Never mind, he paid up,' but now the collector is hot because he's got time and money into this. So he says to AmEx, give me the guy's name, at least that way I can cover my costs by squeezing him for some of the other credit cards he walked away from, so that's what they did. I mean, they're not supposed to, but the collector had a rabbi inside AmEx and the guy took care of him."

"How'd you get him to give you all this?"

"I was lucky, I was posing as a collection agency myself. The guy is still steamed because Jake cleaned up all of his old bills and the guy never got any money out of the deal. You know how it is, you stiff somebody, they never forget you."

"So where is Jake now?"

"J. Austin Smits, Woodstock, New York," Sarah said.

"How about that? You tell Mrs. West about him yet?"

"Noooo…"

"Why not?"

"I got a funny feeling."

"Yeah? About what?"

"You coming in? I'll show you when you get here."

Whatever, Al thought. Mrs. West was Sarah's customer, so she figured Sarah could make the call. "Okay. Be a couple hours, though, while I still got the car I'm gonna take a ride out to Greenpoint. If we're gonna hold off going to the cops about Frank, I'm gonna have to get TJ on board."

"Wait a minute," Sarah said. "No nookie during working hours."

Al wondered if she was blushing, because that's exactly what she had been thinking. She checked her face in the rearview mirror.

"Oh, hey, listen," Sarah said, "I was only kidding…"

"What? No! I was only… Hey, what are you, my mother?"

Sarah laughed, over the phone she sounded like the Emperor from *Star Wars*. "Sorry if that sounded nosy," she said. "It's just that, you know, I'm starving to death over here. I'm about to dry up and blow away."

"When I find Frank," Al said, "I'll put in a good word."

"Thanks for nothing. So will I see you some time this afternoon? Like, late?"

"You're not gonna let this go, are you?"

SHE TOYED WITH the notion, TJ was the kind of guy who slept until noon on a good day, she didn't have a key to his place, but the lock on his door was a hardware store special, she could pull a Pearl Harbor on him, be all over him before he knew what hit him…

What a great idea.

The more she thought about it, the better she liked it. She did not even get upset when she got caught in a jam on the elevated section of the Brooklyn-Queens Expressway, some guy got pranged by a nun driving a station wagon, the nun stood red-faced right in the middle of the road, the station wagon pointing the wrong way, the nun a little unsteady on her feet, waving her arms, yelling at two cops and pointing at the other car. Al just waited in line for her turn to get by. She got lucky in Greenpoint, she found a parking spot just down the block from TJ's building. She was still sitting behind the wheel when TJ came out the front door with a girl on his arm.

Al shut the car off.

She looked like a girl, anyhow, she was tall, thin, nice rack, orange-blond hair, she was probably somewhere between fifteen and twenty. She was one of those kids that had it, it came steaming off her in waves, there wasn't a guy on the street that didn't turn and look her way. TJ hailed a passing gypsy cab, he put the girl into the backseat and then climbed in after her.

The Mitsubishi's engine made ticking noises as it cooled off. The interior of the car was cooling, too, but silently. Alessandra Martillo was silent as well, and still. She thought about following the cab, but that seemed pointless. Got the knife in your chest, she told herself. Why twist it?

She could feel the heat leaching out of the car.

I won't get cold, she told herself, I won't let it touch me.

Some people could do it. Some people could decide not to be cold, and were not. Her uncle Bobby had been like that. He was the one who had taken her in, back when she was twelve, he'd searched the streets, the back alleys and empty buildings of Brownsville until he'd found her, and he had talked her into going home with him. "Come and stay with me and Anthony," he'd told her. "You can have your own room, and it'll be way better than this." She remembered the ride back to his house in Queens, sitting on the back of the stunningly loud Harley hardtail, clutching his jacket for fear of being rattled off the end of the thing. Bobby had been a bear of a man, hairy, tattooed, long thin braid hanging off his chin. In the winter he had rarely worn a jacket. His only concession to the cold had been a vest, and she had watched him clean snow off his van windows with bare hands on days when most people didn't leave more than a few square inches of skin exposed around their eyes.

I don't feel it, Al told herself. I don't feel a damn thing. But her body had already begun to betray her, her feet were beginning to tingle and the tips of her fingers were going numb.

"Aren't you cold?" she had asked him once, not long after he had taken her in. "Can't you feel it?"

He had grabbed her then, dropped what he was doing and pretended to try and stick his thick rough-skinned fingers down the back of her collar. She remembered shrieking, then laughing when he let her go. "I feel everything you feel," he told her. "Every single thing."

"So how come you're not cold?"

"I'm the same temperature you are, I just don't let it bother me."

Al had never mastered the art, never discovered the trick to feeling something without letting it rule her.

She heard Anthony's voice. "Get back in this house and put your jacket on!" Anthony was Tio Bobby's partner, he and Bobby were as different as two people could be. He was Anglo, blue and blond, tall, thin, fussy, self-consciously gay. Tio Bobby simply was what he was, and you could take it or you could leave it.

She remembered Anthony, down on one knee so that he could get eye to eye with her. "Your uncle Roberto," he told her, "is not a normal person. You shouldn't try to be like him."

"Why not?"

"Because you'll catch your death," he told her. "Besides, you need to learn how to be Alessandra. Put on your jacket."

She was shivering despite her best efforts at self-control. No matter how hard she tried to let all the tension drain from her muscles, no matter how much she tried to still the tremors, they returned time after time.

"Tio Bobby," she whispered. "I miss you." She wondered if it were possible for him to miss her as well, and if her absence bothered him. But he might be better off now, she told herself. He might be at peace.

She had not been a gracious house guest. Her time alone on the Brooklyn streets had turned her and she had tested the depths of his desire to save her. As a child she had been a gifted shoplifter, prone to fits of rage, and thanks to her father's lessons, capable of violence beyond her age and physical stature, but all of her anger broke across Tio Bobby's broad shoulders like ocean swells on a stone wall. Rarely had she managed to ruffle his implacable serenity. He had not tried to control her, she could appreciate that now, he had manipulated her, steered her, nudged her gently into a more constructive way of being. Instead of forbidding violence, he had helped her harness it, and there had been a succession of teachers: aikido, kendo, jiujitsu, krav maga, and more.

She had to admit defeat. She hugged herself, shivering uncontrollably. She started the car, sat suffering until it warmed up. "I can't live like this, Bobby," she said to the car. "I need more than this."

"You don't need to steal stuff from the store," he'd told her once. "You have everything. You got your own room, your own clothes, all your own stuff. Anything else you need, you come to me. Okay?"

"Why?" Sullen.

"Because I love you." She had thought, at the time, that he'd misunderstood the question. "And Anthony loves you." She had never been totally sure of that one. "And your father loves you, too, he just doesn't know how to show it." That, too, had seemed a dubious assumption. "You have everything, Alessandra."

That can't be right, she told herself.

There has to be something better than this.

And who fucking needs TJ Conrad anyway, she thought, if that's what he wants why not leave him to it, let him go hang out with some teenybopper who's all impressed because he doesn't live at home and is old enough to buy beer, God, why is it that guys have so much trouble with real women, and if he can't handle being with someone who might give him a little competition for the upper bunk or the steering wheel or even just the TV remote, well then, fuck you, pal, go ahead, go on back over there and eat at the kiddie's table if you ain't big and bad enough to play with the big girls, but then again she had to admit that they hadn't had The Conversation, the one about rules of engagement, and that maybe was you know her own fault, especially if you considered that if someone was gonna have to be the adult and bring it up chances were pretty good it wasn't gonna be him, and maybe she was a little bit guilty of comparing every guy she knew to Tio Bobby and wishing that they could be more like him except you know, straight, but she would be goddamned if she was gonna turn into some old hen that spends all of her time trying to chase off all the other chickens, she was not gonna by God act like some kind of police sergeant and if she could only stop thinking about him all the time and what's the point in wishing he was something different from who he really is and if the guy only has a size 32 waist there ain't shit you can do to try and make him fill up a pair of 38 jeans no matter what you do and goddammit all to hell why is it that life just has to fucking suck so fucking bad sometimes?

EIGHT

ALESSANDRA BARELY GOT through the door before Sarah was on to her. "What's wrong?"

"Nothing," Al said, disappointed. She thought she had a better game face than that.

"Yeah, sure," Sarah said. "What happened, you and the BF get into a fight?"

Al perched her butt on the edge of Sarah's desk. "Something like that." It wasn't that she didn't want to talk to Sarah about it, and it wasn't that she didn't trust her, it was more that she didn't even know what to say: *Yeah, I saw TJ get into a car with this chick...* So what? None of her clients would accept that as any sort of proof, no lawyer and no judge would be impressed with evidence like that. You had to have skin, you had to have contact, you had to have a nice clear picture of the smoking gun.

So to speak.

Sarah squeezed Al's forearm. It seemed like the first friendly human touch she'd had in a while. "Sorry to hear it," Sarah said. "What do you want to do first—Frank, Mrs. West, or Marty's latest threats?"

"God, is he still calling here?"

"Yeah. Doesn't seem like he's calming down at all. If anything, he sounds madder than ever."

"Just what we need. If he says anything that sounds actionable, save the recording. And remind me later to drop by our old building and slip the doorman over there a fifty."

"Okay. Why?"

"Well, if Marty's serious, anybody trying to serve us is gonna go there first. For fifty bucks the doorman will send them off to look in Long Island somewhere. Might buy us a couple days."

"Ohmygod. You think he'll really sue?"

"That would be his next logical step. What do you have on Mrs. West? How come you didn't want to wrap that up?"

"I don't know. I mean, I got a funny feeling about it."

"Yeah, but she's the client, she's paying us to be on her side."

"I know. But take a look at this." Sarah turned to her computer, brought up a site that she had bookmarked. "This is a picture of Mrs. West, back in the day. I found it in the *New York Times,* they were covering some kind of charity thing she was involved with."

"Wow. She was fine."

"Yeah, no kidding. Here's a couple shots of Bats, his picture is all over the Web. I got this one from his kids' website, but he was everywhere else, too, I think he was one of those guys who knows everybody, and not just casually, either. He seems to have had a close personal relationship with every New York politician alive, along with all the movers and shakers, even the backdoor guys you never heard of."

"His kids have a website?"

"Yeah, all squishy, 'We miss you, Daddy,' novenas to Saint Jude, sappy poems, 'roses are red, violets are blue, we hope you're not dead, and we miss you,' and all like that. And this…" She pulled up another site. "Is a picture of Thomas West." It was an unremarkable image of an ordinary-looking, middle-aged guy in a gray suit.

"He looks like an accountant," Al said. "Man, you got to watch the quiet ones."

"Yeah, I guess."

"So how did he wind up with a hot mama like Aggie West?"

"Big investment firm organized a retreat in the Catskills. They were shilling for some Japanese bank that was trying to make a splash in the U.S. commodities markets. Thomas and Agatha were both in attendance. I don't know how the Japanese bank made out, but Thomas nailed Agatha Friday night right after the opening ceremonies. Apparently the booze was flowing like water and they both got into the mood. Saturday morning they both wake up nekkid, perform an encore, and the rest is history."

"You sure it was him nailing her? Could have been the other way 'round. How the hell did you come up with all this?"

"Come on, he's a rich guy, she's a society dame, it was in all the gossip columns. Anyhow, the point is, not everybody was thrilled with the happy news. His sons didn't go to the wedding, and neither did Bats."

"You're gonna tell me they didn't do a City Hall drive-by."

"No way, baby. Big fancy production, West probably spent a couple hundred thou on it."

"Yeah, well… This all more or less backs up what old Agatha told us, doesn't it?"

"Yeah. But check this out."

It was a story from the New York *Daily News* archive, and Al had to lean in close to read the fine text. "Yeah, okay," she said, about halfway through. "The cops are always gonna look at the surviving relatives in a case like this one."

"Yeah, that figures. Keep reading."

"Okay." Al finished the article. "You could have predicted that. I mean, there's a lot of money here, you gotta know some assistant DA is gonna try to pin the father's death on the sons. Says here he pushed for an indictment, but obviously he didn't get one. He couldn't have had much to go on. What's this got to do with—"

"Suppose," Sarah said. "Just suppose the sons did it."

"Suppose they did. Where's the money?"

"No idea, but Isaac West croaks in a yacht race. Last time I looked, yacht racing is definitely a rich boy's sport. Right up there with polo. And Jake West changes his name and drops out of sight. So who knows how fat and happy J. Austin Smits really is? How do we know he's not sitting on a bazillion dollars?"

"We don't," Al said. "I suppose we could go look. But what's in it for us? We can't blackmail the guy."

"Al. Our client's husband and his partner are murdered by her stepsons. In theory. We track down the surviving stepson, give his name and address to the grieving widow, who happens to be suffering with terminal cancer. What would you do if you were her?"

"Ooh."

"Yeah, ooh is right, you'd go make sure J. Austin Smits preceded you down that broad highway to the Other Place, that's what you'd do. And if I'm right, and you and I do have to go apply for a PI's license after Marty pulls the rug out from under us, how's that gonna look on the application?"

"Gonna look like we did our job. Anyhow, society's not exactly losing any huge asset here, are they? The kid got away with murder, he gets whacked by old Agatha, she dies of cancer before she can even go to trial, we get paid. Everybody wins."

"Al, honey, I'm not quite sure everyone else is gonna see it that way. I found that former assistant DA, he's in private practice. He told me he'd been working with some chief of police out on the island, the cop was sure the kids did it.

He gave me the chief's name, I'd like to take a ride out and see if he'll talk to me."

"Okay. You could give that a try. And in a couple more days we'll take a ride up to see J. Austin. First we gotta find Frank, what do you have on him?"

Sarah looked away. "I put everything I had on your desk."

FRANK WATERS, ONLY child of Ida and Francis, both parents now deceased. Born King's County Hospital, Brooklyn, 1975. Minor legal troubles shortly after high school, B & E and simple assault, charges dropped against Frank and four other members of his graduating class. Enlisted in the army, served in Kuwait between the wars. Honorable discharge. Arrested for disturbing the peace with other veterans during several demonstrations, charges vacated. Investigated for inflammatory statements re: U.S. president who served part-time in the National Guard. Married Sarah Rizzo, fathered one child, divorced. Order of protection filed for and granted. Longshoreman, booted from union for non-payment of dues. Worked subsequently as bouncer at Club Mediterraneo, paid off the books. Inherited one-family house after death of mother. Proprietor of several unsuccessful businesses. Whereabouts currently unknown...

Not the dumbest guy in the world, Al thought. Certainly not the smartest. Ordinary Brooklyn kid, chasing the ever-more-elusive American dream, chances of success perhaps less than average. Normal guy, or within hailing distance of normal, anyhow. Remarkable mostly for his size.

Al read through it all again. Probably not a horrible kid, had some bad friends. Went away to war, came back, tilted at some windmills. Lost. Got in some heat for shooting his mouth off about George the Younger. Got married and had a kid.

Lost his job over a dumb-ass thing like union dues.

Got divorced.

Al wondered if there might not be more behind that order of protection. How much did Frank Waters smack his wife around, exactly? Probably ought to talk to the local precinct, see how often they made that particular house call.

Frank Waters looked like an also-ran, just one more schmuck who ran out of gas before he could get where he wanted to go.

Went broke.

Might have gotten a little desperate.

Al looked out her window. Frank Waters, she thought, what the hell did you get yourself into?

"Hey, Al." Sarah's voice rang from the outer office. "I got an address for Frankie."

"Yeah? Where's he at?"

Sarah gave her a street in Queens.

Al got up and stood in the doorway between the two rooms. "Great job," she said. "How'd you come up with that so quick?"

"I called one of Frank's meatball friends. I told the guy that Frankie got a rebate check on a flat-screen TV, but they sent it to me by mistake. Told him I didn't want a dime from Frankie. I think I struck just the right tone, you know, bitter, angry, proud... Told him if he didn't give me Frank's address I was gonna change my mind and spend the money on shoes."

"Wow," Al said. "That's terrific. Where'd you learn to lie so good?"

"Listen, you try raising an adolescent all by yourself, you'll hear 'em all. You want I should come with you?"

Down, girl, Al thought. "No, that's okay, I can handle it."

"You sure? I mean, nobody knows Frankie like I do."

Careful here, Al told herself. "Sarah, I'm not sure if you know how good you are at finding this stuff. I mean, it's getting to the point where I don't know what I'd do without you, but I think we ought to hold off awhile before we get you involved in breaking and entering."

The disappointment showed clear in Sarah's face. "Oh, come on," she said. "Is it really that big of a deal?"

"They send you to jail for it," Al told her. "And take away your kid. That's kind of a big deal."

"I suppose. But, I mean, if this is gonna be my job, and everything…"

"Sarah, honey, I don't want you to feel like you're getting stuck doing the laundry and washing the dishes here, but certain things, you know, you gotta let me do what I do and you gotta keep doing what you do." She remembered her mother, dead on the floor, remembered how it felt, suddenly all alone.

"All right," Sarah said. "I understand."

"Not mad, are you? It's just that, if things get sticky—"

"No." Sarah colored slightly. "What I really wanted, I guess, I wanted to go poking around in Frank's stuff, see what he's been doing without me to take care of him. Be nosy. Check up."

"Yeah? Well, if I find anything juicy, I'll take pictures."

THE SUPERINTENDENT AT Frank Waters's building in Queens was a short round Slavic guy who smelled a little bit like a sweaty dill pickle. His jaw and the top of his head were both covered with short black stubble. "Colombo?" he said, squinting up at Al. "Colombo…"

"Colombo Messenger Service," Al told him.

"You have business card?"

"No," Al said.

The guy put a fat finger on the tip of his nose and pushed it sideways. "Colombo…"

Al took a hundred-dollar bill from her pocket, folded

it lengthwise, held it out between two fingers. "Figure it out," she said. "You got a key? I just need to look inside. Very quick."

"I have key." The guy looked at the bill, but he didn't take it. "Vy they are sending voman?"

Oh, Christ, she thought. Another one. "Because we're smarter than you are," she snapped.

"Impossible," he said.

God must love idiots, Al thought, he made so fucking many of them… "Okay, Einstein," she said. "Where's your kid go to school? What's the name of his teacher? What's her phone number? Hah?"

"I do not concern myself with these thing." But he blinked, and he looked a little unsure of himself.

"No? Then who balances your checkbook? Who pays the bills? Who knows where you left your keys? Who found your wallet last time you lost it? Who finds the car when you get drunk off your ass and forget where you parked it? Hah?"

He grimaced at her and nodded his head, once. "All right," he said.

Shut up, you won, she told herself, but the steam was up and she couldn't stop. "You wanna know how come she's smarter than you, you fat fuck? Because she's hadda listen to bullshit from guys like you ever since the day she grew an ass, that's why. Now, you gonna open up for me or do you want me to go back and tell 'em you don't feel like playing ball? You want to deal with a guy instead of with me, believe me, Paco, we can send you a nice big one, and he'll crack your fucking skull for you before he stands around talking shit in this stinking hallway all this time, I promise you.…"

"Easy," he said, holding up his hands in surrender. He

plucked the money out of her hand. "Easy. I open door for you."

"Fine," Al told him. "You open the door, and then get lost."

APPARENTLY FRANK'S HOUSEKEEPER hadn't been by in a while...

She stood in the middle of the entry hallway, careful not to touch anything, and she stared at the super until he grumbled, closed the door behind her, and went away. You gotta get a handle on yourself, she thought, you can't go around bitching out every guy who pisses you off. This is all TJ's fault, she thought. Whyn't you go yell at him instead of at all these other morons?

When she was satisfied the super was gone she pulled on a thin pair of latex gloves and got started.

Frank liked microwave popcorn, Coors beer, and frozen pizza.

He liked DVDs of Japanese prostitutes.

He didn't have a computer.

He had a speed-dial feature on his telephone, but he'd never bothered to enter any numbers into it.

He had two sets of car keys on his spare key ring, together with a bunch of other keys that looked like hardware store copies.

He had a 52-inch flat-screen TV and a surround-sound system that was not yet hooked up.

He had dishes in the sink, dirty laundry on the floor, food in the fridge, *Juggs* magazines under his bed.

A man in his castle, Al thought. She took her time, but she couldn't find anything related to what it was Frank did for a living or what may have happened to him at Costello's. She pocketed his extra keys and all the paper from his last month's phone bills, credit cards, and bank statements. And she took the last thing she found, a sheet of yellow paper that was taped to the bottom of his desktop. It had a series of numbers written on it. Next to the two top numbers were ATM and BERGLAR ALARM. The others were not identified.

Al went looking for the super when she was done.

"You said very quick," he said sourly.

Al pulled another hundred from her pocket and held it out. "Waters have a car?" she asked him.

He glared at her, but he reached for the money. "Have two," he told her. "One is Audi A4, piece of crap, six, seven years old. Baby-shit brown. Parks on the street. If I vas homeless I vould not sleep in that thing. Other vun is big Chevy, new, black. Beautiful. Parks in back."

"Is the Chevy there now?"

"No. I have not seen, maybe three days."

She stared at the guy, wondered what she was missing. "You never saw me," she finally said. "I was never here."

"I know nothing." He said it without looking at her.

She wondered if he had gotten that from Sergeant Schultz or if he'd thought it up by himself.

AL COULD NOT remember the address of the warehouse on Staten Island where Frank Waters worked, and when she called the office she got the answering machine. She hung up, looked at her watch. Four in the afternoon… She thought about calling Sarah's cell but decided against it. She might be in the bathroom, she thought, or she might have gone home, even though it was not like Sarah to leave early. She likes working, Al thought, and she's got a bunch of hotel bars and restaurants to check out. Actual paying customers… And she likes doing that more than she likes being home, sitting around wondering where she went wrong. Rather be out screwing up someone else's life…

She looked at the "berglar" alarm code. No alarm system

at that dump he lives in, she thought, this has to be for his job. Useful little item… She called information, asked for the address and phone number for Palermo Imports. The computer asked her to wait while it connected her with a human being. A female voice came on the line and Al repeated her request. No such listing, the lady said. Al tried as many variations on the name as she could think of. The closest thing she found was Palermo Machine Tools, and they were in Nassau County, out on Long Island. Doesn't look like I'll be testing that alarm code tonight, she thought.

Besides, she told herself, you're not a teenager anymore, you're not looking to kick a back door open and see what you can grab before the cops get there, you're supposed to be a professional, you're supposed to do your homework, first. Be nice to have some idea what you're going to run into.

You could go see Marty, try to get him settled down…

She recoiled from the idea. Seeing Marty in his current condition was not something you sprang on yourself, it was something you steeled yourself up for after procrastinating for a few days…

But you said you were gonna do it… She sighed, stashed the paperwork she'd stolen from Frank Waters's domicile in her camera bag, looked around for a cab.

"HE WAS OKAY yesterday." The Filipino nurse's dark eyes began to tear up. She really cares about this guy, Al thought, she's really sweating whether or not Marty gets his shit together. Yeah, she thought, but that's only because she doesn't know him, she found out what a prick the guy can be, she'd probably park him in a hallway somewhere and let him starve to death. "After you came, he, he was so animated, he was talking and calling on the phone and pushing himself around… But today he's going back down under." She yanked a Kleenex out of a box on her desk and dabbed at her eyes. "I even thought about what you did." She said it without looking at Al. "I thought about, you know, trying to tempt him, or whatever. But I didn't do it."

"You gotta be kidding," Al said. "If you thought it would work, would you really do it?"

The woman raised her eyes and stared at Al. "You did."

"Yeah," Al said, surprised at herself. "I guess I did."

"Why?"

Al was surprised at that, too, because she didn't have an answer. "I don't know."

"It is because you care about him." Her tone was accusatory.

"No fucking way. I owe the guy." Which was not entirely the truth, she thought, and that makes you a bigger idiot than her, because you do know what a prick he can be. But I worked with the guy, that makes it different, she thought, and then she wondered if it was pathological to argue with oneself or merely neurotic. But when you get to know a guy, even if you don't particularly like him, can you just let him slide under? "Maybe just a little bit," she said. "Where is he?"

MARTY WAS PARKED in his wheelchair on a sunporch that looked south over Ocean Boulevard and Coney Island's ratty boardwalk. The Cyclone, which had looked so intimidating to Alessandra when she was small, looked now more like the sort of thing construction workers would nail together out of two-by-fours so they could climb up and paint the side of a building.

Marty stared straight ahead.

He looked thinner in the face than he had, even just days earlier. He glanced her way once when she came in and perched on the windowsill. There was recognition in that look, and venom, and resentment. But what else? Am I kidding myself, she wondered, or is he glad to see me?

"S'up, Marty?"

He didn't respond.

"Come on, Marty, it's a long-ass cab ride, I'm not dragging myself all the way down here just to be ignored by you."

He turned her way slowly, by degrees, met her gaze. "No dress this time," he said, as expressionless as a snake watching a mouse.

"No," Al said. "No underwear, either."

"Really?" His eyebrows raised up, maybe an eighth of an inch. But it's a sign of life, she thought.

"You really are a jerk, you know that?" But she was relieved, just a bit. Maybe there was something left in him after all.

"Maybe so," he said, and he shifted his gaze, stared back out through the glass. "But at least there's one thing I can still do."

"Yeah? What?"

"I can still piss you off," he said.

She didn't know where to go with that, so she sat and stared at him.

"This is what I do," he said after a while.

"What's that?"

"This," he said. "I sit here. In the sun. Like a yellow jacket stuck behind the storm window. I sit in the sun and I wait."

"For what?" she said. "What the hell are you waiting for, Marty?"

He didn't look at her, and he didn't answer her question. "Mickey Caughlan called me," he said, after a minute. "From prison." He turned and stared at her again. "I didn't ask him about the money."

"No? Why not?"

"No way he paid you," he said, sneering. "No way. You were lying to me."

"What if I was?"

"You ever think about suicide?" he said. She saw it again, that look of distaste and anger passed over his features.

I don't wanna go down this road, she thought, not with Marty Stiles, you open up to him, you're just handing him the stick to beat you with… "Yeah," she said, surprising herself again. "Sure."

"When."

"Early on," she said. "When I was twelve. And a time or two, since. Not often." She stared at him, trying to puzzle out what she was seeing. Distaste, maybe even loathing, but he'd never hated her that strongly, he'd always wanted to have sex with her too badly. Easy enough, she thought, easy to hate the woman but want the pussy so desperately you'd cut off your arm to get it… But she'd never felt that before, not from Marty.

It's himself he loathes, she thought, and another brick came down off the wall. "My mother killed herself when I was twelve," she told him. "They say when someone close to you commits suicide, it becomes more normal for you to consider it."

"I didn't know that," he said, and he looked away from her. "How'd she do it?"

Alessandra sucked in a big breath, held it, blew it out. "Gas," she said. "Head in the oven."

"I can't get into the kitchen," Marty said after a minute. "Three steps down. And there's always somebody around."

She leaned forward and stared into his eyes. "What the fuck, Marty?"

His hands gripped the bars of his chair. "I can't do this," he said, loud. "I want more than this."

"More what?"

"More life!" He yelled it at her.

"Well, then go fucking get it!" she yelled back at him.

He stared at her for a minute, and then the air went out of him. "Easy for you to say," he said.

Maybe you should have worn the dress again, she thought. And then what? God, what a horrible thought. But would you do it? Would you give him a charity fuck if you thought it would bring him back?

"Help me," he said.

"What do you want?" she asked him, suddenly frightened of what he was going to ask. "What can I do?"

"Valiums," he said, and she didn't know whether to be relieved or not. "Tens. Forty or fifty ought to do it. And a fifth of Wild Turkey."

"Oh for crissake, Marty."

"What?" he said. "What are you gonna tell me? Go on, give me the speech. Tell me how great life is."

She thought about it, considered what must be the standard pep talk, they'd probably be great at it in a place like this. Lots of practice. "Aren't you curious?" she asked him.

"About what." He didn't sound curious.

"About anything." He didn't react. "After my mother died, my father was gone, I wound up in a bad place, Marty. You wanna know what kept me going? Curiosity. I had never worn stockings, Marty, and I wanted to know how that felt."

One corner of his mouth lifted. "I never wore stockings neither."

She ignored that. "I'd never had a boyfriend. Didn't have pierced ears. I wanted more, too, Marty."

"If you won't get 'em for me, I'll find someone who will."

"There's a drugstore a couple blocks up on Ocean Boulevard," she told him, louder again. "Why don't you just go get 'em yourself? Can't you think of one goddam thing you still wanna do?"

He stared at her, his expression unreadable. "I already told you what I want," he said. "If you won't help, then get lost. Go away and leave me alone."

SARAH FINALLY FIGURED out what it was that made her love her job so much. "Mr. Jarvis?" she said. "Could I speak to you for a minute?" I am an extraordinary liar, Sarah told herself, and for the first time in my life I can do it with a clear conscience, and get paid for it besides.

Jarvis was just getting out of his car in the parking lot behind the police station in Port Washington, Long Island, New York. He looked like what he was—an aging policeman: gray brush cut, starched white shirt, blue trousers with a sharp crease. Despite the cold he stood there with his jacket draped over one arm. He regarded her with pale blue eyes. "How can I help you?" he said.

She walked up, shook his hand, introduced herself. "I'm with Houston Investigations," she told him. She had spent an hour or so thinking about her approach to the man. A regular policeman, she thought, probably would find it easy and maybe justified to look down on any private investigator. She thought she'd found a way to neutralize that. "We specialize," she told him, "in finding missing children."

It worked. She could tell from the changing expression on his face that he had initially dismissed her, then reconsidered it. How could you look down on someone who finds lost kids? "How did you get into that," he asked her.

"They originally hired me as a typist," she told him. "But none of those guys has ever been a mother. I am. I know kids, I know how they think. And they generally trust me." He nodded. Sarah watched his face as he placed her in the box labeled harmless, might even do some good.

"Come inside," he told her. "I'll buy you a cup of coffee."

"Thanks," she said.

"Station house coffee," he said.

"If it's warm, I'll drink it."

HE SAT BEHIND an enormous desk littered with papers. She sat across from him. "This is a bit beyond my comfort zone," she said.

"I can see why," he said. "Jacob West is not exactly a child anymore."

"Well, it's not just that," she said.

"No. He might be a murderer."

"I read the newspaper coverage," she said. "According to the papers…"

He nodded. "No secret that I thought Isaac and Jacob killed their father," he said. "And probably Barry Tipton, too."

"Do you still think so?"

"Yes," he said. "In my experience, these cases are generally much simpler than most folks make them out to be. Follow the money, Miss Waters."

"Sarah."

"Sarah. It's an old principle. Isaac and Jacob West each stand to inherit significant trust fund assets when they reach the age of thirty. I had information that Thomas West intended to change the terms of his will to the benefit of Agatha, his second wife. It is my belief that Isaac and Jacob discovered that and murdered Thomas in order to prevent it."

"Didn't he die in a car accident?"

"He certainly did, Sarah, but accidents can be arranged."

"Mess with the brakes or something," she said, nodding. "But you must have had something more to go on."

"I did, initially," he said. "I had Barry Tipton, up until he disappeared."

"You knew Tipton?"

"We played golf twice a month."

"So you don't think—"

"That he embezzled funds and disappeared? Not for a second. First of all, Barry was well off in his own right. Second, if you knew Barry…" He shook his head. "Barry was a good man. Damn good golfer. Had a big heart. He was a soft touch, Sarah, maybe not the most intellectual guy God ever grew legs on, but he was personable as hell. There is no way, Sarah, no way he could have pulled something like this off on his own. And he certainly could never have kept his mouth shut about it all these years. He would be constitutionally incapable of that kind of restraint."

"So you think he's dead."

"I do. I think that he was probably murdered by the same person or persons who killed Thomas West, and for the same reasons."

"Jacob and Isaac."

"Well, I certainly can't prove it," he said. "And Agatha thinks I'm insane. But then, she never liked Barry, and he didn't care much for her."

"So anyhow, if I do find Jacob for her—"

"Use extreme caution," he told her. "Isaac was the brainier of the two, but Jacob… There was always something about him that disturbed me. If you do discover his whereabouts, and if you're asking my opinion, I would tell you not to make contact. I would tell you to keep a safe distance." He fished a business card out of a little plastic stand on his desk, handed it to her. "I assume you report to Agatha," he said, "but if you would let me know, if and when you find something, I'd take it as a personal favor. I would truly hate to see anything else happen to her."

Sarah took the card, rubbed its raised letters between her fingers. "I'm sorry about your friend Mr. Tipton," she said.

"Thank you," he said. "So am I, believe me."

AL WATCHED THEM from the bus stop at the top of the hill. Got to buy a decent pair of binoculars, she thought, the ones Marty used weighed a ton. Down at the bottom of the hill, the valets worked the cars and the patrons of Costello's. Gotta be a sweet gig, she thought, particularly if you happened to be undocumented, the restaurant management might throw you a few bucks, but you could count on at least one or two monster tips to make your night. The guy who'd been there the night of the shooting, however, was not in evidence. Scared away, probably. She thought about walking down there and asking after him, but she knew the others would tell her nothing, not even his name.

Give him a day or two, she told herself. He's gonna miss the money, a gig like Costello's would be very hard to walk away from…

NINE

SARAH WATERS SAT behind her desk and looked at one of her lists. "Agatha West called."

Alessandra was in the client's chair, she had it leaned way back, she had her feet on the corner of the desk. "Yeah? What'd you tell her?"

"I put her off," Sarah said. "I told her all about the places I looked where I didn't find Jake, and she seemed to think that was progress. And I told her about the guy in her practice, the one who was rude when I called. 'He's a problem,' she told me, and she asked me not to call there anymore, that I should get her on her cell."

"So she's happy, for the moment?"

"Seems so," Sarah said. "But if you and I can grab an afternoon to drive up to Woodstock to see Jake, maybe we can put this thing to bed and send Mrs. West a bill."

"Okay. As soon as we get a line on Frank, we'll do it."

"Did you, um, you know, what was—"

"I found Frank's apartment," Al told her. "The super let me in. Cost me two hundred bucks."

"Okay." Sarah reached for a pen. "I'll write you a check out of penny cash."

"It's all right," Al told her. She told Sarah she had taken the two hundred out of the twelve and change she'd lifted from her subway assailants.

Sarah's eyes went wide. "You never told me you got attacked on the train!"

"Wasn't a big deal," Al said.

"Maybe not to you," Sarah told her, "but when I go see Marty, I'm taking a cab. I'm still writing you a check from penny cash."

"Why?"

"Al, we gotta do business the way it's supposed to be done, it was a legitimate expense, we got enough money for that, and whatever you make assaulting muggers on the subway is personal income. What did you find at Frank's place?"

"He's not an overly fastidious individual."

"I coulda told you that for free," Sarah said.

"And I grabbed all his bills for the past couple months, including his phone records." She plopped her chair to the floor, dug the papers out of her camera bag, and handed them to Sarah.

"Good," Sarah said, riffling through the pages. "I'll see if there's anything I can dig out of this."

"Okay. That yellow sheet is a list Frank kept, I'm guessing they're all his passwords."

Sarah found the yellow sheet. "The man has a head like a sieve," she said. "Let me keep the original, I'll copy out the numbers for you. I'll even spell 'burglar' right." She looked at Al. "He's not as dumb as this makes him look. You can't measure every kind of smarts there is with an IQ test."

Al kept her opinion to herself. "Okay."

Sarah breathed out a defeated sigh. Frank's reputation, it seemed, was not worth the time it would take her to defend it. "We got a check from Lamborghini of America," she said. "That's from a job you did before I got here. How do you want to handle it?"

"Same as all the others, just like we agreed," Al told her, "except we have to pay a fifteen percent vig to Pete's Towing Service."

"Okay. By the way, Lamborghini is asking for a certificate of insurance."

"What?"

"Liability insurance," Sarah said, nodding.

"Oh shit, I never even thought of that," Al said.

"That's what I figured," Sarah told her. "I went through Marty's records, he's got a policy that's good for another four months. It's under the old company name, so I don't know…" She shook her head. "As far as real coverage goes, I'm sure it's useless, because it's you and I now, not just Marty. I mean, I can probably get them to send us a certificate, but you know insurance companies, if they can find an excuse not to pay, they ain't paying."

"Christ," Al said. "So what's this gonna cost us? And will anyone even sell us a policy? I mean, considering—"

Sarah held up a hand. "Leave it to me," she said.

"Are you sure? How—"

"Do I tell you how to beat up muggers on the subway?"

"No."

"Well, then."

"You really gonna go see Marty?"

Sarah nodded. "I know he's probably not your favorite guy in the world, but he did hire me. We can't just, you know, abandon him."

"He was talking suicide yesterday."

"My God! Are you serious? Did you talk to a doctor? Because if he's talking about it, chances are he's thinking about it pretty hard—"

"I talked to the nurse on his floor. I don't know what anyone can do, other than keeping him so high that he can't move." Liar, she told herself, you know what you could have done… If you knew it would bring him around, would you do it? Would it be wrong to hold back? Wouldn't that be like

withholding CPR from someone because they were ugly and
you didn't want to put your mouth on theirs?

"What?" Sarah said, staring at her.

Gotta work on your poker face, Al told herself. "Nothing. Listen, if you're up to it, go on and see him. Maybe
you'll do better than me."

"I can do that. Besides, he's a lot closer to where I live,
I'll look in on him. What's next with Frank?"

"I wanna go check out the import company where he
works," Al said. "Maybe they know something."

"All right, but be careful," Sarah said. "I'll spend a few
hours digging through Frank's bills, then I gotta go bag
some more crooked bartenders."

"Jeez, I'm glad one of us is bringing in some money.
How are we making it?"

"You find Frank for me," Sarah said, "and I'll handle
those restaurant and hotel accounts until the end of time.
And I don't know if we're making it or not, to tell you the
truth. Another month, I'll have a handle on what we're doing
from the regulars and I'll know our overhead. Once we get
that to a real number, we'll know what we've gotta pull
down every month to keep the door open without going into
the hole and writing rubber checks and all that."

"God, I hope we make it," Al said.

"We'll make it." Al could hear the certainty in Sarah's
voice, but she still had her doubts.

PORT RICHMOND REMINDED Alessandra of a program she
had seen on the Discovery Channel about a Mayan city
lost in the jungles of Central America. The buildings were
still there, some of the roofs were gone, but otherwise the
place was in pretty decent shape, aside from being empty
and overgrown with weeds. There was no one left to tell
you what the pyramid was for or what function any of the

other buildings served. This blighted Staten Island neighborhood had a similar feeling, except there were a few lost souls wandering through the ruins of whatever the place had once been, and the stunted weeds were not doing that great in the poisoned soil. They were clinging to life, just like everything else.

Al had borrowed her uncle's van for the occasion. Al supposed his estate owned the battered Chevy Astro, but in practical terms the thing was hers, her uncle's partner, Anthony, had no interest in it and Al had decided that she would burn it before she let Bobby's sister Magdalena anywhere near it.

Not that it was a treasure…

Its first lifetime had been spent in the service of the phone company. Tio Bobby had picked it up at auction and customized it in his own uninhibited fashion: it looked plain enough on the outside, but inside it was lined with purple shag carpeting and it came complete with a couch, television, DVD player, and an ice box. Al was somewhat embarrassed by the thing, but she had to admit that it was more comfortable and certainly better furnished than most of the places where she had lived. Plus, if you stuck your foot on it, the sucker could haul ass.

The van was parked on a hill overlooking Palermo Imports. The place looked like it might once have been a repair facility for trucks or buses, but now it was a forlorn single-story brick structure surrounded by a parking lot, which was itself enclosed by a fence fashioned out of corrugated metal sheets painted a rusty pale gray. A single container sat in the parking lot in front of the building, the container was about half the size of the kind normally hauled by a semi. The container doors were open, but the open end of the container pointed at the building, so Al could not see what was inside.

Two of the three men inside the fence were of a type: dark hair, rather short, on the thin side. Immigrants, Al thought, the kind of guys you see all over the city, and the suburbs, too, men desperate for any sort of labor, men whose impoverished and malnourished childhoods showed clearly in their small stature and on their pinched faces. The third guy was a bit larger, and there was something about him that the others lacked. He seemed disinterested, for one thing. Whatever he was getting paid for, unloading containers was not it.

One of the smaller guys sat on a forklift truck. Al was too far away to hear anything, but she assumed the guy was yelling, if for no other purpose than to prevent his relatively constant arm-waving to go without accompaniment. Whatever they were trying to do, it seemed beyond their collective abilities, and apart from the shouting, gesticulating, and an occasional halfhearted head slap, nothing much was going on.

A guy came out of the building, he was older than any of the others, he carried himself with more authority and he was better dressed. The others deferred to him, when he walked over near the open doors of the container they gathered around him in a little knot. Even the presumptive forklift driver descended from his perch and joined in. Immediately the other short guy attempted a coup. More shouting and gesticulating ensued. The older guy said something to the bigger one, who went over and dragged the interloper from his perch.

Uncle Paolo, Al thought. Got to be. But wherever Uncle Paolo's talents lie, the ability to unload whatever was in the container did not seem to be among his gifts. They all moved closer, out of Al's sight. They are probably missing Frank Waters right about now, she thought. Frank, a former longshoreman, would surely know how to solve whatever problems these guys were having getting their stuff out, and he had the size and strength to bully the rest of these budding neurosurgeons into line.

A half an hour later, no visible progress had been made. Al heard the truck before she saw it, it was a big diesel rig and it was pulling a flatbed trailer upon which roosted a container identical in most respects to the one in the parking lot at Palermo Imports. The truck rattled past her, down the hill, and rolled up to the gate of Palermo Imports.

Immediately the focus shifted. The two short guys ran to open the gate. Then the two short guys attempted to tell the driver where to park. Each of them had a plan to get the container off the flatbed...

Al watched for the remainder of the afternoon. The container got off-loaded onto the parking lot, mostly because the driver, who seemed to know what he was doing, ignored all the shouted instructions and did things his own way, but it was almost four before he pulled out, dragging his empty trailer. Al waited for the circus to start back up again, but Paolo seemed to give up on the idea of unloading the containers and he sent his crew back inside the building. Al was disappointed, she had enjoyed the show. She had never had the sort of job where one must cooperate with one's compatriots, she had generally functioned more or less on her own. They need Frank, she thought, the whole bunch of them are probably standing inside yelling at each other right now, with each man trying to grab the steering wheel out of his buddy's hands.

At four-thirty the doors opened and the crew exited, began to straggle up the hill, presumably in search of transport. Al took off before they reached her.

IT WAS TEN-THIRTY at night and there had to be forty or fifty people lined up at the entrance to Club Dredd, the joint where TJ's new band, Indio, was playing. There was no velvet rope, no doorman, just one locked door under a short red awning. Al didn't want to wait in the line so she waited across the street, sipped a glass of wine at a window table in a café. She wasn't afraid of being recognized, she had been instructed in the fine art of disguise by Marty Stiles. "No offense, sweetheart," she remembered him saying, "but none of these guys are gonna be looking at your face, so don't go nuts." And she hadn't, the blond wig, fur coat, and oversized sunglasses that she'd taken out of Marty's office closet was a getup that had worked fine for her in the past.

White Zinfandel, she thought, making a face. Sounds a hell of a lot better than it tastes. Horrible stuff, fit strictly for potheads and winos.

When the door finally opened, the line collapsed, everyone crowded around the entrance, trying to be first. It seemed like it took forever for them all to get inside. Al left her wine on the table, took a couple of mints from the bowl next to the register, mostly to kill the taste. She crossed the street, yanked the club door open. No wonder, she thought. The door opened to a steep, narrow set of stairs that led down into a basement. This place catches on fire, she thought, we're all toast… She paid her cover charge, found a dark corner, and settled in to wait.

The first act started about twenty minutes later. A tall, somewhat unsteady guy in a shiny green suit looked like he'd gotten it from the Starvation Army stepped up to a mike, asked for a big hand, a real Club Dredd welcome for… He was immediately drowned out by a wall of noise. The band was opening for Indio, and Al thought she could distinguish the sound of drums, a bass, and a human voice coming from someone who may have been having his toes bitten off one at a time. Hard to be sure, though. Half the people in the joint got to their feet and cheered noisily at each break.

Relatives, Al thought. Who else would pay to listen to this crap? But the kids in the band seemed like they were having a good time. After a while, though, Al was considering wads of paper cocktail napkin for her ears. Finally, mercifully, they were done. The people who'd been standing applauded wildly, and then some of them began to filter out. During the break, the waitstaff worked the crowd hard, and Al ordered a Cutty that she didn't really want. More people made their way down the narrow stairs, and by the time the lights went down again the place was packed. The guy in the green suit stepped back up to the mike. "People," he said, holding his hands up for quiet. "People! I give you…Indio!"

A single spot lit up a tall black kid who began hammering a three-chord progression on a guitar. Ten seconds later a drummer cracked in, and then the rest of the band jumped in and the singer stepped up to the mike. It was her, it was the white girl Al had seen with TJ, man, she looked like a Creamsicle on a hot summer day, every guy in the place came up on point when she ripped into the vocal.

They were doing an old blues standard, but it was set to a grunge arrangement. None of the musicians seemed that gifted, but collectively the band was spare and tight, they were getting everything there was to get out of what they had.

Typical TJ Conrad treatment, Al thought. You had Conrad, you didn't need any virtuosos, he could make almost any bunch of musicians sound like they had it going on.

But God, the singer was hot. She sang in the smoky rasp of someone much older than herself, and she worked the crowd, she growled, cajoled, tempted, pleaded… This kid doesn't do if for you, Al thought, you probably need some kind of therapy. The men up near the stage looked mesmerized, the women looked stunned. Al thought sure she knew what they were feeling, because she was pretty certain she couldn't compete, either.

TJ Conrad was playing keyboard.

Not his best instrument, that's what he'd told her, but you couldn't tell, not on this particular night.

Alessandra felt too tired to hate anyone. The girl was just a kid anyhow, she didn't know anything, she couldn't. And TJ was just being TJ. Besides, she told herself, you've still got nothing, not in the way of proof anyhow, and all the show had taught her was that God had given the kid a set of pipes to go along with her other assets. Still, it was growing stronger by the minute, this idea that the thing Al and TJ had together was dead. And if that's true, she told herself, then you ought to dig a hole and bury it because pretty soon it's gonna start to stink.

The next time the lights went down Al got up and made her way out.

TEN

"AND WHAT WAS it that you did for Best Foods?" The man behind the desk at Palermo Imports had introduced himself as Paolo Torrente. Up close he was far more handsome than he had appeared from a distance yesterday, he had café au lait skin, a nice smile which he employed often, softly graying hair, a mellow voice, and sad brown eyes. His hands, though, despite the manicured nails, were gnarled and twisted.

Al's head pounded. "I was a warehouse foreman at their facility in Bayonne, over in Jersey." She had a different disguise today, she wore black jeans, construction boots, a Mets T-shirt, and she had her hair in a ponytail. Unfortunately for her, the white Zinfandel and the Cutty Sark seemed to have reacted badly with the Beefeater's gin she'd swilled at the bar downstairs from her apartment the night before. She felt like someone was pounding tenpenny nails into her forehead. Most of her carefully constructed cover story was lost in the fog and pain and she was winging it.

"Ah," said Uncle Paolo. Al made a mental note, for what it was worth, not to call him that. "So much responsibility for one so young and beautiful, no? Did you not find it difficult to convince mortal men that they should listen to you instead of merely drinking in the sight of one so, so…" He waved his twisted hands. "Stunning?"

Only an Italian, Al thought, especially one as suave as Uncle Paolo, could make you feel good about questions like that. "Not really," she said. "The guys I know generally fall out of love with me after a little while."

"But how could that be?" he said. "What on earth could dissuade them?"

"Humiliation works great," she told him, trying not to look at his mitts. "Particularly in front of their friends."

"Ah," he said, laughing softly. He held up a hand. "I should like to explain," he said, "how I got these."

"No, no," Al told him. "I was trying not to stare. And it's none of my business."

He grinned broadly. "But they would always come between us, and that must never be. You are human, like me, and we must understand each other. Truly."

This guy should give lessons, she thought, and she nodded.

"Some years ago," he told her, "when I was young and stupid, I worked for the Italian government. They send me to Libya. I try to do the job they give me to do, but before I could get home, the colonel was a make me his guest." His smile had gone. "The colonel could be very persuasive."

"I'm sorry."

He shrugged. "Well, I survived," he said. "I was a pay for my ideals, but after some time Italia was a trade some smuggler for me. My injuries get me out of the government and into the family business. So how could I be unhappy, buying and selling wine? Wine is a gift from God."

"You don't seem bitter," she said.

He shrugged again. "In his own time, God will see to Colonel Qaddafi," he said. "Meanwhile, you must explain to me how Best Foods is allow such a creature as you to escape them."

"Layoffs," she said. "It's a union shop. First hired, last fired."

Paolo nodded. "Sensible," he said. "I, too, feel loyalty

to the men I have hire. I know that some of them may not be the most ideal of workers, but even they have families to feed."

"Very compassionate," she said.

Paolo shook his head. "Is a weakness," he told her. "In Palermo, we are almost all *famiglia*. Since one cannot fire one's relative, we are force to coexist. I am in hopes we can forge the same spirit here."

Al grimaced. "Good luck with that," she said.

Paolo laughed. "Fool's errand," he said. "May I ask you one more question? How did you hear of us? We are still so small, I thought no one could know of us."

Her head swam. She'd had an answer for this one, but her head was thundering too hard for her to come up with it, so she improvised. "Your forklift shop," she said. "I have a buddy who works for them, he told me you looked like you could use some help."

"Very astute," Paolo said. "Like I'm a say, we are still very small here. I have no need for foreman, not yet. Maybe soon, if God is a smile on us. But I do have a lilla problem, some crate we have shipped is a get stuck inside the container. Maybe you help us out for today, okay, you get my stuff unload for me, I pay you cash."

"I can do that," she said.

"Beautiful!" he said. "And you leave you phone number, when we get a lilla more business, I gonna call you right away."

"Deal," she told him.

The wooden crate inside the metal container was almost as big as the container itself. It was mounted on long wooden sleeper rails, and it was one of those sleepers that had caused all the problems. It had come loose from the bottom of one side of the wooden crate and it was jammed behind the container door frame.

"Everybody," Paolo yelled, "everybody, listen to me. I want to introduce—Raffi, you fuckina mongey, shut uppa you hole ana listen to me." Raffi was the smallest of the three guys that Al had watched wrestle with the crate yesterday, he was also the loudest, and from the look on his face, the angriest. "You hear me?" Paolo demanded.

Raffi grimaced. "Okay, okay," he said, impatient.

"From now on," Paolo said, addressing them all, "English only. You understand?"

He was interrupted by a howl of protest from Raffi, but he shouted it down. "English only! No Italian, no Spanish, English. Only. You understand?" He didn't wait for answers. "You don't speak English today, okay, tomorrow you are gone from here, I send you home." Raffi and the larger guy stared sullenly at Paolo. The third, who looked like he hadn't reached drinking age yet, had a hard time taking his eyes off Alessandra. Or off her body, anyhow. He didn't seem to be able to make eye contact.

"Okay, next," Paolo said. "Raffi, do you listen to me? You hear what I'ma say?" Al noticed that the more agitated Paolo got, the worse his accent became.

"Yeah, yeah, yeah, yeah, English. I catch," Raffi said, his face sour.

"Good. Next, this nice young lady, name is Alicia. She gonna help us out today." They all looked at her, then back at Paolo, blank looks on their faces. "For today, she gonna be the boss. Foreman. *Capataz. El Jefe*. You do what she'sa tell you."

The protests over language paled in comparison to what now erupted. The two smaller guys yelled simultaneously in some language Al didn't recognize. She wished, not for the first time, that her Spanish was better. She could sometimes understand a word or two of Italian due to the similarities with Spanish, but she assumed these guys were speaking some regional dialect because she couldn't decipher a thing.

"English!" Paolo bellowed, red-faced. "English! What I'ma just tella you? Cocksuckabasta, English! You don' do what I'ma say, you go home first thing tomorrow!"

They stood in shocked silence. The kid continued staring at Al. "No more talk!" Paolo was pissed. "You do what I'ma say, you hear me? English! Only! And Al isa the boss, she gonna tella you stupida cocksuckabasta how you gonna get that thing outa the box ana insidea the building! That's it!" He turned and stomped away angrily, paused about ten feet away. "English!" he yelled. "You hear me?" He gathered himself, looked at Al. "Raffi," he said, pointing to the shortest. "Tonio," he said, pointing to the kid. "And Vincenzo. Vinnie." Up close, Vinnie was much more intimidating that he had been from a distance. He had the mass and muscle of a pro linebacker.

They all stood and watched Paolo go inside. Raffi looked at Al and sneered. His face betrayed what he felt, it showed a mixture of contempt and hunger. He hates me already, Al thought. She had run into Raffi's type before, he was the kind of guy who regarded her as nothing more than a life-support system for what she carried between her legs. Funny how so many guys found it perfectly acceptable to drool over one small part of her and revile the rest.

Al walked over and looked at the crate. "You guys have a pry bar?" she said, wishing her head didn't pound quite so hard when she bent over to look at the jammed sleeper.

Three of them looked at her blankly while Raffi crawled up onto the forklift. "Pry bar," she said louder, her patience wearing thin. "Crowbar? Pipe? Two-by-four? Raffi, get down from there."

He ignored her, ground the forklift's starter.

She grabbed him by the collar, dragged him down off the

forklift, and pitched him onto the ground. When he tried to get back to his feet, she stuck a booted foot in his ass and shoved. Raffi took two running steps and sprawled face-first in the dirt littering the pavement of the parking lot. Al followed him, seized him by the shirt collar as he scrabbled to his feet, bleeding from his chin. "English!" she yelled in his face. "Only! You get me? Or do I have to explain it to you some more?"

"Okay!" he yelled back. "Okay! I catch!"

"Good!" She let him go, he backed away, and again she followed him.

"Okay!" he yelled again. Raffi was enraged, he couldn't stand still and he couldn't hold his ground, he retreated step by step and Al followed. He kept peering over her shoulder looking for support from the other two. Al did not allow herself to look back to gauge their reactions.

"From now on, you do what I tell you. You catch that, motherfucker?" She stopped, finally, and a step later so did he.

She turned her back on Raffi and walked back over to the container. The other two stood there in silence. The kid's face was white, but Vinnie was impossible to read. She was surprised at that, most men, in her opinion, would be laughing and ridiculing Raffi. "We need pipes," she told them. "As wide as this box, okay, they gotta reach all the way from this sleeper over to the one on the other side." She turned, Raffi was still standing where she'd left him. "Hey, Einstein," she yelled, "get your ass over here! You want me to make you go find this shit all by yourself? We'll all stand here and wait for you, how about that?"

He approached reluctantly, red-faced, bleeding from a cut on his chin, quivering with embarrassment and rage. "Okay!" he yelled. "Okay!"

"All right. I want you guys to look through the piles of

junk in this place, we need some pipes, they gotta reach all the way across the bottom of this crate. We need at least three of them. Four would be better." Her headache seemed to be concentrating itself right behind her eyes. "This big around," she said, holding her thumb and forefinger about two inches apart. If I gotta bust my hump in this place, she thought, at least I'm gonna have a little fun while I do it. She looked at Raffi. "Twice the size of your dick," she told him.

The kid looked like he wanted to laugh but was afraid to. Vincenzo merely turned and walked away. Tough audience, she thought. Well, too bad, I thought it was funny. "What are you waiting for?" she bellowed at Raffi. "A written invitation? Move! Chop-chop! Let's go!"

IT TOOK MORE yelling and cursing, but Al and her three new assistants got the crate unjammed from the container and up on some rollers, and with the use of some long rusty chains they got it started out of its metal prison. Once Raffi and company understood her system, they pitched in, pulling the rollers out as each one of them made its way to the end of the crate, repositioning them back under the leading edge of the crate again, and things progressed at what she thought was a reasonable pace. It seemed obvious to her, though, that the three of them really hated taking instructions from her, and she assumed that it was because she was a woman. Maybe where they come from, she thought, maybe they bring their women up to be silent and compliant. Which, in her opinion, was too fucking bad, because they were in New York now. But it didn't necessarily have to be that, she was willing to admit that perhaps they hadn't cared for Frank Waters any better, maybe they hated New York and everyone in it, maybe they hated everyone who wasn't like they were, hell, maybe they hated everyone, period. The youngest of them, the kid, she thought that maybe under better circumstances they would have gotten along okay, they may have been able to connect, the way normal people do. He still wouldn't make eye contact with her, but when he did stare it seemed that his eyes were filled with a sort of forlorn desire, he looked like a guy mooning at a new car that he desperately wanted but could not afford. It was a small comfort to her that at least he did not seem to despise her the way Raffi did. She continued to ride them all, questioning their family origins, manhood, and sexual preferences. She watched them seethe and squirm, all except the kid, who took it better than the rest of them. She even let him drive the forklift after a while.

Vincenzo, she told herself. The other two are just bodies. Vincenzo's the one you gotta watch…

Once they got the crate in through one of the big roll-up doors and shoved into position, Paolo Torrente came out of his office and fussed over it like a mother hen who'd just located a lost chick. Al ignored him and looked around. There was a shiny new Chevy Suburban parked just inside one of the other roll-up doors. It didn't look exactly like the one Frank Waters had been driving, because it didn't have chrome spinners and the windows weren't tinted. Al tried not to stare too hard at it. As for the rest of the building, it still looked like the former truck garage that it was, but one whole side of the place was devoted to metal racks that were filled with cartons labeled in Italian, French, Spanish, and some other languages she didn't recognize. "Paolo," she said. "No German. How come?"

"German!?" He looked at her, horrified. "German? *Liebfraumilch?* My God! Bleah! Nobody gonna drink that es-stuff ! Never mind German, I give you something special to take home tonight." He approached her, grabbed her by both shoulders, and planted a kiss on each of her cheeks.

"I am so relieve, you don't believe. I thought maybe these guys wasa destroy me."

Raffi and Vincenzo turned away in disgust while the kid watched her from a safe distance.

So, AL THOUGHT, what the hell's in the crate?

Damned heavy, whatever it was.

Come on, Al, she told herself, who you kidding? You got Uncle Paolo Torrente from Palermo, Italy, he comes to New York City looking to expand his family business. Buys a warehouse. Pays cash for it. Hires Frank Waters to clear the way for him. And what then? Did Frank Waters see something he wasn't supposed to see? Did he try to cut himself in for a bigger piece of the pie? After all, Frank was the kind of guy who always dreamed of making it big.

Of course, the crate could be full of boxes, and the boxes could be full of bottles of wine. Hey, that is the business these guys are supposed to be in. Right?

No way to tell from the exterior of the crate what was inside it. There was some writing on the side, but none of it made any sense to Al. And there was one marking in particular that caught her eye, it was a rectangular-shaped set of dots and lines, sort of a bar code but more complicated.

Come on, Al, she thought, why are you making this harder than it has to be? Whatever Palermo Imports is really bringing into the country, a buck buys you ten you either snort it or shoot it or smoke it. And those nutcases working here, their function is not to unload the trucks, that's why they whined so much about having to do it. Vincenzo looked like the enforcer, the hand-to-hand specialist. And that fucking little ferret Raffi, Al bet herself that his real skill was with a garrote or a knife or a pistol, not a forklift. "You don't speak English…tomorrow…I send you home." Al hadn't given a lot of thought to that when

Paolo had said it, but the strangeness of it came back to her now. Why would you say that to a guy you hired off the corner? Why wouldn't you just say, "You're fired, get the fuck out"? No, you said that if you were threatening to put the guy on a plane back to wherever he came from. Wherever they all came from.

Another friggin' dope operation, Al thought. Got real wine being imported and probably even sold, it's the perfect cover. You could bring your shit in with the same containers, who the hell would know the difference? Nobody, not unless they had the machine to read that bar code. And Customs couldn't inspect every container that came into Port Newark, they couldn't even come close. They didn't have the budget and they didn't have the personnel. Al took her cell phone off her belt, flipped it open, toggled on the camera function, held it up to her ear, and pretended to take a call.

AL LEFT PALERMO IMPORTS at four in the afternoon, three hundred bucks cash in her pocket. Uncle Paolo had been effusive in his praise of her, had made a show of writing down her cell number. Her three compatriots lagged behind, probably, she thought, so they could bitch to Torrente about all the abuse they'd had to take from her. Torrente, however, seemed happy as hell that his two crates had gotten unloaded and moved into the warehouse. Al climbed the hill up to the spot where she'd parked her uncle's van, right across the street from the place she'd parked it the previous day. She slumped in the driver's seat for a while, expecting Raffi and his guys to come out, but the doors to Palermo Imports stayed closed.

Maybe Paolo's got those characters sleeping inside the warehouse, she thought. Maybe he just lets them out for an hour or so in the evening so they can get some dinner or something. But no way he hired them off the street. Wherever Paolo came from, whatever he was really doing, those three were a part of the package.

She called the office phone at Houston Investigations, was surprised when Sarah Waters answered. "Hey, killer," Al said.

"Hey," Sarah said. Her voice was lifeless.

"What's wrong?"

"Oh, nothing," Sarah said. "I guess I'm getting down about Frankie. If he was alive, he'd of turned up by now. I mean, the more time goes by, the worse, you know, I mean, the slimmer his chances are."

Al wanted to remind Sarah that Frank was a creep and a deadbeat dad, but she didn't. "Don't start digging the hole yet," Al told her. "Let's wait and see what we find, first."

"But I knew something like this was gonna happen to him someday," Sarah said. "I knew it."

"Sarah, for all we know, he could be shacked up in Jersey somewhere. He's probably sitting in some fleabag motel right now, got his feet up, be drinking beer and watching *Jeopardy*."

"Too intellectual," Sarah said. "*Wheel of Fortune,* maybe, or *The Girls Next Door.*"

"Whatever. Listen, I spent the day at Palermo Imports. I got some pictures, I got head shots of three head cases that work there, and I got some close-ups of the markings on two big-ass crates we unloaded. I don't know what the markings mean, some of it is in some language I don't recognize, and there are some symbols that I couldn't begin to decipher. I'm gonna come in later tonight and download 'em. Can you take a look at them tomorrow? Maybe you can figure out what the hell these guys are actually importing."

"No problem," Sarah said. "Listen, you sound tired. Why don't you just go home and e-mail them to me from there? Save yourself a trip, get some rest."

"I don't have a PC at home," Al told her. In fact, there was very little in the empty room she lived in to make it feel like anything more than a bus-stop shelter with a door and a window. "So if I got to go to the library to download 'em, I might just as well come in to the office and do it there."

"Okay," Sarah said. "Or if you wanna stop at my mom's place… We could use Frankie Junior's computer."

"It's no big deal," Al told her. "I'm all right. Just tired."

"Gotcha. You get a picture of Uncle Paolo?"

"No," Al said. "The other three were no problem, but if I want a shot of Uncle Paolo, I'm gonna have to get it with a telephoto lens."

"We've got something like that here, don't we?"

"Yeah, we do."

"Okay. Listen, you got two calls. One from a guy calls himself Doc, says you and he are old friends. Says he needs to talk to you. And the other was from some guy at something called the Irish-American Mothers and Fathers Association. His accent was so thick I barely understood him. Said he'd call back."

"Oh, great," Al said. "I wonder who the hell that could be. That just sounds like bad news. Listen, I gotta run, the kid from Palermo Imports just came out, he's walking this way. I wanna climb into the back where he can't see me, I'm gonna change clothes real quick, I need to see where this kid goes. Don't forget to look at those pictures for me."

SARAH WATERS DID not like the looks of the cabdriver. "You wan' me to wait for you?" he asked her. "If you wan', I wait and take you back."

"I might be a while," she told the guy. Sarah was Brooklyn born and raised, she had the accent, the survival instinct, and the heightened awareness of a Brooklyn native.

"Is okay," the driver said, watching her in his rearview mirror. "I wait. I don' mind."

"Suit yourself," she told him. The guy might just be looking for a return fare, she thought, maybe he just doesn't want to drive back empty. Still… "Right up here on the corner," she told him, even though she was still a few blocks away from her destination. She paid the driver, exited the cab, and walked into the lobby of a high-rise apartment building, where she gave the doorman five bucks and had him direct her to the back door.

She preached it to her son, Frank Junior, all the time, you don't know these people, don't go assuming they're your friends. You have to watch where you're going, and you have to watch your back. Don't be going places where you don't belong… She came out on the broad wooden boardwalk that ran along the Brooklyn shoreline. There was a wide expanse of sand between her and the dirty waters of Lower New York Bay. The smell was the same one she got near her mother's house in Bensonhurst, a hint of the ocean, a touch of decay. She wished it was lighter out so she could see better because the landmass of Staten Island did not extend this far south and in the daytime there was nothing to mar your view of the clean horizon. She walked across the width of the boardwalk, leaned on the railing, and stared out at the lights winking off the water. It seemed endless, particularly at night, but even in the day the sea seemed to stretch away to infinity. That, she knew, was an illusion. You could only see so far before the curve of the planet dropped the surface of the water below your sight line. She had noticed, as a child, that when freighters left the port and sailed away, the hull of the ship would drop out of view before the superstructure. You think you're looking at forever, but your mind is simply extrapolating the emptiness of your immediate future. There is always something more, something you can't see, it might be just out of your vision but still be close enough to be in your lap tomorrow. Sometimes you gotta hang on to that… She was in the middle of reading a book by a famous neurosurgeon. *Confabulation* was his word for the way the brain papers over the gaps in what it can see, how it fills in the holes with what may or may not approximate reality. It amazed her, last night when she read it, and it continued to amaze her now, the idea that the human condition requires that you become so adept at bullshitting yourself that you lose the awareness that you are doing it…

"Excuse me, Miss…"

The guy took ten years off her life, she turned, he was only six feet away, his stocking cap in his hand. "I'm so sorry to disturb you, Miss, please…"

"Look, buddy, I'm broke," she said, relieved that he was only a panhandler.

"Oh, please," he begged, bending forward at the waist, twisting his cap in his hands as if trying to strangle it. "If you could only help me just a little, I am so hungry…"

So thirsty, more like it, she thought, but the guy's tears seemed real enough. Against her better judgment, she fished a buck out of her pocket and handed it over.

The guy made a great show of gratitude. "Oh, God bless you, Miss, God bless you…"

"Yeah, sure," she said. "Tell your story walking."

"TONIO." ALESSANDRA SAID it softly, but he should have heard it. If it had been his real name he would have reacted. "Tonio!" she said, much louder, and he turned. He was the youngest, the one Al thought still might be worth something. He was coming out of a bodega about six blocks from Palermo Imports, he had a case of beer under one arm and a bag full of sandwiches under the other. He looked at her face and his eyes went wide with surprise.

"Hey," he said. "Alicia... What do you do up here, all alone?"

"I'm not alone, Tonio, I'm with you. What's the matter? Don't you think I can take care of myself?"

His eyes dropped from her face to her chest, and he shrugged. "America," he said, as if that explained everything.

"You don't like it, do you? You think I should be on a leash? Tied up in someone's backyard, like a dog?"

"No, no, I don't say that. I don't say nothing."

"Come on, Tonio," she said. "You and I are friends. Aren't we? Come on, talk to me."

He glanced at her face again. She noticed how dark his eyes were, how long his lashes were, he almost looked like he wore eyeliner and mascara. She wondered how long he would last in an American prison. "They think you are police," he told her.

She was surprised at that. "Police? Come on, Tonio, do I look like a cop to you?"

He looked down at his shoes. "I know nothing of police."

"Can I ask you something, Tonio? If I ask you something, will you tell me the truth?"

He didn't look up.

"What happened to Frank, Tonio? Frank Waters. Great big guy." She held a hand up over her head. "About so tall."

"I don't know anything," he said, and he backed away, edging along the brick wall of the building that housed the bodega.

"Come on, Tonio. You must have heard something." She stepped up, backed him up against the wall, got up in his face. "I thought you liked me, Tonio." She put a hand on his chin, tilted his face up until he made eye contact. "I thought you and I could be friends, Tonio."

He struggled to maintain his grip on the beer. His Adam's

apple bobbed up and down as he swallowed. "I need to go now," he said. "They, they wait for me." He ducked, escaped her like a boxer getting himself out of a corner.

"That looks heavy, Tonio," she said. "You need me to carry it for you?"

His face went white. "No!" he said, and he glanced around to see if anyone was watching him talk to her. "No. I can do it." He took a step backward. "You should stay away," he said. "Um, Raffi, he'sa hate you. He kill you if Paolo lets him."

"You think so? Is that what happened to Frank Waters? Did Paolo let Raffi kill him?"

Tonio swallowed, took another step back. "Don't come back," he said, his eyes pleading. "Please." He turned and fled.

"HELLO, MR. STILES," Sarah said.

Marty Stiles was parked in his chair in front of a south-facing window of a long corridor. It was fully dark outside and there was nothing for him to look at other than his own reflection in the glass. He stared straight ahead.

"Sarah Waters," she said. "I work for you."

He glanced at her, nodded once, turned to the window again. The noises of patients, nurses, and hospital machinery droned behind them.

"You've lost weight," she told him.

He nodded again, just once. "I've taken up jogging," he said, his voice ragged from lack of use.

"Very funny," Sarah said. She looked around, spotted a chair in a corner, went over and dragged it next to Marty's wheelchair, eased herself into it. He turned to stare at her.

"Miss…"

"Sarah."

"Whatever," he said. "What do you want from me?"

She didn't answer right away.

"Sarah," he said, louder. "Why are you here?"

She cleared her throat. "They aren't going to let you stay," she said.

He seemed to come out of himself just a little bit when she told him that, like a turtle poking its head out of its shell to see how hard it was raining.

"A few years ago," she said, "my father had a stroke." She pointed to his wheelchair. "They put him in one of those, with a motor. He couldn't, you know, he couldn't do for himself. Couldn't move, couldn't talk, nothing." She could still feel the tightness in her chest that she'd gotten, seeing him in his reduced state. "They kept him in rehab for a while, but his insurance only covered him for so long. So then Medicaid took him out, they put him in this place." She stared at the glass, at her reflection and his. "Not like here. It wasn't very nice. Four residents to a room, common bathrooms. They, ah, I don't think they paid the nurses or the aides very much." She sighed. "One of my father's roommates would groan all day and all night long. 'Help me,' he'd say it a thousand times. 'Help me, please.' But if you asked him what he wanted, he didn't understand you."

"I spent twenty-two years in the NYPD." He said it as if he were addressing the window. "I have a pension, I have insurance, I have…"

"Mr. Stiles?" Sarah cut him off. "No you don't, Mr. Stiles. Not anymore. Medicaid takes away everything. They took my father's pension, they took his Social Security, they would have taken the house and his savings, too, but my mother divorced him first so she could have something. Otherwise, they'd have left her with nothing at all."

He exhaled. The sound of his breath passing through his vocal cords made a dry rasping sound. It did not sound like a human noise, it was more like a screen door creaking back and forth in the wind.

"She cried when she did it, even though, you know, it didn't mean nothing. He cried, too, but he did that all the time anyhow so it's hard to know if he really knew what was going on."

Marty curled his upper body forward, put his head in his hands, squeezed the bridge of his nose between a thumb and forefinger. "Maybe he just wanted to die," he said.

"Maybe," Sarah said. God, she thought, please don't let me go like my father, let me go in my sleep… "If that's what he wanted, he got his wish, but not right away. He had to lose everything first. His money, his house, his wife, his independence, his dignity, his clothes… In the end, all he had left was a bathrobe and a pair of socks." She wiped at the corner of her eye. "Listen to me, Mr. Stiles," she said, and she leaned in close. "We all gotta go sometime. I know that. But doing it this way, in this place…" She looked around. "This is not an easy way to die. You're gonna hurt a lot, first. It's gonna tear you apart. You gotta get yourself outa here."

"Where am I supposed to go?" He was suddenly loud, angry, on the edge of panic.

Her father had been such a prick, but even he hadn't deserved to suffer the way he did at the end. "Why can't you just go home?" She was surprised at the depth of sorrow she heard in her voice.

He turned forward again. "I lived on the third floor," he said to the blank window. "I can't climb the stairs. I can't drive. I can't…"

"Mr. Stiles," Sarah said, exasperated. "We'll get you a ride home. We'll find you another apartment. We'll move your stuff…"

"We? Who's we?"

"Me and Al," she told him.

He gritted his teeth at the sound of Al's name. "That fucking bitch," he said.

Sarah ignored that. She put a hand on Marty's arm, considered it a minor victory that he did not shake her off. "Don't quit," she said. "If you do, it only gets worse from here. A lot worse. You'll just be one more stray dog at the pound, waiting for someone to give you the needle. I've seen it."

He swallowed once, stared straight ahead. "Go away," he said.

Gave it my best shot, she thought. She patted his arm before she got up to go. "Don't say I didn't warn you."

ALESSANDRA SAT IN her room in the dark, listening to the faint sounds coming from the taproom below. They had the television tuned to a hockey game, she knew that because she had seen it through the windows on her way past. She could not really hear it, though, maybe they had the sound turned down, or maybe its sounds blended too well with the murmur of the Brooklyn night. She thought about calling her father, pictured him sitting in his dark room up in the Bronx, and it frightened her that she was doing the exact same thing, only in a different borough. The realization hit her that she might be the same kind of person he was, and it was like being punched in the stomach. It was horrible, the idea that she might be as cold and as distant as he, so uncommunicative that she drove everyone who tried to get close to her mad with frustration. That's not me, she told herself, I'm not like him…

But she didn't call him. It's only because he's even worse on the phone than I am, she told herself. I can have the whole conversation without him anyway, both sides, without troubling him at all: Hey, how are you? *Great. You?* Yeah, okay. Ahh, how's work? *Eh, well, you know, it's work.* Yeah, mine,

too. You need anything? *No. You?* No, me neither. *Okay.*
Take care. Yeah. See you.

Thanks for calling…

Sure.

It's as much your fault as his, a small voice told her. You
two are peas in a pod… It angered her, the same as it did
when she looked in the mirror first thing in the morning
and sometimes saw his face looking back out at her.

God, please. I'm not like him, I can't be.

And I'm not calling TJ, she thought. It's his turn.

She could call Anthony, he'd be glad to hear from her.
Anthony was her aunt, in a way. He'd been her uncle Roberto's partner for as far back as she could remember. He'd
be happy to hear her voice, and being the soul of convivi-
ality and good manners he would make up for all of her
awkward silences, he'd fill her in on everything that was
going on in the old neighborhood, tell her about everything
he'd done to the house since Tio Bobby's death, inquire so-
licitously after her health and love life… But he knew her
too well, he would know how desperately lonely she was
sometimes. Next week, she thought. Next week, when I'm
in a better head, I'll call him. I promise.

She could call Sarah Waters…

Sarah would be happy to hear from her, too, Sarah liked
talking about as much as anyone Al knew, Sarah would ask
her when she was coming out to the house, she would promise to cook veal and peppers. Sarah would bitch about her
mother, it was funny how the two of them seemed to be always at war. That seemed more the rule than the exception,
it seemed that most women Al knew had the same sorts of
problems getting along with their mothers, they all labored
along under the weight of that maternal disapproval and disappointment… Al could feel the truth of it, she could sense
the approximate size and density of her own mother's unmet

expectations, knew that she, Al, would not have measured up, either, if her mother had lived.

And how bad, she wondered, how awful must life have been, for her to do what she did?

Jesus.

Anyway, Sarah deserves a break from you, she told herself. Leave the woman alone.

And is that where I'm headed, she wondered, will I ever get so down on everything that I would just give up and take the next exit…?

I'm not calling TJ, she thought. The son of a bitch didn't call me back from the last time. And why do I always have to be the one?

An old joke ran across the front porch of her memory: How do porcupines make love?

Carefully. *Verry* carefully…

Am I really that much of a prick? she wondered.

No, man, I'm not doing it, I'm not calling him.

Well, go on downstairs then, said that small voice, reasserting itself. Go on. Go sit at the bar and drink yourself senseless, if that's what you want. Go hang out with a bunch of half-loaded retirees who are sitting together in the same room, not talking, watching a hockey game none of them cared about. Go on, why not?

She picked up the phone, punched up TJ's cell.

"Hello?"

Woman's voice, piano music tinkling in the background, laughing voices, loud, then fading away. Softly, softly, Al asked to speak to Jorge, in Spanish.

"I'm sorry, you must have the wrong number," the woman said.

Al hung up.

ELEVEN

ALESSANDRA MARTILLO CHASED fried potatoes around on the plate in front of her. "So tell me, Doc," she said. "What would your wife say if she could see us right now?"

"She'd say that you're even better looking than I told her you were." Doc was the drummer in BandX, a group in which TJ Conrad had, until recently, played guitar. He was bald, and he wore a pair of sunglasses perched high on his shiny brown skull. "Sheila and I," he said, "crossed that particular bridge a long time ago."

"Did you really?"

"Yep."

"How'd you do it?"

He seemed to consider that for a moment. "Well, I don't know, exactly," he said. "I mean, I'm not trying to tell you that she's a saint, or that I ain't a man. And most men are wired up more or less the same in that department."

"I've noticed," Al said.

"Well, if that's true then you know that it's a lot easier for you guys to hook up than it is for us."

"Oh, please," she said. "You're a musician. You forget, I've seen your tour bus after a show, you guys look at more phony IDs than any bartender in America."

"True enough," he said, nodding, "and I admit that does change the odds somewhat, but if you and I walked out this door and went trolling for a little sumpin', you could be smoking the post-game cigarette before I even get a sniff."

Even if that was true… "Has Sheila seen your tour bus?"

Doc laughed softly. "Al, she knows where I go, and she knows what I do. Hey, listen, I could drive myself crazy worrying about what she does while I'm at work, and she could go crazy thinking about that tour bus, but there ain't no future in it. I know she loves me, if she didn't she'd have tossed me like a dirty paper towel by now. And I hope she knows I'm crazy about her. So for now, you know, unless proven otherwise, me and Sheila are solid."

Alessandra poked at the food in front of her. "Don't say anything to TJ, okay?"

"I got you, baby. I got you." He watched her for a minute. "Did he tell you? They tried to book us into that club up in Boston, that place we were playing when I first met you."

"He hasn't said much of anything to me lately."

"He wouldn't play the gig," Doc said. "He didn't exactly say he was quitting, but he came damn close. The rest of the guys pitched a fit. They're out looking for a new guitar picker right now."

"No kidding. You think they'll find someone?"

Doc sighed. "After what happened to the last one? Anyhow, it don't matter, TJ is the engine that makes the train go. Without him, we're wasting our time. But I talked to TJ afterward. Privately."

"Yeah?"

"Yeah. He told me he wasn't feeling it anymore. Said he didn't feel like a musician anymore, said he felt like a broke, wore-out, unemployed house painter."

She didn't know what to say.

"Help me out with this, Al. I mean, you've heard him, you know what he can do, I don't have to tell you. TJ's got hands from God. What the hell is going on?"

"God should've given him more than just hands, Doc. He should've given him a trust fund or a rich uncle."

"That can't be it," Doc said. "Do you know how much we could clear doing one weekend up at that club in Boston?"

"What do you do, Doc, when you're not playing in BandX? You don't drum for some band doing weddings and bar mitzvahs and shit."

"No," he said. "I work in IT for a consultant."

"I don't think TJ could ever take care of himself that way."

"Maybe not," Doc said. "He needs to play. But, Al, you know what? So do I. And before this, he would always play, even when he was all pissed off at the rest of us, he would always play."

Al put her fork down and closed her eyes. "There's this singer," she said.

She heard the wind go out of him.

"She's, I don't know... She can't be very long out of high school. She's got great pipes, and she, ah, you know... She don't even have to sing, Doc, guys would pay just to see her stand there at the mike."

"Christ." She looked at him, finally, he looked like he'd been slapped in the face. "What's her name?"

"I dunno. The name of the band is Indio. TJ plays piano."

Doc sat up straighter. "No fucking way."

Al nodded. "I saw them."

"These idiots have TJ Conrad and they got him on keyboards?"

"They've already got a guitar player."

"Don't matter," he said. "For real, if he's on piano, he's not... He's just fooling around."

"Is that okay? Is fooling around okay?"

Doc refocused on Al's face. "I'm sorry," he said. "Poor choice of words. Give me a couple of days and I'll find out what's going on for you."

"I hate this, Doc, I hate this backdoor shit. If TJ is moving on for a new band and a new squeeze, why can't he just say so?"

"Sometimes a guy don't know what he's gonna do until he's in the middle of doing it. Gimme two days," Doc told her. "Three, tops. I'll find out, I promise you."

"He's driving me crazy. I can't sleep, I can't work…"

Doc shook his head. "Sometimes it just goes that way, Al. Me and Sheila, we didn't get it right straight out of the box, it took some time. You know what I'm saying? Sometimes the only way through something is through it. Ease up a little bit. Relax. Lemme talk to TJ and I'll try and figure out where his head's at. I'll call you, okay?"

"Sure, Doc. Thanks."

AL SAT BEHIND her desk in the office on Houston Street with her mind in neutral, the street noises of Manhattan flowing past unremarked. Sarah Waters had stepped out when Al showed up, but a series of file folders were neatly arranged in rows on Al's desktop. One file was labeled LIAB. INS., and Al didn't want to look at it because she didn't know how they were going to pay the bill. Another was filled with copies of Sarah's reports on her work with Sheraton Hotels and Marty's other corporate clients. Al didn't want to look at that one because it would remind her how much time she herself was spending on financially unproductive pursuits like the search for Frank Waters and the surveillance of TJ Conrad. Yet another folder was labeled A. WEST, which reminded Al that she had promised to go upstate with Sarah to talk to Mrs. West's stepson, and she didn't have much appetite for that. And the one she really didn't want to look at was labeled OVERHEAD. She didn't want to think about that one at all.

Sarah came back in, Al heard her close the outer office door behind her, and a few seconds later she appeared in the doorway carrying a Dunkin' Donuts bag. She sat down in Al's client chair, took two cups out of the bag, handed one across to Al. "I actually got out of the place without buying anything fattening this time," she said.

"Gee, thank you, Sarah," Al said, reaching for the cup. "When you break a donut in half before you eat it, the calories fall out. Didn't you know that?"

"I'm on a diet," Sarah said, "and you're not helping." She fished a small white bottle out of her jacket pocket, rattled it, then put it down on Al's desk and pushed it forward. "Tylenol," she said.

"God," Al said. "Do I look that bad?"

"You look like you spent the night in the alley. Have you gotten any sleep at all this week?"

Al reached for the bottle, lined up the arrows, snapped the lid off. "Hasn't been a week," she finally said. "Only been a couple days."

Sarah considered that. "BF troubles?"

"You know what my problem is?" Al said, wondering how much of her rotten mood showed on her face and in her voice. "My problem is that I don't know how to take a hint. With you and Frank, how did you know it was over? I mean, when did you really know for sure?"

Sarah took the lid off her coffee, leaned back in her chair, and breathed in the smell steaming out of the cup. "Took a long time," she said. "Too long, I guess. I suppose I had to decide when I'd taken enough of a beating."

"You mean he hit you? You never said…"

"No, no, no, he didn't hit me. I just meant, you know, all the crap. The job, the drinking, those guys he ran with, not knowing where he went or what he was up to, you know, all that shit."

"Did he, um, did he fool around on you?"

"I don't know," Sarah said. "He never did it up in my

face. I mean, by the end I guess I wasn't looking too hard, so maybe he coulda kept it a secret, but you know I doubt it, Frankie wasn't that good at covering his tracks. I know he used to go to titty bars once in a while." She looked at Al. "If he was stepping out on me, I guess I didn't wanna hear it."

"So what was it? What made you decide…"

Sarah sipped at her coffee. "My mother," she said, "took my old man's crap for forty years. She hadda hate him, the shit he pulled. Every day she gets up, every single solitary day, she goes to work, she comes home, she cleans the house, pays the bills, does the laundry, she even cuts the fucking grass, the whole time she's wringing her hands, she's saying the rosary, she's praying to the blessed Saint Jude, worrying about whether or not this old cockroach is gonna make it home or not, is he gonna have any of his paycheck left or not. You know what I'm saying? Every day of her life she's going around with her guts in a knot, and for what? Hah? For what? What's she gonna get from this guy? A little piece, once in a while? Oh, Jesus, Al, I didn't mean to start yelling at you…"

Al stuck two Tylenols in her mouth and swigged coffee. "S'okay," she said.

Sarah was still hot. "Anyway, half the time he probably wasn't even up to that," she said. "So here I am, I'm home with my kid, and where the hell is Frank? Nobody knows. He's out with his asshole friends, he's doing what he wants to do. And then one day it hits me: what is my kid learning? Because you know what, Al, I love the kid to death, but he's just an ordinary kid, you know what I'm saying? He's no dummy, but he ain't no Bill Gates, either, he's just a regular kid, he gets okay marks, he mostly stays out of trouble, and he plays football, but I know what he wants, way down in his gut he wants his father to be impressed with him, even if he never sees the guy, and then one day I just said, you know, fuck this. I packed up and I moved the two of us back into my mother's house. I ain't doing it, Al, I ain't gonna spend my life sweating where Frank is and what he's doing, and I sure as shit ain't gonna have my kid growing up thinking that's the way a real man acts. You told me yourself, just the other day, I want a cheeseburger, I can get one just about anywhere."

Alessandra rubbed her forehead. "Yeah, I remember that."

"The next guy, Al, I swear to God if there's ever a next guy I am gonna tell him straight out: I ain't your fucking mother. If you can't do right by me, if you can't be a grown-up, do us both a favor and make some tracks. You know what I'm saying?"

"You gonna tell him that on the first date?"

"Yeah, right," Sarah said. "You think my chances aren't bad enough? I start out with that, I got no shot. So tell me what happened. You catch TJ with his hands where they didn't belong or what? The two of you seemed cool the other night at Costello's."

"I didn't exactly catch him," Al said.

Sarah waited. "So?" she finally said.

"Well, he's playing in this band."

"Yeah? That's what he does, right?"

"Yes… But there's this girl. In the band. She's the singer."

"Yeah? You see the two of them sucking face or some-thing?"

"No. No, it's just, I don't know, every time I see her, or him, I just…I got a bad feeling about them, that's all. He's been acting funny lately."

"Well, you know the guy better than I do," Sarah said. "But what kinda funny we talking here? What's funny?"

"I don't know, he's just so remote, and he acts so miser-able all the time."

"Maybe he's got hemorrhoids," Sarah said.

"Oh, will you be serious?"

"What, you never heard of 'em? They're in the dictionary, you could look 'em up. Means, if he's got 'em, he ain't the first guy. What I'm saying, if he's not happy, it could be anything at all. Plus, you know what, Al, the world is about half full of women. Give or take a couple. You know what I'm saying? That's just the way it is. You can't go nuts on the guy just because he knows a few."

Al was silent.

"Listen, I ain't saying you're wrong," Sarah said. "You know him better than me. But I know you, and you don't wanna cut him loose, you wanna cut off his Johnson. Am I right?"

"No."

"Hah! Who you kidding? You can't do it, Al, not yet. You need more than a bad feeling. Right now you got nothing."

Al didn't want to admit it to Sarah, but she was both right and wrong. She was right in saying that all Al had to go on was her gut feeling, but Al knew in her heart that she and TJ had gone off the track, and she didn't understand how or why. But she didn't want to hurt TJ, not really, she hadn't yet felt an urge to cut off any of his appendages. What she did want was to stop feeling like she had opened herself up, that she had given the guy a stick to hit her with, and that he had used it.

And she wanted to stop feeling lonely. "When my mother was alive," she said, "she never let me out of her sight. And after, you know, after she was gone I was too messed up. I was too scared. I've never had to do this before, Sarah."

"You're a big girl now," Sarah told her. "You'll figure it out."

"Maybe. Listen, all this stuff on the desk here, do I have to deal with any of this today?"

"Not if you don't want to," Sarah said. "But it ain't really that bad. First, the guy I deal with at Sheraton Hotels, he recommended us to someone he knows at Hyatt. The guy from Hyatt called here yesterday, he wants to talk. I put some sample pictures and reports together for him. He says he wants to give us a trial run. You might want to look my stuff over before I show it to him. And if we pick up Hyatt, we're gonna have to do something about liability insurance."

"Go ahead and send your stuff to Hyatt. Can we afford the insurance?"

"Sort of. We might have to skip some paychecks. Like one a month, at least until we find out how fast Hyatt pays their bills. I think it's worth a shot. Can you swing it?"

"For a month or two, I guess, yeah. How about you?"

"Same answer. Plus, if I buzz up to Woodstock to look for Jake West, I can wrap that up and bill his stepmother, which ought to get us a step closer to solvent. How about it? I'll borrow my mother's car, drive up this afternoon, have a talk with the guy, drive back. I should be okay, I think. How about it?"

"I don't know. It's just, you'd be all alone. What if something went wrong? I'd come with you today, but I'm meeting this cop down in Brooklyn. I want him to stick his nose in at Palermo Imports, and I don't know how long it'll take to talk him into it…"

"I'll be fine," Sarah said. "I'll knock on the door, tell the guy his stepmother is about to go under for the third time or whatever, she wants to leave him some money. What could go wrong? When you first started, wouldn't Marty send you on something like that?"

"I'm not Marty, Sarah. I want to be sure you're going to come back in one piece."

"Come on, Al, you gotta be kidding, Jake will be glad to see me. Wouldn't you be? Some long-lost relative is trying to leave you a big pile of money, why would you have a problem with that?"

"I suppose… Okay, we'll do it like this: call me when you're leaving, call me when you get there, call me when you're done talking to the guy, call me when you get back. I don't hear from you, I'm coming for you."

"Yes, Mom."

Al choked on her coffee laughing, because there was one thing she was pretty sure of: if there was a rational, mature, adult, maternal person in the room, it was Sarah. No matter how hard she tried to change, Al was still the adolescent, she was still the unattended package left at the airport, the one making the ticking noises.

THE CAR WAS a turquoise Pontiac Sunfire which had not been driven much of anywhere in a very long time. Its normal commute was from parking spot to parking spot within a three-block radius of Sarah's mother's house. Sarah got in and started the car, sat there wondering, while it warmed up, what aridity, what dearth of imagination, what poverty of spirit would motivate one to go out and pay actual money for such an appalling vehicle. Sarah had driven it before and she knew what it was like: it waddled along like a duck too short to walk properly and too fat to fly. It astonished her to realize that some designer had dreamed the thing up, that a team of engineers had made drawings and scale models, that some executive had pitched the thing to a design committee. "Fat, slow, and ugly, that's what the American consumer wants this year! Everyone on board here?" But it was free, except for the gas she would burn and the tolls she would pay, so she clunked it into gear and eased away from the curb.

Sarah chose to ignore the advice of MapQuest, Yahoo! maps, and all their on-line brethren and, instead of heading north through the city, she pointed the thing in the direction of the Verrazano-Narrows Bridge. Her way might be longer and slower, but she would rather cross Staten Island over into New Jersey than brave the peculiar sort of vehicular combat that too often categorized traveling by car into or through New York City. It wasn't that she didn't know how to drive, but she knew that she could not compete with the commuters, many of whom seemed alternately suicidal or homicidal.

The Jersey Turnpike would be bad enough.

Staten Island smelled like sour milk. It was home to a series of huge earth-covered mounds. They were the ghosts of garbage past, and could no doubt be seen and perhaps smelled from space. Still, people lived in the area and Sarah supposed that after a while they got used to the stink, but to her the whole island was redolent of something that should have been taken out to the curb a couple of weeks ago. She finally reached the narrow, antiquated bridge that spanned Arthur Kill over into Jersey. She didn't know how the waterway had gotten its name, perhaps some poor soul named Arthur had been foolish enough to drink the water and thus met his untimely end...

New Jersey's chemical reek was not much of an improvement. Sarah closed the car's vents and shut the fan off, hoping the rancid smell would die down. She watched the signs carefully, she needed to make sure she took the correct exit ramp, the one that would put her on the northbound side of the New Jersey Turnpike. The other cars bleated at her, impatient because she did not take the exit at twice the posted speed limit. The honking and impolite gesturing did not bother Sarah in the least. She did what she needed to do, calmly and rationally.

Like always.

As she headed north, the city lay off to her right. It was

beautiful in its own way, silent witness to the artist inside the soul of man, but over in Jersey it seemed as though someone had ripped the covers off the machinery that made it all work, exposing the guts, the necessary miles of plumbing and wiring that spanned the oily swamplands, the twisted intestines of oil refineries that were dotted with gnarled towers tipped with oddly hued flames, and huge metal fans blasting yellow-tinged air into the sky. City life was really all Sarah had ever known and she thought she was used to the costs, but it was distressing to see the fuming steel entrails that made it all possible. She looked at the bright towers of Manhattan, glittering on the far side of the Hudson River. You cannot live there, she thought, without being responsible for at least a part of this, and it was no good pretending that it didn't touch you. She drove for another hour before she got clear of it, up where the industrial forests finally gave way to thickets of houses and apartment buildings. So easy, she thought, so easy to hide inside your little place in Brooklyn and pretend that none of this existed.

She was almost to the northern end of the turnpike when she got off and headed for the Garden State Parkway. She paid her toll to get on and immediately the aura of the state changed abruptly. Jersey looked like Eden from the parkway, it was all trees and rolling swells of carefully tended grass, but the lights from the shopping malls winked at her through the green, reminding her not to be fooled by the façade. And the parkway was far more than just another highway, it did not simply lie there and ease you on your way, the parkway was a machine in its own right, with armies of caretakers, maintenance men, toll collectors, and cops. New Jersey politicians have refined the art of conniving to a level not even dreamed of by your average Brooklyn mobster, and now there was an

Authority dedicated to the parkway, lest it get up and decamp to friendlier locales. The Authority was dedicated as well to the employment and prosperity of everyone who'd been appointed to said Authority by some local or state politician. Indeed, almost every road worth its salt had a similar Authority and was similarly staffed. There must be something in the water in Jersey, because every little piss-ant town and borough had its own separate police force, Jersey had state cops, town cops, county cops, Port Authority cops, parkway cops, and sheriff's deputies. In Jersey, working for the government was a growth industry.

Another hour and she reached the New York Thruway, and somewhere in the foothills of the Ramapo Mountains her radio station turned to static, so she shut the radio off. The Thruway speed limit was sixty-five, but no one seemed to pay it much mind. Sarah found a semi that wasn't speeding too much and she slotted herself in behind it. She wasn't afraid to go faster, but apparently her mother's Pontiac was, it quivered in fear at anything much over seventy-five. The traffic roared past Sarah and her guardian like water flowing past two rocks in a stream. Nobody thinks too much about the law, she thought, not really. The real rules that we follow are the unwritten ones. You can exceed the speed limit, but not too much, call it ten miles per, just to be safe. You can beat your wife and kid, her father had done it for years, just don't do it in public. Try not to draw blood and you'll probably be all right.

And so on.

Her truck deserted her, got off, and left her on her own. She continued on at more or less the same rate and pretty soon a station wagon fell in behind her. You are the leader now, she thought, not the follower, and it made her a bit uncertain. She was uneasy for a mile or so, but then she lectured herself. Really, Sarah, grow up. You're on your own, it's up to you to decide how fast is fast enough, and all the rest of it. Your father is gone, your mother has no sense, and Frank is not around. No one can tell you what to do. You've got to figure it out for yourself.

She thought back to her Catholic childhood, Sunday School, and the story of Adam and Eve in paradise. *"You guys see this tree?"* God said. *"This is the tree of the knowledge of good and bad. Don't touch it. You hear me?"* The nun teaching the class had missed the entire point of the story, even as a child Sarah had been sure of it. *"Follow the rules! Listen to your elders!"* But Sarah had seen through it, she had been sure that the story was not about coloring outside the lines, because the surest way to get someone to try something is to tell them they can't have any. How dumb could God be, not to see that? He had to know, he had to have done it on purpose. Even as a child she'd had the impression that Adam and Eve hadn't become fully human until they'd broken the rule. Up until then they'd been children doing what they were told and staying out of trouble, but after that they had finally become fully human, with not only the right but also the obligation to decide what they would do, and become.

It's no good waiting for Frank or your father or some other asshole to come along and tell you what to do.

You're a big girl now, Sarah. It's on you.

She held it to just a hair over seventy, all the way to her exit.

TWELVE

"I HAVEN'T FORGOTTEN how much I owe you." The speaker was a black man, Salathiel Edwards, a detective in the NYPD.

"I don't look at it like that, Sal," Alessandra told him. They were in a coffee shop on Henry Street in Brooklyn.

He shrugged. "I don't know another way to see it," he said. "You walk into the station house, I don't know you from Adam, you hand me a murder, an attempted murder, a major drug operation, and an organized crime figure, all wrapped up with a bow. I mean, come on. Get real."

"I'm telling you, Sal, that's just the way it worked out. Those guys came after me, I wasn't on some kind of crusade."

"Don't matter," Salathiel said, shaking his head. "Amounts to the same thing either way. I got a commendation out of the deal, the assistant DA got a nice shiny 'Hero' badge to wear on his chest, and what did you get? You got a hearty 'Thank you' from the city. You got screwed."

"So okay, tell you what, get me one of those parking permits they're always screaming about on the news radio stations."

He looked at her. "I can't promise it, but I'll work on it. You have my word."

Al didn't know whether to believe him or not. "Cool," she said. "I was surprised when you guys got Caughlan, though. What did you put him away for?"

"Spitting on the sidewalk. They got him for tax fraud, he'll be out in eighteen months."

"You're kidding." In the course of her work on Daniel "Mickey" Caughlan's behalf, Al had uncovered a traitor in his inner circle. She could only surmise what had happened next, but odds were good that it wasn't pretty. "I figured, you know…"

"Some of his former, ah, associates have not been seen in some time. We were all pretty energized, for a while we had fantasies of taking him down. Silly us. We were on him and his, Al, we were on him tight, and we came up empty. He must have hired someone to come in and clean up for him."

"Really?"

"Come on. Please. There was even a certain faction within the department that liked you for it."

"You're kidding, right?"

"Listen, you had the motive, probably had the opportunity, sure as shit had the means. I hadda do some checking up on you, but we didn't have any bodies, so nobody got too serious about it."

Funny, she thought, they let Sal do the footwork on me, even though they knew she had handed him the case. "You find anything interesting on me?"

"Absolutely," he said. "Fascinating. Among other things, I found out you got booted out of the academy, and I found out why."

"Didn't like getting groped," she said. "I coulda told you that."

"Not sure I'd like it, either," Sal told her. "That instructor you tagged had it coming. He'd been smart enough to knock it off after you got the door, he might have got away with it."

"Yeah, well, all I did was bruise his ego. He got off easy."

"Bruised his ego, and knocked out a couple of his teeth, but I ain't talking about that. He just kept it up after you were gone, and he got himself suspended late last year. Now he's facing a departmental hearing and a class-action civil suit."

"Couldn't happen to a nicer guy," Al said.

"Agreed. But the relevant point here is, you want back into the academy, I can get you in."

"Are you serious?" Alessandra was stunned. She had thought that the book on that part of her life was closed forever.

"Dead serious," he said. "I can hook you up, big-time. You could probably even join the class-action suit if you wanted to." He stared across the table at her. "You should consider it," he said. "The pay isn't horrible…"

"No," she said.

"Retire after twenty."

Twenty years was far too long a span of time to have much meaning to her. "I dunno, Sal," she said. "Maybe six months ago I'd have done it. Now… Now I got this partner, you know, and I don't wanna run out and leave her hanging. Plus, I'm beginning to think this thing we're doing might work out. I think we got a chance to make it. So, no, but thanks for thinking about me. I'm good."

"Great opportunity," he told her. "I don't know how long this window stays open."

"I got you," she said. "I've really got to think about this."

"Well, don't think too long," he told her. "What was it that you wanted to see me about?"

"New business," she told him. "Calls itself Palermo Imports. Just opened a warehouse on Staten Island."

"Never heard of 'em," he said.

"The paint is still wet," she said. "Palermo Imports is owned by this guy calls himself Paolo Torrente. What they do, in theory, they bring in wines from all over Europe and they sell 'em in the U.S. Or they plan to. I think it's just a cover, I think they're bringing in something a lot more profitable than wine." She told him about the two big crates she'd helped them unload.

Salathiel Edwards took out a pad and started writing in it. "Palermo Imports," he said as he wrote. "Paolo Torrente. Okay, we'll get someone over there to take a look. I'll even let you know what we find."

"I got pictures of the crates," she said. "I can e-mail 'em to you if you want."

"No need," he told her. "We can send a Fire Department guy to go look at their sprinklers or some shit, and we'll have a Narcotics guy tag along. Those guys, you don't have to get fancy with them, all you do is point and shoot. If there's something there, they'll find it."

"Okay," she said.

"But there's something you ain't telling me about this," he said. "You got a client mixed up in it?"

Sarah Waters, she thought, or Frank, or even Frank Junior. "Someone in trouble," she told him.

"Yeah," he said. "What is it about you and trouble? Listen, for real, this place comes up dirty, you are gonna have to sit down and be straight with me on this."

"Yeah," she said. "All right."

"One last thing," he said, and he hesitated.

"What," she said.

"This thing with you and Mickey Caughlan…"

Alessandra held up a hand, closed her eyes.

"I know, I get it, he's a client. It's business. But if you seen things about Caughlan that he didn't want you to see, he might be thinking you're just one more loose end he needs to get cleaned up. You get what I'm trying to tell you? So watch your back."

"Sal, you're making me paranoid."

He shook his head. "If they're really out there, it ain't paranoia, it's self-preservation."

THINGS GOT A little more complex once Sarah got off the Thruway. The exit ramp dumped her onto a traffic circle, her directions said nothing about a circle, she went around it twice before winding up on a road that took her across a bridge and into Poughkeepsie. She pulled over, read through her printouts again, then turned around and went back to the circle. You would think, she told herself, that a place as famous as Woodstock, New York, there would be a big sign pointing you in the right direction, but there wasn't. She found the route number she was looking for, though, and forged on.

Five minutes later she was shaking her head. You've been in Brooklyn too long, she told herself. You need to get out of town a little more often. God, who knew that you could be in the middle of a wilderness, practically, in so short a time? Okay, it wasn't exactly a wilderness, but there weren't many houses, there were trees growing all over, not many other cars, and hardly any traffic lights at all. She found herself looking at the houses, wondering what kind of people lived in them, what their lives were like, how she really really needed to get Frank Junior out to some kind of a camp this summer, and God, how much was that gonna cost?

Woodstock, when she finally found it, was nothing like what she'd thought it would be. She'd been expecting a sort of neo-hippie, new-age Disneyland, maybe even with a big toothless statue of Wavy Gravy, but it was just a dozen or so blocks of touristy stuff, T-shirt stores, arts and crafts, T-shirt stores, places to buy fringed leather jackets, T-shirt stores, health food emporiums, T-shirt stores, and so on. She found the side street Jacob West lived on, passed it by, found a parking spot two blocks farther on. She got out, locked the car, wrapped her coat tightly around her against the cold wind, and headed back.

She found it. It was a small, dove-gray Victorian house set about fifteen feet back from the road behind a matching gray picket fence. The first floor was occupied by something called The Austin Gallery. The second floor was apparently an apartment. Sarah went up the walk and climbed the steps to the porch. The front windows on the first floor went almost all the way from the floor to the ceiling, and she was drawn by the bronze figures she saw through the window next to the entrance, so she opened the door and entered the gallery.

There didn't seem to be anyone home.

Standing inside the front door, she looked into the room to her right at a statue of a nude woman right in the center of the room. It was done in about three-quarter scale. The woman was down on one knee, bent over with the knuckles of one hand on the ground. Her head was turned, almost as if she were watching Sarah come through the entrance. Even though she was not full-sized, her presence filled up the room. She was well muscled for a woman, which made Sarah think briefly of Alessandra, wondering, you know, but it was really the look on the woman's face that gave the figure its power. There was something in the expression, Sarah could not quite put her finger on it, but the longer she looked the surer she became that there was something unhealthy about this woman, that in life a wise man would not be drawn by her nudity.

A wise man would back away, slowly.

She turned, was startled by another sculpture hanging on the wall next to the door. It was also bronze, perhaps two feet square, it was a man's face, he was emerging from the base metal like a man coming up from a deep pool. The face was tired and drawn, it was the face of a man beyond pain, who not only knew that he was lost and beaten but had accepted it, given himself over to it. There was a line down low on his neck, a scar…

It was the face of defeat.

It pulled at her, she stopped a foot away and stared.

What she saw there was not the look of death but of a life sentence, she knew that this was the face she would wear every day for as long as she lived if something should ever God forbid happen to Frank Junior. The feeling surged over her, she stood rooted to the spot, fumbled blindly in her pocketbook for a tissue to wipe her damp face. She heard footsteps behind her, but she did not turn around.

"He does that to some people," a voice said.

Sarah turned her head and looked. He was a slim man, a bit taller than average, dark hair and eyes, a trim goatee shot through with a trace of gray, a hooked nose.

"Jacob?"

He went pale. "Who are you?" he said, backing away, his voice wild. "Who…" He started to run, tripped over the bronze nude woman, went down awkwardly, his head made a hollow thunk when it hit the wooden floor.

He lay motionless.

Sarah wiped her nose on her tissue. "Oh for crissake," she said.

THE EXHIBITION SPACE took up most of the first floor, but there was one back room that held a desk in one corner and a couch in another. Sarah thought about dragging Jacob West in there and wrestling him up onto the couch, but that seemed, upon reflection, like it might be beyond her, so she took a pillow from the couch, brought it out, and put it under his head. Then she wet the towel that she found hanging next to the sink in the tiny bathroom in the back hallway behind the office, sat down next to West, and began to wipe his face.

He came out of it a minute later, came out of it like a man in agony. Groggy, he rolled over on his side and retched, curling up like he had a sharp pain in his stomach, but when he was fully awake he rolled back, his eyes wide. "She sent you, did she send you… Are you…"

Sarah held on to him, gave him the towel. "Not exactly," she said. "Here."

He took the towel and mopped his face. "What do you mean, not exactly? Is she here? Does she know—"

"She hired me to find you," Sarah told him. "I haven't told her anything yet."

He flopped back down on the pillow and closed his eyes. "God," he said. "God, my head hurts."

"Who is he?" Sarah said. "That man, the one by the door."

Jake opened his eyes and looked up at her. "My father," he said.

RIGHT AROUND THE corner from Al's old apartment on Pineapple Street there was a pizza joint named Fascati's, and she missed it. It was about a half hour's walk from there to the place she lived now, and there were a couple of pizza joints that were closer, but she had tried one and been unimpressed, looked in on another one and decided that it maybe wasn't the cleanest place in the world. So it's not that far away, she told herself. Why settle? Why not get what you want? In the matter of pizza, at least, what she wanted was easily defined and perfectly attainable. She wanted a couple of slices of heaven served up by a surly counterman, so she decided to take herself there.

As she walked up Henry Street from Atlantic Avenue toward the Brooklyn Bridge, the closer she got to Pineapple the stronger her feelings got, alienation and regret kept in check by a sense of the familiar. I used to belong here, she thought, and not that long ago. This was my neighborhood… She had loved everything about it, right up until the night she was assaulted, right over there in an alley you couldn't even see from Henry Street, right by where that gypsy cab was parked half up on the sidewalk. Even though the thugs who'd attacked her had moved on, some to jail, some to parts unknown, and one or two to whatever hell one inhabits between incarnations, she had never felt the same afterward, never quite attained the same level of comfort. It was very close to the same feeling she'd had on that cold day when she had found her mother on the kitchen floor: This was my place, this was where I belonged. This used to be home, and now it isn't… Still, she told herself, if I ever make a million bucks I'm going to come back here, I'm going to get a place in one of these buildings and I'm gonna stay there until I get the feeling back…

A guy came out of the front door of her old building on Pineapple, crossed the street, sat on the hood of the gypsy cab, the one that was halfway on the sidewalk. He yanked a BlackBerry off his belt, punched a few buttons, held it up to his ear. Tall guy, white hair, big nose, half a belly, red face.

He didn't look like a Brooklyn guy.

Dublin, maybe.

You could, of course, move to Brooklyn from Dublin, but it would not take too long before you lost that wide-eyed, apple-cheeked, hiya buddy openness. Your elbows got a little sharper, your eyes got a little darker, you walked with a little more tension in your shoulders. Brooklyn does that to you, it enforces its own standards, and either you adapt or you go home.

And the guy stood right across the street from that alley… She remembered Sal's warning.

No way, she told herself, no way a guy that looks like an Irish folksinger is gonna be a hitman...

Pass it by, Al told herself, keep walking, forget Fascati's for now, go get your dinner someplace else and be disappointed, Fascati's has been there for a long time, odds are decent it'll still be there when this is all over.

Whatever the hell it is that's going on here...

She stayed on the far side of Henry and walked on. A block and a half away she stopped and looked back, imagining she could smell the dough and the garlic and all the rest of it. She could see the rear window of the tiny fifth-floor apartment she had lived in. The light was on. Her rent was paid through the end of the month, but the landlady was a sharp-eyed, flinty old crow, she would probably know that Al was gone, and she would, no doubt, already have begun the business of finding a new tenant. Could be her, in there...

Still, that guy parked out front was no cabdriver.

Al kept walking.

Her stomach growled.

"WHAT DO I call you?" Sarah said. "What do you like better, Jake or Jacob or Austin or John or Mr. Smits or what?" She was trying to be funny, trying to lighten the mood, but it didn't seem to work. The two of them had left the gallery, they were walking up the side street, away from the noise and lights of Woodstock's main drag. He walked next to her, a brooding figure, taller than her, and thinner, shoulders hunched, hands shoved into the pockets of his oversized black wool jacket, collar turned up. It seemed to Sarah that Jake had to make a conscious effort to remember she was there, and to modulate his gait to match her much shorter strides.

"I don't know," he said, and he seemed to withdraw

deeper into the folds of his jacket. He swallowed. "I don't know." He glanced down at her. "Maybe I haven't found the right name yet. Hard to know what's real anymore, and what isn't."

Sarah reached out and touched his elbow. He started away from her as though he'd been jolted by house current. He stopped, and so did she. "I'm real," she told him.

"Sorry," he said. "Sorry. Yeah. You look real enough." He squeezed his elbows tight against his body, as though if he compressed himself hard enough he'd be able to disappear.

She held out her hand. "Walk with me, Jake." She smiled her most innocent smile at him. "How about if I call you Jake?"

He nodded. "Okay."

Sarah sensed that he didn't know whether or not to take her hand, or maybe how, even. He was too tall, she couldn't put her hand around his shoulders so she settled for patting him on the small of the back, turning him to walk next to her again.

"Izzy used to call me Jake," he said. "My brother. I remember my real mother calling me Jay-Jay, but I hated that."

"What do the people in Woodstock call you?"

"Mr. Smits." He glanced at her again, then looked away. "I guess, you know, I guess I keep them too far away from me to call me anything else." He stopped again and she turned to face him. "What are you going to tell Clytemnestra?"

Sarah stared at him, eyebrows raised.

His lips twitched, the beginnings of a smile, maybe the first sign that he might have a sense of humor. "Clytemnestra," he said. "My stepmother."

"I don't know yet," she said. "Tell me about her."

He scowled, knit his black furry eyebrows together. Sarah had a moment of fear, being, after all, a long way from home, in the middle of nowhere, and in the company of a strange guy. She trusted her intuition, though, and the moment passed. She was pretty sure she was okay with Jake.

"You're gonna think I'm crazy," he told her.

"Try me," she said.

He started walking again, the gravel along the verge of the road crunching beneath his boots. He shook his head. "Evil," he said. "That's the first word that comes to mind. I don't know how else to say it. She's evil. She feeds on other people's miseries. She feeds on despair. And if that isn't enough, I'm pretty sure she killed my father."

"I thought he died in a car accident," she said. "No one ever really nailed down what happened. And then his partner, Tipton, he's missing and presumed dead. Some of the cops thought you had something to do with all of it," Sarah told him. "You and your brother."

"Hah." It was a percussive sound, a small detonation of something, anger, maybe, or bitterness. "I know. Unbelievable." He looked away from her, off into the darkening afternoon. "We were kids, for God's sake. She controlled us completely. Anyone could have seen it. Anyone who was thinking straight."

"How could she control you? You guys weren't exactly babies."

"Twelve or whatever," he told her. "But you have to understand. Right after they got married, her and my father, she pulled us out of school so she could homeschool us herself. Agatha West, the great clinical psychologist, needed to have absolute control over all the men in her life. So she took us out of school and she isolated us, even from each other sometimes. It was like..." He scratched his head. "It was like being raised inside a locked room. You got out once in a while, if you were good. She had the last word over everything, what we read, what we ate, what we watched on television, everything."

Sarah thought of Frank Junior and the video games that he loved. Their cartoonish violence and gore repelled her, but she had not been able to bring herself to take them away from him. "Why?"

"Her great theory." He looked down at her and attempted a smile, but it didn't come off. "To her, you and I, right now, walking up this road, we are not people. Not as I understand the word. We are not individual humans. We are simply biological phenomena, more intelligent than orangs, of course, but still, simply the products of our respective brain structures and our conditioning. We may consider ourselves free moral agents, you and I, but really, that, uh, that exalted status is reserved for a very select few who've demonstrated the mental acuity and the intellectual courage to break through to a higher plane. But for that statistically insignificant minority, the human race is comprised of breeders. Evolution and our environment have equipped us to eat, to procreate, to labor in service of society, and to die. Mastery or servitude, that is the only important choice any of us will ever make. You have no free will, you have no soul. There is no spiritual dimension to man, not outside of his imagination. We are..." His voice trailed away.

"Ants?" Sarah said, after a moment.

"Perfect!" Jake said. "Exactly!" He wanted to laugh, she could sense it, but his face was a mask of revulsion. "You must have read my mother's work."

"No," she told him. "I guess evolution and my environment didn't program me to give a fuck about any of that."

He did laugh then.

She looked around, took stock of where they were. From the Woodstock side, it looked like the crest of a small hill. The town lay behind them, a cluster of buildings clinging to the fringes of the main road, petering out into forest in all directions. In the other direction, the road they were on ran down a long steep slope and disappeared into the woods.

"So, Sarah Waters," he said. "What do I do now? I really like this place. I sort of like J. Austin Smits, too, he's not a bad sculptor, he's starting to do some okay work. I would hate to lose everything again."

"She's dying," Sarah told him. "She has ovarian cancer. She's not going to get better. She sort of gave me the impression that it was your father's memory she longed for, and she wanted to leave her estate to someone connected to him. You're the only family he has left."

"Of course," he said. "And Santa Claus is real. His workshop, contrary to popular belief, is not at the North Pole, it's actually right around the corner from here." He looked down at her. "How can I persuade you to go back and forget all about me?"

She shook her head. "Doesn't work that way, Jake. If I found you, the next guy could do it, too. And there's some money involved here, too. Might be a lot of money."

"You can't spend the money if you're dead. I have to run."

"No you don't," she said. "Let's go back down, I'll buy you a cup of coffee and we'll talk about it."

"You all right?" Alessandra sounded tense.

"Yeah, I'm fine," Sarah told her. "I found Jake West. He's pretty spooked. He thinks—"

Al interrupted her. "Anybody following you?"

"No. Why? What's going on?"

"I don't know. Maybe nothing. I went up past the building where I used to live, there was this guy hanging around. He didn't look right. Are you sure that no one followed you? Do you think you'd notice?"

"Well, nobody followed me up the Thruway because I

stayed behind this truck most of the way and everybody passed us like we were walking. What did this guy look like?"

"Where are you now? Are you safe? You're not out on the street, are you? Take a look around. Look for someone hanging out, pretending to look in store windows or whatever. Jesus, I never should have let you go up there alone. And check the parked cars, look for a guy sitting behind the wheel of a parked car..."

"Al, honey, relax. I'm inside Jake's studio. We went out for a walk earlier and nobody followed us, I'm sure of it, there's no place to hide out here. This guy by your old building, what did he look like?"

"Oh, man." Sarah listened to Al exhaling in relief. "God. I didn't wanna call in case the phone ringing would have drawn attention to you or something. I was picturing you, you know, knocked in the head or whatever, I was trying to figure out what to tell your kid, you know, 'Frankie, I'm sorry about your mom, I shouldn't have let her go, but I did it anyway,' Jesus. Are you positive there's nobody showing any unhealthy interest in you? Or your mother's car?"

"Al, I promise, nobody followed me. You're getting all neurotic and shit. Will you tell me what this guy looked like?"

"Yeah. Yeah, sure. Phew. Just let me catch my breath. I was thinking I got to dig through your desk to see if you left West's address here someplace, and I don't even know what your mother's car looks like..."

"The guy," Sarah reminded her.

"Okay. Okay. He was, ah, a white guy, tall, red-faced, white hair. A little on the porky side. Probably in his sixties."

"Oh, wait. An old, fat white guy? Was he wearing a red suit?"

"Oh, shut up."

"With black boots? Carrying a big sack?"

"I swear to God, Sarah, I am going to smack you so hard…"

They both dissolved in laughter. Sarah sensed Al's tensions draining away. "You were really sweating this, weren't you? I'm touched."

"Yeah, well, it ain't because I like you or nothing, but for real, Sarah, in this business things can go south in a big hurry. One minute everything's cool, you think you got all your shit covered, the next minute it's going bad, everything spins out of control. And I know that guy was looking for me, no matter what he looked like. I know it. So just you listen to me and be careful. Okay?"

"Scout's honor. The old white guy, you make him for a cop?"

"No. Not really. And process servers are usually young guys working in pairs, you know, one to serve you and one for the witness. No, it was weird, Sarah, I couldn't figure it. Anyhow, what were you going to tell me about Jake?"

"You know what? It's a long story. How about I tell you tomorrow? You coming into the office?"

"Yeah, late morning. I'll see you then."

"Okay, but let me ask you something. Why do you get so wigged out when I get off on my own? I'm a big girl."

There was no reply for a few seconds. "We'll sit down and talk about it someday. You leaving now to come home?"

Sarah turned, looked over her shoulder at Jake West, who was in the little office in the back corner of the gallery. "Not just yet," she said, dropping her voice. "I think I'm gonna hang out here a little while."

THIRTEEN

PARATRONIX WAS LOCATED on the second floor of a grubby three-story building on Manhattan's Avenue B, just south of Fourteenth Street, over a liquor store. Once upon a time the crumbling edifice would have been called a tenement, a firetrap, and a blight on the neighborhood, now it was a charming pre-war walk-up in need of some TLC. Al climbed one flight of stairs, walked through the front door of Paratronix, and was greeted by the sight of a man's shoulders and head on a large-screen monitor, he was a fat middle-aged white guy with a red face and he was shouting. A guy with short, pointy, sandy blond hair and a couple days' worth of beard on his face sat at a computer station and peered at a second monitor, his hands poised over a keyboard. He had a Bluetooth headset on. He glanced once at Alessandra, held up a finger, then went back to what he was doing. After a second he touched a button on a teleconference console and while the fat white guy looked like he was still shouting, Al couldn't hear him anymore. The guy glanced at Al again. "If a tree falls in the forest," he said, his voice rueful, and then he was gone again, lost in what he was doing. "George," he said to the headset. "Why do you guys keep doing this? No. No. Look at your screen. Look at your... Wait, I'll highlight it. What does that tell you? Well, it tells me that you've got compatibility issues again. George, come on, you can't just throw another driver in there, it'll corrupt... This is not like adding a printer onto your home network, George..."

Al walked over to the window and looked down at Avenue B. Beneath her, a tall, fierce-looking dark-skinned man with scars on his face and wearing African garb walked up toward Fourteenth. In one arm he carried a bundle roughly the size and shape of a human infant, and in the other a bright yellow SpongeBob SquarePants diaper bag. You see? Al told herself. Goes to show you, there's a wrench for every nut... On the other side of the avenue, two guys emerged from a Greek bakery. They were drinking coffee out of blue-and-white paper cups, those same ones that every Greek diner and coffee joint seems to use. Al turned, caught the attention of the guy with the headset, pantomimed tipping a cup, pointed at him with eyebrows raised. He nodded energetically, mouthed the word "black" at her.

He was still at it when she got back. She went over, left the coffee next to him, returned to the window to watch the world go past, but after a while she turned to watch the proprietor of Paratronix. He looked vaguely European, was not in bad shape, had intense eyes, thin face, looked like some sort of mad, hyperkinetic Polish soccer player. He might have been a few years older than her. His hands flew over his keyboard in a manic dance made all the more remarkable because he was not a touch typist. You could never call his style hunt-and-peck, though, it seemed to be a system of his own design, involving two or three fingers on each hand. This is him, Al thought, this is his favored form of communication. His default mode, because he seemed much less proficient in spoken English. He left most of his sentences unfinished and included a lot of grunts.

"Okay, okay, you're good," he spoke into the headset. "It's rebooting... You see it? Okay, good." He reached over and suddenly the fat white guy regained his voice. "Corgi," the white guy said, exasperated, "what the hell happened? What did—"

"You're good now, Mr. Ellis," he said.

"Yeah, but what the fuck—"

"You really want to know? One of your vendors down-loaded a driver and it corrupted—"

"No, you're right," the white guy said. "I'm good. Thanks."

A minute or two later he was unlinked. "Hey," he said, looking at Al. "Thanks for coffee. I really need it, after that. I love it when they screw up their shit and then yell at me about it. What can I do for you?"

Al walked over to him. "Robbie Corgin? I'm Alessandra Martillo. I got a problem and I'm told you're the man."

"Depends," he said. "I mean, some problems I might be your guy, some others, maybe not. How can I help?"

Al took out her phone and pulled up the images she'd taken at Palermo Imports. She handed it to Corgin, and he was immediately more comfortable.

"Okay," he said. "Well, that's interesting. Like a bar code or something." He looked up at her. "Can I upload, uh, well, yeah, stupid, that's why she brought it… Never mind me." A few minutes later Al had her phone back and the bar code image was displayed on the large screen recently vacated by the fat white guy. "Check that out," Robbie said. "Cool. Never seen anything like that. Wonder what the hell it is."

"Do you think you can break it?" Al asked him. "What?" It was almost as though he was surprised to see her there, like she had suddenly materialized out of the air.

"Break it? No. I don't know. Maybe. Take too long, anyway."

She tried to keep the disappointment out of her voice. "Oh. Really? Then how do I—"

"Post it," he said. "Post it. A sign is not a sign if nobody can read it. No useful function. And look, obviously it's there for a reason. Someone has to know what it is. Is it okay? If I post it, I mean."

"Why not?" she said. "But just because someone can read it, why should they tell you?"

He stared at her, aghast. "You're kidding. Right? Are you messing with me?"

"No," she said, a bit confused.

"Oh, boy." He reached out for her hand, stopped just short of actually touching her. "Um, sorry, you said your name, before—"

"Alessandra Martillo."

"Okay, Al—ah—Aless…"

"Al is fine," she told him.

"Good," he said emphatically, obviously glad to be relieved of so many superfluous syllables. "Al. Come on." He waved vaguely at the workstation behind him. "The Web. What's it do?"

"I'm not sure I understand—"

"You know, what has it done? What's the biggest, you know—"

"Oh, I get it. What's the biggest change the internet has had on us, that's easy. Porn, for free, accessible anywhere."

He blushed to the roots of his hair. "Okay okay okay. Right. Yeah, so what's the second, you know—"

"Tell me," she said.

"Information," he said. "Free."

"What information?"

He waved his arms. "Any of it. All of it. Wanna know where the missile bases are in Kamchatka? Who writes code for the NSA? The questions on next year's bar exam? How to say 'go fuck yourself' in Urdu? What would happen if Michael Jordan tried to post up Bill Russell? How many Ping-Pong balls—"

"Okay," Al said. "I get it."

He shook his head. "You don't get it yet. Nobody does. Listen to this. Here's a piece of skull candy for you. There are…" He paused for effect. "No…secrets…anywhere." He looked at her. "Anywhere. None."

She stared at him, her mouth half open.

"Yeah. Yeah. Now you're starting to… We ain't just talking account numbers and credit scores, either. Just, you know, play with that. Bounce that around for a while. Privacy is dead. In fifty years nobody will even remember what it was. Nothing is safe, nothing is the same." He laughed. "Everyone walks around, like, hey okay, whatever, because they don't get it. We're naked. Totally. All of us."

"You're not serious."

"Naked. You want me to prove it? You want… Watch."

"No!" she said, unable to keep the urgency out of her voice. And then quieter, and a bit afraid. "No. I believe you."

"Oh," he said, alarmed, "I didn't mean… I mean I wouldn't…" He rapped the side of his head with his knuckles and addressed his monitor as though it were a third person. "You see? This is why we never get the girl."

"That's not why," she said, half to herself.

"What?" He seemed stunned. "What? Why, then?"

"Well, hey, if you knew a witch," she asked him, "and she asked you out, would you go?" She watched the light of caution dawn in his eyes. "If you knew she could turn you into a newt."

"Or an Apple," he said. "No wonder most of them were virgins." His half smile was quickly replaced by a look of chagrin. "Well, that sucks," he said, louder.

"Robbie, you give up so easy," she said, stunning him again. "Are you going to post my pictures?"

"I did already," he said, still sounding awed.

"Don't lose my phone number," she told him.

"Never," he said. "Will you come back to check or should I—"

"Watch for me," she told him. "What would happen if Michael Jordan tried to post up Bill Russell?"

"Russell," he told her, "would make himself a nice Michael sammich."

"Ah," she said. "Okay."

ALESSANDRA PAUSED JUST inside the office door. "Sarah, when you came in, were those two tall skinny white guys standing around outside the Starbucks across the street?"

"What?" Sarah had, apparently, been miles away. "Sorry. I wasn't listening."

"Two guys," Al said. "White, both of them six foot six or so, dressed out of the 'business casual polyester' page of some catalog. They were standing around the Starbucks across the street when I got here. Paying a lot of attention to everybody coming in or out of this building."

It seemed an effort for Sarah to drag herself back to the present. She glanced at the office window, but there was no view, it faced a row of empty gray windows across an airshaft. "I, um, I didn't notice."

"Let's get out of here," she said. "I don't like how this feels."

"Well, okay," Sarah said, rousing herself. "But I should probably catch up on billing for a while this morning—"

"No way," Al told her. "Come on, grab your jacket, you and me are gonna find a back way out of this building. I need to watch these characters from a safe distance. We can deal with all that other shit later."

"You really think—"

"Yeah, I do," Al told her. "Come on, we got to go, right now."

"I DON'T KNOW." Sarah held a pair of Marty Stiles's heavy binoculars up to her face, squinting through the dirty glass window of a men's clothing store down the block. "I mean, if this was Brooklyn, okay, I could guarantee you for sure those two ain't neighborhood guys. But, you know, Manhattan, who could tell?"

"Yeah," Al said. "I hear you."

"I was wondering," Sarah said. "How bad do we really need a Manhattan address?"

"Marty always thought it was a big deal."

"Marty doesn't think we got any good pushcart food over in Brooklyn," Sarah said. "He's just afraid he won't be able to get any nice BBQ horse meat on a stick if he moves across the river."

Al wondered which of them was right. Another business issue, she thought, another question for which I have no answer, and not a lot of interest, either. Fine businessperson I'm gonna make...

A guy who looked like a salesman in the men's store wandered up to the two of them, eyeing Sarah's binos. "Bird-watching today, ladies?"

Sarah didn't look at him. "Do I come to your office while you're working and bother you?" she said.

The salesman shrugged. "Whatever," he said. "Long as you're not scaring away the customers."

Sarah still didn't look at him. "What customers?"

The guy looked at Al.

"We'll only be a few minutes," she told him. "And we won't bother anyone."

He craned his neck to look out the window to see what they were watching, shrugged again, then turned and walked away.

"You want my opinion," Sarah said, "these two look like they're from one of those rectangle states out in the middle."

"Hard to figure," Al said. "They don't look like cops, but they don't look like bad guys, either."

"Either way," Sarah said, "I think they know we're in here."

"What? How do you know?"

"The one with the blue jacket keeps glancing over here at the front door," Sarah said. "Like, once every ten or fifteen seconds. Like he's watching to see if we come out."

"Damn," Al said. "What's the other one doing?"

"Talking on his phone." She looked back at Al. "That mean they know we're in here?"

"Keep watching," Al told her. "Yeah, it probably does. Also means there's more than just those two. They must have had someone inside the building to follow us out."

"Who do you think they are?" There was a trace of fear in Sarah's voice.

"That's the first question," Al said. "Second question, what the hell do they want? They could be working for Uncle Paolo, although I doubt it."

"Why?"

"Not his type. I'm thinking he'd use someone from the old country. These guys are too All-American. My best guess, they got hired on by one of Paolo's customers. Whatever Uncle Paolo is really importing, he's not into the retail end of things, he can't be. So he's basically a supplier. The real heavies would be whoever is buying his product, cutting it up, and selling it to the street-level guys. Those guys might not want to hit us, be too easy to follow us back to Uncle Paolo through you being Frank's ex. They might hire it out."

"One other possibility," Sarah said.

"I'm listening…"

"Jake. Jacob West."

"I thought you checked him out last night."

"Very funny," Sarah said. "The other guy just hung up his phone, that can't be good. Listen, I just thought, you know, when Aggie West came along, here was my chance to show I could do something. Maybe I got in over my head. Maybe…"

"Maybe," Al told her. "We are gonna have to figure it out later. Right now we gotta get out of here."

"How about a cab?" Sarah said.

"That could work, but those two bozos see us trying to hail a cab, they might decide to take measures. Know what I'm saying?"

"Here," Sarah said, handing Al the glasses. "Take these." She fished out her cell phone.

"Who you calling?"

"Dial Seven," Sarah said. "That limo company that runs ads on the radio all the time." She punched buttons on her phone, and when the call went through, she changed completely. "Aah, hello? Um, can you, um, can you help me?" Her voice quivered with uncertainty and fear. And it wasn't just fear in her voice, it was the barely contained squeak of someone on the verge of panic. "Um, thank you, um, I'm in this store near West Houston, okay, and I think my husband is out there waiting for me. My ex-husband, I mean. No, no, if the police come, he'll, oh God, I just wanna get back to my dad's house, and if you have like a driver who could get me back to Queens in sort of a hurry, my ex couldn't get me there, my dad would…"

Alessandra watched in amazement. Sarah wasn't imitating a character, she had embodied one. She'd gone pale, her hands shook, she looked like a frightened bird. Al wondered, again, how bad things had gotten between her and Frank. Maybe this was a character Sarah knew all too well…

"Could you? Oh, that would be so sweet, if I have someone to talk to until he gets here. Thank you so much…" She glanced at Al and the frightened bird disappeared. She held out a hand, fingers spread, mouthed the words "five minutes" to Al. Then she turned back to the dispatcher and was at once terrified again as she gave the name and location of the store.

Pitch-perfect, Al thought. A woman, all alone, afraid of her ex-husband, thinks he's gonna kill her, or at least beat the fuck out of her, but no, she doesn't want to call the cops, doesn't want to get the pathetic loser in trouble… Fucking women. And then she shook her head, realizing that Sarah's act was so good that she, Al, was getting pissed off at a nonexistent fictional husband. She looked back through the glasses at the two men down the block, watched the guys who were watching her. A few minutes later she heard the snap of Sarah's phone as she ended the call, felt Sarah's fingers soft on her arm. "Come on," Sarah said, once again herself. "He's here."

They headed for the door. "Where'd you learn how to do that?" Al said.

"Do what?"

AL TOOK ALL the money out of the front pocket of her jeans and handed it across to the driver. "Go," she said. "Please, just go."

"Where the boah at?" The driver, a heavy black guy, had a broad Southern twang in his voice. He tromped his gas pedal and the car screeched away.

Perhaps sensing the driver's suspicion, Sarah reached across the front seat with an unsteady hand and gripped the man's shoulder. Who woulda known? Al thought. Seemingly ordinary person, turns out to have an extraordinary ability. What else could she be capable of? "Thank you," Sarah said, a tear rolling down her cheek. "Thank you so much... I don't see him now, he was standing right there on the corner. Do you think he could follow us?"

"Don' worry, sugah, we gon' leave him scratchin' his butt and wonderin' where the hell evahbody went."

Al sat back in the seat as the driver bulled his way through Midtown traffic, heading for the Triboro Bridge. He was right, no one would catch them: there couldn't be two men in Manhattan this crazy...

SHE HELD SARAH close in the back of the car and whispered in her ear as the aged Town Car roared over the ruts and potholes of Flushing Avenue, down on the border between Brooklyn and Queens. Sarah's face was a study in concentration as she listened to Al's instructions. It's not supposed to be this way, Al told herself, you're supposed to be calm, detached, ready to do what you need to do but wishing no harm or evil on your opponents, you are not supposed to feel this insane rush of fear and elation... She was a skier teetering on the precipice, gone just past the point of balance, committed to jumping in, and you better nail that first turn, honey, because if you blow it you got a long way to fall before you land on those rocks down there...

There was a Korean version of a Home Depot right on Flushing, just inside the edge of Bushwick. The neighborhood was a warren of ancient low-rise industrial buildings. The Brooklyn renaissance had stalled a good half-mile away and it was hard to see how it would make it this far, or why. There wasn't much here to work with, the buildings would never be turned into lofts, they were too small, too old, and too far gone, had been so for perhaps the past century. Nice to know, Al thought, that there are things you can still depend on, Bushwick was always gonna be Bushwick... She pointed, the cab lurched to the curb, she and

Sarah jumped out of the backseat and ran into the truck-sized warehouse entrance.

There was a chopper in the sky somewhere over Brooklyn, but Al paid it no mind, it was far away, only a sound, like the distant echo of a train somewhere. She hurried Sarah past pale rectangular stacks of fragrant pine boards. "You know where you're going?" Sarah asked her, breathless.

"More or less," Al told her. "I grew up around here. Kinda. This way." They ran down a long aisle, drawing odd looks from the Oriental guys who staffed the place and from the various members of the genus *Contractorus newyorkus,* who came in all sizes and colors. At the far end of the place she slowed them to a walk. Al held up empty hands to the security guard and the lady working the counter, universal sign language for "hey, we didn't take anything." The guard and the counter lady looked at each other, then blankly at Al and Sarah, but neither made a move to stop them.

The alleyway out back was paved with cobblestones rounded over by two hundred years of abuse and the cracks and ruts between bricks were filled with ice, making the entire surface slippery as hell. "This way," Al said. "You okay?"

"Yeah, great," Sarah said. "I knew I shouldn'ta ate that second bagel this morning." They half walked, half ran down the alley, keeping close to the row of ancient brick factory buildings. The buildings had been built to fit the needs of another time, they were too small now, and too short to accommodate a modern truck's height. Some of them did seem to be occupied, but all of them were shuttered up tight against the cold. And against the sidewalk entrepreneurs, Al thought. No shelter here, no place to hide. They got to the end of the row, where the alley would dump them back out onto a main street, but just as they got to the corner one of the two men who'd been watching them from the coffee shop in Manhattan barreled around the corner straight at them. He seemed as surprised at they were, he showed the naturally uncoordinated gawkiness of a tall man, all flapping elbows and knees as he groped frantically in an inside pocket and tried to stop.

Al had no time to wonder where the hell he'd come from or how he'd managed to track them here, but she also had none of his loose-limbed gracelessness, either. She lowered a shoulder and charged into him, hitting him in the chest. His feet went up in the air and he went down awkwardly, cold-cocked himself on the frozen cobblestones.

The sound of the chopper was no longer just an echo.

You gotta be kidding me, Al thought. A helicopter? In Brooklyn? It would have to be a traffic copter.

Or cops.

"Holy shit!" Sarah said. "How did he—"

"Listen to me," Al told her. "When I say go, I want you to run for that bodega across the way over there, you got it?" She peered around the corner of the end of the alleyway. "This asshole's partner ought to be behind us somewhere, they probably wanted to catch us between the two of them. I'm going back for the guy. You got money? Good. Whoever's in the bodega, wave a couple of twenties at them and get them to find you a ride. Make up a story, but don't wait for a gypsy cab, they got to have someone who'll drive you out of here. Got it?"

Sarah nodded. "Okay. Are you sure…"

You should run away with her, Al thought, if that chopper has anything to do with these guys, you are about to blow this, big-time. "Yeah. Go now. GO!"

Sarah ran. Al watched her until she hit the bodega's front door, then she turned and ran back down the alley. She'd thought it would lead them to safety, but it was a trap now so she ran hard for the back door to the Korean lumber store, staying close to the buildings, as she had before. She skidded to a stop just inside the place, breathing hard.

The security guard jabbered at the counter lady, then took a step in Al's direction. Al turned in his direction and pointed a finger at him, "do not fuck with me" in any language. He looked at her face and froze. "Smart man," she said, and she headed into the store.

She walked cautiously down the long aisle that ran across the back of the place, peering down each of the intersecting aisles as she went. All the wood in this place, she thought, and not one good stick, all of it too long and too heavy… The same guys who'd eyed her suspiciously before did so again, but she ignored them all, she was looking for a tall white guy looked like he just got off the bus from Des Moines. She began to second-guess herself. What if you're wrong, she thought, and what makes you think you can understand how some strange man thinks, particularly some guy dresses like a mannequin out of an old Sears and fucking Roebuck catalog…?

He didn't seem to be anywhere inside the place, and Al knew she was running out of time. She hunkered down behind a big pile of five-gallon cans of roofing cement up near the Flushing Avenue entrance.

She heard some commotion outside the entrance and it was too late for second guesses. She peered over the top of the pile of buckets and there the guy was not fifteen feet away, he must have caught her movement out of the corner of his eye, he had his gun out, pointed up at the ceiling, he opened his mouth to shout as he began to bring the gun down to bear on her, she held a can of asphalt with both hands and she swung in a half circle, pitched it at the guy with all the force she could muster. It took his knees out from under him and he began bellowing before he even hit the floor, he bounced once, lost his gun in the process, screamed, and grabbed his knee. Behind him the can fetched up against the register stand and the top burst open, splattering black goop. Lumber patrons danced out of the way as Al ignored the shouting voices and ran for the door.

She stopped when she hit the sidewalk.

The chopper was hovering low over Flushing Avenue. An NYPD blue-and-white screamed down the hill and slewed to a stop in the middle of the street.

"Shit," Al said. She'd had it all wrong. This is a fuckup, she thought, she'd figured it wrong all the way around. She should have known these guys were cops, but they'd looked wrong…and why couldn't they have just talked to her?

A young cop jumped out of the cruiser, pointed his pistol at her. He had it in both hands, combat stance, just like they teach you in the academy. Al. raised her arms straight out, palms open. "GET DOWN ON THE GROUND!" he yelled at her. "RIGHT NOW!"

Frustration and anger bubbled in her bloodstream. "Defiance," Tio Bobby had told her a hundred times, "generally gets you nowhere," but she couldn't help herself. She stared at the young cop in disdain as he shouted his instructions again. "DOWN ON THE GROUND! RIGHT NOW! DO IT!" Command voice, she thought, just like they teach you in…

"Don't wet your panties," she yelled back, anger and fear making her voice loud.

The young cop's partner was out of the car now. Both Al and the young cop looked over at him. The guy held a set of cuffs in one hand, and he gave Al the eye.

She nodded, resigned.

"Turn around," he said.

She complied. Inside the store, someone was down on his knees talking to the guy Al had hit with the bucket. A red-faced Korean was looking at the black mess on the floor and yelling at the top of his voice. Some sirens called to one another in the distance. She felt the cuff snap around her right wrist, heard that funny ratcheting sound it made as the cop clicked it shut. "Behind your back," the guy said. "That's good. Nice and easy. Gimme your other hand now, that's a good girl. Okay, sister."

Al stared at the tall man writhing on the floor just inside the lumber store. "Who's he?"

"This way, Miss," he said, his voice formal, telling her he wasn't giving her anything, and he walked her over to the cruiser. He looked at his partner on the way past. "You can put that away now," he said.

FOURTEEN

INHALE. ONE. EXHALE.

She was conscious of the guy screaming, she couldn't be in the same room and not hear him, but she wasn't distracted.

Inhale. Two. Exhale.

She held her hands folded in her lap, one held loosely in the open palm of the other.

Inhale. Be aware of the sensation of breath, of the air rushing in, filling up, giving life. Three. Exhale. Feel it leaving, taking the soreness in your back with it...

Through half closed, heavy-lidded eyes she could see the far edge of the perp desk, she could see the man's blue cotton shirt, red striped tie. She was aware that his voice was growing hoarse. He and his partner had been taking turns going at her for hours. "You assaulted a federal officer! Do you have any fucking idea how much trouble you're in?" She was surprised they let him say "fuck," her surprise broke her concentration, and she had to go back to one.

Inhale. One. Exhale.

Bad enough to get rousted by professionals. She could accept that, the NYPD did not always appreciate privateers like her and Marty, and a certain amount of conflict with cops was a part of the business, always had been, but it was gonna be a cold day in hell when she allowed herself to be intimidated by some chump from Kansas City.

She had come to think of him as Number Two. The other

one was the friendly guy, this one was the screamer. Screw you, pal, she told him silently. You push me, I push back.

"He's gonna need reconstructive surgery on his knee! You're looking at a mandatory ten-year term! Mandatory! In a federal pen!" She knew what he wanted, he wanted her to spill her guts, he wanted to give her nothing in return, he wanted her so scared that she could hardly stand.

Inhale. You don't know who you're dealing with, douche bag, she thought. Exhale. He was overconfident, too close, she could have had her hands around his throat in a half second, and for an instant she burned to do it. Control yourself, she thought, for maybe the hundredth time since they put her in the chair. Control yourself. She remembered the words of one of her grade-school teachers, she'd been using the phrase like a mantra. "She who loses her temper, loses." It had not had the intended effect when she'd first heard it, but it seemed to be working a bit better now. Swallow it, she told herself. Keep it inside. Don't forget your objective…

She shifted her gaze, raised her eyes to look him in the face. Middle-aged white guy, receding brown hair, the beginnings of jowls despite his lack of a paunch. The worried look in his eyes told her she was doing it right. He was gonna be the one who broke, not her, and when he was done for, maybe they'd bring in someone she could talk to.

"One," she said.

He shut up immediately. To his left and to her right was a large mirror. One-way glass, naturally, and no way to know how many were watching.

"I was the one who was assaulted," she said, "and by two of you, not one."

"There were surveillance cameras in that place, and we've got footage that clearly shows—"

"Two," she said, and he shut it just as quickly as he had the first time. Again, he reinforced her judgment that she

was playing him correctly. Whoever these guys actually
were, they really, really wanted to hear whatever she had
to say, but they had no leverage, because if they did they'd
have used it by now. "You've got nothing." She said it without inflection, merely stated the facts as she saw them.
"If you have any footage at all it will show that your men
failed to identify themselves in any way until after they
were disarmed." She opened her eyes slightly wider. "And
incapacitated." She apologized silently to her meditation
teacher, a tall bald-headed Jewish guy named Bernie. She
had gone to him for advanced instruction in aikido, but he
had maintained that she wasn't ready and had bullied her
into meditation practice instead. Unable to shake her anger,
she had not done well. She thought she'd be learning something practical, not some mystical crock of transcendental
bullshit. She had considered it all hocus-pocus at the time,
figured Bernie for a fraud, but in the intervening years she
had been unable to get his teachings out of her head, even
though up until now she had completely missed his point.

"Three." She allowed herself a small smirk, but it was
not a slip, not a lapse, it was a part of the act, a deliberate
goad. A tiny pinprick. "You guys ought to be more careful. Someone could have gotten seriously hurt." The smirk
went away. "You still could." She leaned forward slightly.
"You're not in Kansas anymore, Dorothy." Her quiet threat
was unmistakable.

Number Two jumped to his feet, knocking his chair over
behind him. He slammed his hand on the desk and began
screaming again, but from a safer distance.

"She who loses her temper, loses." She tuned him out.
Her eyelids drifted back to half-mast. Inhale. One. Exhale.
Inhale. Two. Exhale. She tried to feel which muscles were
tense, tried to relax in the chair, tried to let her breath ease
her aches and anxieties away. "Sit like a stack of bricks,"

Bernie had told her, and she thought she might be getting it, except the nagging ache up the left side of her spine was beginning to get to her. Inhale. Three. Exhale. Her hands felt warm in her lap, almost hot. Inhale. Four. Exhale.

He departed some time later. They left her alone, for how long she could not have said, and then Number One came back.

Good cop, bad cop. It was still all they had, and these two were playing it like they'd only seen it at the movies. A real cop would know how to do this right… She'd heard stories, suspects hung upside down in a holding cell, getting worked over by some fat old sergeant who knew exactly where to hit, and how hard. She wondered how she would have fared, back in the day. But those old cops were long retired and gone, and when the new ones held a "tattoo party," it was generally an impromptu affair triggered by someone's frustrated loss of control. When that happened somebody generally got messed up badly enough to require a trip to the emergency room.

Or, occasionally, the morgue.

If they'd sent in a fat old sergeant, things might have gotten interesting.

But they didn't. Number One was just another college boy. Actually, he wasn't a boy at all, he was about forty, just going gray, just getting a belly. His name was Figueroa, they must have decided that she'd identify with him easier, but he was a second-generation Mexican, not Puerto Rican. She could hear the broad nasal twang of upstate New York in his voice.

Didn't speak Spanish.

Probably lived in fucking Westchester.

He picked up the chair that Number Two had knocked over, set it on its feet. Sat down, lowered his head, tried for eye contact. "Alessandra?" he said. "Al? Look at me, please. Please, Al."

She complied, slowly, didn't vary the cadence of her breath.

"We can't keep this up," he said.

"No shit." She said it without heat.

"Your partner," he said. "Mrs. Waters."

Al felt a tickle of fear, a tiny worm chewing at her gut. Tune it out, she told herself, tune it out. They were bound to try this. Surprised it took them this long. She needed to count on Sarah's instincts and her ability to keep her trap shut.

Had to rely on Sarah Waters...

Oh, Jesus Christ....

Come on, she told herself, the girl's Brooklyn, born and bred. She would never...

"We only need one of you. And we're not handing immunity to someone who won't work with us. I just want to give you this one last chance, Alessandra. You really do need to tell us your side of things." He leaned in closer. "We know about Frank. We know what happened at the restaurant. Sarah's talking, Al. Someone is going to answer for that poor bastard who bought it in that parking lot. Sarah wants out, and if somebody has to take the fall, she's going to let it be you. Accessory to murder, conspiracy, assault, and that's just for starters. Probably got some RICO statute violations we can work with."

I'll kill her, Al thought, I swear if the bitch says one damn word I will cut her goddam tongue out... That worm in her gut got a bit larger, and it took another bite.

Number One was still talking possible charges. Accessory. Assault with intent. Illegal flight. Conspiracy to commit. Concealing evidence. And given her record, the possibility of conviction was better than average, especially given the current political climate...

He added up the time, and he didn't just lump it all together the way reporters did, either, he gave her what sounded like a fairly honest assessment of probable sentences, some consecutive and some concurrent. He even hacked off the normal number of years for good behavior, being confident, he told her, that she would be a model prisoner... "You could be looking at ten, minimum, probably more like twelve or fourteen."

Inhale. One. Exhale. The muscle in her back tightened into a knot. It was no good, the best she could manage was to hold on and pretend.

She looked at his eyes, and the anxiety she saw there seemed real enough. That sealed it. Hold on, she told herself. Almost there.

"This is a one-time offer, Miss Martillo. Good for today only."

Inhale. One. Exhale. Her gut told her that they were out of ammunition. "Arrest me," she said.

THE KINK IN her back was becoming intolerable.

Inhale. One. Exhale.

She hadn't asked for a lawyer, purposely, hadn't demanded they charge her or let her go.

Inhale. Two. Exhale.

The muscles that ran up the left side of her spine were doing their best to bend her over backward. It took an effort of will for her to remain motionless. She derided herself. You pussy, she thought. Bodhidharma did this for days at a time. Years, if you believed the stories. Wonder how many times he had to go back to one.

Inhale. One. God it hurt. Exhale.

Number Two opened the door and held it for an older

man. Number One's act was over, though, his face was etched with flop sweat. Whatever it was they'd counted on him to extract from her, he hadn't gotten it done, and now he was worried. And here comes the fat sergeant, at least metaphorically, she thought. The guy in question was a comfortably overweight man, round rosy face, blue eyes, potato nose. His tie was askew and he had a pale brown stain on the belly of his yellow shirt. Al, baby, she told herself, this guy looks like he's for real, we just stepped up in weight class, but maybe we'll finally find out what they're looking for…

He sat down across from her. "Seven hours, twenty-six minutes in a hard chair without moving a muscle," he said. "I'm impressed. Buddhist?"

She shook her head once. She wanted to stretch the kink out of her back, but she resisted the impulse. No giving away points, she told herself, not this close to the end of the game. "Couldn't get with that nonviolent shit," she said.

He snorted. "I'll bet."

She reached out her right hand. "Al Martillo," she said.

"I know," he said, but after a moment he shook her hand. "Bobby Fallon."

She had to ask. "Sergeant?"

"Looie," he said.

"NYPD." It was a statement, not a question.

He nodded. "Yeah."

"Where'd you find these Gomers?"

He glanced over his shoulder at Number One, who clenched his teeth and looked away. "Be nice," Fallon said, looking back at her. "The law enforcement community is one big happy family these days. Al, can we cut the bullshit?"

She shrugged. "Your call."

"You been around. How come you didn't ask for a lawyer?"

"I didn't do nothing wrong."

Fallon laughed at that. Number One looked like he was going to crack a tooth. "You didn't sit in that chair for seven hours and—" Fallon looked at his watch "—twenty-seven minutes to show us how tough you are."

"No."

"Or to make us see what a mistake the department made when we let you get away."

She shook her head. "Look, Fallon," she said. "Why can't you just be straight with me and tell me what this is all about?"

"You're working without a license," he said.

"I work for Marty Stiles."

"My old pal Marty. How's he doing?"

"He has good days and bad days."

Fallon gave her a look. "I must have caught him on a bad day," he told her. "Okay, suppose you skate on the license, there's still this minor matter of assaulting a federal officer. We can probably get that to stick."

"Get real," she said. "It's a bullshit rap, he never identified himself and you know it. Two helpless women, all alone in the world, we still got the right to defend ourselves. You can charge me, but you'll never get a conviction, after I get off I'll bring civil suit, and I'll do it in Brooklyn, because I live there, not Manhattan, and we'll try the case in front of a jury of my peers, from Brooklyn. Twelve ordinary guys just like the ones from that store on Flushing Avenue, you guys are nothing but a pain in the ass to them. You know what that means. You lose, I win."

"Take you twenty years to collect," he said.

"I got time." She remembered back to her academy days, Interrogation 101. How funny would it be to read him the next line in his script? Establish contact, use his first name, try to build a bridge. Make it easy for him to trust you… She leaned in. "Bobby," she said, peering into his blue eyes, "help me out, here. Why don't you just tell me what's going on? Hmmm? Then we can all go home."

He snorted. "You got a pair of fucking balls, you know that?"

"Whatever," she said. "Do it your way, that's what you want. Go ahead. What's next?"

He sighed, examined his fingernails. "Next I appeal to your sense of patriotism."

"I pledge allegiance," she said. "What else you got? 'Cause pretty soon I'm gonna walk."

He sighed again. "All right," he said. "What can you tell me about Frank Waters?"

At least it's a start, she thought. "Father of Frank Junior. Ex-wife named Sarah, who happens to be my client in this matter."

"You can give up more than that," he said. "The guy's apartment was ransacked. You do that?"

"I was there," she said, "but I looked, I didn't ransack. If the place was trashed, I'd start with that dirtbag building super."

"The Serbian female?"

It was her turn, and she gave him a look. "No, Sherlock, the Serbian female's husband."

Fallon shifted in his chair to glare at Number One, whose face turned red. "Okay," he said, turning back to her. "Okay, you got us, that's one. What did you find?"

"Keys. Some handwritten notes, looked like passwords or entry codes of some kind."

He exhaled, like he'd been holding in his breath too long. "I'll need those."

She nodded. "And you got his service record."

"And his arrest record."

She shook her head. "Come on, Fallon, you know what kind of guy Frankie was. He might have been a dope, but he wasn't a bad guy. He just ran with some bad people, that's all."

"Was? You figure he's dead?"

"You got me," she said. "That's one."

"Yeah." He shifted in his chair, uncomfortable. "Maybe the guys he ran with were worse than you know." He turned and grimaced at Number One, then stood up. "Let's go somewhere so we can talk."

About time, she thought. "All right." She stood up slowly, one hand on the back of her chair. "What did you do with Sarah?"

"She went home hours ago. Had her goddam lawyer on the phone before they even got her into the cruiser."

"You didn't take her phone?"

Fallon grimaced at Number One again. "Okay, that's two," he said. "Come with me."

"Lieutenant Fallon?"

"Yes, ma'am?"

"How come you guys couldn't just ask me this like seven hours ago?"

"The ways of the federal government are deep," he intoned, "and past understanding. But when they've failed, we go back to what we know."

"I see." On her way out of the room she stared into Number One's eyes, mentally added him to her list, the names of those whom God would surely not let die before she got her chance at a little payback.

THE COLD WIND howled in off the ocean and roared up Bay Parkway. Al headed for the warmth of a Dunkin' Donuts joint, but she felt the gentle pressure of Sarah's hand on her elbow so they continued in frozen silence for another block until Sarah guided them through the front door of a Zabar's Bakery. Al found a seat behind a rickety table, sat shivering, clutching her thin jacket around her while Sarah waited at the counter. A moment later Sarah was back with coffees and a bag full of chocolate croissants. Al took the plastic lid off, wrapped her hands around the tall paper cup. "Happened to your diet?" she said.

"Screw the diet," Sarah said.

"That's the spirit. Fallon told me you did okay, lawyering up so quick. What was it he said? 'You might have something there.' Pretty high praise, coming from a guy like him." She watched the anger flare in Sarah's eyes.

"Fuckers," Sarah said. "They treat you like you're a piece of dog shit, and then they wonder why everybody fucking hates them." She shook her head. "I know, they're all heroes now... Which one was Fallon?"

"Older guy, heavy, blue eyes. NYPD, not federal."

"I don't think I saw him."

"He saw you. Said they couldn't rattle you."

"First thing you learn, right?" Sarah looked down into her coffee. "Fucked-up-family rule number one: don't tell 'em shit."

"Whatever. You did good."

"Thanks."

"You really have a lawyer on speed dial?"

"No. I called my mother, actually, and she called her cousin."

"He a lawyer?"

"She. Yeah, but disbarred, on account of conspiring to have a jury member's wife beat up. But she called some guy she works with, and, you know. You know how it works."

"Yeah. I do."

"What the hell did they want?" Sarah looked up from her coffee, stared across the table at Al. "What the hell was this all about?"

"Frank," Al said.

FIFTEEN

"I DON'T GET IT," Sarah said. "Not for nothing, okay, I mean I did love the man once upon a time, but Frank was never worth following with no helicopter, not on the best day he ever had."

"They weren't following Frank, they were following us. Me and you," Al told her. She wasn't warm yet, but the coffee was helping.

"You get what I'm saying. It's Frank they're after. Who are those guys, anyhow?"

Al shook her head. "I'm still not sure. Bobby Fallon is NYPD, no question of that, and he's older and smarter than all of those other guys, but I got the impression it was him working for them instead of the other way around. The cops that hauled me in were from the local precinct right there in Bushwick, but those two goofballs who came after us weren't NYPD, no way. And that was not an NYPD chopper."

"Do you think they could have been FBI?" Sarah said. "What the hell could Frank have done…"

"I don't think so," Al said. "They ran that interrogation like they just read the manual yesterday. They kept accusing me of assaulting federal agents, but when I asked Fallon about it, he wouldn't answer."

"The other thing I don't get," Sarah said. "What's up with the surveillance? What could you and I be doing that's worth whatever it costs to have, what, three guys following us around?"

"Three that we know of," Al said. "Plus the cost of the helicopter. Do you suppose they got home movies of you boinking J. Austin Smits—"

"Ohmygod," Sarah said, turning pink.

"—the famous sculptor? I gotta check YouTube the first chance I get."

"Ohmygodohmygod," Sarah said. "You don't think... Wait. There was no helicopter. We were out in the middle of nowhere for crissake, there was nobody there but us. You're a dog."

"Come on," Al said. "They don't have to be anywhere near you, they could record you from a satellite. You got to catch up with the times."

"Oh, shut up," Sarah said, going from pink to red. "You were just... I don't care. I ain't gonna be a nun for the rest of my life. I waited long enough already."

"Are you serious?"

"I like Jake," Sarah said, a bit defensive. "He's nice. I mean, I don't understand why I always wind up shopping in the dented-can store, but I don't care, I like him."

"Wow," Al said. "Good for you. I guess you're pretty sure he didn't off his father."

"Yes. Thank you. Where were we? Oh yeah, we were trying to figure out why these guys from Cleveland or whatever spent all day sweating you instead of just telling you what they wanted. What do you think?"

"Well, they weren't NYPD and they didn't know what they were doing. I just wonder how long it took Fallon to persuade them to let him talk to me."

"What did you give Fallon?"

"He wanted to know what happened at Costello's, so we talked about that. He wanted to know what I came up with at Frank's apartment. I told him what I found. I know they were there after I was, but I'm guessing they'll go back and look again, and they'll work the building super over a little better than they did the first time. They didn't know anything about Palermo Imports or Paolo Torrente, either. They got all hot in the pants when I started talking about that, and about a half hour later Fallon handed me off to two other gerbils, and I went around in circles with them for a while."

"Did you give up TJ?"

"You know something? I told them I was there with my boyfriend, and they weren't at all interested in him. Now that I think about it, these guys act like they've already got everything they need on Frank, now they just wanna grab him." She looked at Sarah. "I feel like a rat."

"Don't," Sarah said. "Listen, if these guys can afford a helicopter, then they can afford whatever it takes to find Frankie, which means they'll probably turn him up quicker than we can do it. And whatever he did, that's on him, not me."

"So what do we do now?" Al asked her.

"Look at what they did just because we were at Costello's with Frank. I bet they told you to leave this alone before they let you go, didn't they? Did they warn you off?"

"They reminded me how much trouble they could cause for us."

"We could let it go. If they find Frankie, fine, at least I know where he is or what happened to him. If they don't, they'll get bored and go away, and then we can pick it up again. In the meantime, we got bills."

"Insurance," Al said.

"Yeah. And it ain't gonna be cheap," Sarah said.

"You don't really want to drop this, do you?"

"No. But I don't wanna be selfish about it, either. We can't afford for either one of us to go to jail for screwing up a federal investigation. Or God forbid, even worse, get hurt or something."

"You know what, Sar, if I thought these guys knew what they were doing, I could think about letting it go. If they were for real, maybe they would have a better chance of finding Frank, but they don't look to me like pros at all. Have they called you or your lawyer since they let you walk?"

Sarah shook her head.

"You see what I'm saying? They should be all over you," Al told her. "Whether you wanted to help them or not, they should have two or three guys assigned full-time to making themselves the best friends you ever had, they should be shoveling your sidewalk and everything. And they haven't even called?"

"No."

"You see? I don't think we should back off yet."

"All right. I'm gonna go back to the office and finish my paperwork, and then I'm gonna go back out there. Just do me one favor, okay?"

"What's that?"

"Be careful."

"Yeah. Will do."

THEY HAD GIVEN Marty a new wheelchair, one with drive wheels so he could push himself around. Al figured that the chair, together with the vindictive look on his face, was a sign that he had turned some sort of corner and was now on the road to recovery. And even if he wasn't, on a guy like Marty, spite looked better than self-pity. "I wondered how long it would take," he said.

Al decided to feign innocence. "How long what would take?"

"Don't try to bullshit me," he said, sneering. "You're in trouble now, so you've come crawling back to see if I can bail you out. Ain't that right?"

She sat down in one of the empty chairs in the dayroom. "I'm not in any trouble, Marty."

"Don't give me that shit, Martillo. Bobby Fallon came down to see me a couple days ago, and he wanted me to talk about you. Fallon is out of the police commissioner's office, in case you don't know. I don't know what the hell you did to attract his attention, but trust me, it ain't good news. You musta fucked up big-time if you got Bobby Fallon up your ass."

"I thought Mr. Fallon was very nice," she told him, glad to see some of the self-righteous smugness wiped off his ugly puss. "I've been working this case, and it so happens that Fallon was looking under some of the same rocks."

"I didn't tell him anything," he told her. "I played stupid." He doesn't know how to spin this, she thought. He knows if he comes on like too much of a hard-on, I'll walk. And if he cares about that, maybe he is getting better… "That shouldn't have been too difficult," she said.

"Oh fuck you, Martillo," he said, but without any real heat. "What can you possibly be working on that a guy like Fallon would be interested in?"

This is it, she thought, this is where we find out if he is gonna come back to life or not. If he really wants to hear it, he's got a shot, and if he sits there busting my chops, he'll probably die in this place. "If I tell you," she said, "can I trust you to keep your mouth shut?" He has to decide, she thought. He knows it and he knows I know it. So is he gonna pull himself together or does he sit here feeling sorry for himself for the rest of his miserable life?

Stiles rocked his upper body back and forth slightly, his hands clutching his armrests. He wrestled with himself in silence.

"Come on, Marty," she said. "What's it gonna be? You gonna help or you gonna sit here and rot?"

He looked at her, swallowed once, steeled himself. Recovery would be the more difficult choice, she knew that. It would mean a fight, a hard one and one that would last just as long as he did. Much easier to give up, grow old and bitter, immobile and useless. He swallowed again, then nodded, surprising her. "You have my word," he said. "Tell me."

She started with the night at Costello's, ran through all of it, right up to her interrogation and the subsequent encounter with Fallon. He sat in silence until she was done. "Great," he finally said. "You've been on this thing for days, and what are we making out of it? You and your fucking crusades, Al, I swear to God. I don't see any way we turn one single stinking dollar on this. Who gives a shit what this guy was into? Let it go, for crissake…"

"Frank is Sarah's ex," she told him. "Like it or not, Marty, she's one of ours. That makes it our business."

"Al, I know you wanna do the right thing, but she answers the fucking phone, okay? She types invoices. Don't make her out to be—"

"Yeah," Al said. "And she also does all the hotel and bar business, Marty. I taught her how."

"Are you nuts? Are you out of your mind? If she fucks that up, how do we keep the door open? How do we pay the rent? Have you thought about that? I know you think those mercenary-type considerations are beneath you, but you have got to—"

"Hey, you know what, she's doing such a shit job with it, Marty, she just landed Hyatt Hotels. Those ops managers love her, Marty, they love her. They think she walks on water." Another choice, Al thought, another turning point. If he accepts her, we go forward. If he doesn't, I walk.

The depth of her feeling surprised her.

She wondered if he knew.

He thought about it. "Hyatt," he finally said.

"Yeah."

He shook his head. "I never wanted a partner."

"Nobody gets it all their own way."

"And you figure I need you now. Both of you."

"Why is that so awful, Marty?"

He looked around the dayroom like he was trying to find the exit. "What about you?" he finally demanded. "What about you? You two wasn't the best of friends, if I recall correct. I hired her to take your job, and she took it, you forget about that? And look at me. I can't even get up the steps and into the office no more. Is this what you want?"

"I told you, we moved the office, Marty. The new place has an elevator."

"I thought you were kidding," he said.

She didn't respond.

"You do that for me?" he sneered.

"Look at it any way you want," she said.

"Fucking bullshit," he said.

"Yeah. But that's life, Marty. It might suck, but it's the only game in town. Take it or leave it."

"What'd I do to deserve this, will you answer me that? Two partners now, and both of them women. Christ. Somewhere my ex-wife is coming all over herself."

"For crissake, Marty, get off the pot."

"You're all heart, you know that? All right all right. Christ Almighty. All right." The muscles in his jaw clenched. "Okay already. Tell me what Fallon asked you. Word for word, if you can."

SHE LOOKED OVER at Stiles's face when she was done. From the side he looked different, human in a way she hadn't thought of him in a while. Or maybe it was the fact that she'd given him something to think about besides himself. For several moments he held the silence, rocking his upper body back and forth in his chair. Finally he coughed. "Any markings on the helicopter?" he said.

Al closed her eyes, tried to take herself back through it. "Logo on the door," she said. "Some sort of stylized animal head inside a circle. Corporate name on the tail. Can't remember the name. Weird name."

"Lots of Italians in this mess," he said. "Was it Italian?"

"I don't think so."

"Those guys from Kansas. They show you any ID?"

She ran back over the sequence of events. Could they all have been phony? No way, she thought. A helicopter flying at street level, even in Bushwick, would be sure to draw questions, and besides, the guys who'd picked her up had taken her straight to the station house. But… "No," she said. "No, they didn't."

"Ya dope ya," he said.

"Yeah. But wouldn't that be a felony? Impersonating a federal agent? And they did it right in the middle of a police station. They had to be for real."

He gave her a look.

"All right then," she said. "Who were they?"

"I'll try to find out," he said. "But I don't think they were cops."

"What, then?"

He shrugged. "If they were any kind of policemen, you'd still be answering questions. Wherever those yokels come from, it's a new one on me."

"Was Fallon alone when he came to see you?"

"Yeah. Probably thought I woulda had too many questions if he'd brought his pals along."

"Did you talk to him?"

His eyes flicked over at her, then away. "I do the catatonic thing pretty well."

"Tell me," she said. "What is it about those guys that makes you say they aren't cops?"

"What they asked you," he said. "What they didn't ask you. Even Fallon, when you come down to it, he didn't sound like he was trying to build a case. All they really were interested in was, where is Frank Waters? Think about it, Al. Did they seem like they cared at all about the man? Were they curious about who he was? What he did? What he talked about?"

Al shook her head. "No."

"That ain't the way cops go through life. It ain't the way they do business. Even if they already got something on the guy, there's a curiosity cops have that these mutts aren't showing me. You take your ordinary citizen, he walks into a bar, he's looking for a beer. He goes in and gets his beer, he drinks half of it, then he looks around. Maybe. And you know, maybe not, maybe he don't give a fuck. Maybe he just drinks his beer. A cop walks into the bar, what's the first thing he does? He stops just inside the door. Tell me, Martillo, what's he doing?"

"Yeah," she said. "He's gathering information."

Stiles nodded. "Being a cop changes your head, it changes the way you move. Okay, you come for a beer, fine, but you ain't Joe Six-pack anymore. Your eyes have been opened. What kinda joint is this? Who are all those guys at the table over in the corner? Is the bartender carrying? Anybody in the joint selling dope? Where's the back door? Where's the shit house? Anybody in it? Anybody looking at you funny? Why's that kid at the bar getting all fidgety? That's all in the first half second. Then, maybe, you go and you get your beer. It's how you stay alive." He pointed at her. "That's why Fallon come alone. He knew those guys wouldn't smell right."

It galled at her that she had missed it and he had seen

it so quickly. "They weren't interested in Frank after all," she said. "They only wanted to know where to find him. That's why they took off so quick when I told them about Palermo Imports."

"They're not trying to make a case," Marty said. "Find the guy, put him in a box, bring him in, that's their job description. That means you still got the edge."

"How do you figure that?"

"We all know how good you kick ass, Martillo. That ain't all there is to the job, though. You know what you have to do now? You have to go ask the questions those clowns should be asking but ain't. You hear what I'm saying? You find the right answers, you might find out who Frank Waters is, and what he did. Because those other guys find him, it'll be by tripping over his dead body."

"Even with Bobby Fallon helping them?"

He looked at her sourly. "Fallon ain't helping nobody, he's babysitting, that's what he's doing."

"All right," she said. She stood up to go.

"Martillo," he said.

"What."

"The other night, when you come down here. You didn't come just so you could piss in my face. You wanted to see how much juice I got left."

"So?"

He glared at her. "So I want what's mine. Houston Investigations belongs to me. While I been in here, you been driving around town on my license, but once I get my shit together, we go back to the way it was. I got the right to what's mine."

"Oh, really?" she said. "You got the right to kiss my ass, Stiles, that's what you got."

"Goddammit—"

"You listen to me, you fat sack of shit, as of right now

you got nothing. You get yourself out of this hole you're in, okay, you prove that you can haul your own weight, you quit acting like a jackass, maybe me and Sarah will work with you. Maybe. Asshole." She walked out.

"Martillo!" She could hear him yelling after her. "You ain't got the license! You can't get one! You don't qualify! You ain't put in the time! I won't help you! Goddam you, Martillo! MAR-TEE-YO!"

IT WASN'T THAT far from the hospital to Costello's. Al double-parked on the hill and watched the lot. The original valet was still not back, they had a tall skinny kid parking the cars.

Suppose it was you, she thought, suppose you were the new guy. Someone comes along, gives you a story about how they owe the other guy money or something. What would you do?

Play stupid, of course. "Sorry, lady, I don't know the guy, I only got here day before yesterday." And then warn the first guy off, "Hey, dude, some people were here looking for you…" Salve your conscience, assuming you've got one, "Hey, I did the right thing, sort of. And now I get to keep the gig."

"You know how these Italians are, gotta impress the lady, right, throw the kid a fifty, just like all the other tough guys do."

"They're coming for you, bro. What was I supposed to do?"

Wait, she told herself. Give him some time. He'll be back.

SIXTEEN

SALATHIEL EDWARDS PARKED his car in the doctors only section of the lot behind the Wyckoff Heights Hospital in Brooklyn and walked inside. He showed his badge at the security desk, where the guards nodded him through. He took an elevator to the cafeteria level, bought two coffees, carried them out into the courtyard garden where Alessandra Martillo waited for him.

"Thank you," she said.

"My pleasure," he said, sitting down. "Very nice, here. Quiet. Secluded, even. Samatter, you don't wanna be seen out in public with me?"

"I thought it might be the other way around."

"No, I got no problems there, it's part of my job, you know, development of contacts and informants among Brooklyn's street criminals, organized crime figures, and other sundry and assorted malefactors and undesirables such as yourself."

"What did I do now?" she said, trying to sound innocent.

"Oh, you set it off, sister, you lit the fuse. And the shit-storm continues."

"I do what I can," she said. "No, really, what happened?"

Edwards put his booted feet up on an empty chair. "Well, it's like this," he said, in a passable imitation of Foghorn Leghorn. "An undercover operative from the DEA, together with an inspector from the FDNY, working with the full, I say the full, knowledge and cooperation of the NYPD, conducted a review of the facility being operated as a bonded warehouse of Palermo Imports, of Richmond Terrace, blah blah blah. Under license, I should add, of the United States Customs. At ten-oh-six yesterday morning the facility was found to be unoccupied. The gate in the fence was ripped off its hinges and the truck bay door had been rendered inoperative, allegedly by the expedient of driving a forklift truck through it, allege, I say allegedly, because said forklift truck was missing and presumed stolen. Contents of said warehouse being, I say, being approximately twelve thousand, four hundred, and twenty-eight bottles of wine, with an unknown number of bottles smashed all throughout the interior of said warehouse, leaving a carpet of broken glass and wine residue. Crime scene evidence contaminated and rendered useless due to the multiplicity of footprints, fingerprints, ass prints, tire tracks, pee tracks, turd piles, and vomit puddles, all assumed to have been left behind by the local teen-aged and wino populace after security was breached."

"Oh, shit," Al said.

"No shit," Edwards said. "We ain't even got to the good parts yet. In the course of their inspection, the aforementioned agents of the DEA and the FDNY were interrupted and interfered with in the dispatch of their appointed duties by the arrival, at approximately ten-forty-eight, by the arrival, I say the arrival, of individuals see attached addenda who orally and by voice identified themselves as federal agents and who was riding in vans, a helicopter, and an urban assault vehicle."

"What? Urban assault—"

"Vehicle," Edwards said, nodding. "Winnebago with a hard-on. Said agents refused to produce identification. The FDNY inspector notified his superiors as well as the captain of the local precinct, who having been previously banished to the wastelands of Staten Island due to his combative, obstreperous, and dare I mention alcoholic nature. Said captain arrived at the crime scene at approximately eleven-twenty-three accompanied by every available on-duty officer of the law." Edwards laughed softly. "You know something? I'm sorry I missed it. Sound like the charge of the dumb-ass brigade."

"Wow." Al shook her head. "Any footage from the security cameras?"

"Al, come on. You get the picture, if it wasn't stolen, it was smashed, if it wasn't smashed, it was drunk up. No cameras, no tapes, no PCs in the office, shit, even the office chairs was gone. We're talking the aftermath of the biggest, baddest, most-fucked-up frat party in the history of mankind. They ain't gonna find anything usable in there, particularly as how they ain't got around to looking yet."

"How about interviews with the local—"

Edwards was laughing.

"No interviews?"

"Will you get serious? As we speak, the NYPD, FDNY, U.S. Customs Department, the DEA, and the Office of Homeland Security are all embroiled in a full-on, knockdown, bitch-slapping, dick-measuring party. By the time the cockfight is over anything and anybody useful will be long gone. Besides, from what they tell me, the place looked like a herd of wildebeests stampeded through there."

"You gonna get any heat behind this?"

"I don't see how," he said. "I got a tip from one Giuseppe Rigatoni of Forty-seventh Avenue, Brooklyn, New York, and I passed it along. I might get my toes stepped on for not going through official channels, but I doubt that. I'm golden."

"Thank God for that," Al told him. "I'd hate to get you into hot water."

"Baby, I got twenty-one years in," he said. "I got good

numbers, I got two commendations, one thanks to you, and I got a good record. My ex-wife is remarried and my youngest daughter graduates from Fordham this fall. You hear what I'm saying? No more alimony, not a hell of a lot of child support left, and I have put in my motherfucking time. I'm a free man, sister. Anybody gives me shit, I walk."

"So how come you're not out on a fishing boat somewhere?"

"I got a place down in South Carolina," he said, nodding. "I go down two, three weeks every summer, drink beer and play golf. Scare the bejesus out of the white folk. 'Cornelius,'" he said, in a quavering old woman's voice, "'there's a Negro on our golf course.'" And then, in Foghorn's voice again, "'Don't look, I say don't look at him, dearest, it's O.J. Simpson.' But it's quiet there, beautiful, peaceful. Boring as hell. One week and I'm ready to come home to Brooklyn, where I like what I do, and I know what I'm good at." He peered at her. "It ain't a bad life, in spite of all the shit you hear about it. You can make a good living on The Job. I know I talked to you about this before—"

"Yes, you did. Did I hear you say 'Homeland Security'? Is that who those guys are?"

"You did hear that, but that is not who those guys are. Matter of fact, they work for something called The Harkonnen Group, which is a contractor in the employ of the aforementioned Office of Homeland Security, which makes them, under some obscure law passed back in '02, de facto agents of the government, although they do not have subpoena power nor can they arrest anyone. Not even you. So that makes them legit, except, maybe, in Staten Island. That is not how interdepartmental cooperation is supposed to work, but in these times of economic insecurity, I say, I say they have a budget that is as deep and wide as the Atlantic Ocean, which insures them undying friendship and free donuts wherever they go."

"That's how come they get Bobby Fallon chauffeuring them around," Al said.

"Can't say I ever made the acquaintance of Mr. Fallon."

"Stupid question, I know, but were there any large shipping containers at Palermo Imports?"

"Nope. Wine bottles. Broken glass."

"Whatever it was in those containers," Al said, "they must've moved it before they cleared out."

"How do you know it wasn't just more wine?"

She shook her head. "No way. Torrente, the guy ran the place, was sweating those containers way too much."

Edwards shrugged. "Well, as soon as everyone's done throwing their rattles at one another, someone will get back up in there with drug dogs, and if there was anything good in the containers, at least we'll know what it was. And don't be surprised if someone, sooner or later, wants to sit down with you and have a long conversation about Torrente, Palermo Imports, and whatever else you know about that warehouse."

"Bet you're wrong. Marty Stiles says the Harkonnen guys are not cops. They just want to find Frank Waters and his buddies and put them in a box. He says Harkonnen acts like they already have everything they need. Says they're not investigating anything."

His face clouded over. "Ain't that some shit," he said. "Gonna be their case, you watch, and they're gonna drop the ball."

"I wonder who really owns the warehouse," Al said.

"Probably some shell corporation out of the Dominican Republic or someplace," he said. "These guys covered their tracks too well to leave something like that to trip them up. Someone will go check, I'm sure, but it'll be a waste of time."

They might if they were cops, she thought. "You're probably right," she told him. "Thanks for the coffee."

SARAH WATERS SETTLED in behind her computer in the outer office of Houston Investigations and started in. She had gotten so used to the task that she could generate invoices while her mind was on autopilot. The invoices were all in the same format and generally said the same things, so for the most part all she needed to do was to change the names, dates, and some of the details on her invoice template, save it, and move on to the next one. That left her mind free to dig around in her mental trash cans, and on this particular day that did not seem to be an asset.

The door to the inner office was just behind her, and it was open. Ever since Marty had left she had thought of it as Al's, through seniority if nothing else, but Al never spent any time in there. The issues that Sarah had organized and laid out for Al still lay unmolested in their various file folders on the desk, no closer to resolution than they had been when she had first generated the paperwork. Alessandra, Sarah thought, might be great at her job, she was smart, tough, and seemingly without fear, not to mention being younger, taller, and with a nicer ass and better hair than Sarah, but she was not the model executive.

You're doing it again, she told herself, you're comparing her exterior to your interior. Means nothing. And your hair is not so bad... Alessandra has her insecurities, you can bet on that, it's just that she simply excels at keeping them hidden. The point being, Sarah told herself, that you can't keep leaving everything for Al to make the decisions on because if she doesn't want to deal with it, she procrastinates, and nothing gets resolved. Their liability insurance was one example, Agatha West's case was another. You've asked Martillo about both of them at least three times now, Sarah thought, to no avail. Why not just be a big girl and deal? Easier to get forgiveness than permission anyhow. She got up, went into the inner office, retrieved two manila folders and brought them out to her desk.

She had gotten four quotes on the insurance policy. Two of them were outlandishly expensive, the third merely exorbitant. The fourth one seemed almost reasonable, but she was not quite sure the agent who'd quoted her had really understood what she'd wanted. Insurance is worthless if it doesn't cover what you need it to... She looked over the paperwork again, both her letters to the agent and his replies. She couldn't find any obvious holes, but you really needed to be a lawyer or have OCD to figure out the gobbledygook... Forget it, she told herself. We need a certificate to send to Hyatt before we can start doing their work, and we really need to start doing their work. Besides, nothing is going to go wrong.

Hopefully. What could happen?

She called the agent who'd quoted the cheapest price and told him she was sending him a binder, then she generated the check, sealed it in the proper envelope, and put in into the outgoing mail.

There, she thought. One down.

She really didn't need to look at the West file...

JAKE WEST LIVED *in the apartment upstairs from his studio. The place had been decorated in a style that might have been lifted straight out of the pages of* Men Without Women Monthly. *The walls were white, the floors were black. Black leather couch, white bookshelves, black-and-white area rugs done in an abstract geometric pattern. Ginormous widescreen television. Aseptic kitchen done in black, white, and stainless steel, looked like it had never been used. Sterile, she thought, nothing in the place to give you any real clue as to the nature of the man...*

Her knees were unsteady, her palms damp, and her pulse thumped so loud in her temples that she was sure he could hear it. All the usual "what if" questions raged through her mind, one after the other. Her fear and self-consciousness stopped just short of paralysis, though, she did not trust herself to speak, but she could still walk. She didn't know what to say anyhow, all of the real negotiations between Jake and herself had, thus far, been nonverbal, consisting of fleeting eye contact, a gentle touch here and there, electricity in the space between them, generated, she hoped, mutually. She walked next to him as he showed her his place. "It's on the small side, but I like it," he told her, seemingly oblivious to her torment. Maybe he's not feeling this the way I am, she thought, maybe he's still thinking about his stepmother... But then he turned, looked at her, and she knew. Your eyes tell on you, Jake... "Lots of light," he went on after a moment. "And a great view from the back porch. Can't see it now, of course, it's too dark, plus, it's a real disaster out there. It's been converted into a sunroom and I use it as my work space, so, you know, it's a complete mess."

"Show me," she said, hoarse.

"Really? It's just clay, you know, paints and easels and sketches taped up, it's not..." He met her eyes again. "Right this way," he said. He walked her over to a door, opened it, hit a light switch on his way into the room. He walked over and stood by a wooden table that had a smooth steel top. A rough clay bust of a man's head and shoulders stood on the table. The features were not yet well-defined, but from her spot in the doorway Sarah thought she could feel something coming from the sculpture, a sense of strength, lessons learned, time gone past. For sure she could smell the

faint damp earthy scent of the clay, the tang of the oil paints, even the dusty cotton smell of the canvas. "This room is what sold me on the place," he told her. "I love this room."

"Yeah," she said, swallowing with difficulty, trying to re-imagine what she had been thinking when she'd made her decision. You already made up your mind once, she told herself. You even told Martillo what you were going to do... Desire was a half-wild mare that she'd kept shut up too long in the barn. She looked at Jake, who stood with his back to her, one hand just touching the clay bust, his fingertips barely caressing the hair as though it were his child's... For once she allowed herself to feel what she wanted instead of merely thinking about it. Thus unchained, her desire leaped past her fears and overpowered her reason. You're here once, she thought, don't let your doubts ruin everything... With a shaking hand she reached for the light switch.

She needn't have been afraid.

They retired to the bedroom in between the first rush of madness and the second, although the second time it was not like true insanity, it was slower and more deliberate, which was better in a way because you didn't fall off the cliff before you got where you needed to go, and in another way it was worse because she couldn't blame it on the moment...

Black sheets, she thought, after. Guys are so funny. She sat up in the bed, reveled in the sensation of cool air on her skin. Jake pretended not to stare. "Tell me about your brother," she said.

"Izzy?"

"Yeah," she said. "Was he like you? Did you guys hang out? I never had a brother or a sister, I always wondered what it would be like."

Jake nodded, stared off into space for a moment. "Well, we were much different," he said. "I was never any good in school because I couldn't pay attention, and in any sort of math class I would just lose consciousness. But I always knew what my thing was gonna be. Izzy, he was the opposite, he aced every class he ever took, especially the ones that had to do with numbers. I guess he got that from the old man. And you know, he was a couple years older than me so he was always bossing me around when we were kids, and I resented that, so we would fight. And then, when Clytemnestra came along she got between us. We didn't, you know...When you're trying to..." He turned and looked at her.

Lord, those dark eyes... Thank you, God, she thought.

"I shouldn't generalize," he said. "Sloppy thinking. Here's what I was trying not to say: I got so focused on, on, ah, keeping my soul safe where Clytemnestra couldn't get at it, on survival, and then finally on breaking loose, Izzy and I lost each other. In my heart I always felt guilty about that, you know, like I ran out on him or something."

"Did you leave before he did?"

"No, he got away first."

"So how could you feel like you deserted him?"

He reached over, underneath the sheet, put a hand on her thigh. She shivered under the touch of his rough skin. "What you feel about somebody," he said, his eyes boring into her, "it's not about the facts, it's not about the sequence of events. It doesn't have anything to do with words. The feeling comes up out of where you live, it is its own truth. We only grope for the words afterward, when we're trying to explain it to someone. Or to ourselves."

"I see." She slid her hand over his.

He smiled. "If Izzy were here, well, all right, if he were here he'd be really embarrassed, but if he heard that statement he'd call it fuzzy sentimental hogwash. He'd say that humans can't conceptualize without words, that we'd only have vague generalized urges with no tools to properly understand them."

"The artist and the mathematician."

"Funny, though," he said. "Izzy called me just before he died. 'There's more to life than work,' he told me. 'Let's get together and go fishing or something.' We probably hadn't talked in over a year."

"That is funny," Sarah said. "What do you suppose came over him?"

"His birthday," Jake said. "He was turning thirty, and he said all he'd ever done in his life was work. So we made a date, okay, second week in August or whatever it was. And a week after I talked to him he lost control of his bike and he was gone."

"I thought he was killed in a sailboat race."

He looked at her. "Please. The only way to die on a sailboat these days is to get drunk, fall off the boat onto the pier, and break your neck. But actually, he was on his way up to Newport, Rhode Island, he had signed up to crew on a boat. He never got there, and when they went looking for him they found him in the trees alongside the highway. They said the front tire on his bike blew out and it must have thrown him off. He loved going too fast. I guess he got that from the old man, too."

"Wow. I don't even know what to say."

"You see?" he told her. "The feeling has primacy, it comes first. You only figure out the words for it later. But I just wish I could have been different, that I could have been a bit less focused on just getting by, you know, more, I don't know..."

"Be different now," she told him.

He stared at her, the question in his eyes, unasked.

"Can't you feel something that you want right now? Something alive?"

"Yeah," he said. "Yeah, I can."

"Me, too," she said, and she kicked the black sheet down out of the way, reached for him just as he reached for her, and she knew he was right, she would never have the words to nail down exactly what she felt, right then.

And she was sure he hadn't killed anyone.

GOD, HE'D BEEN so different from Frank. Jake was quieter, for one thing, he didn't rush, for another, and he seemed interested in all of her, physically, and not just the usual targets. Not Frank, in other words. It was an unfair comparison, she knew, but she'd had no interest in fairness at the time, and little since. Frank would always be Frank, and somehow she no longer felt it her responsibility to nudge him along the path into adulthood. Could one night with Jake West really be so liberating? Still, Frank had done it to her again, he'd insinuated himself back into her life because now she couldn't stop worrying about what the hell had happened to him.

You idiot, she told herself, you think Frank went through all this crap just to get back under your skin? But that hardly seemed to matter. Just when she'd nearly gotten him crammed into the mental closet labeled ex-husband, he had broken free and once again occupied way too much space in her head. She was almost sorry she'd gotten Martillo involved, almost wished that she'd been able to walk away clean. Should have given him the room to sink or swim on his own, she thought. Whoever those guys outside of Costello's had been, if they had just gotten to him before he'd reached the restaurant she could have stood outside in the freezing cold for maybe another fifteen minutes and then felt justified for forgetting all about him and going on home, and about her life.

Oh, Sarah, she told herself. That's cold…

The phone rang, jarring her back to the present. It was Al. "Hello, Miss Martillo," she said.

A pause, then: "Mrs. Waters. How the hell are you?"

"Al, I sent a check to an insurance company for the liability policy."

"Did you? Great. Good job."

You see, Sarah told herself. Handle your business and let Al do what she does. Al does not care about liability insurance…

"Listen, Sarah, can you do me a favor? See if you can find out who owns that warehouse Palermo Imports was using. And see if they own anything else. Look under Palermo Imports, but try Paolo Torrente, too. Can you do that?"

"Of course," Sarah said. "Listen, what would you think about me setting up a meeting between Jake and Agatha West? He said he'd be willing to talk to her under the right conditions. Basically, what that means is that you and I would have to be there to make sure nothing too weird goes down."

"Sounds all right to me. Refresh my memory, here. She thinks he's a nut job and he thinks she's a psycho. Was that about right?"

"Yeah," Sarah said, "more or less. He thinks she killed his father. She says he blames her for everything that went wrong with his life, mostly because she's the last one standing."

"It's all coming back to me," Al said. "Didn't the cops think Jake and his brother had something to do with his father's death?"

"Yeah, that was one of the theories."

"So what do you think?"

"I think that because I found him I'm done with the case, Al, and I think we won't get paid if we don't deliver, and I think we're too close to broke to let that happen. I think we should get the two of them in the same area code, let them do what they need to do, and get our money."

"Can you do it?" Al asked her. "Can you set it up so everybody feels safe? And walks away with a whole skin?"

"Yeah," Sarah said. "I think so."

"West residence." It was a deep male voice.

"I'm sorry," Sarah said. "I thought I was calling Dr. West's cell phone."

"They're linked," the man said in his cultured baritone. "How can I help you?"

"I'm Sarah Waters. Would it be possible for me to speak to Dr. West?"

"Please hold."

No music while they have you waiting, Sarah thought. One minor point in their favor… She'd heard the voice before, though, the one that answered the phone, and she tried to remember where. The guy came back on the line. "Mrs. West is feeling particularly unwell at the moment. Is there a message? Or perhaps I could help you with something…"

"I don't think I want to leave a message," Sarah said. "Maybe she'll feel better tomorrow, I'll try back then."

"We've met, Mrs. Waters. My name is Mitchell Haig. I am Mrs. West's personal assistant and driver. I'm quite sure you would not be violating any confidences by leaving a message with me. I am aware that she hired your firm to locate her stepson."

"Oh, I remember now." He was the former Bentley mechanic. "You were with the car that day. You're, ah, folically challenged."

"Bald. That would be me."

"I see. Well, you can tell Dr. West that I have good news for her."

"You found him?" Haig's tone of voice changed completely. "Wow. That's great news." He sounded, suddenly, less educated, more human. His careful demeanor must be like the coat he wears to work, Sarah thought, and it just slipped. She wondered who the real Mitchell Haig was, and what he was like. "And she could use some good news, let me tell you."

Made his day, Sarah thought. You'd have thought it was *his* son I found. Nice, when the people who work for you like you that much. "Well, don't overpromise, Mr. Haig. Jacob is willing to meet with her, but he does have certain conditions. My partner and I would have to guarantee his safety."

"I am certain whatever guarantees he requires will not be an obstacle. Mrs. West is most anxious to see him again." He recovered, got some of that dispassionate distance back. "If I could trouble you to hold for me one more time…"

He came back. "I am truly sorry, Mrs. Waters, but she really is feeling rather ill this afternoon. I must tell you, though, you did manage to put a smile on her face. Mrs. West spends her weekends at her estate in Manhasset, and she swears that this weekend will be no different, regardless of how she's feeling. It's rather a large property, I'm sure we could satisfy Jacob's requirements. If he's uncomfortable in the house, we could arrange for the two of them to see one another in the driveway, or the gazebo, or on the beach behind the house, or in the middle of the village, if that's what he'd prefer. Just let me know."

"I'll try to arrange it, Mr. Haig."

"Thank you very much," he said. "Very much. We'll be waiting for your call."

Well, you made a sick old lady smile, she thought. But now you have to go back to work…

Some time spent searching told Sarah that there were a lot of Paolo Torrentes and that some of them did indeed live and own property in the city of New York. None of them, however, had any vested interest in a warehouse on Staten Island. She organized her results and printed them out, even though nothing there seemed promising or even relevant.

She didn't do much better looking under the name Palermo Imports. Again, she found pages of results that had nothing to do with prospective wine merchants on Staten Island or anywhere else, but she did find an item in the archive section of the *Staten Island Advance.* When she read the story, though, it didn't tell her anything she didn't already know, except, perhaps, what a positive development Palermo Imports had been for a hurting neighborhood.

How many Torrentes in Palermo, Italy? she wondered, and when she looked she found a whole tribe of them. Another hour of searching, compounded by a balky on-line Italian-English translating program, told her more about the Torrente clan than she wanted to know. Their number included two dentists, a college professor, a whole family of stonemasons, a proctologist, and a twenty-one-year-old who had strangled his father with a wire coat hanger, but no wine brokers or merchants. Poor Frank, she thought, feeling a pang, they were scamming you from day one... If she and Frank had still been together, maybe she would have done this search back when he'd first started working for Torrente. Yeah, she thought, but back before you knew Martillo, would you have been suspicious enough? Or would you have taken it all at face value and simply felt good for Frank, who might finally have caught a break?

Sarah, she told herself, try to focus. You're not supposed to be surfing, here, you're at work. She looked at Property-Shark.com, found the records of the warehouse sale, and discovered her first piece of relevant information: the warehouse had been purchased by one Frank Waters, of Brooklyn, New York.

What the hell? she thought. Frank didn't have enough

money to buy a warehouse. She'd have been surprised if he'd had enough dough to buy a bicycle… How could he have even scraped together enough for an acceptable down payment? And even if he had, what kind of fool would have given Frank a mortgage on a run-down warehouse in a questionable neighborhood in Staten Island? He had no business, no collateral, no credentials. He had a good line of shit, that was true enough, but not the kind that would generally work on a banker.

Maybe Torrente gave him the money, she thought, but why would the guy do something like that? He'd only known Frank for a month or so. You got to figure, she told herself, if the guy is intelligent enough to run a business he has to be smart enough to know better than to give money to a guy like Frank, who despite whatever fine qualities he might possess, had been demonstrably allergic to prosperity his whole life.

Alessandra is right, she told herself. Whatever these guys are up to, the wine was just a cover.

She searched the name Palermo Imports again and could not find anyone doing business in the State of New York under that name, so she found a website for a company that would help you incorporate yourself for twenty-five bucks. After some hesitation she paid the money and requested the name Palermo Imports. The site asked her to wait while its search engine chewed through the databases checking for duplicates. Sarah took advantage of the delay to go out for coffee. She successfully avoided the scones, donuts, turnovers, rolls, cannoli, et al, and when she got back her computer told her that the name she requested was available and that she could register it for an additional fee.

It pissed her off.

Frank had been born one generation prior to the internet revolution. He wasn't really a bad guy, maybe not the best husband or father in the world, but still, he was a guy who had tried, as long as she'd known him, to improve himself. It had been his firm belief, justified or not, that all he ever needed was the opportunity. Torrente, or whoever he was, had seen that, had used it to his advantage.

She burned...

She tried PropertyShark.com again, looked to see what other real estate Frank Waters owned. There were three other properties, two in Manhattan and one in the Bronx, but when she dug deeper she found that the Frank Waters in the Bronx was black and the ages of the other two did not match. Then, out of curiosity, she tried her own name, then her maiden name.

One hit.

Sure, there were other Sarahs, but the sales involving them had all taken place more than six months ago. Paolo Torrente hadn't even hired Frank until after that...

The property in question was an enormous Victorian wreck on the southwestern shore of Staten Island. The property taxes had been in arrears at the time of the sale, so Sarah called the city. "My husband," she told the surprisingly helpful clerk who answered the phone, "must be the most disorganized man on the planet. I know the bank was supposed to clear up the property tax situation after the sale, but the bank we dealt with was merged with Citibank and my husband misplaced the paperwork..."

"If you hold for just a moment I can look that up for you," the man said. She waited, and a few minutes later he came back on the line. "Eighty-four hundred and twenty-six bucks," the guy told her. "Probably a shock, I know, but you still have some time. Shall I send another copy of the bill?"

"Can you do that? Thank you so much. Wait, let me give you my work address..."

The sale of the house was fairly recent, so she checked

the listing agent's website, and sure enough it was still there. At the time the pictures had been taken the place had apparently been occupied by a very old man. Sarah surmised that the guy's wife had died because when she looked at the shots of the interior it seemed to her that the dust everywhere and the dogs lying on the couch did not go with the yellowed lace doilies or the badly tarnished silver tea set. A woman had lived there, certainly, but not recently. Another sad story, another lonely guy playing out the hand, waiting for the game to end.

The house was set on a large lot that looked like it had been created by dumping gravel into a swamp, because out behind the place the tall reeds stood in a row just beyond the huge detached garage that sat near the back property line. In the distance the Arthur Kill reeked, Sarah wrinkled her nose at the thought of the wind blowing in off the bay. God, she thought, is there any water left out there at all? When you looked down on it from one of the bridges, the Arthur Kill sometimes looked like it ran with automotive anti-freeze. And on the far shore loomed the enormous oil refineries of Jersey, and the concrete wastelands and vast parking lots of Newark Airport beyond that. Paradise on earth… Who would want such a place?

She supposed that one might get used to the smell, eventually…

She searched for the seller's name, spent some time looking at the hits, but she couldn't decide if any of them might be the right person so she went back to the agent's website, looked up his phone number, and called him up. He wasn't there, of course, but he returned Sarah's call about a half hour later. Family pictures, she told the man, I'm sure the family would want to have them… They might, the man told her, sounding doubtful, you could send them along. It's the assisted-living facility down in Cherry Hill, New

Jersey…But he might still be angry about how long it took that check to clear. Six whole weeks! Why on earth couldn't you transfer the money out of the Bank of Dubai into an American bank? It would have made everything so much easier. God, the phone calls he'd had to endure…

Sarah thanked him and hung up.

No mortgage, she thought, not if they all had to wait for a check. If there had been a mortgage company involved, they wouldn't even schedule a closing until they had the money in their hot little hands. So Sarah Rizzo, whoever she was, either she or her benefactors, had paid for a ramshackle firetrap on the crusty side of Staten Island, using money from a long ways off.

You could go knock on the door, she told herself, pretend to be the Welcome Wagon lady, just to see what the other Sarah looks like…

She called up Google Earth, looked at the satellite view. Big house, swampland out behind, not a lot of other houses around it, truck parked in the driveway.

And so what? she thought. Quit wasting time. She refocused her searches, trying to get more information on the other sale on Staten Island, the warehouse on the opposite side of the borough. Eventually she tired of that and went back to what she'd really come to the office for, which was to catch up on invoices, and then, around dinnertime, she checked her list of hotel restaurants pending investigation, picked one, locked up, and left for the day.

ALESSANDRA MARTILLO PAUSED at the top of the hill on Atlantic, two blocks from her building. The cab had just pulled to a stop, half on the sidewalk, right outside the bar on the first floor. A guy got out, from the distance she could not be positive, but the dude looked too much like the man who'd been looking for her over on Pineapple Street.

You've got to be kidding me, she thought. When am I gonna catch a break? If it was the same guy, he was still using the cab, which stood to reason, he could drive it anywhere, park it anywhere, and no one would think twice about him, and there were thousands of other taxis to help him blend in. But when she thought about the old guy driving it she could not believe this cab had been hired by The Harkonnen Group, whoever the hell they really were, whatever the hell they were really after. She'd been thinking of them as The Rectangle State Brigade, and a fat old Irish guy flying under the radar definitely did not fit their mold.

A government contractor, being paid by the Homeland Security department. And why the hell would the government use a contractor, anyhow? Maybe because you could get a contractor to go where cops wouldn't or couldn't go and, more important, do things a cop wouldn't or couldn't do.

All right, she thought, if this guy isn't with Harkonnen, what the hell does he want? Could he have something to do with Daniel Caughlan? Caughlan was in prison, true, but while she had been on Caughlan's payroll Al had annoyed some rather unpleasant people, including, at times, Caughlan himself. It was not outside the realm of possibility that one of them might have paid for a hit, but it was difficult for her to believe they'd hire a gunman who looked like an Irish Saint Nick…

Not that it mattered at the moment, out on this dark and cold evening. You're gonna have to deal with this guy sooner or later, Al told herself, but it had been a long day and she was tired. All I really want, she thought… Yeah, sure, okay, but I'll settle for a nice warm bed. She walked over and stood in a restaurant entryway to get some shelter from the cold damp wind blowing up the avenue off Upper New York Bay. You really need to find a safe place, she told herself, but how are you gonna manage that when you can barely swing the rent for one lousy room over a bar? But insecurity, both financial and personal, seemed to be the price she had to pay for her independence.

Which did not make her feel any warmer.

She turned and walked east on Atlantic, away from the cab, away from her bed, away from warmth. Her cell started ringing, but when she looked at the screen she did not recognize the number so she didn't take the call. Her paranoia in high gear, she searched until she found a working pay phone. They were much less plentiful than they used to be.

She didn't need to look at her cell, her memory gave her the number she wanted to call. As she punched it in she was flooded with sorrow, because the man whose number this had once been, the man she really wanted to talk to, was gone.

A familiar voice answered. "Hello?"

"Hi, Ant." It was about all she could manage.

"Al! Is that you? Alessandra?"

"Yeah," she said.

"Are you all right?"

"Well…"

He knew. Maybe it was because he knew her so well, or maybe it was because she only called him when she was in trouble. "Al," he said. "Come home. Do you need a ride?"

"I can make it," she said.

ANTHONY OPENED THE door of his brick house in Queens and stood aside for her to enter. Alessandra, embarrassed, stood on the stoop. "Oh, come on in," he said with a faint smile. "Come inside." She entered, took off her shoes in the entryway, then went in and took the seat he offered her at his tiny dining room table. "Just a moment," he said, and he vanished into the kitchen.

She could smell tea. He knows I hate that stuff, she thought, but when he came out bearing a tray laden with a daintily flowered china teapot and matching cups, the kind with handles too small to stick your finger through and saucers to match, she relented. He took so much pleasure in the acquisition, preparation, and serving of his favorite beverage that she would drink it just so she didn't spoil it for him. And it was the real thing, too, no tea bags in this house...

He sat down opposite her. "Are you all right?"

"Yeah," she said, dispirited. "I'm okay."

He smiled again. "Really?"

"Ah, you know, it's just work."

He laughed at that.

"Well, you know what I mean," she said. "Somebody wants to talk to me and I'm not particularly interested in hearing what they have to say. When I got back to my building tonight, the guy was camped out on my doorstep."

"When I don't feel like talking," Anthony said, "I don't answer the phone."

"Well, this guy seems a bit more persistent than that."

"Oh, well, you know you can't be too careful."

"You're messing with me, aren't you."

"I?" He went all wide-eyed and innocent. "Alessandra, please, you're a trained investigator, I would never dream of attempting to mislead you in any way. Besides, I know you can take care of yourself, but after all, honey, you are still a woman all alone in the big city, you have to be cautious and use your head."

"Now I know you're messing with me."

"Perhaps a bit," he said. "Now I'm going to ask you a serious question, so don't get all proud and insulted, because I want a serious answer."

"I'm ready," she said.

"Are you afraid of this person?"

He'd been right to prick her balloon first, he'd given her a way to put her pride aside and give him an honest answer. "No, I don't think so," she told him.

He steepled his fingers, rested his chin on them. "This isn't like you, Alessandra," he said. "Normally you would have…" He searched for the correct word. "You would have discouraged the gentleman first, then repented later when you discovered he was only the Fuller Brush man attempting to leave off some coupons."

"Come on, Ant, I told you guys I was sorry. How long am I gonna have to keep paying for that? That had to be ten years ago, at least—"

"Really? Seems like only yesterday. But still, you haven't found a way to properly communicate your lack of interest to this gentleman, such as rupturing his spleen, for instance. Why not?"

"I just wanted to go lay down, you know what I mean? And there he was. I guess he was just the last straw."

"Bad day?"

"It's been a lot more than a day. Ever since Roberto died…" She looked up, sorry at once that she'd said it, sorry to have caused more pain, but Anthony just regarded her gravely. His self-control was cast in steel and he would do his mourning in private. The face Anthony wore was the one he wanted you to see, and it was probably all of him you would ever see. She had never gotten past it. She wondered, growing up as an outcast the way he had, a gay child in a straight world, if that had been the only way he'd found to survive.

Talk about lonely…

"In my job," she told him, "I don't get to see the good side of anyone. You know what I mean? Most of the people who come to us, it's like they're on fire, they're all worried the other person is going to get over on them. 'Find the money,' they say, and then it becomes 'Find my money. And catch him with his whore.' And when I do it they hate me, too. Plus, I have a new partner now, all the time she's out there, Ant, I'm scared to death that something bad is going to happen to her. And her ex, he got involved with some bad guys from Palermo, I'm pretty sure they're smuggling something into the country, I don't know what yet, and I don't know what they did to him, either, but he's missing. So his chances of seeing his kid ever again are not too good."

"Palermo, Italy?"

"Yes."

"Heroin?"

"Probably," she said. "Most of the time the easiest answer is the right one."

"I suppose," he said. "But you think your partner's ex stumbled across what they were doing and they killed him for it."

"That would be the charitable assumption," she said. "I mean, you take this guy, never had any money, he's waiting for his big break—"

"I get it," he said. "So all you really need to do is just get through with what you're doing now, and then take a few days off. You deserve a break."

"I don't know, Ant, it isn't just the case, it's everything. I mean, I wanna call my father, but I can't, it's like trying to talk to a bag of walnuts. My boss is an asshole, he's in a wheelchair in this place down in Coney Island and I really think he's gonna sit there in a puddle of his own wee-wee until he finds a way to die, this guitar player I was seeing is fucking the singer in his new band, I've got these pricks from the Department of Homeland Security trying to put me on a leash, I can't sleep anymore, I haven't been eating right, when I moved I lost my fucking winter coat…"

He was smiling at her. "A sea of troubles," he said.

"I should know who wrote that, right? I guess they must have covered that in English class after I dropped out."

"Don't get huffy," he told her. "I'm sure you've encountered the principle somewhere along the line, all the great writers have covered it, Buddha, Jesus, Shakespeare, Popeye the Sailor. Life is suffering. When you ask God to take all of your problems away, what you're really asking for, when you think about it, is to die. Because right up until the very moment of that unhappy occasion, you will have problems. So do you gulp down your spinach and fight with Bluto or do you lie there while he carries Olive Oyl off into the bushes somewhere to have his way with her? That is the question. When Hamlet finally decided to fight back he was all but too late. I always thought if he had acted with a bit more dispatch he might have survived the play."

"I never liked Olive Oyl," Al said. "I didn't mind her being all skinny and whatever, but that voice would drive me out of my mind."

"Well, yes, if she had only shut up once in a while." He eyed her. "You already know all of this, Alessandra. Why don't you tell me the real problem?"

He waited while she wrestled with it. "Roberto was my anchor," she finally said. "With him gone, there's a hole, and I don't know how to fill it."

"I miss him, too." Anthony's control might have slipped just for a second, ever so slightly, but then he had it back. "Your uncle was never one for a lot of introspection, you know. I'm sure you can tell me what he'd say to you if he were here."

She nodded. "Turn off that television," she said, making her voice as low and raspy as she could. "Get out of here and go do something."

"Give it hell," he said. "That's the way he lived his life."

She nodded. "He didn't seem to worry about much."

"Thank you," Anthony said, "for drinking the tea. I know you are just indulging me, but you know this is the first chance I've had to use my new tea service. It was Lady Di's favorite, you know."

"How the hell did you get your mitts on it?"

"Not this exact one, you cretin."

"Ah. And you couldn't use it before now because…"

He held the dainty cup up to the light. "Perfectly acceptable when one has company," he told her. "But I could never use it when I'm here alone. Too gay."

"You know something, Anthony, I can never be sure whether or not you're jerking my chain," she said.

"There's a comfort," he said. "Your bedroom, madam, is where it has always been. I do wish you would use it more often."

"Thank you. Did you really like Popeye when you were young?"

"Honey, when I was young all the sailors were crazy about me…"

SEVENTEEN

AL SAT IN her uncle's van with the engine running. She was parked next to a hydrant on Smith Street in Brooklyn and it was cold out, cold, cold. Even with the defroster running, the windshield was rimmed with ice. There were no legal parking spots available anywhere on Smith Street, but she sat there waiting, working on the theory that someone would eventually have to come out and drive somewhere, otherwise why have the car? Twenty minutes later she had a shot when a spot opened up on the opposite side of the street, but she got aced out by a bread truck. She tried to be angry and curse the guy, but he was just doing his job, after all, so she circled the block, meaning to go back by the hydrant again, but she happened upon someone leaving in a minivan on one of the side streets and she outgunned a Toyota Camry to get the spot. The guy behind the wheel of the Toyota honked his horn and yelled at her, but when she got out of the van and began walking in his direction he pulled out and drove away.

The business card Bobby Fallon had given her was in her bag. She'd tried calling the number on it, but her call was taken by someone who claimed, with definite traces of irony in his voice, that he'd be happy to take a message to relay to Mr. Fallon. She thought about hanging up, but she gave him the message instead. "Please tell Mr. Fallon that I remembered something about the parking valet from that night at Costello's, no, I'd much rather talk to Mr. Fallon about it myself, please have him call me back and I'll be happy to discuss it with him…" The man's tone left no doubt in her mind that he felt confident Mr. Fallon had more important things to do with his time.

Hey, I tried, she thought.

It was too cold to lurk somewhere nearby and wait for her guy to come out so she walked up to the building, paused in the urine-scented entryway to look at the broken mailboxes, then pushed open the inner door, which should have been locked, and stepped into the first-floor hallway.

Right then she realized that it was going to be tougher than she'd planned on, because while the entryway had smelled bad, the first-floor hallway was worse. To Alessandra, it smelled like poverty. It smelled like a communal toilet down the hall, like too many people in too small a space, like bad food, dirty diapers, mice, misery. It smelled like her aunt Magdalena's place. The reek wrapped itself around her senses like a wet bedsheet. Living on the street, she thought, would be better than this. She had made that choice, once.

At the far end of the dimly lit hall a fat woman with thinning hair pushed herself through a doorway on a wheeled office chair. "Who are you looking for?" Her voice was a hostile screech that went high and thin with fear as Al, suddenly angry, strode in her direction. "What do you want? What business do you have here?" She shoved with her feet and she and her chair disappeared back from whence she'd come. "Leave us alone!" she howled, and the door slammed behind her.

Al pounded on the door with a fist when she got there. "Open up!" she shouted, enraged. On her way down the hall she had looked through an open door and seen what had been done to the building. The apartments had been chopped up and what had once been individual rooms was now a warren of tiny cubicles crudely fashioned out of two-

by-fours and particleboard. A one-bedroom apartment that
had once housed a small family was now home to dozens of
men. These places spring up in the viler corners of the outer
boroughs, and they are generally patronized by immigrants
sending money home to families in China, Central America, or India, families they might not see again for years.
Newspapers and police call them illegal rooming houses,
but the term falls far short of accurate description. They
are firetraps, diseased carriers of blight and human misery,
sinkholes of despair. Al had seen them before, and as always she was incensed by the poverty of human spirit that
would lead a landlord to do such a thing to fellow human
beings, let alone a building. "Open this fucking door or I'll
be back here in ten minutes with a housing inspector and a
warrant for your arrest!"

Empty threats, but they got the door opened a crack.
"These are poor people who live here! We have nothing for
you! Leave us alone!"

The woman's accent troubled Al, she was not Hispanic
or Italian. Al put a shoulder against the door and shoved as
hard as she could, knocking the woman's chair over. The
woman sprawled on the floor next to her overturned chair
in the doorway of what was probably the only real living
room left in the building. She flopped over onto her stomach in an attempt to get to her feet, but Al put a knee between the woman's shoulder blades. The woman squalled,
sounding more like a crow in distress than a human. "Shut
up!" Al told her. "Shut up!"

Shutting up was apparently not high on the woman's list
of life skills. "Get out! Get out! We are calling the police!"

"Yeah, sure you are," Al said. "You know what would
happen if the cops ever came to this shithole?" The woman's
use of the word *we* bothered her, though, and she looked
around. There was a door to one of the inner rooms that

had just begun to ease open, and Al saw the yellow wooden baseball bat before she really saw the man holding it, and she leaped up off the fat woman just as he emerged. He held the bat vertically, the business end up next to his ear, all Al had to do was slap the barrel of the bat at his head, which she did, stunning him. She got him twice more in the same manner and he went down, without his bat. He lay where he'd landed without moving.

Al turned back to the woman, who had made it up to her hands and knees, still squalling. Al calmed herself, walked over and laid the head of the bat next to the woman's temple. She went silent at once.

"Better," Al told her.

"We have no money!"

"Yeah, you do," Al told her, "but I don't have time to look for it." She squatted down: "Maybe I'll beat you silly until you tell me where it is. Where are you from?"

"What? What?" the woman sputtered.

Al slowed her words down. "Where do you come from."

The woman spat out a word that Al didn't understand. "Okay. Where is that?"

"Yemen."

"All right. Get up. You and I are gonna take a tour through your little corner of paradise and we're gonna see who's home."

They made a slow tour of the place, the woman muttering and complaining the entire time. The stairs were particularly hard on her, and Al guessed it was the first time she'd seen the upper floors of the building in a long time. Al prodded her along with the bat. The men living in the place were oddly silent, they watched the two women with the passivity of sheep watching the farmer carry his knife to the barn. Maybe they had been behind the bars of the zoo so long that they didn't know, any longer, what to do when someone left the cage door ajar. Al couldn't escape the impression that the woman was an obese black spider sitting at the center of her web, sucking out the soul of anyone who got too close.

The man Al was seeking, the parking valet from Costello's restaurant, was not in evidence. On the way back down, Al paused in the center of each floor and gave the same speech. "Okay, listen up!" she yelled. "One week from today! One week! Seven days! I'm coming back with Immigration! You understand? Seven days! Immigration!" She looked into lifeless eyes, not knowing if they understood her or not. "Don't come back here! Run away, this place is no good for you! One week, don't be here!"

"You're killing me," the woman whispered. "Why do you do this?"

Al stared at the pinched and drawn faces of the men they passed on their way out. "Because these men are human beings, and you are a pig." No one deserves to live like this, she thought, no one. "This is worse than usury."

"No!" the woman shouted. "No! They are…" She went silent when Al hefted the bat.

"There's a room in hell with your name on it," she told the woman, who went pale. "You'll burn for this."

IT WAS WONDERFUL to get back out into the cold clean air. Al hacked and spat, trying to clear the taste of despair out of the back of her throat. Maybe that wasn't a complete waste of time, she thought. Maybe some of those guys will get away, maybe they'll move on, maybe they'll find something better.

SHE DROVE PAST Costello's, still in her uncle's van. There were a few cars in the parking lot, but the lunch crowd would not begin to arrive for at least another hour. Al looked in the cars parked on both sides of the street as she went by, and then she did a slow tour of the neighborhood, doing the same thing. She was looking for someone sitting in a car, someone parked in a spot that gave them a decent view of the restaurant. Finding nothing, she parked up the hill, got out, and took a walk. She saw nothing out of place, no one eyeing her through drawn curtains, no tall guys from Nebraska. Thoroughly chilled, she went back to the van, got inside, fired it up, and cranked the heat to max.

The parking valet arrived on a bicycle about twenty minutes after she got back to the van. She was about a block away, but she was sure it was him, the real one, she had watched him for hours that first night at Costello's and she had a good fix on him. She wondered how to approach the guy. She could knock him in the head and throw him in the back of the van, she could pretend to be with Immigration, she could even dragoon Salathiel Edwards and get him to help out, but in the end she decided on the simple approach, which entailed a trip to an ATM. When she got back, her parking spot was taken so she double-parked nearby and waited for the noonday crowd at Costello's to dissipate.

I should take up knitting, she told herself, it would help me pass the time. And wouldn't that be funny? Me, knitting, that would be like your sweet old grandmother smoking a cigar.

Confuse your enemies, she thought. Mystify your friends.

Probably already doing that...

Finally the parking lot dwindled down to eight cars and Al drove down the hill, pulled up in front of the restaurant, and rolled her window down. The valet trotted over smiling, but he lost the smile when he saw the fifty-dollar bill protruding from Al's fist.

"Senorita?" he said, uncertain.

"I need to talk to you," she told him, and she waggled

the fifty like it was a worm on a fishhook. "This is for your time."

He didn't lunge at the bill, instead he walked around to the front of the van and peered inside.

Cautious man, she thought. He's making sure I'm alone in here.

He went the rest of the way around, opened the passenger-side door, and climbed inside. She handed him the bill. "I'm gonna drive up the block," she told him. "Not far," she said, noting his look of worry. "I don't wanna sit here at the restaurant. They might not like you talking to me."

He nodded. She went back up the hill, pulled a U-turn, and parked pointing downhill. "The other night," she said, "when that man got shot. You were working here that night."

He nodded. "I heard the noise of the shooting. I was parking a car down in the way far end of the lot, I stay over there until everything is finish. I don't see nothing."

His story sounded well-rehearsed. "That's what you told the cops, right? What's your name?" she said.

"Juan," he told her, unhappy.

"Juan what?"

"Juan Castro."

"Any relation?"

"In case he's my uncle, I don't gonna be parking the cars," he said.

"I guess not," she said. "Juanito, you see that red Toyota right there?"

He nodded, looking bleak.

"That night," she told him, "I was parked right there, where that red car is, so I know that you're full of shit."

"No, Senorita, I swear, I was working…"

Sometimes a good lie works better than the truth. "Juan, stop. I saw them drive up in the Lincoln, I watched you park it for them. Then they set off the alarm on that Chevy Suburban, and when the big guy came out they grabbed him and took off. Am I right?"

He just looked down at the floor of the van.

"Juanito, I am not with the police. There's nobody here but you and me. Tell me what happened. I know you were right there, I know you saw everything, and I need to find those guys."

He looked over at her. "Bad people," he said.

"I know," she said. "And they're gonna get what they got coming, but you have to help me find them first."

He sat there thinking about it.

"Juan…"

"Yes," he said. "Yes, okay. The old man with the limp, he comes the day before, he gives me two hundred. His hands are all broken. Somebody work him over good, long time ago. He says, okay, they gonna come tomorrow, they wait for their friend, then they gonna go away with him, please for me to take their car, bring it to such and such a place."

"Smith Street," she said. "Brooklyn."

He looked at her, his eyes wide. "Smith Street."

"So far so good, Juan. How did they trip the alarm on the Suburban?"

"Break the weendow," he said.

"Okay, they broke the window. The big guy came running out. Then what?"

He nodded. "The big guy comes to check his truck, they have guns, they make him get inside and they drive away."

"Okay. How did the one guy get shot?"

Juan swallowed. "His friend, behind him, he is pointing the gun and yelling. His gun shoots, I think he is surprise by that, he jump, like, 'oh shit.' His friend is hit here, in the back." He pointed to his own back, just above his belt.

"Then what?"

"The old man say something, the rest of them shut up and

get into the truck, then the old man shoots the one lying on the ground. Two times in the head. Pop, pop. Then he gets in the truck and they drive away."

"Killed his own man."

He shrugged. "No doctor, no hospital, no police."

"The old man tell you his name?"

"No."

"You sure? Was he Italian?"

"No."

"Not Italian? Are you sure? How do you know?"

"I hear them talk to each other. No Italia."

Son of a bitch, Al thought. Uncle Paolo, who are you? "And then you drove the Lincoln to Smith Street, up off Atlantic."

He nodded. "Bad people in that place. Very bad people."

"Why you say that, Juan?"

He sighed. "Those men inside. They bring those men to the United State. Fifteen thousand each."

"Fifteen grand? Where do guys like that get—"

"The families pay," he said. "They save up, maybe they sell one daughter. Send one son over here to work, he send the money home. From Lebanon, Syria, they do this."

"Sell the daughters? To who?"

He shrugged. "Saudi Arabia. Kuwait. Plenty rich men wanting young girl."

"How do you know all this, Juan?"

"We park your car," he said, shrugging again. "Cook your food, cut your grass. We come here for the working. But we are not stupid. We talk to each other."

"Land of milk and honey," she said.

"Finish now?" he asked her. "I go now?"

"Yeah," she said. "But why'd you do it, Juan? Why'd you deliver the car? You could have sold it."

Juan looked down at the floor again. "Two hundred dollar

more, from the *bruja* up in that house. Plus, that old man, he say he find me. Kill me if I back out."

"You believe him?"

"Yes. I go now? Please…"

"Yeah. Thank you, Juan."

He got out, paused before he shut the door. "Bad people," he said. "I go away from here now. You don't gonna see me anymore."

She watched him walk back down the hill.

"WILL YOU ACCEPT a collect call from Mr. Daniel Caughlan?"

"Yeah." Al was surprised to hear from him. "Yeah, sure."

"Miss Martillo," Caughlan said. "How're you keeping yourself these days?"

"All right," Al said. Caughlan was upstate, in prison, he had to be calling her from the pay phone in jail. Her natural caution kicked in. They have to be taping this, she thought. I sure would, if I had his ass in my jail… "How much time do you get for this call?"

"Time enough," he said. "Talked to Marty the udder day."

"Yeah, he told me," she said. "He tell you what kind of shape he's in?"

"No. Mostly he wanted to talk about how you was fookin' him over, ye ungrateful scut." His Irish accent was noticeably broader than usual. "On yer own now, is it?"

"No. Not yet. Could go either way. You knew he took a bullet in the back at the end of that job we did for you."

"Yeah."

"Well, he's in a wheelchair, and it looks like he's gonna stay in it. He decides to pull himself together and come back, I'll work with him. If he decides to sit in that chair and stare at the wall, there's nothing I can do for him."

"You know something," Caughlan said, "you step on a cockroach, you hear his bones breaking, half the time when you let off he'll get up and run away, broken back and all. I always thought Stiles had plenty of roach in him."

"He hasn't gotten up yet."

"Walk away, then."

"Doesn't feel right."

"Ye've got a generous heart, Martillo. Most men would have walked away already. Don't be a sap. He used you, you hafta know that. Walk away, you don't owe him a t'ing. You ever wonder if walkin' away might not be the kindest choice? Leave him be."

Marty's old buddy, Al thought. "Maybe I'll give him a few more days."

"Listen, Martillo. Don't keep making yeself so hard to get hold of, fer fook's sake."

It clicked then. Caughlan's exaggerated accent went too well with the phone call Sarah had taken in the office from the "Irish-American Mothers and Fathers Association," whatever that really was, and with the rosy-faced cabdrivers who'd turned up on her doorstep, twice. They were all linked, but she would get nowhere asking Caughlan about it, he would never talk about it over the prison phone, and he might not, regardless of the circumstances. "I get nervous when people I don't know show up asking for me," she told him. You never knew with guys like Caughlan. She'd always had the feeling that he genuinely liked her, but that would not necessarily stop him from selling her out if the conditions were right. Caughlan had risen to the top of his chosen field of endeavor by climbing over bodies, some of them his friends'. "Everyone keeps telling me I'm paranoid, but then every once in a while somebody shows up and tries to kick my ass."

"I do understand," he said, "but I got every confidence that they'll have a hard job of it. Anyhow, do me this one favor, Martillo, since I'm stuck in this God-awful hole for anudder year, go on and have a pint for me."

"Sure," she said. "Be glad to."

"And none of this damn drinking it out of a paper bag in some bodega, neither," he said. "Go on and sit downstairs from yer place and sit down inside a proper saloon like the civilized girl I know ye'd like to be."

Downstairs? He knows where I live? And he wants me to meet someone there. But for what? Is he setting me up? "You're such a sweet talker."

"Good," he said. "Monday afternoon, say. Listen, Martillo, I never thanked you properly for seein' after my son."

"I just did what I thought was right."

"Yeah, I know," he said. "Don't forget about that beer."

He hung up.

AL WALKED ACROSS the park and got into the front passenger side of a black Chevrolet gypsy cab that sat curbside on Cadman Plaza in Brooklyn. The car looked like it had been painted with a brush and the windows were darkened. Salathiel Edwards sat behind the wheel. He looked over at Al, then pulled away from the curb without comment.

"What's up?" Al asked him.

"Thanks for coming," he said.

He turned onto Tillary Street and drove down to the entry ramp to the Brooklyn-Queens Expressway. It was an elevated section that ran past the Fort Greene housing project. The cars on the clogged highway were barely moving.

"We going somewhere?" Al said.

"No," Edwards told her. "Just need a safe place to shoot the shit."

"Okay."

He let a minute pass. "Alessandra," he finally said. "Are you a patriotic American?"

She was surprised by the question. "What?"

He elbowed his way into the center lane, settled in behind a UPS truck. "Do you," he said, "consider yourself a patriotic American?" He shifted in his seat so he could stare over at her.

She shrugged. "I guess. I never thought about it much. Why?"

He didn't answer right away. "That sounds like a truthful answer," he finally said.

"Sal, what's going on?"

"I could be suspended for talking to you," he told her. "Actually, I could be fired. I want you to understand how serious this is. I could lose my pension over this conversation."

"You got my attention, Sal."

"Good," he said. "The Harkonnen Group."

"What about 'em?"

"They were contracted by Homeland Security to map the arms trade. What's on the table, what's under the table, gray market, black market, who's got what, where it is, where it came from, who's buying, how it gets from point A to point B, how does the money change hands. What Homeland Security wanted was a second opinion from an independent source, one with no axes to grind. The Harkonnen Group is completely separate from the intelligence community."

"Okay."

"The job took almost two years. Cost the government something like seven million bucks."

"How do you know all this?"

"I was briefed," he told her. "Your name came up. Matter of fact, that's the only reason I was in the room."

"You gotta be kidding me."

"No," he said. "One of the active groups in the market is a bunch that specializes in weapons delivery. They're smugglers, basically. They are not particularly political, but they work mostly in Africa and the Middle East. They've worked for just about everyone except the Israelis. They used to be based in Libya, but they moved out when Qaddafi lost his enthusiasm for the business. We don't know precisely where they call home now."

"What's all this got to do with me?"

He sighed. "One of their operatives turned up in New York. In the parking lot of a restaurant in Brooklyn. Costello's. You know the place, I believe. The man was dead, professionally done, one in the torso, two in the head, two separate weapons. You were there."

"Yeah," Al said. "I was inside."

"What the fuck were you doing there, Al?"

"My partner got a phone call from her ex."

"Frank Waters," Sal said.

"Yeah," she said, surprised. "He said he wanted to see her, but she was afraid of him. I went along so she'd have someone on her side if things got weird."

"Frank Waters," Sal told her, "is on a watch list. He is associated with a group of far-right-wing nuts. Ex-military, white supremacist, burn down Washington D.C., and start over again lunatics. So he meets with two or more members of a known group of arms smugglers, he caps one, the rest of them drive away. You figure it out."

"No fucking way. Frank Waters would never—"

"We have him on video, Al, marching, protesting, making speeches. He's made no secret of his opinions about the U.S. government. Now he's been seen with people who move weapons systems around the world. We're not talking M-16s and hand grenades, either. We're talking some serious ordnance, Al."

"You think he's trying to import what, bombs or something? Into New York City?"

"No," Sal said. "We think he's already done it. Homeland Security considers Frank Waters to be a current, active, and genuine threat."

"You can't be serious."

"Serious as death."

"So you want to know what I've got on Frank Waters?"

He surprised her again. "No. Not unless you know where he is."

"Well, I don't, but—"

"Drop the ball, Al. I mean it. Right now Frank Waters is the object of the full and righteous attention of the U.S. government. There are agents crawling over every aspect of his life, and they are gonna know everything there is to know about him in very short order. I already told you, if anyone sees you and I talking in this car my career is over. And I'm telling you right now, unless someone shows you video that demonstrates otherwise, this meeting never happened. As things stand at the moment, there is no safe way for me to pass along any information you might have without getting burned for knowing it. I mean, if you know where Waters is, I'll go ahead and take the fall for it, but barring that, this case is radioactive. Don't touch it, don't go near it, don't do any more digging, don't call anybody up. Let it go. There's no way for you to come out of this clean."

"So what am I supposed to do?"

"Go back to your life. It's not your fault that you work with Frank Waters's ex-wife, and it's not her fault that she married the son of a bitch. Not really. If you two just go on about your business you just might squeak by, but the last thing you need right now is to get any more stink from Frank Waters attached to your name. Walk away, Al. This could ruin you."

"All right. Thank you, Sal."

"I'm gonna take the exit up ahead into Williamsburg.

You can catch the G from there, okay? I'm sorry to dump you, but—"

"No problem. Tell me one thing, if you can. What is it exactly that they think Waters is trying to do?"

Edwards stared out the window. "The president," he finally said, "is due to address the United Nations on Monday. He's flying into Newark Sunday afternoon. What's that tell you?"

"You think Frank Waters is trying to assassinate the president?"

He looked at her, bleak. "Can you even imagine," he said, "what something like that could do to this country?"

EIGHTEEN

IF THERE WAS anybody watching the entrance to the building where she and Sarah had the office, Alessandra did not spot them in the flood of humanity outside the building. She went inside and did not see anyone lurking, no one followed her when she went up the stairs. She wished she could be sure they were gone, but she could not. She went on up, went into the office, sat down in Sarah's client chair. Sarah was tearing through invoices. She did not even glance at the monitor when she typed.

"You know what," Sarah said, "I think I know what happened to Thomas West. You remember him, the late husband of our client Agatha West. Him and his son Isaac."

Alessandra was grateful she did not have to talk about Frank Waters yet. "What do you mean what happened to him? He died. Didn't we know that already?"

"Yeah, but he didn't die accidentally, he was killed. Probably Isaac, too, but I can't prove it. Anyhow, I think I know who did it."

"Okay," Al told her. "Lay it on me."

She did.

Al listened to the whole thing without interrupting. "You're nuts," she finally said.

"Maybe," Sarah said. "But I'll bet my house I'm right."

"You ain't got a house."

"Yes I do, on Staten Island. Someone with my maiden name bought one a month ago. Never mind that. Here's how we can prove my theory."

Again, Al listened without interrupting. "If you're right," Al told her, "you're gonna get us all killed."

"Bitch bitch bitch," Sarah said. "Jake and I will pick you up in the morning. I've got it all set up."

"Jake is in town?"

Sarah flushed slightly. "Well, umm…"

"Don't tell me. All right, we'll do it. Hopefully that wraps up the Agatha West situation. Listen, about Frank, I have bad news," Al told her.

Sarah listened to Al's story, her disbelief plain on her face. "That's total bullshit," she said when Al finished. "Those guys Frank was with were trying to get better treatment for returning veterans. Health care, Al. They were not interested in killing anybody or blowing anything up. So do what the man says, back off and let them look. They won't find anything."

"Yeah, maybe not. Here's my problem with that approach: if something bad does go down, God forbid—"

"God forbid," Sarah said. "But Frank won't have had anything to do with it.'

"You might feel that way," Al said, "and I might, but if someone decides we need a fall guy, there's Frank, right in the middle of everything. You don't think they'd jump on that?"

"What could they do? The truth is bound to come out eventually."

"Sure, like it did with Kennedy."

"So what are we gonna do?"

"Right now," Al told her, "let's just let them think we went back to business as usual."

Sarah thought it over for a minute. "Do you think they'll find Frank?"

"I wouldn't wanna bet my life on it."

"Okay. And even if they do, they'll never get it right. Do

you remember those searches you wanted me to do? Well, I got some strange results. For one thing, Frank owns that Staten Island warehouse. At least on paper, anyhow. I mean, in real life, please, there's no way. I checked with the city, there's no mortgage on the property. Or at least no record of one. And it's in arrears, whoever owns it for real owes like nine grand in back taxes. I mean, Frank never had anything, money runs through the man's hands like it was water. If you gave him nine grand right now, he'd be broke before he got to the corner, and he wouldn't be able to tell you what the hell he spent it on. But it's too much of a coincidence, this guy he worked for, Paolo Torrente, he can't know two Frank Waters. Can he?"

"No," Al said. "It's a set-up. Torrente, or whoever he really is, wasn't importing wine, he was importing weapons. The wine business was just a cover, whatever he really brought into the country, once he got his hands on it he disappeared. I don't know what these guys are trying to pull, Sarah, but Frank is all set up to take the heat for it."

Sarah went pale.

"Listen," Al said, "I'm sure he didn't have anything to do with—"

"How's anyone supposed to know for sure what really happened? If those guys snuck some kind of a bomb into the city and they blow up a building or whatever, Frank will end up being famous for being the guy who did it, whether he really did or not. Shit, I'm not even sure and I know him better than anybody… God. My kid's gonna have to change his name. How the hell do I explain that to him?"

"What do you mean you're not sure?"

Sarah's fingers went back to her keyboard. "Look at this website. I found it last night."

Al got up, went to look. "For a Rebirth of America," she read. "Is that Frank's picture?"

"Yeah."

"Did you read all the rest of this crap? What's 'the second American revolution' supposed to be? 'Aryan heritage'? Is all this for real?"

"Looks real enough, doesn't it? I never thought he cared about any of that, Al, but we been apart for a couple years now. Who the hell knows what he could have gotten into? He's… He was always gullible, Al, he was always easy to sucker into things. If he met some of these neo-Nazi dingdongs and they treated him nice, he'd follow them around like a lost puppy. So to answer your question, no, I can't be sure he's not mixed up in this shit or not. And I guess that makes him just about the perfect patsy."

"Damn. Was this site hard to find?"

"No. All I did was type his name into a search engine and this came up down near the bottom of the first page."

Al shook her head. "I'm not buying this, it's too easy. It's bogus, Sarah. Look, someone went to a lot of trouble and expense with this whole situation. They bought an old warehouse? Even if the place is a wreck, it had to cost them a couple hundred thou. And they bought a boatload of wine and then they just walked away from it? And now this. It's a scam, Sarah, it's the classic scam technique: they distract you, look here, look here, keep your eyes on the right hand, and you never see the left coming. When their bomb goes off, the cops backtrack, and what do they find? A home-grown American, an army vet with a history of anti-government protest, ties to a foreign arms supplier, and the whole thing financed by persons unknown. Whoever's behind this, they're gonna get what they want. Some damage, some dead people, and fingers pointing at the wrong guy. And major unrest, if they're lucky."

"What can we do?"

Al shook her head. "I don't know," she said. "They've got

us in a box. If we're not careful, we'll wind up looking just as guilty as Frank. Listen, tell me about this house of yours."

"It's nothing," Sarah said. "Someone else named Sarah Rizzo bought an old shack on the stinky side of Staten Island, down by Arthur Kill. Place looks like the house from the friggin' Addams Family."

"How do you know it's nothing?"

"I don't, but do you know how many Sarah Rizzos there are in New York City?"

"No. But when you look at the transaction, does the sale of this house look anything like the sale of that warehouse? Time frame's about the same, am I right? Did Sarah Rizzo take out a mortgage on the place? Where did the down payment money come from? Does she owe back real estate taxes on the place?"

"Jesus," Sarah said. "I didn't look. Oh, shit, the agent told me they hadda wait like weeks for the check to clear, because it was on the Bank of Dubai." She glanced at her watch. "I scammed the clerk to get the details on the warehouse deal," she said. "I gotta come up with something else for this one, but they should still be open—"

"Before you get into that, tell me what you know about the place."

"I can do better than that," she said. "I can show it to you." She called up the real estate agent's website and took Al on the virtual tour. When that was done, she pulled up Google Earth and got the satellite view. "Same shot they had last time," she said. "I thought Sarah Rizzo was moving in. Doesn't that look like a moving van, parked in front of the garage?"

Al peered at the indistinct image on Sarah's monitor. "Yeah, that could be Sarah, moving in," she said.

"You suppose she's got a couple spare rooms she might like to rent out?"

"I don't know," Al said. "I'll ask her when I see her."

"You going down there? You want me to come?"

"No. You still need to get the details of the house sale, if you can. And when you're done with that, write up a report on this whole goddam catastrophe, just like you were doing it for a client, from Costello's right up to now, and e-mail it to Rod Benson."

"That reporter from last time?"

"He's not a reporter, he's a schlock-meister, but he's gonna have to do. I got his e-mail address on a card in the other office. I'll get it for you, then I'm gone. Okay? What time is this thing you wanna do tomorrow? I don't know how late I'm gonna be up, here."

"Ten," Sarah said. "Ten. I forgot all about that. You think we ought to put it off?"

"No. If we can finish up the West business, let's at least do that."

"What about the house? Shouldn't we, you know, talk to someone about all of this?"

"Like the cops?"

"Yeah."

"I was warned by my contact in the NYPD, yesterday. He told me to stay away. Don't call anyone, don't do anything, walk away. That's what he said. Otherwise, we get pulled into this, we're in trouble."

"I know, but… You know."

"Yeah. I know. Listen, right now, they don't wanna hear anything we got to say. I made some calls to that number Bobby Fallon gave me and nobody called me back. I gotta believe they know everything we do. My guy told me to stay away, don't even think about calling him unless I got something concrete."

"You mean, like something at the Addams Family house."

"Yeah." Something like Frank Waters, done up with a bow.

"All right. How do I contact this Rod Benson character? And are you really sure you want me to send him everything we have?"

"Yeah." Al walked into the inner office to get Rod Benson's e-mail address for Sarah. She was still digging for it when her phone went off. "Shit," she said. "Now what?"

HE DIDN'T HEAR Al when she stepped through the door of Paratronix. She stood in the entryway, watching him. He still had that Euro look, blue eyes in a thin face, beard growth that seemed no longer and no shorter than it had the last time she'd seen him. She was surprised, again, that he differed so much from the nerd cliché, he was not skinny, pale, or out of shape, he was built more or less like a racing greyhound. Despite the stress she was under, she could sense the tension between them, almost like a living presence that grew stronger the longer she stood there. Something's gonna happen, she thought, if I let it…something's gonna happen with me and this guy… After a moment, he must have sensed it, too, felt it somehow. He looked up.

"Robbie," she said.

"Ooh," he said. "Wow. I get that jolt, I mean, every time I see you, okay, all two times. But you know, wow."

She smiled. It felt like the first good one in a while. "I bet you say that to all the girls."

"Never," he said. "Thanks for coming. Listen, we got a hit. On the pictures, I mean. Check this out." She walked around behind the counter and looked over his shoulder. He was scrolling down through a message board. "Where is it? Shit, man, it was right here. Damn. And they took the pictures down, too. I wonder who… Son of a bitch. Doesn't matter…that code, it was military. Military code. They used to use it, back in the day, to track shipments. Not anymore. Now it's electronic, satellites." He laughed.

"LoJack. Whatever. And they only use secure transport. But back when, you know, they were all worried about Soviet tanks in Eastern Europe. Which probably didn't run. But they were afraid, 'cause we didn't have as many. And they shipped stuff. You know, by truck."

Al looked at him. "What the hell are you talking about?"

He gave her a look. "Show you." He lit up his favorites list, clicked on the bottom entry. Seconds later Al was looking at two squat, squared off olive drab vehicles. "Each one of these is about the size of a senior-citizen bus," he told her.

"So what are they?"

"What? Oh, yeah. Well, this one is like power and radar. Targeting system. This other one is the launch vehicle."

"What?"

"Launch vehicle. See those tubes, right there?" He tapped the screen. "Right there. The missiles…"

"Missiles? Are you fucking kidding me?"

He shook his head. "Swear to God. Surface to air. I mean, this is nothing, we got much better stuff now, this is like the eighties. Much more compact these days. I mean, we've had shoulder-fired stingers for a long time, okay, but these things, man, they got some serious range to them. You don't have to have anything like visual. Contact, I mean. Okay, they're old and whatever. Still, you were on approach, flying some big old Boeing cattle car, got your wheels down, I'm guessing you saw one or two of these babies coming up after you it would give you a serious rush. This particular one, okay, not the one in the picture. The one with your code, it got stolen in Austria back in '86. On its way to a depot or something. You know, somebody, ah… They hijacked the truck. Somewhere near Innsbruck. Where'd you find it?"

"My picture came off a crate in a wine wholesaler's warehouse," she said.

"Holy shit! Are you kidding? We gotta... Who do we call? We gotta call somebody. I mean, we can't have this. I mean, it's old and whatnot, but if it still works and everything, Jesus..." He stared at her, blue eyes wide. "Don't we? Um, who, you know... Who do we call?"

"Okay, Robbie, listen to me carefully. Here's your story. I came to you with these pictures, okay—"

"Well, you did. Come to me, I mean."

"Quiet. I came to you, you found the answers, okay, and you're calling the authorities. Okay? Official story, you didn't wait to show them to me, you called right away, because this is too serious. You got that?"

"Got it. Oh, man. Yeah. I should have thought. Right? I should have. Called, I mean. Um, who? The cops?"

"No," she told him. "Military Police. I don't know where—"

His fingers flew across the keyboard. "I got it," he said, but then he stopped abruptly. "Do you know, like...where this thing is?"

She shrugged. "I know where I saw the crate, and I know it ain't there now." All she really had was her suspicion. Certainly not anything like concrete... "No. Not really. But whoever you get, tell 'em I went to Staten Island to look for it. Tell 'em I saw it out there."

"You got it." He took his hands and his full attention away from the computer, stood up straight, focused completely on her, maybe for the first time. "Al," he said. "Um. You know...this is probably not the right... Well, anyway. Am I gonna see you again?"

She could feel it, whatever it was, and so could he. And your musician, she told herself, just dumped you for an orange-haired teenager... Polish soccer player, she thought. I'll have to ask him some time.

"I sure hope so," she said.

AL POINTED HER uncle's van down Arthur Kill Road, which ran down Staten Island's western verge. You couldn't exactly call it a shore, there were no beaches, no sand, just a wide muddy expanse of tall pale brown reeds standing stiff, tall, and dead in the frozen mud. CHEMICAL LANE, she thought, reading a passing street sign, Jesus Christ, they don't even try to hide it. And no matter how long she'd lived in New York City, it seemed to always have one more wonder to show her, and one more horror... The hills to her right blocked off the lights of the city, and to her left the island sloped down to the oddly tinted waters of Arthur Kill. She drove past the address she wanted, saw only a dark neglected Victorian that looked like it had been built on a stony apron of rubble dumped into the swamp. Three-story house of no discernible color, oversized detached garage. Another hour, she thought, and it'll be dark down here, there were few other habitations to provide any illumination, just a couple of streetlights and a few poison-blue mercury vapor lamps casting their unhealthy pallor across the parking lot of a metal-sided industrial building across the way. A thin layer of snow lay over everything, gray in the dying light of day, dirty up near the road.

Lovely.

A hundred feet farther down the road a body shop occupied another patch of gravel surrounded by reeds. There's my parking spot, Al thought, her uncle's aging van would look right at home there. Whoever worked in the body shop was already gone, the place was shuttered up and dark. She drove on by. A half-mile farther on she drove under a highway where one of the major arteries ran over a bridge, one of the tethers connecting Staten Island to New Jersey. It gave the locals on the Jersey side their connection to the city, it was their bane and their lifeblood. Gotta be hell, Al thought, gotta be, fighting your way through that mad crush every morning and every evening, God, how can you keep from going insane?

She kept going, followed Arthur Kill Road all the way down to where it ended in the tiny enclave of Tottenville, a thumb on the far end of Staten Island that stuck out into Raritan Bay. It was only a half-dozen blocks wide. Al found a parking spot, got out and stretched.

Cold air rolled gently up off the water, flowed on past her and pushed the vapors fuming out of Staten Island's toxic garbage dumps away northward. For today, at least, there was no smell. Look at us, Al thought, shivering as she wrapped her arms around herself, look at us, ain't we something? Even here, we build our little houses, we shovel our sidewalks, and we tend our yards. No matter what, inspired or insane, we keep on planting things regardless of the odds against them taking root, or of us surviving long enough to see them grow. Goes to show you, she told herself, you might as well go ahead and do what you can. What the hell…

NINETEEN

THE SUN VANISHED somewhere on the far side of New Jersey, the racket of rush hour faded and ordinary people took refuge inside their warm houses. Al got back into the van and drove up Arthur Kill Road. She parked the van next to the driveway of the body shop. Someone drove up the road while she sat there, it was a big Mercedes sedan. God, she thought, what the hell can they be doing down here? Then she realized that if they had seen her, they would be wondering what the hell she was doing. Traffic was sparse, but it wasn't nonexistent…

Too bad, Al thought. All you've gotta do is get a look at what's up inside that garage, and then you can call in the cavalry.

SOMETHING WAS ALIVE inside the garage, there was some mechanical thing humming, something working. Alessandra put her palms up against the side of the building and she could feel it. She found the single window in the side of the garage, but it was so black inside that she could not be sure she saw anything or not. Maybe the suggestion of a dark looming shape, and then again maybe not, she could not be sure. I've got to get inside, she told herself. They've already warned me away twice, if I call the cops out here and this turns out to be a false alarm, I will have put myself and Sarah in the path of Harkonnen's freight train and we'll get run down, and for nothing…

There was a single garage door in the front, it spanned

nearly the width of the building, easily wide enough for two vehicles side by side, even oversized ones, like a landscaper's trucks or like the two separate modules that Robbie had showed her on his computer. Each one would have been towed here, possibly behind a behemoth Chevy Suburban such as the one Frank Waters had been driving. Once in place the two modules would be mated by their umbilical cords and the power unit would be started, rendering the radar unit, and presumably the missile launcher, operative. They would wait until just before the anticipated launch time to power up, because according to Robbie, you couldn't just light up some stray radar signal without attracting immediate and unfriendly attention from the military, who might even recognize the signal for what it was. "They'll wait," he'd told her. "If they have some way of knowing when the president's plane is coming, they'll wait until it's on approach, then they'll crank that bitch up and fire off their missiles because you got to know someone will be honing in on that radar source within minutes. If they're lucky, they'll have enough time to launch and then get clear before the counterstrike."

"You can't be serious," she'd told him. "You really think we'd fire a, what, an anti-radar missile into a metropolitan region? There would have to be civilian casualties..."

"Don't you think they've game-planned all of these scenarios already? They already made that decision. Bet on it. If Air Force One gets lit up by an unknown radar source, I sure as hell wouldn't want to be anywhere near where it's coming from."

Or the garage could be totally empty.

Find out first, she told herself.

There was a personnel door set into the big roll-up garage door in the front so that you could enter the building without opening the big door, but it seemed to be locked.

She made a slow, careful circuit around the garage. There were no other points of entry, just the window and the door. There was, however, soft yellow light coming from two windows in the back of the house, and the reflected, flickering blue of a television in a front room.

This place is empty, she thought, it's another dead end. Otherwise they'd have posted a sentry, she thought. If you spent a small fortune just to get to this point, you bought the missile system, paid someone to go over it to make sure it still worked, then you smuggled it over here and got your people into place, you had to be way past committed. You had to be ready to die or to spend your life in prison before you came on a mission like this. So where was the guard? She made another slow circuit, but there was no one.

Break the window? Too loud, she thought. You can't have them come running while you're still inside. That only left the two doors… She went back around to the front, tried the personnel door again, with no better result. The bigger door, however, had certainly seen better days. It was locked and latched, but only on one side, when she tried hoisting on the extreme left side, it had about six inches of give. She put her back to the door, squatted down, got both hands under the bottom and heaved. She put all of herself into it, strained with everything she had, and she got about another inch. She stopped, rested for a moment. When she was ready, she did it again, strained against the door with every muscle fiber at her disposal, strained until she thought her bones would crack, but she couldn't tell if she'd gained any ground or not. She rested again, longer this time, then did it again. It did not feel to her that she was capable of exerting the same force one more time, or that the door had moved any more. She knelt down and measured the opening with her hands. That's all you're gonna get, she told herself. You are gonna have to make it through there. She lay on her back in front of the opening, turned her head sideways and inched her way under. Dirt from the bottom of the door fell onto her face, into her mouth and one of her eyes. She ignored it and wormed her way farther under, kept going until her rib cage was wedged into the opening. Collapse your chest, she told herself, exhale all of the air out of your lungs and push hard... But you better make it through, you better not get stuck or you'll suffocate, they'll find you here dead in the morning...

She exhaled as hard as she could, pushed herself farther into the gap. She could not breathe, her feet slipped on the frozen driveway, she saw sparks of light somewhere behind her eyes, she felt the rough bottom edge of the door digging into her chest. I'm screwed, she thought, I really did it this time, but then she pushed again, got an inch, then another one, and then enough of her ribs cleared the door for her to suck in some air. I made it, she thought, but then she thought she heard something, she was blinded by a sudden burst of light.

A harsh voice said, "Don't move or I will cut your throat."

THE TWO OTHERS came in response to his phone call. Alessandra couldn't really see their faces, but she was sure it was them, these were the guys she had tormented, the ones who'd hated taking orders from her so much, the ones who worked for Paolo Torrente. One of the new arrivals unlocked the roll-up door and then the two of them heaved it open. There was a second of blinding pain because Al's side of the door dropped back down even before it went up and for a moment the flashlight in her face had nothing on the lights exploding in her brain. She could hardly breathe through the pain in her chest as hands hauled her roughly erect, and then she nearly passed out when they jerked her arms around behind her back. One of them held her arms, a second one grabbed a handful of her hair and then they marched her out into the driveway and through the snow, over to the side entrance of the house. They stopped just inside the door. She was vaguely conscious of excited speech and some laughter, as well as some distressing noises that might have been coming from her. They were in some kind of a mud room, not yet in the house proper. She fought for breath, fought against the pain, but she did not struggle against her captors, she stood no chance against them in her current shape. She went rigid when she felt them lifting her up, they threw her onto her back on a counter against one wall. She felt one of them leaning down on her chest, pinning her down, and then a second one sat on her ankles.

Not exactly what she'd been expecting.

She heard water then, flowing out of something and splattering all over the floor. The third man came into view, he was carrying a garden hose, it had water pouring softly out of the end. He grabbed her hair and held the hose in her face.

The water was so cold it was almost like being hit with an electrical current. She closed her eyes and held her breath. No big deal, for maybe ten seconds.

God, they could drown her like this.

It wouldn't take more than a minute or so...

Her body began fighting her. Her mind screamed, how can you drown on dry land, Jesus, what if they didn't let her get another breath, God, what a stupid way to go... She did her best to counteract her body's insistent demands that she inhale, but it was an involuntary reflex, a mindless overwhelming command that bypassed her higher consciousness, the part of her brain that knew there was no air for her, only water. Her control slipped and she got a nose full of water, she tried to cough it out but got more in instead, she began fighting against the men holding her down, bucking against them like a wild thing, but they had her good. She felt a knot of white-hot pain right in the center of her chest as she lost the battle to keep her airways closed. She was dying...

She came to on the floor, one of them had his knees on her stomach, she coughed and then threw up. The one on his knees jumped back out of the way to the sounds of laughter and then they grabbed her again, lifted her back up onto the counter.

One of them went for the hose, she heard the water, and she screamed.

They were doing this for fun...

THE FOURTH TIME they did it she had no more strength. Maybe this is it, she thought, this must be what it feels like to die, to lose awareness of the world, of the air just out of reach, to forget why you came, who you are, even, to sense your spirit ebbing away, to feel the enveloping darkness... It ended, though, after only seconds the water stopped, the other two let go of her and she rolled over on her side and coughed the water out of her nose and throat. They grabbed her and dropped her to the floor where she kept coughing until her throat was raw.

She noticed a voice yelling, it was not hers and it did not belong to any of the other three, either. Out of the corner of her eye she caught a glimpse of him, a polished black shoe, a tailored trouser leg, a crippled hand. It was the man she knew as Paolo Torrente, and he had come to yank back the leashes on his dogs.

"Idiots!" he shrieked. Al heard the unmistakable sound of a hand striking flesh. "What are you doing? Did she come alone? Did you even look?" One of them tried to answer him and he shouted the man into silence. "Have you completely lost your mind? Have you forgotten our purpose?

When we leave here tomorrow she must walk out with us! We cannot leave her here!" He went on, then, in a language she did not recognize.

She lay on the floor, breathing shallowly. The awareness of her body returned slowly, she felt her hair matted on her face, her sore ribs, she was once again able to command her hands and feet. She stayed still and gathered what strength she could.

Paolo ended his tirade, but then continued a moment later in a more normal tone of voice, in English. "After tomorrow," he said, "I do not care what you do with her. Until then, put her with the other one."

She didn't move. Whatever it is that makes you alive, she could feel it flowing back into her. She remembered Caughlan's words, thought she might just have enough cockroach in her, too, and then she knew at that moment that Paolo's first mistake had been to leave his dead comrade in the parking lot at Costello's. His second was this one, not killing her while he had the chance. If I let them march me out of this place tomorrow, she thought, I am really and truly done for...

IT WAS A SMALL unlit basement room, rough concrete floor, exterior walls of stone, interior walls of concrete blocks, a thin layer of dirt on everything. They rolled her in there onto the floor, left her in the pitch darkness, locked the door behind her. She spat the dirt and hair out of her mouth and sat up slowly, head throbbing.

There was someone else in the room. "Frank," she said. "Frank Waters. Is that you?"

"Wow," a voice said. "How'd you reckanize me in the dark? And what the hell is going on? Can you tell me what's happening?"

"Yeah," she said. "You been set up. They want you to be the next John Wilkes Booth."

"John what? What the hell are you talking about? Where are you? I'm reaching out, I'm right here." She felt his hand brush against her face. "God, you're freezing," he said. "What the hell did they do to you? C'mere. No, it's all right, c'mere, you could catch your death in this place."

"Yeah, you got a point. Be a little careful, okay, I think I got a cracked rib or two."

"I got you," he said, and she let him pull her to him. She had to admit it felt pretty good, she had forgotten what warm was like. "Tell me," he said. "Who the hell are you, and what's going on?"

She told him. They sat in silence awhile after she finished.

"You warm enough now?" he finally asked her.

"Yeah, I'm good. Thanks. Did you get all that, Frank?" She eased away from him, found a block wall, leaned back against it.

"I got it all right," he said. "I got it. There's water here if you're thirsty."

"Hell, no," she said. "Thanks anyway. How can we get outa here, Frank?"

"We can't," he told her, his voice quiet. "The room is too small, they can see clear into every corner from the window in the door. Do you know how to fuck up that launcher if you get clear?"

"I'll find a way."

He thought about that for some time.

"Well, listen," he said, going on in a quieter voice. "You need to rest up. I got a jacket here, you can use it for a pillow."

She felt him thrust a soft cloth bundle into her hands. "Are you sure there's no way out of here, Frank?"

"I had plenty of time to figure it out, believe me."

"Do they ever open that door?"

"Yeah, sure," he said. "When they bring breakfast. One guy with a gun and one with the food. And the guy with the gun is on the ball, you ain't gonna surprise him and you ain't gonna jump him."

"We might have to try," she told him. "That might be our only chance."

"It ain't no chance at all," he told her. "Listen, you lay down and try to get some sleep."

SHE WOKE UP with a start, confused first and sore second, felt his hand on her knee. It took her a second or so to put it all together. She couldn't see him, but she sensed him close, heard his hoarse whisper. "How ya feeling?" he said. "I know ya slept good."

"Yeah?" God, it even hurt to breathe. "How do you know that?"

" 'Cause ya snore like a truck driver."

"Sorry. I keep you awake?"

"S'all right. I needed the time to think. Here's what I got: if these guys with Paolo really want me to take the fall for this, they need me alive and without any bullet holes in me. I didn't know that before. Ya know what I mean?"

"I don't think I like the sound of this, Frank."

"Listen, I ain't nuts about it neither, but if we don't do something, the shit just goes downhill from here. I mean, it just gets worse. So the way they do it in the mornings, the guy with the gun shows up, he opens the door first and then stands to the left of the door there while the kid brings in the food. Just cereal. Anyhow, I didn't know the guy couldn't shoot me, ya know what I'm saying? Not if they want me to be the patsy. So I'm gonna bum-rush the guy. Ya gonna have to get past the kid."

"You're betting your life on this, Frank."

He was silent for a minute. "When they come," he finally said, "I take out the soldier. Raffi, the one with the gun."

"Raffi," she said. "He look like a fucking ferret?"

"Yeah, that's him. The kid's name is Tonio. If ya can get past the kid, ya might have a chance. I mean, it won't be a great chance, there's one more soldier and he's a real hard-ass, ya gotta stay away from him. But we need to catch a break somewhere along the line here. Ya know what I mean? We might get lucky. He might be busy doing something else."

"Frank…"

"Listen to me," he whispered harshly. "I had plenty of time to dope this out, and I ain't goin' down this way. Swear to God I'm not. These guys think they can use me and then just throw me in the garbage. I ain't goin' for it. Get ready, here they come."

"I didn't hear anything."

"They're in the kitchen. Listen, this asshole Raffi has any brains, which is debatable, okay, he's gonna try to shoot you first hoping that'll stop me."

"I thought you said he wasn't gonna shoot."

"Quiet, get around behind me."

There was some creaking of ancient wood and then the lights in the basement went on. The window in the door to the tiny room they were in was a small bright yellow square. Al saw Frank for the first time since Costello's. He was a big man, broad shouldered, barrel chested, short growth of beard, dirty face. He was down on one knee, leaned on the knuckles of his right hand, his left hand dangling, twitching slightly. Looks like a defensive end, Al thought, late in the game and he's tired, he's waiting for the last moment to get set. He glanced at her. "Behind me," he said softly. "Down on your knees. Don't look at 'em. Be ready."

"Get back!" a voice said. "Both of you, get back!" A key rattled in the door.

Frank didn't move, but Al could feel him tense up. There was a shadow of a face at the yellow window, then the door opened outward.

It was Raffi, and he carried a semi-automatic in one hand.

I should stop this, Al thought, I should say something, but then Frank exploded out of his stance like a bull in the chute. Al had never seen anyone his size move that fast. He had called Raffi a soldier, but Raffi had his non-gun hand on the door, he had to let go of the door, reach up, and rack the first round into the chamber. Frank Waters blasted into him, drove him over backward and knocked the door the rest of the way open. Behind Raffi, the kid Tonio dropped the tray he carried and he stumbled backward. Al ignored the pain in her chest and vaulted the two men on the floor in the doorway. Tonio was up on his knees, he had a knife in his right hand. Al never slowed, Tonio slashed at her, but she went high over the blade and kicked him in the chin as hard as she could. The kick sent her down to the floor and the impact took what breath she had. She rolled over onto her hands and knees. Tonio lay on his back, eyes wide, watching her, but nothing below his neck moved.

Just a kid.

Behind her, Raffi's gun went off twice.

Overhead, a door banged, footsteps ran across the old wooden floorboards. Frank Waters lay like a dead weight on top of Raffi. The smaller man squirmed hard, trying to get his gun hand free before Alessandra reached him. He did manage it, but not quite fast enough, she got to him in time to grab his gun hand in both of hers and twist it until the muzzle pointed at the side of his own head. The acrid smell from the first two rounds filled her head. Raffi's mouth opened, but no sounds came out, his eyes went wide as she helped him pull the trigger. Her ears rang with the sound of the shot as the far side of Raffi's head blew out and blood and brain matter splattered across the basement.

Al wrestled the pistol out of Raffi's hand, put it aside, took Frank by the shoulders and rolled him off Raffi and over onto his back. He had two entry wounds in his chest, but they didn't seem to be bleeding much. His eyes met hers and then he looked up at the ceiling. He was trying to say something, she had to lean down close to hear. "Hurry." She could barely make it out. "Hurry."

She took his hand, but there was no life in it. He stared at the ceiling. "I'm going," she told him, and she squeezed his hand but got no response. "You hang on, I'm coming back for you," she said, but she could not tell if he heard her or not. He didn't look at her again. He might have been staring upward in an attempt to urge her on, or he may have been thinking about the sun he would never see again, she didn't know, but when she let go of his hand it fell limp to the floor. She reached over and picked up the pistol that killed Raffi, the one that had her prints on it now. She looked at Frank one more time, but he was not responsive.

Tonio was paralyzed, unable to breathe, dying for air. She walked past him.

There was no way to creep up the stairs, they groaned every time she shifted her weight. Other than that, the old house was silent. Either the other two had left, run off to fire their missiles, or else they were waiting for her... She kicked the cellar door open and rolled out onto the floor, scanning wildly for them as her ribs registered their objections once again.

She didn't see anyone.

She breathed in quick, shallow, painful gasps.

The house phone was dead.

The kitchen window blew inward, something dug long gouges in the ceiling, and then she heard the gun.

THEY WERE PARKED on Atlantic Avenue in Brooklyn, out in front of Alessandra Martillo's building. Sarah's mother's car did not seem happy. Sarah revved the engine, hoping the thing would cough the phlegm out of its throat and run smoother. "She's not answering," Sarah said, and she ended the call. "I wonder if she's okay."

Jake West sat restless in the front passenger seat. "Maybe she forgot," he said. "I have to ask you something. How did you know I didn't, you know… How do you know it wasn't me?"

"She'd never forget," Sarah said, but she called the office phone just to check. "No answer there, either."

"Sarah…"

"What?"

"The police suspected me and Isaac, you said so yourself. How do you know we didn't do it? You could be sitting in this car with a terrible person, someone who would kill his own father."

"Yeah, but I'm not."

"How do you know?"

She put the phone away and looked over at him. He had dark shadows under his eyes. The closer this meeting had gotten, the more haunted he looked. It was almost as if the very idea of seeing his stepmother again was poisoning him. "I know," she said.

"Don't tell me it's intuition," he told her. "You can't just… When did you start to trust me? Do you trust me?"

She sighed. "This really bothers you, doesn't it?"

"Yes," he said. "People look at you differently when they think you might be guilty of murder, even if there isn't a shred of evidence, even if it's only speculation. I could see it in people's eyes after those newspaper articles came out. Even my friends. They didn't look at me the same way anymore. Because they couldn't be sure."

"I know you better than they did, Jake."

"Sarah, that's not an answer. Talk to me, please."

"All right." It was not so easy, explaining. Sarah knew that she saw things other people did not notice, but, more important, she felt things that they did not or would not feel. And there were times when she just knew what she knew. "Your father's face," she said.

"My father's... Do you mean the piece in the gallery? By the door? What's that got to do with anything?"

She looked at her watch. "That piece isn't just a hunk of brass," she said. It was so hard, sometimes, to put into words something that her mind told her was true. Words could be blunt objects sometimes, it was like trying to build a bicycle out of bricks. "Every single emotion inside that face," she told him, "you had to feel it first. You had to feel it, live with it, understand it. You had to feel it hard enough to get it down out of your head and into your hands. Otherwise, no one would feel a thing when they looked at it, like I did. When I saw that face, I knew something about you. Do you get that? Haven't you ever looked at a painting and felt that you knew something about the artist, just from what he did? I don't think you can hide, not when you're an artist, Jake. Besides, you wouldn't be able to live with emotions that strong if you'd really done it. You'd have to do something about them."

"I would have to kill myself, you mean."

"Well, I was thinking you'd have to find a way to pay it back if you could, like, 'fess up and do the jail time. But I suppose suicide would work, too. Anyhow, I know who did it, and it wasn't you." She glanced at her watch again. "At least, I think I do. We're gonna have to go soon."

"I will never understand you," he said.

"Keep trying," she told him. "Besides, if you did have all that money that disappeared, you wouldn't be living in a garret above your gallery in the middle of nowhere, with no car. Jake, I dropped a piece of tinfoil on your kitchen floor and the wind blew it across the room."

He nodded. "It's an old building."

"Old? It's a wreck. Someday it's gonna fall down, hopefully without you inside it. Listen, we're gonna have to make a call pretty soon. If Al doesn't show, do we go ahead without her or do we try to reschedule?"

"Reschedule?" He looked horrified. "God. Aren't we, you know, all ready to go? Could you even get this all arranged another time?"

"I don't know. I'm just worried about Al."

"Let's just do it," he said. "Get it over with. Then if she hasn't turned up, we'll go find her."

"All right."

SOMEWHERE NEAR LAGUARDIA the fourth spark plug must have spit off its carbon raincoat and begun to fire because the engine lost its roughness and the car seemed to settle more comfortably into the business of transport. And wouldn't it have been something, Sarah thought, you get these two to agree to get together after all this time, but then you wind up stuck by the side of the road somewhere. But that didn't happen. She followed the directions she'd downloaded carefully. They made a stop in the village first, then they proceeded to Agatha West's weekend house.

It was a big old Dutch Colonial, sided with brown cedar shingles and trimmed with red. It sat not far from the shore of Long Island Sound. The water was cold, gray, and rimmed with a coating of stuff that looked more like dirty shaving cream than sea ice. Sarah turned in between two brick pillars and went up the long driveway. A garage door jerked into motion as she neared. She waited for it to open all the way, then pulled into the empty slot next to Agatha's Bentley. There was another car on the far side of the Bentley, a small red two-seat convertible. Sarah didn't know what it was, and Jake had his mind on other things. He looked like a man in shock.

Sarah shut the engine off and got out. Mrs. West's chauffeur stood in the doorway that led into the house. If he found the sight of Sarah's mother's car next to the other two incongruous, he gave no sign of it. "Hello, Mr. Haig," she said.

"Mrs. Waters," he said. "Jacob. Please come in." The garage door closed behind them.

TWENTY

ALESSANDRA DANCED BACK out of sight.

The firing stopped. They're not interested in me, she thought. They just want to get that bitch cranked up... But how to see them without getting shot? The stairs leading to the upper floors were just steps away.

She ran upstairs. It looked and smelled as if no one had been up there in ages. She edged into an empty room just over the kitchen. Bedroom, she thought, one small closet, linoleum floor that curled up in the corners. Two old windows.

It was about the same size as her room over the bar.

They had pulled the two vehicles out into the driveway. They were olive drab, dull, gave little clue to their intended purpose. A gun can be beautiful, like an old flintlock produced by a single craftsman, a work of art forged by a man who cared about his work. Or they can be ugly. These things were utilitarian, she would never have guessed what the long tubes were for if Robbie Corgan had not told her. The man she knew as Paolo Torrente was down on one knee in the snow. He was pointing an M-16 at the house.

Not a lot of elegance in the look of the M-16, either.

Break the glass, Al thought. Break the glass with the barrel, then focus on him and shoot, because you're seriously overmatched in the firepower department, and the thin walls of the old house are not going to give you much protection. Go ahead, she thought. Break the glass... Funny how easy it is to break something. When she'd been on the street as a child she'd done it many times, never pausing to think how she was destroying something that she'd had no power to create. How do they even make glass? How had they done it a hundred years ago when they built this place? And wasn't glass supposed to be a liquid, so slow to move that it still stood there smooth and vertical after the passing of a century? And would you be able to tell if that was true? You could go around with calipers, measure the thickness of window glass in old houses, in theory it ought to be a bit thinner, up at the top…

Paolo checked his clip.

Alessandra punched out the window glass, pointed Raffi's gun, and fired.

Torrente dropped the clip. He jerked the gun up, pointed it in Al's direction, and fired, something blew through the plaster about a foot to her right.

Missed, she thought, both of us. Torrente took his eyes off her, leaned over for his clip. Al aimed carefully. What was that thing about shooting downhill? She'd heard about it in an old Western movie… And who knew if that was real or just made up? She focused, lined up Torrente's feet in the sights, pulled the trigger.

Recoil bounced the barrel skyward, but suddenly Torrente was down on his side. He struggled for the clip frantically. Al's hands began to shake.

I hate this, she thought.

I never wanted this.

Paolo had seemed like a decent guy…

She focused the sights on him again and shot. He forgot about his clip and began worming his way across the yard, leaving a thin red trail on the snow in his wake. She fired at him twice more. He got almost all the way to the garage before he stopped moving.

She felt sick.

There was a pair of feet behind one of the two vehicles, and a thick black umbilical linked them together. It's him, she thought, the big one, the one they call Vincenzo. The soldier. He's out there getting his missiles ready to fire.

This ain't over yet...

AGATHA WEST SAT in a white wicker chair at one end of a greenhouse appended to the rear of her weekend house. She had a great view of Long Island Sound, but she didn't look like she was enjoying it all that much, her face was lined with pain and her color was bad. She grimaced when she saw Jake, then tried to smile, but it didn't come off well. Sarah felt Jake stiffen. She put a hand on the small of his back and urged him forward. "It's all right," she said.

"Easy for you to say," he told her.

"Hello, Jacob," Agatha said. "Come now, I don't bite." He didn't answer her.

"I'm sorry you still feel like that," she said. "Would you feel better if you searched me? Make sure I don't have a handgun?"

"Nah," he said. "You'd never use a gun. Slow poison would be more your style."

She pursed her lips. "I had hoped you'd outgrown your bitterness by now," she told him. "It's Tipton you should hate, not me. He's the one spending your inheritance." She shifted her gaze to Sarah. "Could you excuse us, my dear? I'd like to..."

"No way," Jake said. "I want her where she can watch you stick the knife in."

Agnes sighed. Jake didn't move. "What if I go down the other end, there?" Sarah said, pointing at the far end of the greenhouse. "That way I can see, but I won't be able to hear. How would that be?"

Jake looked at her for a second, then nodded.

"Thank you, dear. Mitchell, perhaps you could get Mrs. Waters a chair. Make her comfortable."

"Ma'am."

Jake went over and perched on the windowsill, his back to the frozen bay. He looked at Sarah. "Go ahead," he said.

Sarah and Mitchell Haig walked down to the far end of the greenhouse. "I'll be right back," he said, and he went into the house.

Sarah looked out at the water. Million-dollar view, she thought, and most of the time there's no one here to enjoy it. You couldn't afford to even pay the property tax on this joint, she told herself, and that's just the smallest part of what it must cost to keep the place operating. And although the house and grounds appeared to be maintained well enough, the place didn't give you the feeling that anyone really cared about it. Certainly no one loved it. She could see cobwebs in the high corners, mouse cookies in the low ones. And wouldn't you schmear a little paint around here and there if you loved the place? Hire one of those decorators from HGTV to come in and spiff up the joint.

But then again, Agatha West had her mind on other matters.

Still…

Haig returned after a while, he carried an old-fashioned, undersized dark wooden rocking chair. "I hope this is all right," he said.

"Fine, thanks," she said. "How about one for you?"

He looked down at the other end of the greenhouse. Jake was still perched stiffly on the windowsill, his upper body inclined away from Agatha. She sat still, hands in her lap, head downcast, talking softly. "I think there's a ditch out back I need to go dig," Haig said.

"No fun here," Sarah said, agreeing with him. "If I hadn't

said I would watch, I'd come help you shovel. Nobody can do you like your family."

"Ain't that the truth. But I do need to beg off, Mrs. Waters. One of the circulators for the heating system is leaking water and I need to go see to it before we have a flood. Ag— ahh—Mrs. West will buzz me when you're ready to go."

"Thank you," Sarah said.

After he left, Sarah watched Jake and Agnes for a while. Agatha never raised her voice, but she seemed to be getting to Jake, some of the starch seemed to go out of his backbone and his posture softened. I suppose, Sarah thought, being told you were going to inherit an estate like West's might do that to you...

Her mind wandered.

Gotta cost a bloody fortune to heat this place... And as much as she disliked her mother's basement, at least it felt real there, you could walk through the door and tell that it was home to somebody. Mrs. West had the money, no question, plus a certain amount of notoriety. She had done something with her life. You might disagree with her conclusions, but you had to respect her for doing the work, particularly considering that she'd done it by choice, not necessity. She probably could have retired twenty years ago and spent her time playing tennis or whatever. Still, Sarah thought, I've got something she doesn't, I've got time. Or at least I assume that I do. Providing, of course, that I refrain from certain risky behaviors, like this little expedition. And my son doesn't hate my guts yet...

Got to be almost through, don't they? How long could it take you to say, "Hey, I'm checking out so I'm gonna leave you a little something. Oh, and sorry about the old man..." Sarah looked at her watch. God, please let them get this over with. And get us through this in one piece. Please? Haig had been gone a little over twenty minutes when Agatha stirred, reached down into her bag.

Sarah felt her heart stop.

Agatha pulled out her cell and punched a key, held it up to her ear. As she spoke into it, she turned and waggled her fingers at Sarah.

All done, finally.

Almost home...

SARAH BACKED HER mother's car out of the garage carefully. "You okay?" she said to Jake.

He swallowed. "I need a drink."

She shifted into Drive and inched slowly back up the driveway. "Well, you're fat now, you can buy me one, too."

He snorted. "I'll buy you a beer," he said. "But don't hold your breath waiting for the check from that one. The only thing she's giving me is a ticket to the undertaker." He looked out the window. "Everything all right?"

"So far." She kept her speed down to a crawl, all the way out to the street. She stopped just outside the stone pillars. Two police cruisers and a tow truck were just down the road. One of the cruisers blipped its siren.

Sarah stopped and shut off the engine. "Get out here," she said to Jake. "Nice and easy. Don't close the door behind you, leave it open. Nice and easy, now."

Three cops approached, two of them wearing suits that made them look like astronauts.

"Those guys look like bomb squad techs," Jake said.

"Yeah," Sarah said. "Nice and easy, like I told you."

ONE OF THE ASTRONAUTS came over to the cruiser. Chief Jarvis rolled his window down. "It's on the firewall," the astronaut told him.

"Holy shit," Jarvis said, and he glanced in his rearview

mirror at Jake West, who sat in the back. "I'll be damned. Let's move everybody back." He twisted in his seat to look directly at Jake. "Mr. West," he said, "it seems I owe you an apology." He turned to Sarah. "You got a pair of balls, you know that?"

Sarah looked back at Jake. "You all right?"

He stared at Sarah, his mouth open. "You never mentioned a bomb," he said. "You said Haig was gonna sabotage…"

Jarvis was talking to his radio. "Go get 'em," he said. "The West woman and her driver. Get 'em both, and keep 'em separated." He dropped his radio. "Hey!" he yelled, pointing at a figure running diagonally across West's backyard, angling toward the boathouse down in the far corner. "Hey! That's Haig!" The astronaut backed out of the way, Jarvis flung his door open, jumped out, yelled at the other cops as he ran.

Jake watched them go. "You drove the car? After you let him rig it to blow up? Are you nuts?"

"Relax," Sarah said. "He wasn't gonna blow us up right there in Aggie's driveway."

"I suppose not," he said. "But you're still nuts." He stared over at the house. "She was telling me how much she missed him. Told me to go have a son. Call him Thomas." He reddened. "The old snake. She was just keeping us there long enough to give Haig time to do your car." He was getting angry now. Sarah figured that was progress. "How did you know she'd do it?"

"Your brother was twenty-nine when he died."

"Yeah. So?"

"How old are you?"

"Thirty—"

"And a very grown-up thirty, too," she told him. "Your

father set up trust funds for the two of you. You get the money at age thirty."

"Yeah, but…his company went under. There was all kinds of money missing. They tried to say—"

Sarah shook her head. "They stuck Tipton with embezzlement and fraud," she told him. "Your father's estate took a big hit, but the trust funds were locked in. And when Isaac died, his money reverted to the estate. And to Agatha."

"How do you know all this?"

"It was in the papers, Jake. You guys were big news for a while."

"Jesus. Well, all right, fine. How'd you know she'd put a bomb in your car?"

"I didn't. But when I talked to the service manager at the Bentley dealership where Haig used to work, he told me that Haig and Agnes used to be embarrassing. Which, I guess, so what? It's a free country, you can suck face with whoever you want. Right? But that was before your father's accident. So they weren't exactly shocked when she hired him away from them. And Haig is a mechanic. Must've been pretty good, too, he made manager. And your father died in a car accident. There were accounts that said he was racing another car. What if he wasn't racing? What if he was trying to get away?"

"God. And Izzy—"

"Thrown off his bike on the way to a yacht race. Agatha told me it was a boating accident. Not that far off, but it felt funny. I mean, wouldn't you make the distinction, if it was you? You didn't say anything about a boat when I asked you. You even knew which tire supposedly blew out. The Connecticut police crushed the bike when they closed the case so I guess we'll never know for sure unless Agatha and Haig cop to it, but it fits. And then when I talked to Haig to set this meeting up, he wanted to be sure I drove you out here. That's when I knew."

"Well, wouldn't it be suspicious if your car just blew up?"

"Yeah," Sarah said. "I'm sort of curious to see how he worked that out."

A YOUNG MILITARY-LOOKING COP with short hair and bright brown eyes stuck his head around the office door. "Hey, Chief," he said. "Ah, Mrs. Waters, we're gonna have to hold on to your car. You guys should probably look at picking up a rental."

"We can give you a lift anywhere you want," Jarvis said.

Jake shook his head. "I'll get a car." He seemed anxious to be gone.

"You get it disarmed?" Jarvis asked the cop. "You gonna detonate it?"

"No need to blow it," the cop said.

"Why not?" Jarvis sounded disappointed.

"Chief, this thing is a work of art. Haig is a goddam genius. Pardon me, ma'am. But what you got, you got two plastic canisters, okay, one's a carbon monoxide generator, feeds gas in through the heater. Everyone passes out, right, or dies. The second canister is an incendiary."

"So the car crashes and burns."

"Yeah. But here's the kicker: the plastic canisters burn up in the fire. Who's gonna notice? There's a ton of plastic in the car. I mean, the inner fenders on that piece of shh—ah—on the car, they're plastic. The detonator is attached to the outside of the canisters, not the firewall, so when the incendiary goes off, the detonator falls off on the road. If they were going sixty or seventy, it could wind up a mile or two back down the road. Probably get run over a couple hundred times before anybody noticed it."

"What kind of detonator did he use?"

"Short-range radio. Yeah, he'd be tailing. Pick a good spot, okay, push the button, the first canister goes, then the second one. He'd be right there to give the car a little nudge if it needed one."

"Nice," Sarah said.

"Brilliant," the cop said. "And when the tox reports come back, they show high carbon monoxide levels in your blood, they blame it on the car. And on your mom," he told Sarah. "You know. For not getting a tune-up."

ALESSANDRA RAN BACK down the stairs.

He has to know I'm coming, she thought.

She heard her father's voice in her head. "You think I haven't taken on guys bigger than me? A lot bigger. And tougher." She'd had a difficult time believing that at ten years of age, but she knew a lot more now about Victor Martillo's particular brand of ruthlessness.

Still, doubt had her stomach tied up in knots.

She did a quick tour of the kitchen, looking for anything she could use, but the place had been thoroughly cleaned out.

Quit stalling, she told herself.

She went out the back door instead of the one closer to the garage. Out in the side yard, a diesel engine cranked and then caught, revved high for about five seconds and then settled. Generator, she thought. He's getting ready.

No more time.

She ran across the short backyard to the edge of the swamp, then crouched low and ran until the garage was between her and her target. The sounds out front covered the noise of her approach, she hoped, and she went around the far side of the garage, crept forward, and peered around the corner.

He was there.

He had his back to her, a sheet of stiff paper in his hand, he was punching keys on a control panel mounted shoulder-high on one of the modules. At the same time he was trying to watch for her, he kept glancing at the side door of the house, even crouching down to look under the vehicle. Al heard a new noise, it had to be a gear motor because the six tubes of the launcher, which were welded into one single unit, had begun to move. It looked like a giant dull green candy bar that was slowly pivoting on one end and elevating, one glacial degree at a time.

Al aimed Raffi's gun carefully and fired.

He dropped abruptly to the ground.

She fired again. The tubes continued to move, no faster and no slower. You've gotta be kidding me, she thought. They armored the control panel? Both of her rounds had apparently bounced off without causing any damage. Vincenzo rolled over on the ground, eyes wide, looked like he couldn't believe his good fortune. She fired at the control panel once more, it was the last round in the pistol and the slide locked back.

His face lit up.

Al reversed her grip, threw the pistol at him as hard as she could, but he dodged it. Grinning, he rolled onto his feet, drew a black-bladed knife, and came after her. He was a good six inches taller than her, probably close to twice her weight, and he came hard, slashing with the knife and grabbing for her with the other hand. He was an order of magnitude quicker than Diego Ponce, the guy from the subway platform, and Al was willing to believe that he'd spent a significant portion of his life training for occasions like this one.

She wondered what her father would do...

Big, sweeping horizontal slash with the knife. She dodged back, spun the other way, got his wrist. His momentum carried him, all she had to do was let his weight and his movement bend his hand back. She felt the steel of the back of the metal blade cold on her forearm, felt his wrist snap...

He didn't lose his grip on the knife.

He went past her, surprised, his face contorted. Quicker than she thought possible, he had his knife in the other hand. He planted his left foot to arrest his forward motion. The broken wrist did not seem to slow him at all. Al pivoted again and kicked out hard, aiming for the side of his knee, but he saw it coming and flexed the knee forward so that her kick caught him on the meat of his thigh just above the joint.

Had to hurt like hell, though.

He spun and slashed at her again, the knife in what had to be his nondominant hand, but the angle was wrong and she had no shot at getting his unbroken wrist. And she had surprised him the first time...

He doesn't have to beat me in order to win, she thought, he just has to keep me occupied until his missiles fire.

She risked a glance at the missile launch vehicle. Mistake.

He was too close.

She feinted, but he anticipated that, his left hand, the one with the knife in it, was out of position but his right wasn't. His wrist was turning purple, she saw him tuck it up against his collarbone and drive his elbow at her throat. She tucked her chin and dodged, it was a glancing blow, but it took her down just the same.

I was ahead on points, she thought, and then she was on her back just inside the open garage doorway, her head spinning. She kicked at his knee, got it this time, she saw it bend the wrong way, but then he was falling on top of her, out of balance. She got both hands up, got both hands on his knife arm.

The impact of his body falling on her drove the air from her lungs.

Nothing to hit him with. There was an old spade leaning inside the garage doorway, maybe four feet away. Might as well have been in China.

She felt his knife enter her abdomen.

Not much pain at first.

She pushed back as hard as she could. He screamed in rage and triumph. He knew something about momentum, too, and instead of resisting he went with her, reversed direction, pulled the knife back out, held it high for another strike.

She could see *her* blood on the blade.

This is it, she thought, forget the knife, this is your last shot… She stiffened the fingers of her left hand, jabbed at him with everything she had left.

Surprised him again. Her fingers went in past the wet soft eyeball, her hard fingernails deeper yet, and she curled them and raked backward.

He screamed.

All of his attention went to his face.

She took the knife out of his shaking hand.

Stuck it into him, just below his navel.

He rolled off her, but she rolled with him, once on top she ripped savagely, cut him open all the way up to his sternum. The knife stuck in something there and she couldn't pull it out.

Didn't matter.

A jet flew by so low she could feel it, the noise of the engines was an assault on her ear drums. The one they'd called Vincenzo lay on his back next to her, hideously transformed, his heels thrumming on the ground. Her hands were covered in his blood. Her head throbbed and despite the temperature outside, she didn't feel cold at all. Her air came back then and she inhaled, the pain from her ribs receding to some far corner of her consciousness.

She felt enormously tired.

There was a stain spreading slowly on her shirt, a warm sticky feeling running down past her waist.

Get up, she told herself. Get up! You can sleep later. She crawled over to the edge of the garage door opening, grabbed the spade, used it like a cane to help her climb to her feet.

Another thundering roar close overhead.

She ignored it.

She focused on the rubber cord that linked the two modules together, it was just long enough to droop on the ground between them. Unhook it, she told herself, and she looked at where it connected to the launch vehicle, feeding it power and data, but she was no longer functioning well enough to figure out how it came apart. Serve you right, she told herself, you let that asshole get his blade into you...

Down to her knees.

Focused on the cable.

Direct approach, she thought. Just go stone age on it... She raised the spade high, still another roar just above the house, she brought the blade of the spade down as hard as she could manage on the cord.

Mother was tougher than it looked.

Come on! she told herself. Hit it like you mean it... Same result.

Third time was the charm, the cord parted with a loud bang and a shower of sparks. The generator shut down, the gear motor stopped, the big green candy bar went still. She looked at her spade, the electricity had vaporized a baseball-sized hole at the bottom of the blade. She turned slowly, collapsed, leaned back on the launch vehicle.

Choppers, faint in the distance.

Inhale, one, exhale...

Darkness fell.

TWENTY-ONE

He was an older guy, he had snow-white hair, but it was punked. He was probably about sixty, but he had the bright and curious eyes of a four-year-old and a nice smile to go with them. He was there when she woke up in a haze, but she was only conscious for a second or so. He was there again when they brought her out of it, he was dressed in blue scrubs. There were two or three others around, too, but she only remembered him. A while later they got her off a gurney and into a bed. The effort didn't seem to bother them, but it exhausted her and she fell asleep again. The third time she woke up gradually. She was in bed in a small room that was dominated by tubes, wires, and machines, most of which seemed to be connected to her. Her mouth was dry and her head was banging. Seemed to her that she could still hear choppers somewhere.

The door to her room was open, it was almost as wide as the room itself. It fronted onto another room, a bigger one, where there were people. A nurse looked up from a monitor and over at her. Seconds later the white-haired guy was there. "Don't try to sit up," he told her. "Just take it easy. How are you feeling?"

"Thirsty," she said.

"Here," he said, reaching for a pitcher.

Something was bothering her, something important, but it took her a minute to figure out what it was. "Did they fire?" she asked him.

"I don't want to go getting you excited," he said. "And

they're waiting to debrief you. I guess they've got a lot of questions. I'm not supposed to tell you anything."

She looked into those eyes. "Hey, Doc," she said. "Who gives a fuck what those guys want?"

When he laughed, he laughed with all of himself. "Well, all right," he said. "I suppose the nurses will tell you anyhow. No, they didn't fire. You got them shut down in time."

Exhale... She felt the tension drain out of her. "When do I have to talk?"

"I'll keep them away until you're ready," he told her.

"I'm not ready."

"Can't say I blame you. I'd like to look at your stitches, if that's okay."

"What stitches?"

He waved to a nurse, who came over to stand next to him. "You came here with a pretty deep stab wound," he told her. "We almost lost you. Two members of the assault team were qualified medics, they got you stabilized, got the bleeding slowed, they brought you here on one of their helicopters." He flashed that smile again. "A big green National Guard helicopter landing on the roof! You made all the news shows. But without them, you'd have bled to death."

"If any of those guys are still around," she told him, "send them up."

"I'll have a nurse do it," he said. "They go nuts down there whenever they see me. You've made me a celebrity. If this keeps up I'm going to hire a nutritionist, some bodyguards, and someone to hold a parasol over my head." He pulled her covers back. She realized that all she was wearing was a thin hospital gown. And it seemed forever since she'd had a shower.

The nurse's eyebrows went high on her forehead and she murmured something to the doctor. "Yes," he said. "Healing nicely." He covered her up again.

"Will I have a scar?"

He nodded. "About two and a half inches. When it's fully healed, you won't notice it. Friend of mine happened to be in the ER the other night. Plastic surgeon. Teeny, teeny, teeny stitches."

"How long are you guys gonna keep me here?"

"Why are you in such a hurry to leave us? Is it so terrible here?"

She thought of her room over the bar on Atlantic Avenue, the medical bills she was surely racking up, and the thin finances down at Houston Investigations. Suddenly she understood why Marty Stiles was in no hurry to complete his rehab. "No," she said. "It's not terrible at all."

He smiled. "Anyhow, we won't keep you any longer than we have to. Administration would love for that circus downstairs to leave."

"Circus?"

"Media," he said. "Police. A couple of guys from the assault team that brought you here. Various and sundry." He pointed at the television. "Turn on CNN. You'll see."

SHE FOUND THE REMOTE, thumbed the power button. On the screen, two women and one man stood in the kitchen of an empty house. One of the women looked around the room, her distaste plain on her face. "I want granite," she said. The man looked sick. The other woman, presumably the real estate agent, pasted on a smile.

"We'll keep looking," she said.

Alessandra hit the channel button, surfed until she caught one of the twenty-four-hour news channels. A young black man wearing a suit and tie stood in front of a police barricade on Arthur Kill Road. "Speculation continues to surround this blighted neighborhood on Staten Island," he said. "The initial statements coming out of the NYPD stated that this was an incident of home-grown terrorism, but these statements were contradicted by a reporter for the *SoCal Insider,* which is normally an entertainment source in Los Angeles. The reporter, Rod Benson, claims to have information that there was a foreign terrorist cell operating here in New York City."

The picture on the tube switched to a sober-looking news anchor. "Brian," the man said, "isn't it a fact that the *SoCal Insider* is not exactly an ideal model of journalistic integrity? Can we place any credence in the news we're hearing from that source?"

The black guy nodded. "David, while it is true that the *Insider* might not be ranked very high as a traditional news outlet, their reporter, Rod Benson, is a solid professional with a decent reputation. Plus, included in his reports are these pictures." The television cut to a paste-up of the pictures Al had taken of the men at Palermo Imports. "These two men are still unidentified, but this one is apparently a man known as Hassan El-Hamidi, a Syrian national who was cashiered out of the Egyptian military eighteen years ago. He has been linked to the embassy bombings in Africa. While we do not know if Mr. El-Hamidi has actually been sighted, here's what we do know: Air Force One was due to touch down at Newark's Liberty Airport when it was suddenly rerouted to Philadelphia. No explanation has yet been given for this. All takeoffs and landings at Newark Liberty, LaGuardia, and JFK airports were held up for three hours, snarling air traffic up and down the East Coast. And, U.S. Air Force fighters made a series of extremely low passes just over Arthur Kill, the body of water behind us which separates Staten Island from New Jersey. The residents here are alarmed, to say the least, and some windows were broken…"

She muted the set, reached for the phone next to the bed,

and called Sarah Waters's cell. "Hey. Sorry I missed the trip to Long Island."

"Never mind that," Sarah said, her voice hushed. "You're a hero! Were they really going to blow up the president's plane? Are you okay? What the hell happened? First they were saying that Frank was a terrorist, then they were saying he died trying to stop it, and now they won't say anything about him at all. Pending investigation. Are you all right?"

"Why are you whispering?"

"Because I'm just downstairs from you. Reporters and camera guys are crawling all over this place like a bunch of goddam roaches. Hey! Buddy! Do you mind? This is the ladies' room! What is wrong with you? Get the fuck outa here! Hang on, Al, I gotta find a safer place to talk. Call me back in one minute."

"Gotcha."

Al waited, called back. "Better?"

"Yeah. I'm in the stairwell, one of the security guys is a sweetheart, he unlocked it for me. Are you okay? What happened?"

"I got stabbed. I think I'm gonna be all right. Probably stuck here for a few days. Listen, I need you to do me a favor. Tell your kid not to believe a thing he hears about his dad. When I get out of here, we're gonna sit down and I'm gonna tell him the real story about the kind of guy his old man was. And I know you two were on the outs, but, you know, I'm sorry."

"Thank you. And for Frankie Junior, too."

"How'd you make out with Mrs. West?"

"She's in jail."

"What?"

"Yeah. When Jake and I went to see her, her driver wired up my mom's car while we were talking."

"Are you kidding me?"

"No. Anyway, I kinda figured he would, him and Agatha were in it together. That's how the two of them did Jake's father and his brother, Izzy. Her driver got away in a boat, but they arrested him on the Connecticut side when he tried to land. Now he's in jail in Bridgeport and he's rolling over on Agatha almost as fast as she's rolling over on him. They found Bats, by the way. And would you believe it? West doesn't have cancer at all, it was all an act."

"She lied to us? I'm shocked. And I am never letting you out of the office again, ever."

"Too late for that, kiddo."

"Jesus. So where was Tipton?"

"In her wine cellar, wrapped up in a sheet. They kept it so dry in there, they said he was like, mummified. You know, like a dead fly on your windowsill. They're reopening the old case."

"I would hope so. Did we get paid?"

"You know, that's exactly what Marty said. But, um, no, we didn't."

"How broke are we?"

"Broke on our ass broke. But I charged a laptop on Marty's credit card and I took it down there to him and I put his fat ass to work. We got a lot of face time in the papers behind Agatha West and we've been getting a lot of missing-person calls. Marty can do a lot of that stuff on-line right from where he is. And we got the Hyatt account."

"Wow. So we're broke, but we won't starve."

"Not this month."

"Okay. I'll be out of this place in a day or so, Sarah, so we'll—"

"Don't you dare. You just lay your sweet little *boo-tay* right back on them sheets, baby. You get some rest. You deserve it."

"You know what, Sarah, I take back all those mean things I wrote about you on the men's room wall."

"Was that you? No wonder I'm so popular lately."

THREE COPS SHOWED up just as one of the hospital staff was clearing away the wreckage of her lunch. As usual, despite the lack of taste in the food, there was nothing edible left over, no scraps, no little cellophane packages of crackers, nothing, and she was still hungry. The two younger cops were decked out in standard NYPD blue, they looked new, fresh, just graduated, they both looked at Alessandra like rookie zookeepers venturing into the tiger cage for the first time. The third guy was Al's fat sergeant, Bobby Fallon, the guy who was attached to the commissioner's office, the guy who knew How It All Really Worked. They stood in the doorway waiting for the orderly to finish up and leave. Behind Fallon's back, one of the younger cops caught Al's eye, raised his fingertips to the corner of his eyebrow, and saluted her. Al nodded back, just a millimeter or so, but Fallon caught it and turned to stare at the younger man.

"Pardon me, gents." The orderly pushed his rack of empty trays out into the hall, paused, and looked back. "You gents be polite to Supernatural in there, you hear? She ain't 'posed to get all excited. We don't want no trouble."

"Okay, Doctor," one of the uniforms told him, sarcastic. "Don't worry about it."

"You two meatballs wait out there in the hall," Fallon said. "We don't want to be disturbed." The two younger cops stepped back and Fallon closed the door with a bang. There was a patient chair down by the foot of Al's bed and he flopped down in it.

"S'up, dog?" Al said.

The television over Fallon's head replayed footage of the National Guard helicopter on the hospital roof, rotors turning lazily. Figures in green uniforms and white uniforms rushed Alessandra onto a gurney and into the hospital. The picture zoomed in close, but the images were too blurry to identify her. A CNN reporter doing voice-over talked about the conflicting reports coming out of the NYPD. Al picked up the remote and thumbed the mute button.

"Thank you," Fallon said, and he sighed. "You really fucked us up, all that stuff you fed to Rod Benson. That goddam reporter."

"Yeah, the truth is a bitch, ain't it? You were all ready to stick this whole thing in Frank Waters's back pocket, just like Torrente wanted you to. And you'd have let me and Sarah go down with him."

He shrugged. "Be that as it may. Looks bad, bunch of foreign guys taking a run at the president. Gets people all stirred up. Not that it matters, but just between you and me, did you do the one out in front of Costello's, too?"

"No," Al said. "One of his own caught him with a round by accident so they finished him so he couldn't answer any questions."

"Nice," he said, irritated. "How do you know that?"

"Got it from the valet parking guy."

"How the hell did you find him?"

"Followed him back to his rooming house."

Fallon glared at her. "The guy was gone when we went looking for him."

Al shrugged. "Guess you got there too late."

The muscles worked in the side of Fallon's jaw. "How much trouble am I gonna have with you?" he said.

"Figured it was gonna come down to this," Al said.

"Yeah?" She heard the challenge and the frustration in his voice. "Why?"

"Because they're all dead," she told him. "I mean, good or bad, I don't know how you wanna look at it, bottom line is they ain't talking to anybody. But someone sent them here. Someone paid for all this. And the way it stands right now, the guy's gotta figure he wasted his money because the best police force in the world, which would look like youse guys, got wise to the operation and blew it up. Killed everybody. Took the missiles. Am I right?"

He just stared at her.

"You can't afford to let 'em know how close they came," Al said. "You can't let anybody know that two chicks from the hood pulled your onions out of the fire. You're here to tell me that me and Sarah have to keep our fucking mouths shut."

"Some would call it your patriotic duty," he said.

"Call it whatever you like."

"So what do you want? What's it gonna take?"

"What do you got?" she asked him.

"We can't let you back into the academy," he said. "Not after this. That what you're asking? You really wanna put on the blues, ride around in a patrol car chasing radio calls?" He leaned forward, enunciated carefully. "Taking orders? Following procedure? Doing what you're told?" He leaned back in the chair. "Ain't gonna happen. That ain't what you want anyhow. Can't be."

"What are you gonna do about Rod Benson?"

He glanced up at the television. "Nothing. He's gonna write a book, and every conspiracy theorist fruit basket between here and Mumbai will buy it, but nobody with any sense will believe him. He'll get rich, he can retire to spend his money, quit chasing Britney Spears and UFOs. Everybody wins."

"What about The Harkonnen Group? What about Homeland Security?"

Fallon looked like he wanted to spit. "Fuck them," he said with some heat. "They came in here like John Wayne on his fucking horse, they get what they deserve, which is nothing. You let me handle them. I ain't letting them get near you." He stared at her for maybe ten seconds. "You with me on this, Martillo?"

"Yeah. Because it's my patriotic duty."

He stood up, obviously not sure if she was messing with him. "The department," he said, "is picking up your tab in this joint."

"Wow. Thanks. I think." She waited for it: there is a price tag on everything.

"The debriefing is gonna be brutal."

"I been wondering when that would start," she said.

He just gave her a look.

"Come on, Fallon, spit it out. I'm not in the mood for games."

He walked over to the window, stood there with his back to her. "This is your turf, Martillo," he said, and he pointed out at the streets of Brooklyn with his chin. "You were born here. You couldn't function anywhere else. Any other city in the world, you couldn't be what you are."

She hadn't been anywhere else long enough to know the truth of that, but it sounded like he might have a point.

Fallon turned and stared at her. "We're gonna have to live with you. And you're gonna have to live with us."

"I'm not gonna lie for you guys, Fallon. I'm not telling anybody I was working for you."

"Oh, no. Nothing like that. But you have long-standing ties to the department. Long-standing, ongoing. And the department is gonna be right by your side throughout this whole ordeal."

"The debriefing, you mean." He nodded once.

"I am beginning to worry," she said, staring at the silent television, "what this is really gonna cost me."

"Come on, Martillo, what do you care? Ain't neither one of us gonna get our picture in the paper over this. Do it our way, everybody walks away from this clean. No inquests, no repercussions…no dirt. And the undying admiration of the few of us who know what really happened."

"Undying."

"Yes. For whatever it's worth."

"How do we work this?"

"Your lawyer will be with you the whole time."

"My lawyer?"

"Well," he said. "Our lawyer. Yours and ours. Don't worry, you'll like her."

She sighed.

"Come on, Martillo. You with us on this?"

"You're too slick for me, Fallon. But send your lawyer up. We'll talk."

"Fine." He headed for the door, paused long enough to toss a manila envelope on the foot of the bed without looking at her.

"Hey," she said, "if that's about those parking tickets, I already told you guys it wasn't my car."

"It's an investigator's ticket," he said.

"What? A license?" she said, disbelieving.

"So you can work." He glanced at the television. "Listen. Between you and me, we really ought to tell everyone who you are. What you did. But we can't, and so you're getting screwed. I'm sorry, but the PI license was the best I could do."

"It's okay," she said. "I'll take it."

He nodded to her and walked out.

Spin management, she thought. The truth stays buried. To everyone except the conspiracy theorists, the NYPD looks like they were on it.

And I get to keep my job.

THE WHITE-HAIRED doctor came to see her about a week later. "Hey," he said. "Supernatural. How are you?"

"Bored," she said. "Tired of talking. Ready to go home. Why do they keep calling me that?"

"Supernatural? Because we are impressed. Very few people heal as fast as you do. Professional athletes, other freaks of nature, such as yourself. Listen, Homeland Security says they're not done with you yet, but the NYPD says we need to get you out of here. We're going to blame it on hospital administration, those people could screw up a free lunch any day and twice on Sunday. We're gonna take you down the freight elevator and sneak you out past the loading dock."

"Wow, Doc, you really know how to sweet-talk a girl, you know that?"

"I got an A-plus in bedside manner. But there's someone here you ought to talk to first."

Had Conrad come to see her? For a moment she hoped. "One more lawyer, cop, or politician, Doc, I swear to God I can't be held responsible for what happens…"

A tall chubby white guy stepped into the room. "Alessandra Martillo?"

"Who are you?"

She flinched when she saw him reach into the bag he carried, but he only came out with a thick sheaf of papers. "I," he said, sucking in his stomach, "am a duly appointed representative of the Irish-American Mudders and Fadders Association, and as such—"

"What? The Irish what?" Then she remembered the beer she'd agreed to have for Daniel "Mickey" Caughlan, the one he couldn't drink on account of being locked up. "Oh, right," she said. "I stood you up a while back. Sorry."

"Well, we're all here now," he told her. "Look, they give me two hundred bucks to deliver these papers, doll, and I swear to God it's the hardest two hundred I ever turned. I been chasin' you all over Brooklyn. So do me a favor and sign wherever you see them yellow stickies and here's the bloody keys. The good doctor already signed for the witness, and he give me the dollar besides, so it's all legal. You owe him a buck."

"What the hell are you talking about?" She took the pile of paperwork he handed her. "This is a deed…" She looked at the address, remembered Caughlan's call from prison. "This is the studio Caughlan bought for his son, isn't it?"

"Which you just bought for a dollar, plus other valuable considerations. So I'm told. And I never heard of no Mickey Caughlan, nor his son Willy Boy, neither, God rest his soul. May he rest in peace. Sign, there, for the love of Christ's aching balls, and initial by them checkmarks. Every one a them yellow tags." She complied. "And on the last page, there. Now take the top copy, the rest are mine." She handed them back and he stuffed them in his briefcase. "Done, by Jaysus. Sometimes, mind you not always, just every now and then, Miss Martillo, good t'ings do happen to them tha's done the right t'ing."

He winked at her and walked out.

* * * * *

REQUEST YOUR FREE BOOKS!

2 FREE NOVELS
PLUS 2 FREE GIFTS!

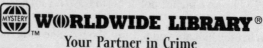

MYSTERY
W**O**RLDWIDE LIBRARY®
Your Partner in Crime

YES! Please send me 2 FREE novels from the Worldwide Library® series and my 2 FREE gifts (gifts are worth about $10). After receiving them, if I don't wish to receive any more books, I can return the shipping statement marked "cancel." If I don't cancel, I will receive 4 brand-new novels every month and be billed just $5.49 per book in the U.S. or $6.24 per book in Canada. That's a savings of at least 31% off the cover price. It's quite a bargain! Shipping and handling is just 50¢ per book in the U.S. and 75¢ per book in Canada.* I understand that accepting the 2 free books and gifts places me under no obligation to buy anything. I can always return a shipment and cancel at any time. Even if I never buy another book, the two free books and gifts are mine to keep forever.

414/424 WDN F4WY

Name		
	(PLEASE PRINT)	

Address		Apt. #

City	State/Prov.	Zip/Postal Code

Signature (if under 18, a parent or guardian must sign)

Mail to the **Harlequin® Reader Service:**
IN U.S.A.: P.O. Box 1867, Buffalo, NY 14240-1867
IN CANADA: P.O. Box 609, Fort Erie, Ontario L2A 5X3

Want to try two free books from another line?
Call 1-800-873-8635 or visit www.ReaderService.com.

* Terms and prices subject to change without notice. Prices do not include applicable taxes. Sales tax applicable in N.Y. Canadian residents will be charged applicable taxes. Offer not valid in Quebec. This offer is limited to one order per household. Not valid for current subscribers to the Worldwide Library series. All orders subject to credit approval. Credit or debit balances in a customer's account(s) may be offset by any other outstanding balance owed by or to the customer. Please allow 4 to 6 weeks for delivery. Offer available while quantities last.

Your Privacy—The Harlequin® Reader Service is committed to protecting your privacy. Our Privacy Policy is available online at www.ReaderService.com or upon request from the Harlequin Reader Service.

We make a portion of our mailing list available to reputable third parties that offer products we believe may interest you. If you prefer that we not exchange your name with third parties, or if you wish to clarify or modify your communication preferences, please visit us at www.ReaderService.com/consumerschoice or write to us at Harlequin Reader Service Preference Service, P.O. Box 9062, Buffalo, NY 14269. Include your complete name and address.

WWL13R

Reader Service.com

Manage your account online!

- Review your order history
- Manage your payments
- Update your address

> ### *We've designed the Harlequin® Reader Service website just for you.*

Enjoy all the features!

- Reader excerpts from any series
- Respond to mailings and special monthly offers
- Discover new series available to you
- Browse the Bonus Bucks catalog
- Share your feedback

Visit us at:

ReaderService.com